Praise for
LEGENDBORN

An Indies Introduce Selection

★ "Rich and explosive debut."
—*SLJ*, starred review

"Don't look over sea or under stone—*this* is the fantasy novel
for all once and future fans of suspense-filled storytelling."
—*KIRKUS REVIEWS*

"*Legendborn* is a thrilling and tense fantasy that weaves
Arthurian adventure with southern Black culture into a story that
had me shouting. It will hook readers from the very beginning and
leave them breathless until the final, mind-blowing revelation."
—**KWAME MBALIA,** *New York Times* bestselling author
of the Tristan Strong series

"*Legendborn* is a remarkable debut that should firmly place
Tracy Deonn on every fantasy and contemporary YA reader's
radar. Deft and insightful blending of Arthurian legend and
Southern Black American history make for an engrossing tale of
mystery, romance, and finding your place in the world—
an absolute must-read!"
—**ALYSSA COLE,** award-winning romance author

"*Legendborn* is an enthralling, standout modern fantasy about history
and power, and Deonn is an author to watch."
—**KIERSTEN WHITE,** *New York Times* bestselling author

"Perfect for fans of Cassandra Clare and Kiersten White, Tracy Deonn's unique reimagining of Arthurian legend is full of magic and heart. A brilliant debut!"

"A King Arthur reimagining that adds seats to the Round Table, inviting new readers to find themselves within its lore, Tracy Deonn's *Legendborn* braids southern folk traditions and Black Girl Magic into a searing modern tale of grief, power, and self-discovery."

"*Legendborn* is intoxicating and electrifying, and resonates with a deep understanding and vulnerable adoration of what it is to be a Black girl searching for the magic of herself. Tracy Deonn captivates you from page one with her perfect pacing, exhilarating plotting, and a command of storytelling that cannot be ignored. This book will hold everything you are hostage until, page by page, you discover how it has actually set you free."

LEGENDBORN

TRACY DEONN

SIMON & SCHUSTER

First published in Great Britain in 2020 by Simon & Schuster UK Ltd

First published in the USA in 2020 by Margaret K. McElderry Books, an imprint of
Simon & Schuster Children's Publishing Division
1230 Avenue of the Americas, New York, New York 10020

1 3 5 7 9 10 8 6 4 2

Simon & Schuster UK Ltd
1st Floor, 222 Gray's Inn Road
London
WC1X 8HB

www.simonandschuster.co.uk
www.simonandschuster.com.au
www.simonandschuster.co.in

Simon & Schuster Australia, Sydney
Simon & Schuster India, New Delhi

A CIP catalogue record for this book is available from the British Library.

PB ISBN 978-1-3985-0187-4
eBook ISBN 978-1-3985-0188-1
eAudio ISBN 978-1-3985-0189-8

Printed and bound by CPI Group (UK) Ltd, Croydon, CR0 4YY

For my mother

PROLOGUE

THE POLICE OFFICER'S body goes blurry, then sharpens again.

I don't stare at him directly. I can't really focus on one thing in this room, but when I do look, his face shimmers.

His badge, the rectangular nameplate, his tie clip? All the little metal details on his chest ripple and shine like loose silver change at the bottom of a fountain. Nothing about him appears solid. Nothing about him feels real.

I don't think about that, though. I can't.

Besides, everything looks otherworldly when you've been crying for three hours straight.

The police officer and nurse brought me and my father into a tiny mint-green room. Now they sit on the other side of the table. They say they are "explaining the situation" to us. These people don't feel real, but neither does "the situation" they keep explaining.

I don't cry for my mother's death. Or for myself. I cry because these strangers in the hospital—the nurse, the doctor, the police officer—don't know my mother, and yet they were closest to her when she died. And when your people die, you have to listen to strangers speak your nightmare into existence.

"We found her on Route 70 around eight," the police officer says. The air conditioner kicks on. The sharp scents of hospital-grade hand soap and floor cleaner blow across our faces.

I listen to these people I don't know use the past tense about my mother, the person who brought me into this world and created my present. They are past-tensing my heart—my whole beating, bleeding, torn heart—right in front of me.

It is a *violation*.

These uniformed strangers carve me open with their words, but they are just doing their jobs. I can't scream at people who are just doing their jobs, can I?

I want to.

My father sits in a vinyl padded chair. It creaks when he leans forward to read paragraphs of fine print on pieces of paper. Where did this paperwork come from? Who has paperwork on hand for my mother's death? Why are they ready when *I* am not ready?

My father asks questions, signs his name, blinks, breathes, nods. I wonder how he is functioning. My mother's life has stopped. Shouldn't everything and everyone stop living too?

She was crushed inside our family sedan, body half-crumpled under the dashboard after a hit-and-run. She was alone until some nice, probably frightened Good Samaritan saw her overturned car on the side of the road.

Bloodred twine connects the final words I said to my mother—last night, in anger—to another night in February. A night when my best friend, Alice, and I, sitting together in the basement of her parents' split-level home, decided UNC-Chapel Hill's Early College Program was our dream. *Bright high school students can earn college credit at Carolina over the course of two years, experience life in the dorms, and become independent.* At least, that's what the brochure said. For Alice and me, Early College was two minority girls' ticket out of a small town in rural North Carolina. For us, Early College meant bigger ideas and classrooms—and *adventure*. We'd filled out our applications together. Marched right into the Bentonville post office after school together. Dropped the envelopes in the chute together. If we could get into EC, we could leave Bentonville High and move to a university dorm four hours away from home—and away from parents who held us so tight that sometimes we couldn't breathe.

A decade before I was born, my mother was an undergraduate at Carolina. A burgeoning scientist. I'd heard the stories for years. Seen the framed photos of elaborate chemistry experiments: beakers and glass pipettes; protective goggles resting across her high cheekbones. It was her fault, really, for planting the idea in my mind. That's what I'd told myself, anyway.

Our letters came yesterday. Alice's parents knew she was applying. They'd beamed like *they* were the ones who'd been accepted.

I knew it wouldn't go that way for me; I'd applied behind my mother's back, certain that once I got in, once I had that letter, she'd let go of her need to keep me close. I'd handed her the letter on blue-and-white Carolina stationery, grinned like it was a trophy.

I'd never seen her so angry.

My brain doesn't accept where my body is sitting. It catalogs the last thirty-six hours in an attempt to find the *how* of this hospital room.

Last night: she'd roared about trust and safety and not rushing to grow up. I'd screamed about unfairness, about what I'd earned, and how I needed to get away from dirt roads.

This morning: I was still fuming when I woke up. In bed, I made a silent declaration to not speak to her all day. That declaration had felt good.

Today: a nothing, normal Tuesday, except that, for me, it carried the stubborn undercurrent of *We'll talk later.*

Tonight: she drove away from work at the end of the day.

Then: a car.

Now: this pale green room and a disinfectant smell that burns when I inhale.

Forever: *We'll talk later* is not the same as *We'll never talk again.*

The twine from February closes tight around me like I will never take another breath, but somehow the police officer is still talking, shimmering and shining.

The air around him looks alive. Like he is drenched in magic.

But when your entire world is shattering, a little bit of magic is . . . nothing.

THREE MONTHS LATER

PART ONE

ORDER

1

A CAROLINA FIRST-YEAR sprints through the darkness and launches himself off the cliff into the moonlit night.

His shout sends sleepy birds flying overhead. The sound echoes against the rock face that borders the Eno Quarry. Flashlights track his flailing body, all windmilling arms and kicking legs, until he hits the water with a cracking splash. At the cliff line above, thirty college students cheer and whoop, their joy weaving through the pine trees. Like a constellation in motion, cone-shaped beams of light roam the lake's surface. Collective breath, held. All eyes, searching. Waiting. Then, the boy erupts from the water with a roar, and the crowd explodes.

Cliff jumping is the perfect formula for Southern-white-boy fun: rural recklessness, a pocket flashlight's worth of precaution, and a dare. I can't look away. Each run draws my own feet an inch closer to the edge. Each leap into nothingness, each hovering moment before the fall, calls to a spark of wild yearning inside my chest.

I press that yearning down. Seal it closed. Board it up.

"Lucky he didn't break his damn legs," Alice mutters in her soft twang. She scoffs, peering over the edge to watch the grinning jumper grasp protruding rocks and exposed vines to climb the rock face. Her straight, coal-black hair lies plastered to her temple. The warm, sticky palm of late-August humidity presses down on our skin. My curls are already up in a puff, as far away from the back of my neck as possible, so I hand her the extra elastic band from my wrist. She takes it wordlessly and gathers her hair in a ponytail. "I read about this quarry on the way here. Every few years kids get hurt, fall on the rocks, drown. We're sure as hell not jumping, *and* it's getting late. We should go."

"Why? 'Cause you're getting bit?" I swat at a tiny flickering buzz near her arm.

She fixes me with a glare. "I'm insulted by your weak conversational deflection. That's not best-friend behavior. You're fired." Alice wants to major in sociology, then maybe go into law. She's been interrogating me since we were ten.

I roll my eyes. "You've best-friend fired me fifty times since we were kids *and yet* you keep rehiring me. This job sucks. HR is a nightmare."

"*And yet* you keep coming back. Evidence, if circumstantial, that you enjoy the work."

I shrug. "Pay is good."

"You *know* why I don't like this."

I do. It's not like I'd *planned* to break the law our first night on campus, but after dinner an opportunity had presented itself in the shape of Charlotte Simpson, a girl we knew from Bentonville High. Charlotte popped her head into our dorm room before we'd even finished unpacking and demanded we join her for a night out. After two years of EC, Charlotte had officially enrolled as a Carolina undergraduate this year and, apparently, she'd turned party girl somewhere in the interim.

During the day, the Eno River State Park is open for hiking, camping, and kayaking, but if you sneak in after the gates close like all the kids here have, it's probably-to-definitely trespassing. Not something I'd normally go for, but Charlotte explained that the night before the first day of classes is special. It's tradition for some juniors and seniors to host a party at the Quarry. Also tradition? First-year students jumping off the edge of the cliffs into the mineral-rich lake at its center. The park straddles Orange and Durham Counties and sits north of I-85, about twenty-five minutes away from Carolina's campus. Charlotte drove us here in her old silver Jeep, and the entire ride over I felt

Alice beside me in the back seat, shrinking against the illegality of it all.

The jumper's unfettered laughter crests the cliff before his head does. I can't remember the last time my laugh sounded like that.

"You don't like this because it's"—I drop my voice into a dramatic whisper—"*against the rules?*"

Alice's dark eyes burn behind her glasses. "Gettin' caught off campus at night is an *automatic* expulsion from EC."

"Hold up, Hermione. Charlotte said a bunch of students do it every year."

Another jumper sprints through the woods. A deeper splash. Cheers. Alice juts her chin toward the other students. "That's them. Tell me why *you* want to be here?"

Because I can't just sit in our room right now. Because ever since my mother died, there's a version of me inside that wants to break things and scream.

I lift a shoulder. "Because what better way to begin our adventure than with a *pinch* of rebellion?"

She does not look amused.

"Did someone say rebellion?" Charlotte's boots crunch through the leaves and pine needles. The sharp sound stands out from the droning background of crickets and the low bass thump pulsing our way from the party's speakers. She comes to a stop next to me and brushes her auburn ponytail away from her shoulder. "Y'all jumpin'? It *is* tradition." She smirks. "And it's fun."

"No," damn near leaps out of Alice's mouth. Something must have shown on my face, because Charlotte grins and Alice says, "Bree . . ."

"Aren't you pre-med or something, Charlotte?" I ask. "How are you this smart *and* this bad an influence?"

"It's college," Charlotte says with a shrug. "'Smart but a bad influence' describes like half the student body."

"Char?" A male voice calls out from behind a raggedy holly. Charlotte's face breaks into a wide smile even before she turns around to see the tall red-haired boy walking toward us. He holds a red Solo cup in one hand and a flashlight in the other.

"Hey, babe," Charlotte purrs, and greets him with a giggling kiss.

"Char?" I mouth to a grimacing Alice.

When they separate, Charlotte waves us over. "Babe, these are new EC kids from back home. Bree and Alice." She curls around the boy's arm like a koala. "This is my boyfriend, y'all. Evan Cooper."

Evan's perusal takes long enough that I wonder what he's thinking about us.

Alice is Taiwanese-American, short, and wiry, with observant eyes and a semipermanent smirk. Her whole MO is dressing to make a good impression "just in case," and tonight she chose dark jeans and a polka-dotted blouse with a Peter Pan collar. Under Evan's scrutiny, she pushes her round glasses up her nose and gives a shy wave.

I'm five-eight—tall enough that I *might* pass for a college student—and Black. Blessed with my mother's cheekbones and curves and my father's full mouth. I'd pulled on old jeans and a tee. Shy isn't really my thing.

Evan's eyes widen when they take me in. "You're the girl whose mom died, right? Bree Matthews?"

A trickle of pain inside, and my wall snaps into place. Death creates an alternate universe, but after three months, I have the tools to live in it.

Charlotte jabs Evan in the ribs with her elbow, sending him daggers with her eyes. "What?" He puts his hands up. "That's what you sai—"

"Sorry." She cuts him off, her gaze apologetic.

My wall works two ways: it hides the things I need to hide and helps me show the things I need to show. Particularly useful with the Sorry for Your Loss crowd. In my mind's eye, the wall's reinforced now. Stronger than wood, iron, steel. It has to be, because I know what comes next: Charlotte and Evan will unleash the predictable stream of words everyone says when they realize they're talking to the Girl Whose Mom Died.

It's like Comforting Grieving People Bingo, except when all the squares get covered, everyone loses.

Charlotte perks up. *Here we go . . .*

"How are you holding up? Is there anything I can do for you?"

Double whammy.

The real answers to those two questions? The *really* real answers? *Not well* and *No.* Instead I say, "I'm fine."

No one wants to hear the real answers. What the Sorry for Your Loss Crowd wants is to feel good about asking the questions. This game is awful.

"I can't imagine," Charlotte murmurs, and that's another square covered on the bingo board. They *can* imagine it; they just wouldn't want to.

Some truths only tragedy can teach. The first one I learned is that when people acknowledge your pain, they want your pain to acknowledge them back. They need to *witness* it in real time, or else you're not doing your part. Charlotte's hungry blue eyes search for my tears, my quivering lower lip, but my wall is up, so she won't get either. Evan's eager gaze hunts for my grief and suffering, but when I jut my chin out in defiance, he averts his eyes.

Good.

"Sorry for your loss."

Damn.

And with the words I most despise, Evan hits bingo.

People lose things when they have a mental lapse. Then they find that thing again from the lost place. But my mother isn't *lost.* She's gone.

Before-Bree is gone, too, even though I pretend that she's not.

After-Bree came into being the day after my mom died. I went to sleep that night and when I woke up, she was there. After-Bree was there during the funeral. After-Bree was there when our neighbors knocked on our door to offer sorrow and broccoli casserole. After-Bree was with me when the visiting mourners finally went home. Even though I can only recall hazy snippets from the hospital—trauma-related memory loss, according to my father's weird, preachy grief book—I have After-Bree. She's the unwanted souvenir that death gave me.

In my mind's eye, After-Bree looks almost like me. Tall, athletic, warm brown skin, broader-than-I-want shoulders. But where my dark, tight curls are usually pulled up on top of my head, After-Bree's stretch wide and loose like a live oak tree. Where my eyes are brown, hers are the dark ochre, crimson, and obsidian of molten iron in a furnace, because After-Bree is in a constant state of near explosion. The worst is at night, when she presses against my skin from the inside and the pain is unbearable. We whisper together, *I'm sorry, Mom. This is all my fault.* She lives and breathes inside my chest, one heartbeat behind my own life and breath, like an angry echo.

Containing her is a full-time job.

Alice doesn't know about After-Bree. Nobody does. Not even my dad. *Especially* not my dad.

Alice clears her throat, the sound breaking like a wave against my thoughts. How long did I zone out? A minute? Two? I focus on the three of them, face blank, wall up. Evan gets antsy in the silence and blurts out, "By the way, your hair is *totally* badass!"

I know without looking that the curls springing out of my puff are wide-awake, reaching toward the sky in the night's humidity. I bristle, because his tone is the one that feels less like a compliment and more like he's happened upon a fun oddity—and that fun oddity is Black me with my Black hair. Wonderful.

Alice shoots me a sympathetic glance that Evan misses entirely, because of course he does. "I think we're done here. Can we go?"

Charlotte pouts. "Half an hour more, I promise. I wanna check out the party."

"Yeah! Y'all come watch me shotgun a PBR!" Evan slings an arm around his girlfriend's shoulders and leads her away before we can protest.

Alice grumbles under her breath and takes off after them, stepping high over rangy weeds at the edge of the tree line. Fall panicum and marestail, mostly. My mother had called the stuff "witchgrass" and "horseweed fleabane" back when she was alive to call out plants to me.

Alice is almost to the trees before she realizes I'm not following. "You comin'?"

"I'll be there in a sec. I wanna watch some more jumps." I jerk a thumb over my shoulder.

She stomps back. "I'll wait with you."

"No, that's okay. You go ahead."

She scrutinizes me, torn between taking me at my word or pushing further. "Watch, not jump?"

"Watch, not jump."

"Matty." Her childhood nickname for me—Matty, short for my last name—twists at something deep in my chest. Old memories have been doing that lately, even the ones that aren't about *her*, and I sort of hate it. My vision goes fuzzy with the threat of tears, and I have to blink Alice's features into focus—pale face, glasses perpetually sliding to the tip of her nose. "I . . . I know this isn't how we thought it would be. Being at Carolina, I mean. But . . . I think your mom woulda come around to it. Eventually."

I cast my gaze out as far as the moonlight allows. Across the lake, treetops are the shadowed fringe between the quarry and the murky sky. "We'll never know."

"But—"

"Always a but."

Something hard slips into her voice. "But if she were here, I don't think she'd want you to . . . to . . ."

"To what?"

"To become some other person."

I kick at a pebble. "I need to be alone for a minute. Enjoy the party. I'll be there soon."

She eyes me as if gauging my mood. "'I hate tiny parties—they force one into constant exertion.'"

I squint, searching my memories for the familiar words. "Did you—did you just Jane Austen me?"

Her dark eyes twinkle. "Who's the literary nerd? The quoter or the one who recognizes the quote?"

"Wait." I shake my head in amusement. "Did you just *Star Wars* me?"

"Nah." She grins. "I *New Hope*'d you."

"Y'all comin'?" Charlotte's disembodied voice shoots back through the woods like an arrow. Alice's eyes still hold a pinch of worry, but she squeezes my hand before walking away.

Once I can no longer hear the rustle of her shoes in the underbrush, I release a breath. Dig out my phone.

Hey, kiddo, you and Alice get settled in okay?

The second text had arrived fifteen minutes later.

I know you're our Brave Bree who was ready to escape Bentonville, but don't forget us little people back home. Make your mom proud. Call when you can. Love, Dad.

I shove my phone back into my pocket.

I *had* been ready to escape Bentonville, but not because I was brave. At first I'd wanted to stay home. It seemed right, after everything. But months of living under the same roof alone with my dad made my shame intolerable. Our grief is for the same person, but our grief is not the same. It's like those bar magnets in physics class; you can push the matching poles together, but they don't want to touch. I can't touch my dad's grief. Don't really want to. In the end, I left Bentonville because I was too scared to stay.

I pace along the cliff, away from the crowd, and keep the quarry to my left. The scents of damp soil and pine rise up with every footstep. If I breathe in deeply enough, the mineral smell of ground stone catches at the back of my throat. A foot over, the earth falls away below my feet and the lake stretches out wide, reflecting the sky and the stars and the possibilities of night.

From here, I can see what the jumpers were working with: whatever cleaved the dirt and rocks to form the quarry had dug at a thirty-degree angle. To clear the face entirely, one has to run fast and leap far. No hesitation allowed.

I imagine myself running like the moon is my finish line. Running like I can leave the anger and the shame and gossip behind. I can almost feel the delicious burn in my muscles, the rush sweet and strong in my veins, as I sail over the cliff and into emptiness. Without warning, the roiling spark of After-Bree stretches up from my gut like a vine on fire, but this time I don't shove her away. She unfurls behind my ribs, and the hot pressure of her is so powerful it feels like I could explode.

Part of me *wants* to explode.

"I wouldn't do that if I were you."

A wry voice from behind startles me and sends a few birds, hidden in the canopy above, squawking into the sky.

I hadn't heard anyone approach through the underbrush, but a tall, dark-haired boy leans casually against a tree as if he'd been there the whole time; arms over his chest and black combat boots crossed at the ankles. The boy's expression is lazy with disdain, like he can't even be bothered to muster up a full dose of the stuff.

"Forgive me for interrupting. It looked like you were about to jump off a cliff. Alone. In the dark," he drawls.

He is unsettlingly beautiful. His face is aristocratic and sharp, framed by high, pale cheekbones. The rest of his body is borne from shadows: black jacket, black pants, and ink-black hair that falls over his forehead and curls just below gauged ears bearing small black rubber plugs. He can't be more than eighteen, but something about his features doesn't belong to a teenager—the cut of his jaw, the line of his nose. His stillness.

The boy who is both young and old lets me study him, but only for a moment. Then, he levels his tawny gaze in challenge. When our eyes meet, a stinging shock races through me, head to heels, leaving fear in its wake.

I swallow, look away. "I could make that jump."

He snorts. "Cliff jumping is asinine."

"No one asked you." I have a stubborn streak aggravated by other stubborn people, and this boy clearly qualifies.

I step to his right. Quick as a cat, he reaches for me, but I twist away before he gets a grip. His eyebrows lift, and the corner of his mouth twitches. "I haven't seen you around before. Are you new?"

"I'm leaving." I turn, but the boy is beside me in two steps.

"Do you know who I am?"

"No."

"I'm Selwyn Kane."

His gaze sends tiny, invisible sparks of electricity dancing across my cheek. I flinch and throw my hand up between us like a shield.

Fingers, too hot, too strong, instantly close around my wrist. A tingling sensation shoots down to my elbow. "Why did you cover your face?"

I don't have an answer for him. Or myself. I try to yank away from him, but his hold is like iron. "Let go!"

Selwyn's eyes widen slightly, then narrow; he is not used to being shouted at. "Do you—do you *feel* something? When I look at you?"

"What?" I pull, but he holds me tightly without effort. "No."

"Don't lie."

"I'm not—"

"Quiet!" he orders. Bright indignation flares in my chest, but his unusual eyes rake across my face. Snuff it right out. "Strange. I thought—"

Suddenly, shouts break the night, but this time they're not from the cliff jumpers. We both twist toward the forest and beyond it, to the party in the clearing. More yelling—and not the happy, drunk kind.

A low growl close by my ear. I jump when I realize the sound is coming from the demanding boy whose fingers are still locked around my wrist. As he stares into the trees, his mouth curves into a satisfied smile, exposing two canines that nearly touch his bottom lip. "Got you."

"Got who?" I demand.

Selwyn startles, as if he'd completely forgotten I was there, then releases me with a frustrated grunt. He takes off, speeding into the woods, a silent shadow between the trees. He's out of sight before I can form a response.

A jarring scream echoes from the party on my left. Raised voices ring out from the cliff jumpers on my right, who are now sprinting for the clearing too. Blood freezes in my veins.

Alice.

Heart pounding in my chest, I race to the trailhead to follow Selwyn, but once I'm under tree cover, the ground is barely visible in the darkness. Three steps in, I trip and fall hard into bramble. Branches scrape my palms and arms. I take two shaking breaths. Let my eyes adjust. Stand. Listen for the sounds of yelling undergraduates. Then, adrenaline shooting through my veins, I jog half a mile in the right direction with quick, careful steps, wondering how the *hell* Selwyn could move so fast through the woods without a flashlight.

By the time I stumble into the clearing, the party is chaos. Undergrads push against one another to run down the long narrow path toward the cars parked at the gravel lot. Beyond the trees, car engines growl to life in a rolling wave. Two guys struggle to lift the kegs and push them onto truck beds while a small crowd beside them tries to help "lighten" the barrels by drinking straight from the hose. Beside the fire, a circle of twenty kids cheer while holding Solo cups and cell phones high in the air. Whatever or whoever they're looking at won't be Alice. She'd try to find me, like I'm trying to find her. I reach for my phone, but there are no missed calls or texts. She's got to be freaking out.

"Alice!" I scan the crowd for her, for Charlotte's ponytail and T-shirt, for Evan's red hair, but they aren't there. A half-naked, dripping-wet undergrad girl shoves past me. "Alice Chen!" Campfire smoke billows thick in the air; I can barely see anything. I push through sweating, churning bodies, calling Alice's name.

A tall blond girl scowls when I shout too close to her face, and I scowl back. She's beautiful the way a well-maintained dagger is beautiful: sharp, shiny, and all angles. A bit prissy. Absolutely Alice's type. *Damnit, where* is *she—*

"Everybody out 'fore someone calls the cops!" the girl yells.

Cops?

I glance up right as the Solo cup–carrying circle parts. It only takes a second to see the cause of the screams from earlier and the reason why someone might call the cops: a fight. A bad one. Four drunken, *enormous* boys are rolling and swinging in a pile on the ground. Probably football players right out of pre-season and fueled by adrenaline, beer, and who knows what else. One of the giants has another's shirt in his hand, the fabric pulled so taut I hear the seam rip. The third is on his feet, rearing back for a kick to the fourth boy's stomach. It's like watching gladiators brawl, except instead of armor they're covered in layers of muscle and have necks as thick as my thigh, and instead of weapons they're swinging fists the size of award-winning grapefruits. The hurricane cloud of dirt they've created has put so much smoke and dust in the air that I almost miss the flicker of light and movement above their heads.

What the . . . ?

There! There it is again. In the air above the boys, something is shimmering and dancing. A greenish-silver something that swoops, dives, and flickers in and out of transparency like a glitching hologram.

The image pulls at a string of memory. The shimmer of light . . . and the very *feeling* of it, punches the breath right out of my lungs.

I've seen this before, but I can't remember *where. . . .*

I turn, gasping, to the student beside me, a wide-eyed boy in a Tar Heels T-shirt. "Do you see that?"

"You mean the jackasses fighting over nothing?" He taps his phone. "Yeah, why do you think I'm filming?"

"No, the—the light." I point at the flickering. "There!"

The boy searches the air; then his expression turns wry. "Been smokin' something?"

"Come *on!*" The blond girl pushes through the circle of spectators, standing between the fighters and the crowd with her hands on her hips. "Time to go!"

The boy beside me waves her away. "Get outta the shot, Tor!"

Tor rolls her eyes. "You need to leave, Dustin!" Her vicious glare sends most of the gawkers running.

The *something* is still there, beyond the blond girl's head. Heart hammering, I take in the scene again. No one else has noticed the silvery mass hovering and flapping above the boys' heads—either that, or no one else can *see* it. Cold dread creeps into my stomach.

Grief does strange things to people's minds. This I know. One morning a couple of weeks after my mother died, my dad said he thought he could smell her cheesy grits cooking on the stove—my favorite and my mother's specialty. Once, I heard her humming down the hall from my bedroom. Something so mundane and simple, so regular and small, that for a moment, the prior weeks were just a nightmare, and I was awake now and she was alive. Death moves faster than brains do.

I exhale through the memories, shut my eyes tight, open them again. *No one else can see this,* I think, scanning the group a final time. *No one . . .*

Except the figure on the other side of the fire, tucked between the trunks of two oaks.

Selwyn Kane.

He glares upward, his expression calculating. Irritated. His sharp eyes watch the there-not-there shape too. Long fingers twitch at his sides, silver rings flashing in the shadows. Without warning, through wisps of smoke rising in eddies and waves over the campfire, Selwyn's eyes find mine. He sighs. Actually *sighs,* as if now that the hologram creature is here, I bore him. Insult spikes through my fear. Still holding my gaze, he makes a quick, jerking motion with his chin, and a vicious snap of invisible electricity wraps around my body like a rope and yanks me backward—away from the boy and the *something*. It pulls so hard and so fast that I nearly fall. His mouth moves, but I can't hear him.

I resist, but the rope sensation *responds*, tight pain in my body blossoming into a single utterance:

Leave.

The word materializes in my brain like an idea of my own that I'd simply forgotten. The command brands itself behind my eyes and echoes like a bell rung deep inside my chest until it's all I can hear. It floods my mouth and nose with dizzying scents—a bit of smoke, followed by cinnamon. The *need* to go saturates my world until I'm so heavy with it that my eyelids drop.

When I open my eyes again, I've already turned to face the direction of the parking lot. In my next breath, I'm walking away.

2

LEAVE. NOW.

I'm leaving. Now.

That seems right. Good. *Best*, even.

Beside me, Dustin is leaving too. "I need to go." He shakes his head, like he can't fathom why he hadn't left the party already. I find myself nodding in agreement. Tor told us to leave and we should do as she says. We're on the gravel path now, the lot a few minutes' walk through the trees.

I trip on a branch, lurch to the side, and catch myself against a trunk, hands slapping against jagged pine bark. The quick, stinging pain from my already-scratched palms cuts through the smokiness of *Leave* and the lingering spice of *Now*, until both words dissipate. Instead of pressing on me like a weight, the command flits gnatlike around my skull.

Dustin is long gone.

I gulp oxygen until my thoughts feel like my own again, until I'm in my body enough to feel the sweat-damp cotton T-shirt clinging to my back and chest.

Memories rise like bubbles through oil, slow and sluggish, until they explode into rich Technicolor.

Selwyn. His bored expression. His mouth spilling words into the night like a cold wind until they swept away *my* intention to stay and replaced it with *his* command that I leave. His will wrapped around my memory of the flying creature and ground it down into a pile of dust and fractured images, then rearranged that pile into something new: an unremarkable blank space above the campfire with no creature in sight. But that new memory doesn't *feel* real; it is a thin, flimsy layer created from silver smoke with the truth visible and concrete underneath.

He gave us both false memories, but now I remember the truth. That's impossible—

A voice sends me ducking behind a tree. "It's just these four. The rest made it to the parking lot." It's Tor, the blond girl who'd yelled at everyone. "Can we make this quick? I have a date with Sar. Drinks at Tap Rail."

"And Sar will understand if you're late." Selwyn. "This one was nearly corporeal. I had to wipe those last two kids' memories just in case."

I stifle a gasp. They're both still there at the clearing twenty feet away. Whatever they're doing, they're working together. Tor and Selwyn are visible between trees, circling the campfire, looking up. The murky green shape is still there in the sky, flashing in and out. The four drunk football players must be absolutely *plastered*, because they're only now coming up for air. They sit back, chests heaving, faces bloodied, expressions disoriented. One of them moves to stand, but Selwyn is at his side in the blink of an eye. His hand drops like an anvil on the kid's shoulder, forcing the larger boy back down so hard and fast that I hear his knees crack against the earth. The boy screams in pain, falling forward onto his hands, while I muffle my own cry.

"Dude!" another boy shouts.

"Shut up," snaps Selwyn. The wounded boy struggles in Selwyn's grip, but Selwyn holds him down without effort, without even looking. Selwyn's gaze hasn't left the flickering thing moving above their heads. After several pained breaths the boy releases a low moan. "The rest of you, over here with him." The other three boys exchange glances in silent debate. "Now!" he barks, and they scurry together on hands and knees to sit next to their injured friend.

In that second, I realize I have a choice. I can go find Alice and Charlotte. Alice will be worried sick. I can leave, like Selwyn told me to. I can put my wall up again, this time against whatever is happening here with these kids I don't know from a school I've barely started. I can hide my curiosity, just like

After-Bree, just like my grief. Or I can stay. If this isn't just a trick of grief, then what is it? Sweat streams down my forehead, stings my eyes. I bite my lip, weighing my options.

"As soon as I get them out of the way, it's going to bolt," Selwyn cautions.

"You don't say?" Tor says dryly.

"Snark later. Hunt now." *Hunt?* My breaths quicken.

"Pot, kettle, black . . . ," Tor huffs, but reaches over her shoulder for something I can't see.

Any choice I had evaporates when silver smoke appears from nowhere. It writhes and coalesces around Selwyn like a living thing, wrapping his arms and chest, blurring his body. His amber eyes gleam—actually *gleam*—like dual suns, and the ends of his dark hair curl upward, topped by bright flames of blue and white. The fingers on his free hand flex and contort at his sides, as if they're pulling and churning the air itself. Impossibly, he is both more terrifying and more beautiful than before.

Silver smoke materializes and surrounds the boys. They don't even blink—because they can't see it. But I can. And so can Selwyn and Tor.

When Tor takes a step back, I finally see what she's holding: a dark metal rod curved in an arc. A downward snap and it extends—into a bow. A goddamn *bow*.

At the sight of her weapon, the taut football players shout and scatter like crabs.

Ignoring them, Tor pulls hard to extract a silver bowstring from one end. Strings the weapon with practiced fingers. Tests the tension. The girl I'd called prissy draws an arrow from a hidden quiver between her shoulder blades and nocks it without looking. Takes a breath—and in one powerful motion, pulls the bow up and the arrow back to her ear.

One of the players points a shaking finger. "What—"

"Where do you want it?" Tor asks, as if the boy had never spoken. Cords of muscle strain at her bicep, in her forearm.

Selwyn tilts his head, assessing the creature. "In the wing."

Tor aims; the string tightens. "On your signal."

A beat.

"Now!"

Three things happen in quick succession:

Tor's arrow flies.

Selwyn swings toward the boys, spreading his arms wide and murmuring words I can't hear.

And the boys stand up. They march around the campfire in a line and walk in my direction.

Tor's arrow has pierced the shimmering mass. For a split second, I see wings in the campfire smoke. Claws. A thud—and it's writhing on the ground, scattering leaves and dirt, half the arrow sticking up. Whatever it is, it's not much bigger than a possum. But just as angry as one. I shudder. A possum, with *wings*.

The football players reach me, and I duck out of sight as they pass. My blood runs cold when I see their expressions: mouths slack, eyes unfocused. They move as if drugged.

Is that how I'd looked?

A screech splits the air, yanking my attention back to Selwyn and Tor. A hiss. A voice like metal scraping across glass. *"Merlin . . ."*

I blink in confusion. *Merlin as in King Arthur?*

Selwyn advances on the flickering creature twitching from Tor's arrow. Five needle-thin points of light appear at the fingertips of his extended hand. He snaps his wrist, and the light spears fly into the ground. The creature screams; Selwyn's pinned it in place like a butterfly to a board. His low chuckle makes me shiver. "Not just any Merlin."

The creature hisses again in pained rage. *"A Kingsmage!"*

A feral grin spreads across Selwyn's face. "That's better." My heart skips. Mage. *Magic.*

"It's just a small one, Sel." Tor pouts, another arrow already nocked in her bow.

"Doesn't matter how small it is," Selwyn—*Sel*—objects. "It shouldn't be here."

The thing struggles against its restraints. A flapping sound.

Sel clucks his tongue. "Why are you here, little isel?"

He says "isel" with a long "e" on the first syllable—and a derisive sneer.

"Nosy Legendborn!" The isel makes a sniffing sound. *"Nosy trai—"* Sel stomps down on its wing. Hard. The creature screeches.

"Enough about us. Why are *you* here?"

"Feeding!"

Sel rolls his eyes. "Yes, we saw that. Found yourself a spark of aggression and *blew on it* until it became a feast. So intent on gorging yourself you didn't even see us when we were right beneath you. But so far away from campus? You're a weak, miserable thing. Barely corporeal. Surely it'd be easier to feed there, closer to your Gate?"

A grating, rhythmic sound comes from the ground where the isel lies trapped. It takes a moment for me to recognize the sound as laughter. Sel hears it too; his lips curl back.

"Something funny?"

"Yesss," the isel crows. *"Very funnnnny . . ."*

"Spit it out. We don't have all night," Sel warns. "Or should I say *you* don't have all night? You're going to die here—or did you miss that, too?"

"Not myyyyy Gate," it rasps.

Sel's jaw clenches. "What do you mean, not your Gate?"

The creature laughs again, the sound atonal and *wrong*. Sel's eyes flick to Tor. Still aiming at the isel, she shakes her head, shrugs. Neither one of them knows what it means. *"Not my Gate. Not my Gate—"*

Without warning, Sel clenches his hand into a tight fist in one hard motion. The glowing pins draw together. There's a quick flash of light and a bone-shaking scream, and the creature's flickering shape explodes into green dust.

My feet are glued to the earth. *They're going to find me,* I think, *because I'm too terrified to run.*

"There could be more." Tor pulls her bow to rest. Sel's head lowers in thought. "Sel?" Silence. "Did you hear me?"

His eyes cut to hers. "I heard you."

"Well, we huntin' or not, Kingsmage?" she huffs.

He turns to face the woods opposite my hiding place, tension radiating across his back and shoulders. He comes to a decision. "We're hunting." He mutters a word I don't understand, and the silver smoke from before returns, swirling around the campfire until the flames die, sending the clearing into darkness. "Move out."

I hold my breath, but Tor and Sel don't turn my way. Instead, they step into the section of the woods he'd been scrutinizing. I wait until I hear their voices recede. Even without the fear of what they'd do if they found me, it takes that long to get my trembling limbs under control. Finally, they're gone.

A beat of silence, two, and the crickets begin singing again. I hadn't realized they'd stopped.

From a limb overhead, a bird releases a quiet, uncertain chirp. I exhale in kinship. I'm pretty sure I know how they feel: the isel was an impossible monster that somehow fed off humans, but Selwyn is something else . . . something worse.

Every living thing in the forest had hidden itself from him.

I stand there one more beat, still frozen, and then I run. I run as fast as I can through the shadows and don't look back.

3

WHEN I BURST through the trees, I slow down, all thoughts of the impossible disappearing.

Lights flash blue and red against the night sky, and dread, heavy and sour, fills my stomach. A Durham County Sheriff patrol car has pulled into the lot, and my friends are standing beside it talking to a deputy holding a notepad.

Charlotte and the deputy both notice me approach. The deputy, a white man in his forties, flicks his notebook closed and puts a hand on his hip, as if to remind me there's no use in running away. The holstered gun on his other hip doesn't go unnoticed.

Alice is tucked behind them, a quiet shadow with her head bowed. Her hair falls forward in a thick black curtain, hiding her face. The sight makes my heart ache.

When I reach the car, the deputy glances at Charlotte. "This your friend?" Charlotte nods, then continues rapidly explaining and apologizing.

I go to Alice and look her over. "You okay?" She doesn't respond or look me in the eye. I reach for her shoulder, but she twists back, away from my fingers. "Alice—"

"Now that we're all here . . . ," the deputy drawls. Aided by a long-suffering sigh, he strides around the driver's side of his squad car—taking his sweet time on purpose, I'm positive—and leans on the hood. "Ms. Simpson, you're free to go with a warning. The next time it'll be a ticket. Ms. Chen and Ms. . . . ?" He tips his head my way expectantly and raises a brow.

I swallow, my heart still racing. "Matthews."

"Uh-huh." He nods at the back seat of the squad car. "You're both with me."

Beside me, Alice's hands shake in her lap. I glance at the squad car's glowing blue digital clock. 10:32. We've been on the dark, empty back road to campus for eleven silent minutes. Neither of us has ever ridden in a police car. It smells like leather and gun oil and something sharp and minty. My eyes land on a round green-and-black tin of Classic Wintergreen–flavored Skoal in the cup holder between the front seats. *Ugh.* Beyond the metal mesh divider, a dusty laptop sits attached to the center console. Below it, there's a pile of electrical equipment sprouting coiled wires and covered with dials and switches. The deputy, whose name tag says "Norris," fiddles with the radio station until it hits the chorus of "Sweet Home Alabama" over the crackling speaker.

I'm sixteen. I pay attention. I listen to the stories from uncles, cousins—hell, my own father—about police run-ins and stops. I see the videos online. Sitting in this car and thinking about those images makes my heart pound. I don't know if there's a single Black person in this country who can say with 100 percent confidence that they feel safe with the police. Not after the past few years. Probably not ever. Maybe there are some, somewhere, but I sure as hell don't know 'em.

Alice sits stiff as a board, gaze locked outside the window onto the endless wall of passing shadowed woods. In the front seat, Norris taps his thumbs on the wheel and mouths, "Lord, I'm coming home to you."

"Alice," I whisper. "Something happened—"

"Not talking to you."

"Come *on*," I hiss. "Back at the campfire, there was a—" *God,* I don't know where to start. "It was the fight, I think—"

"Quit the chatter," Deputy Norris orders. I catch his eyes in the mirror. He raises a brow as if to say, *Say something. I dare you.* I shutter my gaze and look away.

After a few minutes, Norris speaks up. "So, Carolina. My kid applied couple a years ago—he didn't get in. Tough school to crack. Pricey, too."

Neither one of us knows what to say to that.

"How'd y'all swing it?"

We both hesitate. Swing *what*? Getting accepted, or the cost? Alice answers first. "Scholarship."

"How 'bout you, girlfriend?" Norris's eyes find me in the mirror. "I'm guessin' need-based?"

Alice stiffens, and my hackles raise. I'm not his *girlfriend*, and I'm not ashamed to have financial aid, but that's not what he's asking—"Affirmative action?" is written all over his knowing sneer.

"Merit," I bite out through gritted teeth, even though it's none of his business either way.

He chuckles. "Sure."

I breathe through a surge of impotent rage. My fingers curl into my thighs, tensing with all of the things I can't afford to say right now.

After a few minutes, the car slows. We're still miles from campus and there's no intersection or car in sight, just a straight two-lane road illuminated by the squad car's headlights. Then I see why Norris is stopping. Two figures have emerged from the tree line on the other side of the road. As the squad car pulls closer, lights on full, the figures cover their eyes with raised hands. Norris rolls to a stop beside them, turns the volume down, and lowers his window. "Late to be out for a stroll."

"Norris, is it?" The blood drains from my face at the sound of that voice.

Deputy Norris's shoulders tense. "Kane." His eyes slide to the left. "Morgan. Sorry about that. Didn't recognize y'all."

Alice leans against her own window to get a better look at who I know to be Selwyn and Tor. *Nosy Legendborn.*

"I noticed," Sel says smoothly. He bends at the waist, and I direct my eyes straight ahead, face blank. In my peripheral vision I see his gaze linger on me for a moment, then move to Alice. His attention sets my nerves on fire. "Stragglers from the Quarry?"

"Yep," Norris confirms. He hesitates, then clears his throat. "Anything to be concerned about there?"

Selwyn stands. "Not anymore."

"Glad to hear it." Norris's chuckle is tight. Nervous.

Norris knows. He knows.

"Is that all?" Sel asks dryly. If Norris is offended that he, a Durham County Sheriff's deputy and full-grown man, is being as good as dismissed by a teenage boy, he doesn't show it.

"Just taking these two back to campus."

Sel is already walking down the road, his attention withdrawn. "On your way."

On your way. Not a request. Not a suggestion. An order.

Any ounce of security I could have felt in this car is erased in three words. Whatever higher power Deputy Norris answers to, these two teenagers outrank him.

Norris salutes Tor before she follows Sel; then he shifts the car into drive to continue down the road toward UNC. After a minute, he turns the radio back up and hums under his breath. I gather my courage and twist, as subtly as possible, to peer out the rear windshield.

Tor and Sel are gone.

Beside me, Alice slumps back against the seat. I don't attempt to talk to her again. If I didn't know what to say before, then I definitely don't now that I've seen the way law enforcement interacts with these so-called Legendborn. I spend the rest of the drive reviewing my earlier words to Alice and end up both relieved and terrified. Relieved, because I said nothing in Norris's presence to indicate that I knew what really happened at the Quarry. Terrified, because I witnessed something that I was not meant to see, and if Selwyn Kane had wanted to do something about that, Deputy Norris would not have stopped him.

Three thoughts chase one another the entire ride to campus until they bleed into a single stream of words: *Magic. Real. Here.*

Norris drops us off in front of Old East, the historic building that houses

Early College students. We take the stairs up to our dorm on the third floor in silence. Once inside, Alice changes into her pajamas and climbs into bed without saying good night. I find myself standing adrift in the middle of our floor.

On her side of the room, Alice has a row of framed photos of her brother and sisters and parents on vacation in Taiwan on the shelf above her desk. Her parents declared early on that they would pick her up from the dorms every Friday so that she could spend the weekend at home in Bentonville, but that didn't stop her from decorating like she'd live here full-time. Earlier today, she'd hung a few rom-com movie posters on the wall and draped a six-foot string of Christmas lights over her bed.

On my side, there are no pictures. No posters. Nothing decorative at all, really. Back home, it hurt beyond tolerance to walk the halls of my childhood home and see photos of my mother alive and smiling. I even hid her knick-knacks. Any sign of her existence cut into my heart, so when it came time to move to Chapel Hill, I packed light. All I have here are a few plastic bins of books and stationery, a suitcase of clothes, my favorite sneakers, my laptop and phone, and a small box of toiletries.

After tonight, everything looks like an artifact from another world where magic doesn't exist.

Real. Here.

Three other words join the thread: *Merlin. Kingsmage. Legendborn.*

I don't expect to find sleep, but I climb into bed anyway, childhood imaginings colliding with the hellish reality I'd witnessed tonight. When I was little, I loved the *idea* of magic, the kind that lives in Percy Jackson and *Charmed*. Sometimes magic seemed like a tool that could make life easier. Something that could make the impossible *possible*.

But real magic includes creatures that *feed* on humans. A small voice inside me thinks that, if they hunt those creatures, the Legendborn must be good. They *must* be. But when the night slips into early morning, that voice grows quiet. By the time I fall asleep, my ears ring with echoes: that boy's sharp cry of pain when Sel forced him to his knees; Dustin's slurred mumble as he marched to the parking lot; and the isel's scream when Sel destroyed it.

4

ALICE'S VOICE PULLS me awake.

"What is it?" I groan. Sleep threatens to drag me under, and I don't want to fight it.

"Get up!" Alice stands fully dressed with her arms crossed and hip popped. "The dean of students's office called. The dean wants to see us in fifteen minutes!"

My heart seizes in my chest and my thoughts fly. Selwyn. The creature. The ride home with Norris. *Magic.* It was all *real.* Wait—does the dean know too? Is he in cahoots with Selwyn and Tor, like the police? I swallow against a rush of panic. "Why?"

She fixes me with a pointed stare. "Why do you think?" It takes me a long minute to realize what she's referring to—expulsion. Ours. In one motion, I'm upright and out of bed. Alice pivots on a heel and sweeps out the door, her face a mixture of anger and apprehension. "I'm heading over now. Don't be late." The door slams.

I scramble for my phone, find Charlotte's late-night group text.

OMFGGGG holy hsit I'm SO sorry!! cops have NEVER shown up to the Quarry party text me when you get this!!!!

Ignore.

Next, a missed call and voicemail from a number I don't recognize with an

Orange County area code and a university prefix. My own call from the dean's office.

I dash around the room looking for clean clothes. A few minutes later I'm out the door, down the hallway, and taking the dorm stairs two at a time. I hit the crash bar on the exit door and stumble down the stone steps at the side of the brick building.

To my right, students stand in a long line on the red bricks surrounding the Old Well. Waiting for a sip, and good luck, on the first day of classes. Beyond them, the grounds are dotted with old-growth trees, low bushes, and a Confederate statue facing north.

I cross the street and trot between the South building and the old Playmakers Theatre. As soon as I clear both, I've got a picturesque view of Polk Place, the university's main quad. Then, it feels like the seven-hundred-acre campus stares back at me all at once.

Academic buildings hold the border on all four sides of the rectangular lawn, connected via a sprawling network of walkways that stretch long over the grass and cross one another like red brick latticework. A hundred yawning, groggy students drift across the quad like birds in scattered migration. Some navigate the campus by memory, heads bent over their phones. Others move in pairs or groups, cutting across the grounds toward the dining hall for breakfast before their eight a.m.'s. Late summer's early morning clouds cast the sky in muted grays and turn leaves to rich greens.

This is probably only a tenth of the grounds, but it's still more school than I've ever walked. It takes a minute to get oriented. I thumb through the campus map on my phone and take off at a jog through the low-hanging mist and dew-drenched grass for the Student and Academic Services Building.

My mind tosses up images from last night like dark, confusing confetti. I want to tell Alice what I witnessed, but would she believe I saw a golden-eyed boy who uses magic to hypnotize students and a girl who carries a bow and arrow in her back pocket? And what about the deputy—maybe even the entire Sheriff's department—who almost definitely knows the truth and helps keep it quiet? Alice didn't see the isel, but she saw Selwyn dismiss Deputy Norris. She might agree that that hadn't been a typical encounter between a police officer and a teenage boy, but would she leap with me from the shores of *not normal* to the wide, unknown ocean of *absolutely terrifying*?

"Ms. Matthews, Ms. Chen, please, sit down."

Dean McKinnon has a former-football-player look about him: broad shoulders stretch the seams of his blue-striped button-down. I'm grateful that he's offered us a seat and sit quickly. I have at least an inch in height on him, even in flats and not counting my hair, tall in its bun. It tends to make older men uncomfortable when I meet their gaze equally.

Sometimes I wish I could shrink into someone more convenient.

He strides around the desk to take his own seat. The sun sends a wide band of light in through his office window, and it bounces white, blue, and gold off the silver nameplate that sits crooked on the front edge of his mahogany desk. He pulls up a file on his computer and starts to scroll through it while we wait. His hair is shorn close to his temples and graying, but the color looks premature. Like working with thousands of students has aged him exponentially. Probably has. I'm probably one of them.

Beside me, Alice sits ramrod straight and still, but my knee bounces in anticipation. I'd been mentally composing my Don't Kick Us Out speech since the elevator ride up to the second floor of the SASB. I'm *not* going back to Bentonville. Especially not after what I saw last night.

The dean opens his mouth to speak, but I'm faster. "Mr. McKinnon—"

"*Dr.* McKinnon, Ms. Matthews." His voice is so stern I temporarily forget my rehearsed speech. He steeples his fingers. "Or Dean McKinnon. I have earned my titles." Alice shifts uncomfortably in her chair, and her lips press into a thin line.

"Yes, of course." I hear my voice slide into the tone and accent that matches the dean's. "Dean McKinnon. First of all, I'd like you to know that it was my idea to go off campus last night, not Alice's—"

Dean McKinnon's blue eyes flash between us, and he smoothly cuts me off again. "Did you handcuff Ms. Chen to you, thus forcing her to follow you?"

I exchange a glance with Alice. She tilts her head as if to say, *Shut up, Bree!* "No."

"Good." He clicks into another file, and my transcript and student ID appear on the screen. He scrolls without looking up. "Because we aren't in the business of educating students who can't think on their own. While Ms. Chen's academic records are stellar—practically perfect, in fact—if she is indeed so passive as to follow someone into her own expulsion, I'd have doubts about her being here in the first place."

Alice inhales sharply. I could kick this man.

Dean McKinnon leans back in his chair and releases a long sigh. "You're exceptional students or else you wouldn't be one of the thirty high school participants admitted to the Early College Program. It's common for students your age, upon experiencing unsupervised residential life, to make mistakes. Fortunately, the Durham County Sheriff's office has graced you both with a warning rather than a citation. Likewise, I don't intend to expel you. Consider this your first and only strike."

Oh, thank God. We both release a breath.

"However"—something sharp flashes through Dean McKinnon's eyes— "there are consequences for your blatant disrespect for program policies and the disregard for your own written agreement to follow them." I open my mouth, but he silences me with a look. "I will be placing phone calls to both of your parents after this meeting, and you will both report to a peer mentor the rest of the semester. A second-year Early College student who has excelled in the program by making better choices."

I gape, heat creeping up the back of my neck. "We don't need baby-sitters."

"Apparently," Dean McKinnon says with a raised brow, "you do."

"Thank you, Dean McKinnon," Alice says evenly.

"You're dismissed, Ms. Chen." We both stand, but he gestures for me to stay. "Ms. Matthews, a moment."

My stomach sinks like a dropped anchor. Why would he want to speak to me alone? Alice hesitates for a moment and our eyes lock; then she exits and the door clicks softly behind her.

The dean studies me and drills his fingers on the desk in the ensuing silence. *Tadum-tadum-tadum.* My heart races while I wait for him to speak. Does he know what I saw? Does *he* know about the Legendborn?

"Deputy Norris reported that you . . . got an attitude with him last night."

My mouth falls open. "An attitude? I barely said a word to him. *He's* the one who—"

Dean McKinnon stops me with a raised palm. "There are no excuses for disrespect to law enforcement. No excuses for back talk."

"I didn't—"

"If you'll let me finish," he says. I clench my teeth, and my fingers curl into fists on my thighs. Alice is passive and I'm disrespectful? White-hot fury rises in my gut, my chest, my jaw. "Fortunately, I explained to Deputy Norris that this is a difficult time for you, and a new environment that's"—he offers a patronizing smile—"different from what you're used to."

What I'm used to? My mind spirals. First the racist cop, then the dean *believing* him without giving me a chance to explain, and now . . . ?

"Your mother is—"

"Was," I correct him, automatic even as my brain processes the hard turns in our conversation.

He inclines his head. "Was. Yes, of course. Your mother was an esteemed alumna in her department. She was an advanced student: patents for biochemical testing processes, leading-edge work in soil science. I didn't know her personally, but our time as undergraduates here overlapped."

I will my hands to stop shaking, and I inhale slowly. He caught me off guard, but I have my defenses. I close my eyes and imagine my wall stretching up, up, up.

"I just wanted to say that I am sorry for your—"

My eyes snap open. "She's not lost." The words erupt from my mouth.

Dean McKinnon purses his lips. "Alice Chen is an exemplary student. But you, Ms. Matthews? With your mother's legacy and your test scores and transcripts, I'd say that you have the *potential* for brilliance." I don't know what to say to that. I don't know if I'm brilliant. I know that my mother was brilliant, and I know that I'm not my mother. His eyes flick toward the door behind me. "Your assigned mentor will contact you today. Dismissed."

I slip out the door, dizzy with frustration and humiliation both. Alice, sitting stiffly on the bench at the end of the hallway, jumps to her feet. As I get closer, I can see her red-rimmed eyes and tear-streaked face. Her trembling fingers hold a wrinkled white tissue that's been twisted into a rope.

"Alice," I begin, glancing back at the dean's door, "you won't believe what just happened in there. I'm pissed—"

"*You're* pissed?!" Alice breathes. "How do you think *I* feel?"

I startle, confused by her rage. "We're not getting kicked out. It's okay."

"It's not 'okay'!" She claps a hand over her mouth, covering a sob that erupts from deep in her chest.

I reach toward her shoulder, but Alice steps away, out of my reach.

"I—"

"Last night was *not okay*!" Her voice ricochets around the empty administrative building hallway, bounces around the cubicles and tile floors. "We almost got *expelled*. My parents would *eviscerate* me if that happened. It's going to be bad enough after he calls them!" Fresh tears run down her face.

"I know, but—"

"Not everyone is good at school without even studying like you are, Bree. Some of us have to work hard. *I* had to work hard to get here. It's been my dream since . . . since forever, and you *knew* that."

I throw my hands up. "I apologize! We won't go off campus again!"

"Good."

I shake my head. "But, in a way, I'm glad we did, because there's something *really weird* going on at this school. Last night there was this boy—"

"Are you seriously changing the subject right now?" Alice steps back. "To talk to me about a boy?"

"No!" I exclaim. "You're not listening to me—"

"Is that why you're acting this way? Boys? Is school just a big party to you now?" Her eyes grow wide, but her voice turns cold, like she's just found me stealing or cheating on a test. "That's it, isn't it? That's why you registered for those classes."

I blink. "What does—"

She laughs sourly. "English 105: Composition and Rhetoric? Come *on*, Matty! You write papers in your sleep, you've never prepared for a speech in your life, and you still get As. Bio 103: Intro to Plants of the Piedmont? Your mother was a botanist! I didn't say anything about it before, but now it makes sense. You signed up for *slacker* classes, you barely paid attention to the campus tour, and now you're getting us into trouble. You're just screwing around here, aren't you?"

Shame rises up inside my belly. Shame, and not a small amount of embarrassment. I didn't think I'd picked *slacker* classes. Maybe they wouldn't be as hard as others I could have chosen, but just being here at all is *already* hard. Keeping the wall up, keeping After-Bree hidden, and now magic. Anger chases right behind the shame, burning it away in a fiery rush. Alice doesn't even know about After-Bree. Alice doesn't know about any of it!

"You didn't have to go to the Quarry," I spit. "You could have said no."

She groans. "You've been acting like this all summer. Like nothing matters. I couldn't let you go off *alone* with Charlotte Simpson!"

"So, what, you're my babysitter now too?"

"After last night, it's pretty clear you need one! If you—" She stops herself and looks away, her jaw clenched tight around words she's holding back.

I spread my hands wide. "Say what you want to say, Alice."

She turns away. "We applied when your mom was still . . . I know things aren't the same for you. I'm trying to understand, but if you don't want to be here, if you're not going to take this seriously, then maybe you should go home."

It's like she slapped me clean across the face. Hot tears press against the back of my eyes. "Go home? Home to what, exactly? Go back to being the Girl Whose Mom Died in that small, gossipy town?" Carolina had been *our* dream.

She stares back, and I can see it in her eyes: sometime in the last twenty-four hours she'd already imagined doing this alone. Without me.

The wall inside me grows. I let it stretch so tall and wide that I can't see its top or its edges. The barrier slides into place so completely that all of the muscles in my face go still at once. I envision a surface that is flat and impenetrable, and I feel my eyes become flat and impenetrable too. "My turn. How 'bout you grow up and get a life instead of blaming me for your choices?"

Alice steps back, and the crack in her voice goes straight to my heart. "I don't know who you are right now, Bree." She stares at me for a moment longer and then bends to gather her things. I can't move, or speak.

All I can do is watch her walk away.

5

ANGER CASCADES THROUGH me so entirely I can taste it.

I make it halfway back to Old East before I have to pause to catch my breath on the steps of a library. At the edge of Polk Place, it seems like all of Carolina's almost thirty thousand students are rippling across the quad in a steady wave, heading to their first class of the semester.

Before, Alice and I'd talked about EC like a grand adventure we would conquer together. Now, watching all the other students walk to their classes with purpose, it feels like I'm here on my own. A sly, bitter voice appears from a dark corner: *Maybe that's how it should be. One less memory of Before-Bree to live up to.* I swallow against the quiet, raw satisfaction that surfaces, but it doesn't go away. Right now, alone feels . . . *good.*

My phone buzzes in my pocket. A text from a number I don't recognize.

Hi, Briana! This is Nick Davis. Dean McKinnon gave me your number so we could get started today. Want to meet up after classes?

The babysitter already. I swipe it away. Then my phone buzzes *again*. A call. The name on the screen makes my throat go tight, but I answer it anyway.

"Hey, Dad."

"There's my college kid." My father's voice is warm and familiar, but my pulse quickens. Did the dean call him already?

"It's not real college, Dad." I sit on the stone veranda behind one of the library's massive columns, tucking myself away from the eyes of passersby.

"It's a real college campus," he retorts. "They take my real college money."

Damn. No comeback there. What I said to Norris was true: I did earn a merit award. My parents weren't rich, but they'd been good about saving. Even still, the small pot of money they'd saved for my college tuition wouldn't be enough to pay for a four-year bachelor's degree without loans. The only reason Dad could afford the two years of EC was because that partial academic award cut the price in half. He doesn't say as much, but I know he's gambling that the investment in EC now will help me get into colleges later, and maybe earn scholarships, too. I wince, still smarting from Alice's comment about my class choices. "S'pose that's right," I mumble.

"Mm-hmm." He chuckles. "How was your first night in a real college dorm?"

My dad doesn't traffic in subtext. With him, what you see and hear is what you get. If he'd gotten a call from the dean, he'd have let me know by now. Loud and *clear.* I release a quiet sigh.

"First night here? Quiet," I lie. It doesn't feel great, but I don't feel great right now.

I expect the next question, and it's right on time. "Met any Black kids yet?"

The only other Black kids in my high school had been a year older than me. A quiet boy named Eric Rollins and a girl named Stephanie Henderson. Whenever we spent time together, the white kids got nervous or, like, weirdly excited? All the other Black folks I know are relatives or from our church two towns over. Carolina's got a larger Black population than Bentonville High does, that I know for sure. It's one of the reasons I applied.

"Not yet. I haven't even gone to my first class."

"Well, you need a community. When's your first class?"

"Ten a.m."

"Had breakfast yet?"

"Not hungry." I realize I haven't eaten since before the Quarry.

Dad makes an *mmph* sound. I imagine his expression as he does it: mouth curled downward, bushy dark brows furrowed, all the lines in his deep brown face frowning at me all at once. "Appetite still comin' and goin'?" I don't reply, not ready to lie again just yet. He sighs. His voice is slow, careful, and his Richmond drawl drops away. "The book says that not feeling hungry, not eating, is a physical symptom of grief."

I *knew* he'd bring up that book. I can see the title now: *Letting Go: Bereavement, Love, and Loss.* I squeeze my eyes shut and scramble around for my wall. "I eat. I'm just not hungry right now."

"Kiddo, while you're away, I need you to take care of yourself. Meals, rest, grades, make some new friends. If you shut down, you come home. That was the deal, right?" I make my own *mmph* sound, and his voice gets sharp around the edges. "Excuse me? I'm not sure I heard you. That was the deal. Correct?"

"Correct," I murmur. That *had* been the deal. He knew I was miserable at home, and so he let me go, but he'd had reservations. "Dad, I appreciate you asking. I really do. I'm okay, though. Being here is . . ." *Scary. Lonely. Messy.* "Good for me."

"Baby . . ." The tiniest tremor in my father's voice makes my chest go tight. "You keep saying you're okay, but this thing that's happening to us . . . I feel it too. I know it feels real bad."

"I'm good, Dad," I grit out. I stare at the veranda beneath my feet, and my vision tunnels, goes sharp, then blurry.

"Okay," he says with a sigh. "Well, try and get some food in your stomach before your class, okay, kiddo?"

"Will do."

A pause. "Where do we begin?"

I clench my phone tight at my ear. It's what we say when one of us is overwhelmed. "At the beginning."

"That's my smart girl. Talk to you later."

When we hang up, I'm shaking. My breath comes in short pants; heat climbs around my collar. I dig my elbows into my knees and press the heels of my hands into my eyes. *This* is why I left. I love my father, but his words puncture every single layer of my wall until it may as well not exist. His grief makes my own emotions break across my skin like an earthquake, opening me up to—

"No," I whisper into my palms. "No, no, no." But it's too late; the memories swell and take me.

The sharp smell of hospital disinfectant. Raw bile in the back of my throat. Cheap, soft wood in the cranny beneath my fingernails as I dig them into the armrest.

Details from that night spin like a hurricane, blocking out the world in layers. The flashback pulls me from the now and into the past, one sense at a time, until I'm in both places, both times at once—

A blue jay jeering and whistling overhead in a tree.

The piercing beep from a life support monitor down the hall.

The campus Bell Tower chimes nine a.m.

The police officer's deep, even voice . . . "Route 70 around eight . . . a hit-and-run."

Familiar, horrifying, all-consuming—once it starts, this memory is a ride I can't escape. The only thing to do is let it run its course—

The nurse leaves. The officer watches her go. He sighs. "I'm sorry for your loss . . ."

Almost over.

Next, we'll stand, he'll shake my father's hand, and we'll go home without her. I whimper and rock and wait for that awful night to let me go—

But it doesn't.

I gasp as a new image dislodges itself with a violent *crack*, like an iceberg in an ocean.

A silver badge on a breast pocket flashing. A body, shimmering. The officer's blue eyes holding my gaze, then my father's. His thin, drawn mouth muttering words I can't hear. Words flowing into the room. A cold wind sweeping through my mind . . .

Just as quickly, the memory ends.

"That's not what happened—" As soon as the words leave my mouth, I know they aren't right.

For the second time in twenty-four hours, my brain wrestles with two conflicting memories of the exact same moment.

I squeeze my eyes shut. The memory of the isel at the Quarry is still there, opaque under a silver smoke blanket of false images. The truth under Selwyn's lie.

Now the new memories of the hospital wage war against the old ones, until finally, the lies dissolve.

Selwyn and the police officer. Both chanted a spell of some kind. Both bent my mind to their will.

My eyes snap open.

The first time I saw magic was the night my mother died.

My first class, English in Greenlaw, goes by in a blur. I don't remember walking there. I sit at the back of the classroom. Questions run through my mind on a loop:

Was the officer at the hospital like Sel? A Merlin? A Kingsmage? How big is the Legendborn network? Why did I remember what Sel wanted me to forget? Why am I only now remembering what happened then? What other memories did that officer *take? And why?* Was an isel there at the hospital that night too? Did it attack my mother? Is *that* what killed her? How much do I *really* know about my mother's death?

I lose time. The professor talks. I don't write a thing.

My phone buzzes.

Briana. I got a phone call from the Chens then a phone call from the dean. Going off campus? Trespassing? The police? You need to call me back ASAP.

My father's anger barely registers, but I force myself to text back.

He gave us a warning. I'm in class right now. Can we talk later?

You hid this from me on the phone. A lie of omission is still a lie.

I know, Dad. I'll call you after dinner.

Yes, you will!

Two hours later, class is over. I drift through the crowd like a ghost, eyes unfocused and turned inward.

The campus that had seemed large and intimidating now feels tight and claustrophobic. Trees obscure the lawn like curtains hiding secret truths. Towering oaks are sentinels, monitoring our every word. I lose time again while sitting on a bench outside, so far gone that I jump when my phone buzzes.

Hey, Briana! Nick again. Hope your first day is going well! My last class gets out at five thirty. Want to meet up for dinner?

Ignore.

By the time my second class is over, one thought has burrowed in my mind like a splinter:

Someone used magic to hide what really happened the night my mother died, and I'm not going to let them get away with it.

6

WHERE DO WE begin? At the beginning.

Well, by dinner, I have the beginnings of a plan. In the busy dining hall I grab a table and take bites of a sandwich between texting the only person I know who might have answers.

Hey! We didn't get expelled.

The response is instant. Charlotte's the type of girl who lives with her phone in her hand, never on silent, never on do-not-disturb.

YEsssss! I'm serious tho i'm really sorry I almost got y'all kicke out!!! I feel like hsit

I should feel ashamed about using her guilt to my advantage, right?

All good. That party was wild. Lots of different kids there.

For REAL! somebody ratted out those football players! They have to ride the bench our first game and it's against State, too!

That's bullshit! I don't keep up with football, but vulgarity seems like the right response. Who was that girl yelling at everyone to leave? Tall blond ponytail

Victoria Morgan. Goes by Tor. A serious legacy. She adds a couple of thumbs-down emojis.

What's her deal?

Her daddy and granddaddy and whoever else all the way back to whenever went to UNC. Couple years ago, her fam donated so much $ to the B School they renamed a building after them. Old money good ol' boys. Legacy kids waltz in, get whatever grades, and leave 4 years later with great internships and jobs lined up

Old money and good ol' boys. Why am I not surprised? This is the South. Tight-knit groups, lots of loyalty, established networks, plenty of resources. Perfect for the Legendborn, I bet.

What about that guy she was with? I pick out the descriptors that sound the most . . . reasonable. Dark hair. Angry. Yellow eyes.

SELWYN KANE WAS THERE!?!?! AND I MISSED HIM!?? He never parties with ANYONE. Holy Jesus that boy is hottt

A stream of emojis: tongue-out smiley face, both hands up, hunnit, kissy lips.

I shudder. I don't think Charlotte would add kissy lips if she'd seen Sel snarl like a lion and almost break someone's kneecaps with one hand. She texts me back before I can respond.

Selwyn doesn't hang with Tor tho?

He doesn't? They were both standing right near the fight. All true. All things anyone could have seen.

I've never seen them even SPEAK to each other. They don't run in the same circles, babe. Not even close! He's an EC junior like me and Tor's a regular junior.

My wheels spin. So, the Legendborn avoid each other in public, but in private, they're coordinated. Organized. They mentioned a Gate on campus. Is that where they usually hunt? If Sel is an EC junior, he's not ageless; he's eighteen.

Gotta go. Sigma party tonight! Wanna come?

Nope. Already on the dean's shitlist.

By the time I finish dinner, the sun has set and ribbons of deep purple and burnt orange streak through the darkening sky. I push through the doors into the thick soup of a humid evening, lost in thought.

"Briana Irene Matthews!"

I freeze, then pivot slowly to look for the sort of asshole who calls out some-one's full name *in public* to get their attention.

Leaning against the wall just beside the exit is a tall white boy with tousled straw-blond hair and the bluest eyes I've ever seen. He looks like he belongs on the cover of the university brochure: impossibly bright and cheery, wearing plain jeans and a Carolina blue zipped hoodie. When he laughs, the sound is warm and genuine. "Now, that's what you call a murderous expression!"

"Want to help me with the follow-through?" I snap.

He smiles, shoves off the wall with one foot, and strolls toward me. "You're hard to pin down." He looks up briefly, as if considering. Eyes back on me. "And *rude*, too, leaving me on read all day."

My eyes fall shut as I mutter, "You're the babysitter."

"Does that mean you're a baby?" My eyes snap open to find Nick Davis standing right in front of me, eyes twinkling with barely contained mirth. He is at least four inches taller than me, which is saying something, even though as a second-year EC he's probably only a year older than I am. Definitely not built like any seventeen-year-olds I know. With his broad shoulders and narrow waist, he looks like one of those Olympic gymnasts.

I turn on my heel to leave. This boy is not part of the plan. Not the begin-ning, middle, or anywhere in between.

"Briana, wait up!" Nick jogs to follow. "I'll walk you to your dorm."

"It's Bree, and no thanks."

When he catches up, his fresh-laundry-and-cedar scent comes with him. *Of course* he smells good. "Bree, short for Briana." His dimple-edged smile is proba-bly on a poster at a dentist's office somewhere.

"I'd be happy to escort you. Peer mentor and all that," he says without a stitch of sarcasm. "According to the dean, you have a tendency to get lost at night and accidentally end up in the back of police cruisers?"

I huff and pick up the pace, but he matches mine without missing a beat. "How did you find me?"

He shrugs. "I asked Dean McKinnon for your class schedule and campus ID photo." He holds up a hand before I protest. "Not personal information typically shared with students, but the EC consent forms we all signed waive that right between mentors, orientation assistants, and other assigned guides. I found out when your last class ended. Made a guess as to when you'd hit dinner, then estimated how long it'd take for you to get through the buffet line in Lenoir, find a table, and eat at that hour of the day. All I had to do was show up and wait outside the exit closest to Old East."

I stop, my jaw open. He grins, clearly amused and more than a little pleased with himself. "So, you're a creep?"

He holds a hand to his chest like I've wounded him. "Not a creep, just clever! And operating under Dean McKinnon's explicit orders to make first contact with you *today*." Ocean eyes set in a tanned face take me in, and a knowing smile sends a wave of warmth to my ears. "Timed it perfectly too. You walked out five minutes after I arrived."

"Being clever and being creepy are not mutually exclusive."

"Oh, I agree." He scratches at his chin. "There's probably a Venn Diagram or a graph of direct proportionality in there somewhere—"

I groan. "This is, by definition, using your intelligence for evil."

Nick tilts his head. "Correct. On two levels, in fact." He raises a finger. "Using one's cleverness to creep and"—a second finger—"using one's cleverness to diagram the cleverness-to-creepiness relationship."

I open my mouth, close it, turn, and walk away. He follows.

We walk in silence for a few moments, letting the night flow around and between us. I glance back once. Nick's easy stroll reminds me of a dancer: long strides, straight posture. When my eyes reach his face, there's a smile tugging at the corner of his lips. I whip around.

After a minute, he speaks up again, his voice curious behind me. "So, did you jump the cliff? The one at the Quarry?"

"No."

"Well," he muses, "aside from landing in the dean's office on your first day of school—a record, I'm guessing, so well done—it's not the worst thing to do. Cliff's not that high, and it's kinda fun."

I turn back to face him, surprised in spite of myself. "*You've* done it?"

He chuckles. "I have."

"But aren't you the dean's golden boy?"

He lifts a shoulder. "I'm great on paper." A few minutes later, we arrive at an intersection where walking paths branch out all around us in a circle like spokes on a wheel. He steps beside me and we walk together down the path on our right toward Old East. Crickets and cicada song drone in the distance.

I wonder if Alice is back in our room. We've fought before, plenty of times, but nothing like this. Nothing that left me feeling this cold. I imagine Alice's eyes in my mind, angry and scornful. The last person who'd yelled at me like that had been my mom. How am I so good at hurting the people I love? Hurting them so badly that they scream and cry in my face?

"So, Dean McKinnon said you enrolled with a friend?"

This boy is intuitive. Unnervingly so. "Alice. She's always wanted to come here."

He eyes me. "And you didn't?" I blink, unsure how to respond, and he takes my silence as an answer. "Then why did you come?"

"I'm a smarty-pants."

His scan of my face is quick, appraising. "Obviously," he murmurs, "but that's *how* you got here, not *why*. Nobody comes to EC just for the classes."

I snort. "Tell that to Alice. She'll be crushed."

"Not answering the question. I see." His attentive eyes pass over me like he's found my insides and wants to idly peruse them. *No rush. Don't mind me. Just digging out your guts.*

"Dean McKinnon asked me to talk to you about your student activity requirement since some campus groups begin recruiting members the first week of school. See any you like?" I'd completely forgotten about that part of the program. Nick spots the look on my face and hides a smirk behind his palm. "Do you even know what a student group is?"

"I can guess," I growl. "Clubs. Professional degree orgs for pre-med kids or pre-law kids. I dunno . . . fraternities and sororities?"

"Mostly right," he says, "except EC kids can't join frats or sororities. Minors in environments notorious for partying and drinking? That's a no-go. What parent would send their precious underage baby to UNC if they thought we were studying organic chem during the day and doing keg stands at night?"

"Well, which one did you join? So I know which one to avoid."

"A second sidestepped question. Cricket Club."

"Cricket. Club. In basketball and football country?"

He shrugs. "I knew it would piss my dad off."

Something twists in my heart, tight and sharp. "Oh?"

"My dad's an alum. A psychology professor here."

"And he wants you to do something other than cricket?"

"Yep." Nick tips his head backward and watches the tree limbs as we pass under them. "Follow in his footsteps."

"But you're not going to do that something else?"

"Nope."

"Why not?"

He drops his gaze to mine. "Because I don't do things just because my father wants me to."

Suddenly, irrationally, the twist in my chest transforms into something more aggressive. "He just wants a connection."

Nick scoffs. "I'm sure he does, but I don't care."

I stop on the pathway and turn to him. "You *should* care."

Nick stops walking. Uses my earlier response against me. "Oh?"

"Yes," I challenge.

We lock eyes, brown to blue, and something unexpected passes between us. A tug of friendship, a dropper full of humor.

"You're pushy," he observes, and smiles.

I don't know what to say to that, so I start walking again.

Old East appears ahead of us, beige-yellow brick and unremarkable identical windows running in rows down its sides. You'd never guess it had been standing for almost two hundred and thirty years—the oldest state university building in the country.

I don't know why it bugs me that Nick doesn't want to connect with his father. We've only just met, we barely know each other, and he doesn't owe me any details about his life. It shouldn't irritate me.

But it does.

Contempt and jealousy intertwine and slice through my stomach like jagged claws. I want to aim them at this Nick so that he can feel what I think of his wasted luxury: a parent who's still alive for reconciliation. I turn to him, the words on my tongue, when I catch a flash of unearthly light in the distance, just over his shoulder.

Selwyn's magic had been smoke and swirling silver. These flames, pulsing in the sky above the trees, burn a rotting neon green.

"Oh my God . . . ," I whisper, my heart suddenly racing.

"What?" Nick asks.

I'm running past him before any other thoughts fully form. I hear him yelling behind me, asking me what's wrong, but I don't care. I *can't* care.

This time of day on a college campus makes a straight path impossible. Strolling students, sitting couples, and a Frisbee game send me zigzagging. Last night I ran away from magic. Tonight, I *have* to run toward it. For my mom, for my dad, for me. I have to know the truth. I have to know if not getting a chance to talk to her again was my fault, or if—

I round a hedge, and the world drops out from underneath me.

Crouched between two science buildings is something I'd never imagined could exist.

The creature is outlined in thin green light. Its body flickers, gaining density, then thinning, then gaining it again. It could be a wolf except that it stands twice as tall and instead of fur it has a semitranslucent layer of stretched and blackened skin that flakes off at the joints of its four legs. It bares two rows of teeth, curved backward like scythes. Thin rivers of steaming black saliva stream between its lower canines and pool on the grass.

I don't know what sound I make—a gasp, a near-silent yelp of fear—but its head whips in my direction, glowing red eyes and red-tipped ears pointing my way. It howls, and the piercing sound bounces between the buildings until it assaults me from all sides, freezing me to the spot.

The creature drops low, a growl gurgling in its throat, and launches itself at me.

I brace for the bite of teeth, but suddenly a figure barrels into the creature, knocking it off course mid-flight.

The heaving wolf-thing hits a brick wall with a heavy, squelching sound, a smear of black splattering the wall from the impact.

"Run!" It's Nick who stands between me and the creature.

The creature hauls itself to its feet. It shakes its body like a dog, flinging dark liquid in every direction. Where the spray lands, grass sizzles like bacon in a pan.

"Bree!" Nick bends down on one knee. *"Run!"*

Heart pounding in my ears, I stumble—and fall. An arrow of pain shoots up my palms into my elbows.

Nick yanks a thin silver baton from a sheath strapped to his shin. He shifts into a high crouch, then whips the baton down in a slicing motion. The rod extends into a thin, sharp blade.

A hidden weapon. Just like Tor's.

Nick spins the sword in his grip. At the top of the arc, a small silver cross guard pops out over his hand.

The creature leaps off powerful hind legs and Nick dodges, slicing its ribs as he goes. It lands and swings its tail. Nick ducks, narrowly missing the barbed tip.

The two dance faster than I can follow: Nick slashes. The creature swipes black-tipped claws at his chest. Nick opens it up and sickly light pours from its skin.

They circle each other, both panting hard. Then, the pattern breaks.

Nick steps backward; the creature follows. Nick drops his chin and takes another measured step back—into a closed alley between buildings.

There's nowhere to run.

He's trapped, and he doesn't even realize it.

The creature rears back—

Instinctively, I scramble to my feet and yell, "Hey! This way!"

Nick's eyes fly to mine at the same time that the creature's ears flick back toward my voice.

"No!" Nick shouts, but it's too late. I'm running and the creature is sprinting in my direction. I shift, running perpendicular to its path. Out of the side of my eye, I see it change direction to follow me.

It's *fast*. Its teeth snap behind me, less than a foot away. I tuck my chin and push. Faster. *Faster*. A howl of pain—not mine. A heavy thud.

I can't help but look.

Nick's sword is buried a foot deep into the downed creature's spine. The body shudders and spasms, the blade shaking with it. The creature's front paws are splayed toward me. So close.

Nick had speared it mid-pounce.

A millisecond later—

"Get back!"

In one motion, the creature I thought was dead pulls its limbs in and under and springs. I raise my arms. It yelps; the embedded sword cuts its attack short. Its jaws snap, black spittle sprays through the air—I hit the ground.

My hands and arms are on fire.

Someone's screaming.

Me, I think.

The world bleeds black, flowing like ink to the center of my vision.

The last thing I see is Nick, yanking his sword free, then driving it deep into the creature's skull.

7

VOICES FADE IN and out.

What happened?!

Hellhound saliva.

Feels like my head is dunked underwater. Drawn up. Under again.

On campus? Corporeal? That's impossible—

Help me get her on the table!

Falling. Falling down to the cold and the dark. The voices grow faint.

Who is she? Aether isn't meant for Onceborns. If she—

It's eating through her bones. Do it. Now.

The high-pitched, rhythmic trill of crickets pulses against my skull.

My eyes open to find a white ceiling with wide exposed wooden beams and a ceiling fan spinning lazy circles. I try sitting—and fail spectacularly. My arms aren't working.

"You're all right." A gentle palm presses my shoulder down. Nick withdraws his hand. He's standing beside the bed, one sleeve of his hoodie torn to shreds.

A white sheet covers the rest of my body, but underneath it, an intense itch crawls up, around, and over my arms. An awkward roll dislodges one limb; then panic rises. Thick layers of gauze wrap my right arm from knuckle to elbow. I yank my left shoulder back to confirm what the itching is already telling me, but the bedding catches.

"Careful," Nick cautions. He folds the sheet back to expose my left arm, bandaged identically to the first. "You were injured."

"Where am I?" I croak. My throat feels like sandpaper someone set on fire.

"I brought you to our healer." Nick reaches for a glass of water on a bedside table behind him. There's a straw crooked out of the top, and he brings the glass closer. It's awkward, and it makes me feel like a child, but I'm too thirsty to turn him down.

He didn't really answer *my* question, and I'm sure he knows that, but there are other ways to figure out where I am.

The room is comfortable in an expensive ski lodge sort of way, but the building feels *old*: furniture and wallpaper done in heavy fabrics and textures no one uses in updated homes. Tall ceilings, mahogany hardwood floors in wide planks. To my right, an upholstered seat below a tall window cracked open to the night—and the chirping of crickets. No lights beyond the glass pane. In the distance, the Bell Tower erupts in Westminster Quarters—the opening notes of the melody clear, but not close. Near campus, then.

I finish drinking. Nick puts the glass down and moves to the window seat to sit, his expression solemn. Nothing like the Nick I met outside Lenoir. "What do you remember?"

I frown, images coming in quick flashes: light in the sky. Running. Nick, wielding a sword. A *monster*. My eyes key to his in an instant. "You killed it."

He nods. "I killed it."

The Bell Tower chimes the hour. One. Two.

"You saved me." Three.

He holds my gaze—four—nods again. Five.

A realization, clear and true before I even speak it aloud. "You're Legendborn." Six.

He inclines his head. "Yep. You must be a new Page? William said he didn't recognize you."

I shake my head. Seven.

He frowns, studying my face. "But you saw the hellhound——" When the tower strikes eight, Nick goes still as a statue.

I honestly don't know who's more stunned, him or me. We search each other's faces, as if the next step in this conversation might be written on our skin. Nine. Ten. All I see are the hard lines of his jaw and his eyes, wide and wary. The strands of his straw-colored hair are still darkened from perspiration. Eleven. Silence.

Eleven o'clock—not quite three hours since we met. Close to campus. In an old building. Historic home, maybe. All clues, folded together.

He narrows his eyes in speculation. "If you know I'm Legendborn, then you must know you're speaking within the Code. You can answer me freely. How do you know that word?"

I chew on my bottom lip to buy myself time. The way he says "Code" sounds as if there should be formal trust between us. Sure, Tor and Sel possess an easy ruthlessness that I can't, at the moment, find in Nick's face, but that doesn't mean he's safe. If he's Legendborn, he could be dangerous. "What will you do to me if I answer that question?"

Surprise ripples across his features. "*Do* to you?"

I nod, my heart thumping in my chest. "Threaten me? Break something I'd rather keep in one piece? Turn me over to the cops?"

His blue eyes dim, a storm cloud crossing the sky. "I'm not going to do any of those things." He gestures toward my arms. "Why would I bring you here to our healer if I wanted to injure you? If I wanted you to end up with the police, why didn't I drop you off in front of a hospital?"

"Maybe you still plan to dump me at a hospital," I shoot back. "Maybe the police are on the way."

A wide smile spreads across his face, and just like that, he's Nick from the dining hall again: amused and wry. "Bree, short for Briana. Pushy *and* stubborn. She doesn't accept what she sees with her own eyes, won't accept what she hears with her own ears." He appears to turn an idea over in his head before pinning it to me with his eyes to see if it fits. "Or at least, that's what she'd *like* me to believe. Is 'Bree' even your real name?"

Bristling, I ask, "What about my memory? You could still erase that."

His grin falls away. "No. I couldn't."

Fear makes me bold. "Not a Merlin?"

"You know I'm not." His eyes narrow, and the corners of his mouth turn down in a mixture of resignation and disappointment. His low chuckle is laced with fatigue and the tiniest thread of anger. "All right, I get it. You know about Merlins and their mesmers, so you're Oathed, but you're not a Page from our chapter. Who sent you, then? Was it Western? You here to *evaluate* me?"

My mouth opens, then closes, because I have no idea how to answer. Who does he think I am? Who do I *want* him to think I am?

I decide we're playing a strange sort of game, he and I. Each searching for the knowledge that the other has before we reveal any more of our own. I know why I want his answers, but I don't know yet why he wants mine.

I lift my chin, a spark of my earlier determination coming back alongside a tiny bit of After-Bree under the surface, just enough to fuel a wild card challenge that won't make me look ignorant and might be just sharp enough to make him reveal himself. "I know Legendborn love to hunt isels like the one that I helped you find tonight."

The wild card backfires.

"Oh, you want to test me, is that it? Fine." Nick pushes up from the window seat, eyes flashing in a way that startles me. "First, that wasn't just any isel. That was a ci uffern, a hellhound. Lowest intelligence of the Lesser demons, no speech capabilities, but the most ferocious next to the foxes. Partial-corp, so it was still invisible to Onceborns, but able to injure living flesh. Another few aether infusions and it would've been as solid as you and me. And second . . ." He runs a hand through his hair, a gesture that's part disbelief, part frustration.

It's a welcome pause, because even though I'm lying down, the word "demon" has shifted the world beneath me. Nick's unfinished sentence has me perched in terrifying hesitation at the top of a roller coaster. His next one tips me over.

"Second, you didn't help me *find* it, Bree. You ran *straight toward it*. You baited a hellhound, unarmed and untrained, and almost lost both arms for your trouble. Whoever ordered this little recon mission sent you here with more ignorance than I've witnessed in a Page in years. I've changed my mind. If this is a game, I'm not playing anymore. Answers. Now."

A demon.

Both arms.

Aether.

I swallow around the fresh fear swirling in my throat. "I . . . I didn't know they were . . . demons. I—"

"Christ, you're either *incredibly* stubborn and committed to this ruse or you're so brand-new they rushed you out here right after your damn Oath." Nick runs a hand over his face and sighs heavily. "Yeah, they're demons. This is basic information. Kiddie stuff."

Demons. The word raises a childhood memory: my mother, taking us to church for worship in hot, humid summers, all packed pews and paper fans on tongue depressors. I'd sit beside her, miserable, with sweat dripping down the back of my polyester dress, white tights sticking to my thighs, and flip through the pew Bible to take my mind off the heat. The colorful, whisper-thin pages of art tucked in the middle realized what the text could not: St. Peter at gates made of gold, ribbons of sun shining through white clouds that stretch on forever; holy light blazing around Jesus's head; invisible impure spirits— demons—tormenting gaping believers with lies and deception.

"Like in the Bible?"

Nick takes in my expression. When he sighs, the severity falls from his frame one fraction at a time, like a dropped cloak. He steps forward and reaches for me, then stops when I flinch. "Not gonna go through the trouble to heal you and then turn around and hurt you again," he says, and waits for my response. After a moment of hesitation, I nod, and he gingerly takes my right hand in his to unravel the gauze in slow loops. He shakes his head. "Half-educated Page it is . . . I can't believe the jerk who put you up to this without even teaching you the fundamentals. Honestly, you should tell me who they are—they need to be reported for this kind of negligence." When I just stare at him, he scratches the back of his head. "I can't let you leave here without knowing the basics, or else you'll end up in a bwbach pit or strangled by a sarff uffern, or worse.

"The Shadowborn—what we call demonkind—come to our plane through Gates they open between our world and theirs."

Shadowborn. The strange word lingers and loops through my mind, but I'm too frightened to stop him for an explanation.

"No one knows where a Gate will appear, but they cluster in some places more than others, almost always at night. Most of the Shadowborn that cross are invisible and incorporeal. They come to our side to feed on and amplify negative human energy—chaos, fear, anger. Those emotions sustain them. If they get strong enough to use aether, they'll use it to go corp—corporeal—and they can attack us physically then, too. We don't hunt the demons just to hunt them. We don't do it because we like it, no matter what other chapters say. We do it to protect humanity." His fingertips leave warm trails behind on my skin. As the material falls away in his hands, it releases the bright, tangy smell of citrus trees and damp soil.

When I glance down, my skin looks like it was splashed with acid—not tonight, but maybe weeks or months ago. Streams of shiny, pink tissue run in a drizzle from palm to elbow. The new skin is sensitive; when he wraps his palm around one arm, carefully turning it so he can examine me, I feel the calluses from where he's spent long hours practicing with a weapon.

"Hellhound saliva is corrosive enough to melt steel," he explains. "I've seen a few drops burn a hole through a foot of concrete. You're lucky William was home." He places the last bit of gauze and the other loose roll on the nightstand. "The rest will be healed by morning."

"How is that possible?"

"We're really doing this?"

"Yes," I whisper. "Please."

He scoffs. "This type of ignorance is how Pages get hurt or killed. What you saw in the sky was mage flame. A byproduct of aether, an element in the air that only some people can see and fewer still can manipulate. Different Legendborn use aether to do different things. Some create constructs like weapons, armor, shields. William uses it to accelerate healing."

That name again. Their healer. Someone who helped me even though he doesn't know me. Sudden shame washes over me in a wave. Nick rescued me, made sure my injuries were treated, and I'd just antagonized him. "Thanks," I finally murmur, "for helping me. And thank William."

He looks me over again and notes the tremor in my fingers. His face turns patient and open. "I'll let him know. But if you're looking for a thank-you gift, I'm a fan of honesty."

I struggle for words. "I just wanted to know what I saw. What I'm seeing," I say softly. The memory of the *other* Merlin from the hospital rises—and immediately turns sour. The flashback threatens to take me in front of this boy that I don't know. I *need* that memory. And I will use it. But I can't let it have me. Not now. Instead, I strengthen my wall and wrap myself around the easier facts. "Last night at the Eno Quarry, I saw something. Flickering light in the shape of a flying . . . thing. Sel and Tor were there. Sel did something to me and these guys to make us forget and walk away. His mesmer, I guess? But after a minute, it didn't work anymore. I hid. Then Sel and Tor—"

"Wait." Nick's hand shoots up. "Say that again."

"Sel and Tor—"

He waves his hand impatiently. "No, no, before that."

"Sel did something to make me leave and forget, but after a minute it didn't work on me?"

"Yeah, that part. Not possible, Pageling. Mesmered memories don't come back." His eyes fill with an emotion I can't read. "Believe me, I'd know."

I shrug, picking at the edge of the sheet. "Well, *sorry,*" I say, copying his condescending tone, "but that's what happened, Legendborn."

Nick examines my face. He looks at me for so long and the room is so silent that I'm certain he can hear my heartbeat quicken. His eyes drop to my mouth, my chin, my hands still shaking on my lap. He sucks in a sharp breath. "You're—you're *serious,* aren't you? About everything. You aren't a Northern or Western spy."

"No."

"But if you can break *Sel's* mesmer, then he'd . . ." Nick stops, his eyes wide as dinner plates, the color draining from his face with some understanding about me that I don't follow.

I shove myself upright as my adrenaline spikes. "Then he'd what?"

"WHERE IS HE?"

We both jump when a voice booms, the shout echoing outside the room and down what sounds like a long hallway.

Nick's attention flies to the door, tension singing through his frame. "Shit."

Another door slams. Hurried footsteps, and another, calmer voice intercepts the first. "Sel, wait—"

Nick glances rapidly between me and the door. "Listen to me. I assumed you were one of us at first, but if you're telling me the truth right now and you're not, then no matter what happens when he comes in here, *do not* let Sel know his mesmer failed. He's going to try again, and you need to let him. You understand me?"

A second slam, closer this time. "No! Wha—"

"I need you to trust me," Nick hisses. I stare, speechless, and he shakes my shoulder to get my attention. *"Do you understand?"*

"Yes!"

"Stay here." Without another word, he jogs to the door, opening it and closing it behind him.

I do not stay there.

I throw the covers off the bed. Across the room, my sneakers are perched on a stately-looking armchair. I make a beeline toward them and shove them on, but when I stand up, a wave of dizziness sends me slumping against the leather.

Sel's cold, measured tones reach me from just outside the door. "The prodigal son returns. And with such *flare*." He's so close. Too close. My eyes dart to the open window, and I heave myself off the chair to get to it even though the floor threatens to rise up with every step. "Did you even kill it, Davis?"

"Yes, I killed it." Nick's voice is a taut wire ready to snap. "You want to inspect the blood on my blade?"

Sel doesn't miss a beat. "Perhaps if you weren't so busy playing Onceborn, leaving us to do the dirty work, you'd know that I should have been called immediately to find its Gate and close it. Or do you *want* more hellhounds coming through from the other side?"

I reach the window and curse silently. I'm three stories up. Wherever this museum house is, it's surrounded by a dense forest. Even if I were on the first floor and felt steady enough to climb out, there'd be nowhere to go.

"Do you *want* me to pause mid-battle to send a text? What are the emojis for a hellhound? Fire, then dog?"

There's a quick shuffle, and the third voice intervenes again. "This is not helpful! Sel, you closed the Gate. Nick destroyed the hound. That's all that matters."

"That is not all that matters, William. This is the fifth attack in a week. They are *escalating*. And getting stronger. Just last night I tracked a near-corporeal isel miles from the nearest Gate. It is my job to protect this chapter," Sel growls. "Just as it is my job to clean up your mess tonight. William says I'm needed here?"

"She's a human being, Sel." I wonder if Nick is stalling, but his voice sounds too weary. Too familiar with this argument.

"She's Onceborn," Sel retorts. Something about the way he says "Onceborn" makes me flinch, and I don't even know what the word means. "How did she even get wounded?"

"It was partial-corp. She was just in the wrong place at the wrong time."

"A partial-corp demon, capable of hunting—and harming—human flesh. Wonderful. And then you brought her here. *Lovely.*"

"Would you rather I left her on the ground, blacked out from pain?"

"Of course not. Her injuries would raise far too many questions."

"That's your only concern, isn't it? The Code of Secrecy. Not that an innocent was injured!"

"The Line is Law, Nicholas." Sel's voice is low, dangerous. "Our Oaths come first!"

"*Gentlemen!*" William shouts. "Speaking of the Code, may I remind you both that these walls are not soundproofed. The more you argue outside this door, the more Sel will need to erase."

My heartbeat speeds from a gallop to a full-on jackhammer sprint.

"Thank you, William, for that reminder." The knob turns, and Sel sweeps into the room, face full of thunder. When his eyes fasten to mine, his forehead furrows slightly in surprise. "You."

It's only been a day, but I'd somehow forgotten how terrifying this boy is. Even without Nick's height and stature, Sel's presence fills the doorway. He floods my mind with a crackling, swirling cloud of fear—fear so palpable and alive that it holds me in place like a heavy hand. Then, I remember that a man just like him—a *Merlin*—lied to me about my mother's death, and a rising rage burns that fear to ash.

"Stay away from me!" I spit.

"Hm." Sel's head tilts to the side. "Two nights in a row, you've been in the way."

Nick pushes around Sel to look between the two of us. "You know her?" He's quick; anything else and Sel would know I talked to Nick about the Quarry.

I slide along the wall until my back is against the window. The glass creaks against my spine, and I briefly consider whether I'm strong enough to break it. What I'd do even if I could.

"We've met." Something like suspicion skates across Sel's face, gone before it really lands. "But she doesn't remember that."

Sel enters the room, but Nick steps in his path and places a broad hand on the other boy's chest, stopping him. Sel's eyes drop to the fingers splayed against his dark gray shirt. A feral grin curves along his elegant mouth. "There may come a day when you can stop me, but you and I both know it's not today."

Nick's nostrils flare, and for a brief moment I'm certain that he's about to throw a punch. That the warrior I'd seen fighting a hellhound could easily throw Sel over his shoulder or knock him into a wall so hard it'll leave a crack. But Sel's fingers begin to twitch at his sides, silver rings flashing against the black of his pants, and Nick does not strike. His eyes screw shut, and he lowers his hand.

Sel looks almost disappointed, but he steps smoothly around Nick, tossing "You don't have to watch" over his shoulder as he walks. A shadow of some emotion runs beneath the granite of his voice.

Nick meets my eyes behind Sel's back, his earlier plea plain on his face: *Don't let him know.*

Sel moves into my field of vision and peers down with a speculative gleam in his eyes. "I don't believe in coincidences. Perhaps I should be concerned to meet you two days in a row, but no Shadowborn would have made herself as vulnerable as you have tonight, which means you must simply be . . . unlucky." That word again, *Shadowborn*. When Sel says it, his face twists into a sneer.

"You are Unanedig. Onceborn." The Kingsmage's eyes—scientific, assessing— track every tremble of my frame. "So your body isn't accustomed to aether. That's why you're dizzy."

"Screw you."

"Sit." Sel's voice rolls over me like a wave. When I don't comply, he steps forward and that deep-down, primordial fear of him *presses* against me. I sit.

Nick takes half a step forward. "Minimal intervention directive," he urges. "Just the last couple hours."

Sel rolls his eyes. "Orders, Nicholas? As if I am not bound by the same laws you so carelessly neglect?"

My eyes fly to Nick's. He nods as if to confirm what's about to happen. *He's going to erase my memory again.* Sel kneels in front of me, and the same heady, spiced smoke scent swirls around me, filling my nose. "Your name?" he purrs in that same rolling voice.

"Her name is Briana." Nick gives Sel my legal name, not my preferred one.

My mind races. Last time Sel's mesmer worked, but only for a little while. *How did I break it? There was the light, then the pain in my palm—*

Sel watches the fight on my face with interest. "I must admit, Briana, I'm curious. What twist of the universe has set you in my path again?" he asks, his voice quiet, wistful. "Alas, some mysteries must remain forever unsolved."

I flinch when he reaches long fingers toward my face. It gives me just enough time to bite down on the inside of my bottom lip. Hard.

The last thing I remember is the hot skin of his palm pressed against my forehead.

8

A BEEPING SOUND drills into my skull. I lurch upright to play whack-a-mole on the nightstand until I slap the clock alarm. "Ughhhh. Too bright." I drop back and fold the pillow over my face. My brain is a fragmented, floating thing. Fruit in a Jell-O mold.

"You're unbelievable," Alice says from her side of the room.

"My *eyes* hurt," I whine. "My optical everything hurts. The rods and the cones, Alice."

"Well, it's time to get up." Alice's voice drips with acid. "Unless you want to add skipping classes to your streak of delinquency."

I frown, dropping one side of the pillow. "What's your problem?"

Alice stands up from her bed, fully dressed in a skirt and blouse. She'd been waiting to berate me until my alarm went off. An ambush by an evil librarian. "My problem? You almost got us kicked out of school our first night here, and on the second night you don't come home until one o'clock in the morning!"

I squint at her. "No, I didn't. I mean, yes, I did. To the first thing. But no to the second thing."

Alice bares her teeth. A fierce evil librarian. "I can't believe you got blackout drunk."

I sit up, shaking my head. "I didn't."

"You're delusional!" Her screech makes me gulp. I hate it when she gets upset. I hate it when we fight. "Some blond guy brought you back here, stumbling and slurring. He said you'd partied too hard in Little Frat Court. A frat house, Bree? Seriously?"

That makes me jump out of bed. "Alice," I say slowly, walking toward her with my hands outstretched for peace. "I have no idea what you're talking about. I didn't black out."

She stamps her foot, and if I wasn't so rattled, I'd laugh. "Isn't that exactly what a blackout drunk would say the next day?"

"Well," I say, considering. "Yeah, but—"

"I know it's our first real freedom. You always hear about people going to college and drinking too much, not knowing their limits. I just didn't think you were that . . ."

Suddenly, I don't want to laugh anymore. "You didn't think I was that *what*, Alice?"

She crosses her arms and sighs. "Pedestrian."

I blink. "Did you just Jane Austen me again?"

Alice breathes slowly through her nose. "This is what everyone says happens. You go to college with a friend, you each find some new . . . group or whatever, you drift apart. I just didn't think it'd happen to us." Alice snatches the handle of her bag and stomps to the door. It's the resignation in her voice that does me in, and the blow she delivers right before she walks out. "You need help."

Tears fill my eyes almost before the door shuts behind her; then comes a rush of burning anger. My hands ball into fists, nails digging red half-moons into my palms.

Five minutes later, while brushing my teeth in the hall bathroom, I let out a scream so loud the girl next to me jumps.

"What the hell?"

"Sorry," I mumble through a mouthful of toothpaste. The gash in my lower lip is so deep that when I spit, crimson blood and foamy Crest swirl in the sink in equally disgusting harmony. In the mirror, I draw my lip down to check the damage. "I bit myse—"

Another stab of pain. Then, I feel a strange, fluttering panic, like I've just tumbled down a staircase, but instead of hitting the floor at the bottom, I tip forward—into memories.

Where is he?

Genetics 201 starts in five minutes, and Nick isn't here.

I'd arrived early to make sure I wouldn't miss him and have been hovering near the back row of the large lecture hall as students stream in. A girl with stringy black hair scoots by, blocking my view of the door momentarily. After she passes, I see Nick in a blue T-shirt and jeans, walking along the back wall toward the corner of the room.

I weave through the incoming flow of students to follow him. When the clock strikes eleven, a thin, middle-aged man wearing a gray tweed suit steps up from the front row to cross the creaking wooden floor. He pauses at the lectern and frowns as the others and I continue to find seats.

"As the board states, this is Genetics 201. Not Geology 201. Not General Anthropology 201. Not German 201. If you are here for any of those classes, please exit now and take some time to review both the class abbreviations and the campus map."

Amid a low wave of laughter, half a dozen students stand and shuffle down their long rows toward the exit at the back of the lecture hall.

Nick flops into a wooden seat in the very top row in a move that somehow manages to look graceful. I speed toward him, slipping into the seat directly beside him at the end of the aisle. "Nick, short for Nicholas."

He jumps. "Bree. Hi." I don't miss his quick glance at my forearms. "How's my peer mentee?" His smile is so fascinatingly genuine that I probably would have believed him if I didn't know any better. He pulls up the small writing surface attached to the armrest and slaps down a composition notebook that looks like it got wet at some point. He pauses, squints. "I didn't think you were in this class."

"I'm not. I asked the dean for your schedule."

A smile breaks across his face. "Who's creepy-clever now?"

I snort. "Still you. By the way"—I lean back in my chair—"I've never gotten blackout drunk in my life, and I'd die before I set foot in a frat house. Tell Sel to mesmer better next time." I sit up, eyes wide. "Wait, *was* that a frat house? I thought you said we couldn't join them."

Nick's brow lifts a fraction, his eyes widening, but he doesn't respond.

Any further conversation is interrupted when the professor clasps his hands together. Nick faces front, and I smother a frustrated growl. The professor serves all 150 of us a long-suffering gaze. "Now that everyone who is supposed to be here is here, my name is Dr. Christopher Ogren. We will be taking roll today and randomly throughout the semester"—groans all around at this—"by sending around the roster. Please initial beside your name and *only* your name."

"Nick—" I begin, turning to him.

He silences me with a finger, then points to the front of the room. "I'm trying to pay attention." His tone is serious, but I catch the slightest twinkle of humor in his eye. Without another word, he bends over his composition notebook and starts writing who knows what.

Unbelievable.

I lean over and hiss, "I made myself remember."

His pen stops moving, but he doesn't raise his head. "Remember what?"

"Are you seriously—" I'm cut off when an olive-skinned boy with a buzz cut passes the roster to our row. I grab it and scribble *you know what!* before passing it to Nick.

"Your handwriting is atrocious." He signs his initials before passing the clipboard down. Irritation is a barely contained scream behind my gritted teeth.

Dr. Ogren calls our attention again. "All right, let's begin with a thirty-minute pretest." Groans again. Dr. Ogren smiles. "Relax, it won't be graded. It's just an assessment to see, generally speaking, where everyone falls in their knowledge before we begin the term, or what you remember from the last time you studied genetics. Work with a partner, share your ideas, record your answers."

"Work with a partner" is easily the second-worst classroom phrase after "group work." But today I couldn't be happier to hear it.

"Partner?" I ask primly.

Nick studies me, evaluating his options. "Fine." He opens up to a fresh page in his notebook.

The TAs distribute large stacks of worksheets. I grab a copy and send the rest along. We spend the first few minutes actually reviewing the pretest. The worksheets are fairly straightforward and a combination of multiple choice and short answer. Nick is as smart as he is good-looking, because of course he is, but he hasn't covered the material as recently as I have. I stow my questions for now and take the lead to help move things along.

"We're at the short answer portion now"—I flip my own notebook over to a blank page—"and we've got to write these together."

"Mmm, yeah." Nick scratches at the faint white-blond stubble on his chin. "I'm not one hundred percent sure on this one . . ." He reaches across and taps his finger over question ten.

"'Common DNA processes include replication, transcription, and translation. At a high level, describe the distinct functions of these processes.'"

"I can't remember the difference."

"It's easy to get the terms mixed up. Replication is making more DNA, transcription uses DNA to make RNA, and translation has to do with ribosomes. They use RNA to make protein." I sketch a diagram on my notebook. "Visuals help."

Nick examines my drawing, and his eyes flicker up to mine. "Visuals do help. A lot, actually." I'm unprepared for his small, appreciative smile. Even at a low wattage, it is warmth and sunlight and summer and *entirely* distracting and it makes me squirm in my seat.

We speed through the remaining five short answer questions and finish with ten minutes to go. Ripping a sheet out of my notebook, I scribble down a few words. When I shove the sheet into his hands, he braces himself like the

paper might explode on contact. I watch his eyes dart over the list of words—
Shadowborn, Legendborn, Page, Onceborn, mesmer, Merlin, Kingsmage, aether—before
he crumples the page in his fist and shoves it into his pocket.

I lean into his space. "I'm not gonna let it go."

Nick takes a slow, steadying breath, still facing straight ahead. "How are
you . . . doing this?"

"Not sure." I push against the wound in my mouth. "Pain, I think," I murmur.
His eyes snap to mine in concern, but I wave him off and whisper, "Better question: How do the Merlins do it?"

He shakes his head. "Whatever questions you have, I promise you, the answers
aren't worth it. You should act like last night and the Quarry never happened."

"Pens down!" Dr. Ogren directs our attention back to the front of the classroom.

"Can't do that."

He turns to me then, his eyes flashing a warning. "Here's what's gonna happen: *I* am going to ask Dean McKinnon to assign you another mentor, because if
we're seen together on campus, it'll raise suspicion. *You* are going to stop asking
questions and move on with your semester, because this conversation is over.
I'm sorry, Bree, but that's final." He turns back to the front of the classroom as
if that's that on that. Like he's just handed down a decree.

I can't help but snicker into my palm.

He catches it and scowls. "What?"

My smirk grows to a full-blown grin. I lean in close again until he tips his
head toward mine, then whisper, "We may have experienced a life-threatening
demon attack together and you may have saved my complete and total bacon—
again, thank you—but this isn't over. I don't know who you think you are, but
you can't tell me what to do."

His shocked expression is wonderfully satisfying. I shove out of my seat and
push down the row until I reach the aisle and the exit.

Time for Plan B.

It takes all of five minutes to look up a list of historic homes near campus on my phone, and there are a *lot*. But it only takes one minute to pick out the house surrounded by woods: the Lodge of the Order of the Round Table. Not a fraternity. A historic secret society. My mind flies to robes and chants and rituals in catacombs, but before I can keep researching, my father calls.

Oh.

God.

No use in hiding.

"Hi, Dad . . ."

"I don't wanna hear it."

Oh, he's pissed.

"Why didn't you call me back last night? What is your word worth right now?"

What is your word worth? Another family saying. "Not much," I mutter. "I—" . . . *think there's something we don't know about Mom's death. Know for a fact that there's a secret network of magic users who can wipe memories and—*

"You what?" he demands.

I grit my teeth and lean into a lie. "I flaked. I got caught up with some people I met at dinner and just forgot. I'm sorry."

"What's going on here, Bree?"

I tell him the parts of the story that would most likely match the dean's; when I *know* what happened that night, and I can prove it, I'll tell him the rest. He's still angry. "We have an agreement, kiddo. You take care of business, you can stay. If you can't do that . . ."

"Then I come home." I sigh. "I know. I made a bad call. It won't happen again."

During Statistics, I skim through Google results, marking the pages that seem most helpful.

There are five known secret Orders associated with the university, all organized around a central theme—the Gorgons, the Golden Fleece, the Stygians, the Valkyries, and the Round Table. The first three use stories from Greek mythology. The Valkyries, from Norse. The Order of the Round Table is the only society to draw their name from a legend—King Arthur.

I'd shoved that list of words at Nick to get a rise out of him. To get him to crack. But now I tumble the phrases around and slot them into place with what I know of the legend. It'd be easy for someone to dismiss the King Arthur connections as a medieval fantasy about chivalry and honor that the Order founders assigned to themselves to feel bigger, older, greater than they are. But this isn't fantasy. This is real. So, I have to ask: Is the Order based on the legend? Or is the legend based on the Order? I know "Merlin" is a title, not a person. Nick mentioned Pages. Sel's a Kingsmage. How much of the story is true?

The website says little about the societies beyond stating that they exist, and almost nothing about the Order of the Round Table—except that it's not only the oldest society on campus but the oldest known secret society in the *country*.

I have to hand it to the Legendborn; their cover is perfect. Public frats and sororities advertise their rush, host parties at their homes, and have social media accounts, but collegiate secret societies simply . . . exist. And not just at schools, but out in the world, too. There's a Masonic lodge not ten minutes from my parents' house. The casual outsider would never expect to learn what a secret society gets up to, who its members are, or how they recruit. By unspoken agreement, we all just accept that it's not public knowledge.

Maybe the Order of the Round Table recruits sorcerers called Merlins and demon hunters called Legendborn?

I look up. Seated all around me are students who have no idea that they're walking through two worlds every day. One world with classes and football games and student government and exams, and another with Shadowborn and mesmers and aether—and hungry demons from a hell dimension that want nothing more than to devour them. An isel could be flying above my professor's head at the front of the lecture hall, feeding from her energy, and no one here could see it. No one but me. And them.

After class, I walk through campus and past its northeastern edge to the Battle Park forest reserve, on a mission to find a house I've been inside but never seen.

Growing up Black in the South, it's pretty common to find yourself in old places that just . . . weren't made for you. Maybe it's a building, a historic district, or a street. Some space that was originally built for white people and white people only, and you just have to hold that knowledge while going about your business.

Sometimes it's obvious, like when there's a dedication to the "boys who wore the gray" on a plaque somewhere or a Rebel flag flying high out front. Other times, it's the date on a marker that tips you off. Junior high school field trip to the State Capitol? Big, gorgeous Greek revival architecture? Built in 1840? Oh yeah, those folks never thought *I'd* be strolling the halls, walking around thinking about how their ghosts would kick me out if they could.

You gain an awareness. Learn to hear the low buzzing sound of exclusion. A sound that says, *We didn't build this for you. We built it for us. This is ours, not yours.*

The Lodge has a black-and-white historic site marker right at the open gates. *Original mansion constructed in 1793*—the same year as Old East. My dorm is an antebellum building. Not built *for* people that looked like me, but definitely built *by* them. And the Lodge . . . ?

I take a deep breath, ignore the buzz, and walk up the long gravel driveway. After one turn, I see it.

The place is a freakin' medieval castle. A dark sorcerer's keep, sitting isolated on a wooded hill in the middle of a forest. Four circular stone towers at each corner rise to conical points with fairy tale–style blue-and-white flags at the top.

And, like the trail that led me here, it's coated in a faint, shimmering layer of silver aether.

I hadn't *realized* the wisps I'd been watching filter through the trees were aether and not sunlight until I saw it gather in eddies on the Lodge's gravel driveway. When I reach the brick steps, I touch the iridescent layer with a tentative hand. As my fingers pass through the shimmer, I feel a push *away* from the tall double doors. An insistent nudge urging me to move on. Not sinister, exactly, but intimidating. A subtle warning slipped between the folds of one's brain, just like Selwyn's message.

Leave.

My hand lingers inside the enchantment. The now-familiar clove and smoke scent rushes toward me. *"Different casters use aether to do different things."* Does that mean this is a . . . signature? If so, the bright smell from my bandages had to be William's.

Selwyn's signature is so rich here I can taste it: the whiskey Alice and I stole from my dad's liquor cabinet last summer. Cinnamon cloves. A campfire banked low in the woods and smoke carried on winter wind.

After several heavy raps of the bronze lion door knocker, I glance down at my clothing one last time. What does one wear to stake out a secret society? I'd settled on comfort over fashion: jeans, a fading *Star Wars* T-shirt, low boots. My curls are in a cute bun, high and full on my head. Nothing that screams "spy."

The door opens to reveal a pixielike girl with short dark hair in a flowy dress and leggings. Her large dark eyes rake over me, then dart around the steps and up the drive, like she's looking for someone else. "Who are you?" she asks, not unkindly.

"I'm Bree Matthews. Nick told me to meet him here."

9

SEVERAL EMOTIONS CARTWHEEL across the girl's face: alarm, doubt, and curiously, hope. "Nick told you to meet him here? Tonight?"

"Yeah." I add an uncertain frown and waver to my mouth. "Is that . . . is that okay? He said it would be—"

A squeak leaps from the pixie girl's mouth. "Yes! Of course it's okay. If Nick said it, ohmygosh . . . yes." She squirms like a caught mouse, and I feel a little guilt mixed with triumph.

When she opens the door farther to let me in, I notice a blue silk ribbon bracelet wrapped around her wrist. Sewn into the center of the fabric is a small silver engraved coin. "It's just that you're a little early," she exclaims. "No one's really here yet. I can't let you into the great room without your sponsor, but we have a salon for guests. You can wait there while I call Nick."

Sponsor? "Sounds great," I say, and follow her into the foyer.

I immediately recognize the smell and the *Southern Living*–meets–ski lodge decor, but that's where the Tanglys's familiarity ends.

I've never seen anything so grand in my life.

The stone walls of the three-story foyer extend up into open rafters. On either side hang paintings in gold-leaf frames and heavy-looking tapestries in dour browns and blacks. There are actual, honest-to-God iron sconces lining the entryway before us, but instead of flames behind their glass coverings, there

are vintage Edison bulbs. Twin staircases flank the porcelain-white marble floor
and curve up to an open balcony connecting the two wings of the second floor.

Bentonville doesn't have houses like this. Normal people don't have houses
like this. At least not in my world. My parents had renovated an old split-
level from the seventies, and we'd moved there eight years ago. Most of the
homes nearby are rural farmhouses passed down from grandfathers and great-
grandfathers, or middle-class neighborhoods filled with older houses that look
like mine.

As I gape, the girl looks over her shoulder with a dimpled smile. "I'm Sarah,
by the way. But most people call me Sar."

I smile back. "Nice to meet you."

Sarah opens a door tucked under the left staircase. The salon is circular, just
like the stone tower above. Four round tables sit in the center of the room,
each with a wooden and marble inlaid chessboard embedded in its center, and
a leather couch sits in front of a fireplace by the window. Sarah gives a guarded
but polite smile and closes the door, leaving me alone.

I walk the perimeter of the room while I wait, studying the frames on the walls.
Directly across from the door are two prominent portraits hung side by side under
a pair of brass picture lights. The first is a man with bushy brows staring out with
unyielding blue eyes. JONATHAN DAVIS, 1795. The next portrait was painted much
more recently. DR. MARTIN DAVIS, 1995. Nick's ancestor and his father. *Of course.*
The Order must be the organization his dad wanted him to join. Like Nick, Martin
in the portrait is tall and broad in the shoulders, but his eyes are a deep blue that's
almost black. Instead of the sun and straw strands that fall into his son's eyes, he has
a shock of thick, dark blond hair cropped close at the temples.

I gnaw on my lip, adjusting the information pile in my head. No, piles won't
do anymore. I need drawers and cabinets now. Organized places to add new
details that feel important, like the fact that even though Nick seems to despise
Sel and maybe even the Order itself, his family portraits are displayed in a place
of obvious honor.

Another image draws my eye. To the left of Jonathan, there's an old black-
and-white illustration on yellowed parchment behind glass: five men in long,

aristocratic waistcoats with puffy white sleeves, standing around a table in a drawing room. The bronze plate beneath it includes a short paragraph:

PIONEERS FROM GREAT BRITAIN, THE FOUNDERS OF THE ORDER OF THE ROUND TABLE'S CAROLINA COLONIAL CHAPTER WERE STEPHEN MORGAN, THOMAS JOHNSTON, MALCOLM MACDONALD, CHARLES HENRY, AND JONATHAN DAVIS, C. 1792.

The plaque includes brief bios of the men and their achievements:

Served on the legislature. Lieutenant governor. Tobacco baron. Co-owners of one of the largest plantation complexes in the South.

Buzz, buzz.

The door opens, and I turn around with as pleasant a look as possible. This is where my plan gets wobbly; I have no idea what Nick may have said on the phone, so I brace for Sarah's response.

From the look on her face, my gamble has paid off. "Nick's on his way. Can I get you anything? Coffee? Perrier? Wine?"

"No, thank you. Did he say how long he'd be?"

"Maybe ten minutes. He lives off campus, but it's not far." She stands on one foot, then the other, as though she feels required to play host but doesn't know how. In the end, she mutters a quick "Okay" and slips out the door.

Part one of my plan is complete. I drop onto the leather couch and wait for part two.

Ten minutes later, part two surges into the room, his cheeks bright as blood oranges. Nick slams the door behind him and reaches me in two steps.

"What the hell are you doing here?" His normally kind eyes strike me like blue lightning. The force of him, the sheer momentum of his anger, pushes me back against the pillows.

"Getting your attention."

He studies me, his chest rising rapidly like he'd run here on foot. "We need to leave. Now, before everyone else arrives. Especially Sel." He leans down, grabbing my elbow. "Come on."

I can't help but stand when he yanks me up, but I don't make it easy for him.

I pull against his grip and he pulls back. "Let me *go.*" I jerk my arm out of his grasp. Before he tries again, I take a deep step into his space so he'll retreat. It works, and he takes two stumbling steps back.

I take a sharp breath. Because broken hearts strip vocabularies down to their raw bones, and because I don't want After-Bree to show up and turn this conversation into a tear-streaked explosion, I've scripted an admission using as few words as possible: "My mother died three months ago."

Nick blinks, confused dismay overtaking fury until his expression lands somewhere in between the two. Most people say something right away, like "I'm sorry to hear that" or "Oh God." Nick doesn't. It makes me like him more than I should.

"Bree . . . that's . . ." Nick shudders, and there—that response right *there*—makes me worry he won't understand. That he hasn't lost anyone close, so he won't get it. I plow ahead anyway.

"It was a car accident. A hit-and-run. At the hospital, they took me and my dad into this . . . this room with a police officer and a nurse who told us what happened." Hard now. Panic bubbling. Finish fast. "Or at least that's what I thought. Yesterday, a memory came back. Just a snippet, but enough that I *know* that police officer was a Merlin. He mesmered me and my father to forget something from that night. If we know the full story, then maybe . . ." I break off, swallow again. "I just have to know what happened and why he hid it from us. And I need your help."

Nick turns away, rubbing a hand over his mouth.

"Nick?"

"I'm thinking. Just—" He shoves both hands through his hair.

"You don't look surprised."

A hollow laugh escapes him. "That's because I'm not."

I set my jaw. "I need your help."

He's silent for so long I think he might turn around and leave. Shove me out the door for real. Call security, like in the movies. Then he closes his eyes, sighs, opens them—and starts talking.

"Merlins are the Order's sorcerers. Their affinity for aether is so strong they're essentially supersoldiers. Trained from birth, assigned to posts, and sent on missions to hunt rogue Shadowborn, keep Onceborn populations safe, close Gates . . ."

My breath catches. *A mission.* "They never let us see her body. Could—could she have been attacked by a demon?"

Nick doesn't look convinced. "A Merlin can detect a demon miles away, and even then, most are incorporeal isels. Visible to someone with the Sight, but not strong enough to cause physical harm. Onceborn deaths are extremely rare because they're exactly what Merlins are trained to prevent. That, and securing the Code. If Onceborns ever knew the truth, there'd be mass fear, chaos— two things Shadowborn thrive on. No, this doesn't make any sense." His eyes darken. "Unless . . ."

A cold hand grips my heart. "Unless what?"

"Unless the mission went bad. The Code threatened. Merlins are authorized to do whatever it takes to keep the war hidden."

I remember Sel's cruelty with the boy at the Quarry. The near torture of the isel. His disregard for my wounds last night.

"What if she got in his way somehow? Or—or he failed and wanted to cover his tracks?"

When I look up, Nick's expression holds disgust. Old pain, resurfaced. And a question.

Maybe *the* question. The one all the others have led to.

The one that changes *everything* just by the asking.

"Would a Merlin kill someone?"

He doesn't meet my eyes. "I don't—"

"The truth."

He looks at me then, his voice iron. "I'm not a liar. Not outside the Code."

"Would they?"

His eyes slide shut. A single nod.

Everything inside me burns. A furnace, roiling, turning. I draw my shoulders back and steel myself. "I know the date. The time. Location. If I tell you what he looks like . . ."

He spreads his hands. "There are hundreds of Merlins all over the world. Even if I knew every one, they won't tell me anything. Each Merlin takes the Oath of Service to the High Council of Regents. They're the ones that assign Merlins to their missions, and no Regent will speak to an outsider."

"You're Legendborn. Speak to the Regents on my behalf."

A heavy sigh leaves him. "Technically, yes, but procedurally? No. I renounced my formal title years ago—*very* publicly. Upset a lot of people. I'm sorry, Bree, I—"

"I don't care!" I shout, and close in on him until our faces are inches apart. "Let me make this clear. My mother is *dead*, and a Merlin might have killed her. At the very least, he hid the facts. I'm not leaving until I get answers. If you can't help me, tell me who will."

He holds both palms up. "I hear you. I do! But you'll never get near the Regents."

"Because I'm not in this—this club?"

"The Order is a strict hierarchy, all titles and ranks," he explains in a voice meant to calm. "The Legendborn title is sacrosanct. They outrank Vassals, Pages, Lieges, Viceroys, Mage Seneschals, you name it. The Regents have all the functional control, but if a Legendborn makes a demand, they are Oathbound to comply. The Regents won't answer to anyone less."

"So I live the rest of my life without knowing what really happened?" The defeat on Nick's face fills me with desperation. How can I be this close to the truth, and yet it's still out of my reach? Fear is a tight knot in my throat, but I swallow around it. There has to be a way—

Outside, the massive front door swings open with a bang. We both freeze. Sarah's voice, then another. Several feet enter the foyer. Laughter. Someone says, "Welcome!"

And just like that, a solution strikes down into my core. A path. A purpose. Lightning. *Our Brave Bree.*

"Why did Sarah think you were my sponsor?"

Nick's eyes widen, a glint of fear in their depths. "Bree . . ."

"It's the first week of school. Are they recruiting?"

Nick says no. Then repeats himself. But I don't hear it: the idea is already coursing through my veins, hot and heady.

If the Regents won't talk to outsiders, then I won't *be* an outsider.

"It's not possible." Nick groans. "Even if it were, you're the exact *worst* person to appear before the Regents."

I raise a brow. "What does—"

"Listen to me." He reaches for my hands, forces me to look at him. "I've been around the Order *my entire life* and I've never heard of *anyone* like you. An Unoathed Onceborn who can See aether and *voluntarily* resist mesmer, the Code of Secrecy's greatest weapon? All of that means the Legendborn, the Order, and the Regents will see you as a threat, an anomaly. Something to be contained if not eliminated. Not to mention the Merlins. They're an army dedicated to enforcing Order law—and Sel's one of the most powerful Merlins in *years*. If it gets out he's failing at his post here, it's his head and future on the line. He'll report you to the Regents himself, the Regents will put you on trial, confirm what you can do, and then *disappear* you. Now, please, we *have* to leave before—"

"No!" I yank my hands away, walking back toward the door. "The timing is perfect. All I have to do is go out there and confirm what Sarah already thinks she knows. Then I'll join and become Legendborn. Easy peasy."

Nick stares at me, incredulous. "That right there is proof you have *no idea* what you're talking about. I was born into my title, but you're an outsider. If I bring you in, you'll only be a Page. You'd have to compete against all the other Pages to become Legendborn. The tournament lasts months, and *all of it* is rigged. It's a setup to favor certain families, certain kids."

"Kids like you, right?" I'm drunk on the idea now, the solution to everything. I jerk a thumb over my shoulder at the two paintings. "Your ancestor founded the damn Order. You're the textbook definition of a legacy."

He laughs bitterly. "A legacy I *rejected*. I've never even seen a tournament. Even if you do well in the Trials, there's no guarantee you'll get chosen at Selection. The other Pages have been trained to fight, they've studied—"

"And I'm pushy," I retort.

A wry smirk tugs at the corner of Nick's mouth. My heart is thundering so loud I'm sure he must hear it. He paces, stares at me, then paces again. Stops. "Say we do this. Then what? You join, find your evidence, and go? These people don't let members just walk away for good."

The fight in me is still there, but resolve folds around it. "The last words I said to my mother were in anger." He flinches like I've struck nerves in multiple places. "If there's even a *one* percent chance that she was . . ." I swallow hard. "Either way, I can't let our fight be the end. And if you don't help me, I'll just find another way."

His eyes search mine. That *tug* between us pulls tight.

We both jump when the door opens and a new face peeks in. "Davis!" A tanned boy in a dress shirt and slacks ambles into the room, swirling a glass of sparkling water in one hand. His cool gaze lands on me for a second before it flows back to Nick. "Sar said you were here! This your Page?"

Nick's eyes never left my face. I meet them with every ounce of determination I possess. Finally, after a long moment, he answers us both.

"Yeah, Fitz, she's mine. Figured it's about time I reclaim my title."

PART TWO

DISCORD

10

FITZ SLAPS NICK on the back, spilling his sparkling water in the process. "That's what I'm talkin' about, Davis!"

Nick's eyes slide from mine to Fitz's. "Give us a minute, Fitz?"

"Not a problem." Fitz backs out of the room with a wide grin. "My man!"

"That's right!" Nick flashes a smile and points to Fitz, looking for all the world like a fraternity bro at a tailgate. When the door closes, he turns to me, expression solemn again.

"Questions: Was that your bro face? Because I super don't like it. More importantly, *your* Page?" I exclaim, eyes narrowing. "Like I belong to you? Your servant?"

"No!" Nick says, flushing. "Of course not. Sorry. Not that kind of Page. Here—" He fishes under his collar and draws a long silver chain up and over his head. "A medieval Page's service was voluntary, honorable, and mutually beneficial." He nods toward my neck. "May I?"

I eye the jewelry in his palm. "I guess." He drapes the necklace over my hair. A heavy silver coin like the one on Sarah's bracelet drops down to the center of my chest. I run my fingers over the engraving on the still-warm surface: a circle with an elegant diamond shape etched in the center. A line with no end, and four points stretching beyond its curves.

"Calling you 'mine' means I'm the one who tapped you. That my bloodline—my family and I—vouch for you, and you have our protection and blessing." He holds a hand up to stop the question on my lips. "Later. I'll go along with you competing for now, only while I figure out an alternative. But if we're going to do this—and I just need to state for the record, one more time, that this is a *bad* idea—then we're doing it together. You and me. And on my terms. Agreed?"

I cross my arms, but he tilts his head expectantly. "Fine." I relent. "What 'terms'?"

"We literally *just* came up with this plan, Bree, gimme a second."

The lights above us flicker once, twice. Outside, Sarah announces that the event will begin in ten minutes. When I look back down, Nick's eyeing me speculatively. I can't help but feel like he's measuring me for a coat that I'm not going to like.

"Okay. First rule . . ."

When we leave the room ten minutes later, there are over twenty students milling in the foyer. Some are dressed like Nick and me, in jeans and T-shirts; others wear cocktail dresses and suits. Some Pages assess me with not-so-subtle glares, while others stare at Nick, blinking twice as if he's a heaven-sent mirage.

Nick sports an expression I've yet to see on him. With each step into the crowd, he becomes some new iteration of himself: a combination of the confident, warm charmer from the first time we met and . . . something I don't recognize.

A curvy, short girl with wavy red hair and a tall, lanky boy with cropped brown hair approach us. Although they walk close together, they seem like polar opposites: she's dressed in loose slacks and a paisley blouse while his jeans and wrinkled button-down shirt look like he'd plucked them from a sad pile of clothes on the floor. Interestingly, they wear matching red leather cuffs on their right wrists with identical silver coins in the center.

What *are* these coins?

"Nick . . . ," the girl breathes, "Sarah said you were here, but . . ." A soft British accent curves around each word before her voice trails off in awe.

The boy squeezes her shoulder and steps forward with his hand out. "While Felicity here regains the power of speech, I'll say it's good to see you, man." He doesn't sound Southern at all. A New Englander, probably.

"Hey, Russ. Thanks." Nick clasps Russ's hand with a smile and nods in my direction. "This is Briana Matthews, my—" He clears his throat. "I invited her to join the Order."

I shoot him a look that says *real smooth*, and his mouth quirks.

Russ notices our exchange but doesn't comment. His mischievous eyes immediately put me at ease. "Nice to meet you, Briana," he says while shaking my hand. "Welcome to the Lodge."

"Thank you," I say, keeping my tone light. Gracious. I force a goofy smile, hoping that I look overwhelmed and clueless. "I've never been in a house like this before. It's so . . . fancy." Nick's first rule is still ringing in my ears.

"Remember that Sel thinks you've been mesmered twice: the Quarry and last night. So, behave as though you know nothing and have witnessed nothing. Everyone here has to think you're an ignorant Onceborn brand-new to our world. Don't let anyone know what you can do."

"Yeah, well, we don't really do things halfway." Russ follows my gaze. "It has a certain museum-chic, don't-touch-anything-or-else-someone-will-rap-your-knuckles charm, I suppose." I giggle at that. The sound feels completely foreign, but I think I pull it off, because Russ gives me a wink. "Of course, fancy and formal means Flick made me wear something other than a T-shirt."

Beside him, Felicity scowls. "I really hate that nickname."

"Felicity is *way* too many syllables!" Russ exclaims. "Your parents were sadists."

She rolls her eyes. "Ignore him."

Somewhere a small chime rings, and double doors open at the back of the foyer.

As Felicity and Russ walk ahead, Nick and I follow at the back of the crowd. I lean in to him, my voice pitched low for his ears. "What's their deal? And what are the coins?"

Nick replies quietly, without looking at me. "Felicity Caldwell, junior, and Russ Copeland, sophomore." He waves at a tall boy with a gentle face and light-colored hair, who salutes him back with a wry smile. "Both Legendborn. They wear matching sigils because Felicity is a Scion, born with the title like me, and Russ is her chosen Squire."

"Why do you hate them?"

He blinks. "Who said I hate them?"

I gesture over his shoulder to the undergraduates chatting around us, then to the opulent foyer. "Sel called you the prodigal son. You rejected all of this."

A muscle twitches in his cheek. "The reason I renounced my title has nothing to do with the people here."

"Then why—"

"Another story for another day."

I frown but don't feel like I know him well enough to press. *But if I don't know Nick,* I think, *then why do I trust him?*

He bumps me with his arm, nodding ahead to where the crowd is moving into the great room. "We both need to be 'on' when we walk through those doors. Any more questions?"

"A ton." The features of his face are caught halfway between the loose, charismatic boy I'd met last night and the stern, noble Nick whose eyebrows are drawn tight with some emotion I can't identify. "Why are you helping me?"

His mouth quirks. "I like helping people, if I can." The light in his eyes dims. "And I know how it feels to watch your family shatter right in front of you and not be able to stop it."

Before I can ask another question, he turns away—and then I'm struck silent by the massive living room in front of me. Brown leather couches sit clustered in front of a large fireplace on one far end. The fireplace itself is Biltmore House–big; the marble hearth could hold a horse standing upright. I glimpse a bright chef's kitchen through a swinging door to the right, but most stunning are the twelve-foot-high floor-to-ceiling windows that make up the entire back wall and give an expansive view of the forest. The Lodge is high enough on its hill that the darkening horizon is visible through the earthen browns and evergreens.

Nick has paused beside me while I take everything in. Once I'm done, I notice that, again, half of the eyes in the room are glued to Nick and the other half have found me. A few of the more nicely dressed people from the foyer trail curious eyes up my boots to my jeans and T-shirt. Some stare openly at Nick's coin around my neck, and heat rises up my ears. Nick leads me over to a display of beverages in a corner. When the eyes follow us, I find my irritation shifting from the gawkers to Nick.

The moment the voices around us return to idle chatter, I move closer to him and whisper, "Everyone's staring."

His back to the room, he passes a glass of cucumber water to me and keeps his voice low. "As far as they know, I haven't walked into this house since I was twelve years old. Then I show up out of the blue to reclaim my title and sponsor a Page no one's seen before. And . . ."

"And?"

Nick presses his lips into a thin line and pours a water for himself. "And, traditionally, new Pages come from the Vassal families who pledged themselves to the Order decades or even generations ago, so . . ."

I groan inwardly. "So it looks like I skipped the line."

He chuckles. "You could say that."

Nick explained Vassals in the salon: Onceborn outsiders who are sworn to the Code and the Order at large, but pledged in service to one of the original thirteen Legendborn bloodlines that founded the Order in the medieval ages. The Vassals know about aether and Shadowborn, but they don't fight in the war. Instead, their network shores up any gaps in their assigned family's needs and resources. In exchange, the Order grants them favors. Most Vassals start out with power or money and use the Order to gain more. Climbers. Like Deputy Norris, probably. Vassalage creates CEOs, elected officials, cabinet members, even presidents.

I scan the room, hear the buzz again, then mutter into my drink. "And then there's the fact that no one else here looks like me."

Nick follows my gaze, sees what I see—a room full of white kids, not a person of color in sight—and grimaces. His jaw sets in a hard line. "If someone says something to you, anything, let me know. I'll put a stop to it."

I look at Nick's face. He is so certain that he understands what I'm facing. Then I think of Norris, the dean, and how some things, some people, don't want to just . . . stop. I think of what it might cost me to infiltrate the Order. To succeed in an institution founded by men who could have legally owned me, and wanted to.

"Sure you will."

I hear my cynicism, and Nick does too. He frowns and starts to reply, but gets cut off by a new voice at my shoulder.

"Hey, Davis!"

We turn to see a pair of students looking at us with bright, curious eyes.

"Whitty!" Nick smiles and slaps hands with one of them. "Man, is it good to see you. It's been what, two years since the rafting trip?"

Whitty grins. "Not our finest hour." He has a stocky build with wild, pale curly hair, and he's wearing a worn camo jacket and jeans. While the other kids are dressed for classes or the formality of the Lodge, Whitty'd look equally at home on a tractor or up a hunting blind. His casual indifference appeals to me immediately, but then I remember he's probably a Vassal kid, and my guard goes up.

Nick had been disdainful about Vassal families whose sole focus is positioning one of their children to join the Order: "The Order's mission is fighting Shadowborn and protecting humans. It's safer on the outside, but for some the benefits of membership outweigh the risks. Even Pages and their families get privileges Vassals don't. Only Legendborn can recruit new members, so these climbers will do anything to curry favor with their assigned bloodline in hopes that their child will get tapped," he'd scoffed. "But those Vassals don't want to help people, they want the status. And they put their kid in harm's way to get it."

Hence, Rule Two: *"Keep your head down. Disappear. Make them forget you, so they don't consider you competition."*

But Nick seems genuinely happy to see the other boy, so maybe Whitty's not the "sport and glory" variety?

"The Upper Nantahala's class three and four rapids, though. We did all right."

Nick nods in my direction. "This is Bree Matthews. Bree, this is James Whitlock, also known as Whitty. The Whitlocks are Vassals to the Line of Tristan, and they own most of the pig farms out in Clinton."

"We prefer the term 'hog barons.'" Whitty gives me a conspiratorial wink. He offers his hand; his grip is firm and warm. The faded blue cuff around his wrist is held together by a rubber band. "Nice to meet you, Bree. Nick here your sponsor?" I nod, and he whistles low. "Well, all right then."

"I'm Sarah's Page." Whitty jerks a thumb at his companion. "And this is Greer Taylor. They're Russ's."

"Hey, y'all." Greer gives a short wave. They're basketball-player tall and lean, with long, muscled arms and legs. Their dirty-blond hair lies in a single braid over their shoulder, while a few shorter strands fall out the front of their slouchy gray knit cap. An unbuttoned, expensive-looking, slate-colored suit vest over an untucked denim shirt and cuffed jeans puts their look somewhere between designer and hipster. They're also wringing their hands in front of their belt buckle in a nervous gesture that reminds me painfully of Alice.

"Thought we'd come over and introduce ourselves," Whitty says with a side-long glance at the rest of the room. "Plenty o' time to be at each other's throats later, if the tournament stories are true."

Nick starts to reply—to assuage our fears or to counter Whitty's casual pre-diction of violence?—but stops when a tall boy with brown curly hair appears at his elbow.

"Sorry to interrupt, but are you Nick Davis?" When Nick nods, the boy's brows shoot up. He offers his hand. "I'm Craig McMahon, fourth-year Page."

The year of study doesn't affect when a student can be tapped, so someone who joins as a senior will only ever be a first-year Page—and will only get one chance to be Selected as a Legendborn Squire. If Craig's a fourth year, then he was tapped as a freshman.

Nick returns the boy's handshake. "McMahons are Vassals to the Line of Bors, right? Fitz or Evan brought you in?"

"Yep." Craig nods and raises his hand to show off a thin, dark orange leather band wrapped around his wrist with a silver coin at the center. "My family's given five generations of outside service. I'm the first to Page." His eyes dart to me, then back to Nick. "It's true, then? You're claiming your title?"

A slight flush creeps into Nick's cheeks, but his chin tips up. "It's true."

Craig grins. "I'm a senior. Last opportunity to Squire. Didn't think I'd ever meet you, but . . ." His eyes drift my way briefly, something sharp behind them. "I'd like to put my hat in your ring. Officially. Got a minute?"

Nick's jaw clenches, and Whitty smiles into his drink. Craig pulls Nick into a conversation and they drift a few feet away. Greer sees the confusion on my face and leans in close. "You're brand-new to all this, right?"

I have our agreed-upon story ready to go. "Nick and I met through Early College. He thought I'd be a good fit."

"Only Nick could get away with plucking somebody outside Vassalage," they say, and offer an encouraging smile. "He's probably happy you're not one of these." They point their chin discreetly in Craig's direction.

"One of what?"

"Legendborn acolyte. Fundamentalist Line worshippers. Craig there wants Nick to choose him before the Trials've even started. Want some gum? I chew when I'm nervous." They reach into their bag to fish out a fresh pack. I notice their red ribbon choker and make an educated guess that Greer's family serves whatever Line Felicity and Russ belong to. When I decline, they keep talking. "The acolytes are a special kinda believer, that's for sure."

"You say that like the Order's a cult."

"Not far off from one, some days," Whitty interjects, watching a few more people wander in.

Greer shrugs. "All of it's a leap of faith when you're an outsider and don't have the Sight yet. You seem to be taking it pretty well, Bree." Greer assesses me with their brown eyes and kind smile before stuffing another piece of gum in their mouth. "How'd you react when Nick told you about Arthur?"

Arthur? Greer says the name without pause or inflection. Like King Arthur is some guy who could walk through the door at any moment. It takes me a few seconds to put together an answer that doesn't betray the extent of my ignorance. "I was . . . stunned, of course."

Nick and Craig make their way back over, with Felicity in tow. She bounces up to us with a clipboard and an infectious smile. She may have been surprised by Nick's appearance, but now that her event is underway, she's in her element. I'd bet good money that she's in student government in the Onceborn world beyond these walls.

The Onceborn world where King Arthur is just a story, not a person. If Arthur is real, are his knights real? The Round Table? The Holy Grail?

When Nick sees my expression, concern ripples across his brow, but Felicity speaks up and draws our attention. "As this year's recruitment coordinator, I have the pleasure of giving the initiates a tour of the Lodge before we begin. Shall we?" She inclines her head toward the foyer. Another pair of Pages is already waiting.

Whitty and Greer move to follow Felicity, but Nick touches my elbow. He walks me over to the window and out of earshot. "Are you sure you want to do this? It's not too late—"

"King Arthur is a real person?"

Nick pales, blinks. Blinks again. "Yes, but not in the way you're thinking."

"What does *that* mean?" I nearly shout.

A few Pages across the room turn in our direction, their eyes darting between the two of us. Fitz looks like he's considering clobbering me. Nick flashes a winning smile but speaks to me through gritted teeth. "Low. Profile."

"Explain."

His eyes canvas the room as he talks. "What you think you know of the legend, the versions you've read or heard? Almost all of them can be traced back to the Order. They had a hand in most of the stories about Arthur that spread beyond Wales and a pen in every text from Geoffrey of Monmouth to Tennyson. Vassal glaving, writers, archivists worked on misinformation campaigns to keep Onceborns from the truth. This is what I mean by 'bad idea.' The other sponsors have had *way* more than ten minutes to prep their Pages—"

"Stop." I sway on my feet, still reeling from lies and truths. "This is happening. I don't care if it's all real."

"Page Matthews!" Felicity calls from the doorway.

"Be right there!" I wave, a false smile on my lips.

I start in her direction, but Nick steps in my path. "Legends are dangerous, Bree. Don't underestimate them."

The group is already halfway up the curved staircase and finishing introductions by the time I reach them.

"There are common spaces and private residents' rooms on the second floor," Felicity is saying. Her red curls sway behind her as she walks backward up the stairs with ease. "We've also got a theater room with enough seating for twelve and a wet bar." While Felicity leads us across the balcony and down the hall, I study the other initiates.

All told there are five new Pages: Greer, Whitty, me, and two other boys named Vaughn and Lewis. Vaughn, Fitz's Page, is as tall as Nick, but so broad across the chest and biceps that the buttons of his pale blue dress shirt look liable to pop. Lewis, Felicity's Page, is the opposite: small-framed, thin, and a little green around the gills.

When we reach the end of the hallway, Felicity shoves open a pair of heavy doors. "And here's the library."

Rows of bookshelves are filled with great tomes bound in worn browns and blues and green leather. Solemn, heavy crimson curtains drape windows that stretch up into a Gothic arch. One side of the room holds rectangular study tables with green-shaded banker's lamps. On the other side, three leather couches face a fireplace and tall mantel.

I float against the back wall alongside Greer, half listening to Felicity, who is now listing the many perks that Order of the Round Table members receive on campus. She's so bubbly and welcoming that I can't quite imagine her hunting a demon. There are portraits here, too. A floor-length oil painting of a knight on horseback hangs between two windows. Green-and-black gore runs down the center of the blade he brandishes, and his bright, cyan-blue eyes glitter beneath a medieval helmet.

A waist-high glass display case sits on a table in the back corner. It holds tattered, delicate-looking journals and small artifacts made of stone and silver. Nothing seems particularly remarkable about the objects until I see— "What the hell are those?" I blurt. Beside me, Greer gasps.

Felicity and the others walk over to the case to examine what I've found: a chained pair of dented, silver bands resting on a black velvet stand. The info card beneath them reads: MERLIN JACKSON'S MANACLES. SALEM, MASSACHUSETTS. 1692.

"Oh," Felicity says, her bright demeanor faltering. "Those are, er, handcuffs. That Merlins can enchant with aether to restrain individuals."

"You mean aether users from outside the Order," Vaughn says with a nonchalant shrug. "Witches, looks like. From the Trials."

"Merlins use handcuffs?" Lewis breathes at the same time that I say, "The *Salem* Witch Trials?"

Vaughn rolls his eyes at us both. "Only *weak* Merlins need material tools and weapons. The powerful ones can make aether constructs that are hard as diamond."

"It's true," Felicity adds, eager to change the subject. "I've never seen our Kingsmage use metal weapons. My father says Selwyn's constructs are the strongest he's ever seen, and he Squired at Northern in the seventies when Merlin *Jenkins* held that post."

While the others follow her to the door, I linger at the case, shaken by all that had been left unsaid: why the manacles were used initially, why they're on display now, and, most disturbing, what they mean about Merlins and their missions.

Merlins don't just hunt demons.

They hunt people.

BACK IN THE great room, only Pages remain—first through fourth years. Everyone is standing apart. I don't know if the competition has already started and it's every Page for themselves or if people are just nervous. Nick wouldn't know that part. He didn't have to do this step, and he never would.

Most of the crowd looks like sophomores and juniors. Almost all of them look like athletes. A handful are tall and muscled, like swimmers. Some look more like wrestlers, wide across the shoulders and hips. Sturdy tanks built for the mat. Two of those Pages look like particularly vicious Ralph Lauren models, with barrel chests that stretch their powder blue and salmon polo shirts at the seams.

Vaughn, the only Page leaning casually against a wall, catches me staring at him. The leer on his handsome, tanned face—and the wink he sends me—makes it hard to play the lost lamb, because all I want to do is scowl back, teeth bared. I look away.

There's a girl about my build with short auburn hair, her body thrumming with tension. A few of the other girls remind me of Sarah: small, ballerina-like people who stand with both feet planted wide and turned out. Deceptively fast and strong, I bet.

If the Vassal families prepare their children like Nick says, then even a freshman would enter school with some weapons training, if not actual demon-hunting experience. I've seen two demon attacks, which gives me an advantage over someone who hasn't seen one, but I can't let on that I've seen any.

Nick doesn't know about my wall and After-Bree, but he didn't seem to think I'd have any trouble pretending to be ignorant. I *did* lie to Sarah to get into the Lodge.

I wonder what Alice would say.

I think she'd tell me I've bitten off more than I can chew, and that if I don't get out now, I might not be able to when things turn for the worse.

Abruptly, the double doors open and Tor strides into the room. She's wearing a ruched royal-blue dress that hugs her curves, and her hair cascades down her shoulders in sunflower waves.

"Welcome, everyone. I'm Victoria Morgan, the Legendborn Scion of the Line of Tristan, third-ranked." She pauses for applause, and the Pages in the room actually give it to her. Instead of clapping, I notice her blue bracelet. It's identical to Sarah's. And if Sarah sponsored Whitty, Sarah is Legendborn.

"Tonight begins the annual initiation process for our hallowed Order." Her cheery gaze pauses on me for a brief moment, like she's trying to place me. Her eyes widen when she spots Nick's sigil. "Pages, tonight you will take the Oath of Fealty. If the Oath finds you worthy, you will officially become a member of the Southern Chapter and be granted Sight, the ability to see aether. If you are not worthy, you will be mesmered and cast out. In the meantime, not a word until the ceremony, yes? Follow me." Instead of turning the way she came, Victoria strides through the crowd toward the back of the room.

"Tor?" Craig speaks up.

"Yes, Page McMahon?" She answers without looking, already opening the sliding balcony door to let the night air in.

He glances at the rest of us, then back to her. "How many Squire spots are open this year?"

"Oh! So sorry!" Victoria pivots on a heel, pleasure bright on her face. "As I'm sure you've all noticed, Nick Davis has returned." Murmurs, eager nods from the crowd. "Thanks to Nick, tonight our chapter makes history in more ways than one. This year will be remembered as the year he claims his Scion title, the year Pages compete for a record *three* Squire positions, and"—to my surprise, she openly gestures in my direction, a pleased smile on her face—"the year our chapter welcomes its most diverse Page class."

Victoria leads her own applause, and half of the room joins her.

Heat curls around my neck and ears. *Diverse.* Like an award she'd given herself. A gold star. *Diverse.*

We follow Victoria across the balcony and tramp single file down wooden stairs to reach the Lodge's backyard. Here the humid, dark evening swallows us whole, save for the light from a few tall torches around the yard's perimeter. She tells us to line up in the grass and wait, then disappears down a path around the side of the building.

I'm grateful for the poor lighting because Victoria's words are still churning in my stomach, and I can't control my face.

Its most diverse Page class? Ever? And as if that's *why Nick chose me?*

Norris. McKinnon. Tor. Three comments, three assumptions, three people who've singled me out because of how I look and what they've decided I represent. In forty-eight hours.

I close my eyes against a rush of emotions: anger, hot and burning against my cheeks. Disgust at the self-congratulatory expression on her face. Then the deep fatigue my father calls "death by a thousand cuts."

How many cuts am I going to have to endure? I wish Alice were here.

Greer nudges me with their elbow, and I open my eyes. "That's messed up, what she said."

I blink, startled to hear it from someone else this time. "Thanks."

Someone shushes us from down the line. Greer leans in. "People say shit about me, too. But my parents are major donors. I come from six generations of Vassal service and three generations of Pages, and I'm white, so they get strategic about when and where. Some folks just don't care to get better or learn more, and it shows."

"Yeah." I take a shaky breath. "Yeah."

"Just remember, you don't have to be the best. To be eligible for Selection, all we have to do is make it to the end of the tournament without losing or forfeiting. It's good there are three open Squire spots instead of two. Better odds, you know?"

"Wouldn't say that." Whitty is on my right. "The higher-ranked the Line, the more folks'll be gunning for its title." Greer nods, their face solemn.

This is gonna be a long few months.

The air pressure changes, setting off a small *pop!* in my ears. In the next heartbeat, the dark trees in front of us smear and twist into a black-and-green knot, then unfurl with a snap into an identical scene that now includes a line of eight hooded, robed figures. While the Pages beside me gasp in surprise, I scent the air, on edge.

Where is that damn Merlin?

But the smell of Sel's casting never comes, likely carried away by the warm wind flowing across our faces. The figures take a single, unified step forward, their robes dragging in the grass. Shadows deepen between the folds of the heavy material, and the cowls are so full that nothing of their faces remains visible. I'm certain they're all Legendborn, but it's impossible to tell who is who. Beside me, Greer sucks in a breath.

Together, the figures say, "One at a time," and everything goes dark.

Complete, endless black. Before the cinnamon-smoke scent even reaches my nose, I know that Sel's mesmer has taken our sight.

My heart lurches against my ribs. Someone yelps, the sound breaking against the trees.

"Quiet!" Vaughn snaps.

Movement, ahead of me. The soft whisper of one pair of feet moving over dry grass. Closer. Greer's breath, coming in short pants. A sharp gasp far to my left. A pause. Louder steps, shuffling, the sound moving farther away. Two pairs of feet, maybe. Where are they taking us?

One at a time.

The same cycle again, this time to my right. I hear Whitty grunt before he and his escort walk forward. Greer goes next. Then one more. Legendborn sponsors taking their Pages?

Measured paces approaching me now. I hope that it's Nick. Closer. My heart leaps into my throat. I don't want to be touched in the dark. My breath rattles in my ears. A hand wraps around my elbow, holding the joint in a loose grip. That subtle warning is all I get before someone pulls me forward.

They guide me from behind by the shoulders. Twigs snap under feet walking maybe twenty feet ahead of us. The ground transitions from soft grass to soil to pounded dirt. A path. My nose tingles with the scent of tree sap and fresh pine needles. The sounds of nature grow closer, tighter. A barred owl hoots above us. Crickets swell in a high-pitched chorus. We're in the woods.

Two pairs of steps not far ahead of us, shuffling and regular. Another guide, another Page. We walk straight for a few minutes, then turn. Turn again. After a while, I lose track of time. Maybe it's because I'm under, but the smell of Sel's mesmer and the disorienting path make me dizzy. We walk for ten minutes. Or twenty. I think we even double back at one point, but I can't be sure. There's a hundred acres of wooded land behind the Lodge. We could be anywhere.

Suddenly, my guide halts me. They press my shoulders until I lower into a squat; then warm fingers move my hand to a smooth, cool stone surface that drops off after a foot. A step. Stairs. They stand me up and come around to my front, take both hands. We walk down the stairs one careful step at a time. By the time we reach the bottom, there's a river of sweat down my spine. We're back on pounded dirt when the hand on my right shoulder drops down to my wrist and fingers brush across my knuckles.

"It's me."

I release the breath I'd been holding. Nick flips my hand and squeezes my fingers, then steps close. I can feel the heat of his chest against my shoulders, and when he leans in, the stale-smelling cowl brushes my ear. "Squeeze once for yes, twice for no. Can you see?" I squeeze twice. "Keep it that way."

In other words, *Let Sel's mesmer take you. Don't resist it.*

"Listen, Oaths are living bonds sealed by speech. Their words pull aether from the air so that the commitment becomes a part of you. The Oath of Fealty will know if and when you intend to break it, but it works like mesmer, so—" He stops, his words lost to the night.

I whisper, "Nick?"

He releases my hand. I feel him step in front of me. Overhead, towering pines creak in the wind. Nick's feet shift on the ground, like he's pivoting in the darkness, searching. My heart begins to race. I tongue at the still-healing bite in my cheek.

"Wha—"

"Hush." Indignation sparks, then dies when I hear the sound of his sword, extending. I imagine his face: brows tight, eyes and ears intent, weapon drawn. A swell of rustling leaves. A single branch snaps up high and to the right.

The barest whisper of movement—and a palm strikes my chest so hard the air leaves my lungs in a whoosh.

I hit the ground back-first, and pain shoots across my spine.

A low growl from above—the harsh clang of metal on metal.

The high-pitched whine of weapons grinding against each other.

"What are you *doing?*" Nick shouts, his voice strained.

"You bring a Shadowborn onto *our* grounds, to *our* sacred ceremony, and you ask what *I* am doing?"

Sel!

Adrenaline rushes through my veins, along with Nick's voice and Rule Three: *"Never let Selwyn Kane get you alone. He can't find out what you can do."*

I skitter backward in a frantic crabwalk, hands scraping dirt and gravel.

A burning-hot hand seizes my ankle.

A thud, a grunt. The fingers release.

Impossibly strong fingers dig into my bicep. Pain like daggers. I scream.

The hard smack of flesh hitting flesh. A punch?

Sel's fingers let go.

Labored breathing above me. Nick, between us. My heart thunders with panic. How much do I trust him now that I know what Sel can do?

"She's not Shadowborn!"

"Three nights in a row of Order interference is not coincidence. I mesmered her twice myself and yet she stands here. An uchel—"

"Jesus, Sel," Nick groans. "An uchel?"

What is that? Another demon? They say the new word with a short "i" sound at the beginning, then the throaty "ch" from "loch."

"I decided to bring Bree forth today. She is my Page. *Mine*. You swore an Oath to serve—"

"And I am keeping my Oath." The wind picks up just as Sel's casting reaches my nose. There's a tight, rhythmic sound like a small cyclone spinning to life.

"Sel . . . ," Nick cautions.

"It has enthralled you," Sel growls. Electricity arcs across my nose and cheeks. The wind picks up, and something crackles. Ozone enters the air.

"Don't do it—"

"SELWYN!" A man's voice slices through the woods, and the cyclone dies immediately.

Footsteps approach behind me on the path. The steps are low and measured, but the older man's heavy drawl holds barely contained fury. "You wouldn't be callin' aether against my son, now would ya, Kingsmage?"

Another pause. Even in the darkness of Sel's mesmer, the tension in the air raises the hair on my arms.

"No, my lord."

My lord?

Dr. Martin Davis—Nick's father—steps close, and his cologne falls over me like a rich, heavy cape. "Well, that's good. Because if you were, I'd expect that Oath o' yours to be burnin' a hole through your throat right about now." It's part observation, part warning. Sel hears it too; in the following silence, I hear his teeth grind together.

"Yes, my lord."

"Nicholas." The breathless way Dr. Davis says Nick's name makes me wonder how often he sees his son.

"Dad."

"'And there be those who deem him more than man, and dream he dropt from heaven.'"

"Tennyson," Nick says, his voice tight.

"Indeed."

The strain of distance in their voices makes me wonder what happened to their family. What shattered them?

Beside me, the man's body weight shifts in the dirt. "Mercy! And who is this lovely lady?" I'm still half-frozen on the ground, adrenaline thrumming through my body. Light fingers land on my shoulder. "May I help you up?" I nod, and he slips his hand under my elbow, pulling gently until I stand.

Another pair of hands around my other elbow. Dr. Davis lets his son pull me to his side. "This is Briana Matthews, my Page."

Davis inhales sharply. "*Your* Page?" Hope runs through his voice like a quiet current. "Does this mean—are you—"

"Last-minute decision." A clicking sound and the whine of Nick's retracting sword.

"Ah." I get the feeling Nick's father is weighing what words to use next, like the wrong phrase might send his son running into the woods. Finally, he says, "I'm sure you know how much this means to me. And to the greater Order."

"Yeah." The resignation in Nick's voice catches me off guard, and my stomach twists. I'm the one who pushed him here. Am I the reason his voice is that heavy?

Pride and awe mingle in the older man's voice. "My son claiming his title and bringing forth a Page, all in one night. That is . . . somethin' else." His next words are directed at me. "I don't know how or if you're responsible for my son's change of heart, but if y'are, consider me eternally grateful. I'm in your debt, Briana. Welcome."

A pause. *Am I supposed to respond?*

I mumble a quiet, "Thank you."

Davis clears his throat. "Now, I'd like an explanation as to why the two of you were fighting."

Nick doesn't hesitate. "Sel thought he sensed a Shadowborn here in the woods, but he was mistaken. Our Merlin remains vigilant, as always."

I hold my breath, waiting for Sel's outburst and correction, but it never comes.

Davis is shocked. "Here? The Shadowborn have never been bold enough to open a Gate on our land, not with so many Legendborn under one roof. Selwyn, is this true?"

Silence. I wonder why Sel isn't speaking up. Just a few minutes ago he had been so certain, so full of determined rage.

"We rely on your senses, son." Davis makes a thoughtful sound. "Are your abilities becomin' unpredictable, Kingsmage?"

A pause. Sel's terse response comes through clenched teeth. "There is always that risk, Lord Davis."

"You look unhappy, boy. As the Gospel of Luke instructs, let us celebrate and be glad of Nicholas's return, for 'he was lost and is found.'" Another pause in which Sel could counter Nick's explanation, but doesn't. "Bree, I must apologize for both my son and Selwyn here. Oil and water, these two, ever since they were children." I nod. Satisfied, Davis moves down the path. "Let us proceed to the Chapel. Don't want to keep the others waitin'. Not on a night such as this."

Nick guides me forward. I don't hear Sel say or do anything else. In fact, the only footsteps I hear are Nick's and his father's.

12

WHEN SEL'S MESMER lifts, my sight returns all at once. Lights off, lights on. It's so disorienting that beside me Greer falls forward on both hands. All five of us—the first-year Pages—blink the world back into existence while on our knees, integrating sound with sight: the sound of water streaming over rocks nearby—from a creek maybe—deeper in the forest to our right. The waning moon sending light down on us from overhead, turning leaves from green to silver. We kneel before a low, curved altar that protrudes up the slab itself, our faces lit by flickering candlelight.

Eight Legendborn stand before us, arranged along the far arc of the stone circle, their hoods drawn low. Five new figures in robes of gray—the veteran Pages, I'd wager—flank them on either side. In the middle is a single man in a deep crimson robe edged in gold, his cowl pulled back just enough to see his face. Dr.—no, *Lord*—Martin Davis. He looks almost exactly like his portrait.

Davis steps forward, his arms hidden in the deep sleeves. When he speaks, his voice is sonorous and steady. "My name is Lord Martin Davis, and I am the Viceroy of the Southern Chapter and its territories. Each of you has been invited by a Legendborn member who deems you worthy of initiation as a Page. The five of you kneel before us because you have the spark of eternal potential."

The "Chapel" is a circular slate-colored stone slab flecked with shiny bits of silver in the middle of a clearing. The slab *feels* old, worn, and heavy, like a coin dropped by a giant long ago. Pine trees stretch up in a thick ring around the clearing, closing us in on all sides with no marked path in or out. I have no idea where we are or in which direction the Lodge lies. We're isolated here, on a round surface with no end, and at their mercy to get out.

Every instinct I possess yells at me to run. Just a couple of miles and I could be back in the real world, where there are no ritual slabs and robes and magical Oaths. But it isn't the real world, is it? It's the surface the Order works to maintain while they operate below, on its edges, and in the shadows. I can't run. Staying here and playing this role is the only way I'll find out the truth.

"Tonight, in our Chapel, you will pledge yourselves to our Order and its mission by taking the Oath of Fealty. Our work goes unseen and unrewarded by the very lives we protect, therefore no other commitment is more sacred. But first, an introduction."

It's only because we're looking up at Lord Davis that I catch the movement over his shoulder. Thirty feet up and tucked in the trees, darkness bleeds into a shape. Without a single creak of a branch, a black-robed figure descends in a long, smooth arc. Selwyn lands in a crouch, and the other Pages jerk back in alarm. Beside me, Whitty makes a near-noiseless sound of surprise.

Nick said the other new Pages have known about the Order most of their lives, but only in the abstract. Only in stories. They've trained for battles they've yet to encounter, learned about aether they've never seen, but knowledge is not the same thing as experience. I don't blame them for startling. That jump would have broken a normal person's legs, and none of us had detected his presence. I would startle, too, if this was the first time I'd encountered Selwyn Kane.

The Merlin rises in one motion, silent as a panther and eyes just as bright. Candlelight turns the silver thread at the edges of his robe into a living thing: a thin line of white frames his face, a whip of electricity around his wrists. Under the hood, his hair is so black I can barely make it out against the fabric. He belongs to the night as a predator does. And like a predator, he takes our measure. When his glittering golden eyes find me, a line from childhood comes to mind unbidden: *All the better to see you with, my dear.*

Now that I know what the Merlins truly are, all I can see is Sel's arrogance, and through him, the arrogance of the Merlin before him. I see the man who stole my memories. The soldier who may have taken my mother from me.

I should follow Nick's rules. I should be *afraid*. Instead, I lift my chin from where I kneel. Let defiance shine from my eyes. Even these tiny gestures are blood in the water, but I don't care.

Sel cares. A muscle ticks in his jaw and aether *flares* at his fingertips—but when Lord Davis frowns his way, Sel douses the flames inside tightly curled fists. His lips curl at my satisfied smirk.

"The Southern Chapter is fortunate to call Selwyn Kane our Kingsmage. Merlins are the first of many revelations only privy to Oathed members of the Order."

On cue, Sel stalks to the far end of the altar and stands at parade rest.

Davis's legato voice flows over us like a preacher leading his congregation. "Tonight you will echo the ancient vows sworn by warriors of the medieval. In those days, men committed themselves to higher powers and greater missions, and left behind the petty concerns of earthly pursuits. Likewise, our Order is fashioned after the body politic.

"Our Vassal friends and their contemporary fiefdoms are the Order's lower limbs. Without them, we would not have walked through fifteen centuries of this war, would not have advanced from the Middle Ages to modernity. Pages are the left hand: once Oathed, you will be granted Sight in order to hold the shield while we fight in the shadows. Merlins are the right hand, the sword and fists of the Order. Our guardians and weapons against the darkness. The Legendborn Scions and Squires are the heart. The holy text of their Lines has fueled our mission from the beginning. The Regents are the spine, directing our eyes and energies to the urgent matters at hand."

Davis pauses, letting the image of his metaphor settle in our minds.

"And, when he is Awakened, our king is the head and the crown itself, leading us to victory by divine right."

A whisper rises in the night. *Shh-shh-shh-shh.* The sound comes from the other Pages and the Legendborn standing behind Davis. They've raised their hands to chest level, all of them, and are brushing their thumbs over their fingers in steady rhythmic circles. Approval.

When Davis raises a hand, the sound stops.

"Be proud of your invitation, but know that there is so much more yet possible. Tonight, many of you wear the color and sigil of the Line served by your family, and as Pages, you always will. But at Selection, those who earn the title of Squire will take the colors and sigil of their Scion. And this Line, you will serve by choice." A pause. "You have no title, but you do have your names. We must know who you are and know the blood you bring to service."

"State your name and family." Sel's voice catches me off guard.

This is the first time any of us have been asked to speak in over an hour. Vaughn doesn't hesitate. "Vaughn Ledford Schaefer the Fourth, son of Vaughn Ledford Schaefer the Third, Vassal to the Line of Bors."

Lewis speaks up next: "Lewis Wallace Dunbar, son of Richard Calvin Dunbar, Vassal to the Line of Owain."

Greer follows quickly: "Greer Leighton Taylor, child of Holton Fletcher Taylor, Vassal to the Line of Lamorak."

My mind spins while Whitty speaks beside me. What do I say? Not my mother's name, right? No, my father's!

When it's my turn, I open my mouth, but nothing comes out.

The harsh sound of hissing cuts through the night and lashes against me, sends my pulse racing. Disapproval. My ears burn hot. Pressure begins behind my eyes and—No! Wall up! Now is not the time for After-Bree's anger.

Davis raises a hand, and the sound ceases.

"Your name," Sel repeats, his voice low.

This time, I speak. "Briana Irene Matthews, daughter of Edwin Simmons Matthews."

The Chapel is silent, waiting for the final words that they already know I can't claim. No Vassalage. No Line. Someone in the Legendborn row hisses. Vaughn stifles a snicker.

Davis's voice slices across the quiet, stiff with warning. "Do not fall prey to hubris. Affiliation with this Order is not equivalent to sworn fealty. Indeed,

Tennyson said, 'Man's *word* is God in man.' Tonight you sever all other promises but these and serve the Order not as individuals but as one."

My chest unclenches. I say a silent "thanks" to Nick's father, whose imperious glare has cowed even Vaughn.

"Who brings Vaughn Schaefer forward to make the Oath of Fealty?"

A Legendborn figure steps forward, drawing his hood back. "I do." It's the boy from the study, Fitz. He kneels opposite Vaughn and extends one forearm across the stone, palm up, and the other next to it and palm down. Sel takes a knee at the end of the altar and rests long fingers on the silver speckled surface. A ripple of mage flame from his fingertips flows down the altar in a wave, from Vaughn to me.

"Tonight, you make an Oath to us and, through your Legendborn sponsor, the Order makes one to you." Davis nods to Vaughn.

Vaughn grasps Fitz's upturned arm with his left hand and raises his right. When he speaks, a nagging itch crawls up and over my skin. I can *feel* the aether infused in these words, even if I'm not the one saying them. "I, Vaughn Ledford Schaefer the Fourth, offer my service to the Order in the name of our king. I swear to be the shield of the Southern Chapter, the eyes and ears of its territory. I swear to aid in its battles and arm its warriors. I swear to guard its secrets and secure all that I see and hear henceforth."

Fitz clears his throat. "The penalty for breaking this vow is total mesmer and excommunication to the darkness of unknowing, never to return to the light. Do you bind yourself still?"

"I do."

Down the altar, Sel nods, giving Fitz the go-ahead of some kind. "I, Fitzsimmons Solomon Baldwin, Scion of the Line of Bors, accept your Oath on behalf of our ancient Order and welcome you to service. We grant you Sight so that you may see the world illuminated for as long as your heart be true."

A bright flare of silver-blue mage flame rushes up the hand Fitz has placed on the altar. He tenses, and then the flame surges down his other arm and into his Page. It loops around Vaughn's wrists and curves up his shoulders. Now with Sight, Vaughn stares as the Oath disappears into his skin.

Lewis goes next, with Felicity. Then Greer, with Russ. With each Oath, a new thread of doubt winds through my chest, because I know I have no intention of keeping this promise. Nick said Oaths are like mesmer, but how *much* like mesmer? I've never resisted Sel's mesmer in real time, only after the fact. By the time Whitty starts his Oath, my heart is pounding. I can't help but glance down the altar at Sel, who stares back with narrowed eyes as if he can hear the fear in my chest.

Davis interrupts my thoughts. "Who here brings Briana Matthews forward to make the Oath of Fealty?"

"I do."

A tall figure steps out of the circle. Nick pulls his hood back as he walks to the altar, eyes solemn. He settles across from me, and I clamp my hand around his forearm almost as soon as he lowers it, desperate for something familiar, something I can trust in all of this. His eyes find mine, his fingers pulsing reassuringly around my elbow.

I take a shaky breath, raise my right hand, and begin. "I, Briana Irene Matthews, offer my service to the Order in the name of our king."

I pause, gasping. I can feel the words slip down into my body and coil around my ribs. Nick's eyes urge me on.

"I swear to be the shield of the Southern Chapter, the eyes and ears of its territory. I swear to aid in its battles and arm its warriors. I swear to guard its secrets and secure all that I see and hear henceforth."

Nick's voice echoes around the Chapel, louder and clearer than the others who went before him. "The penalty for breaking this vow is total mesmer and excommunication to the darkness of unknowing, never to return to the light. Do you bind yourself still?"

The cool tide of the Oath has wound itself between my fingers. It streams down my back like a waterfall until I'm covered with it. I squirm, shifting my weight from my right knee to my left. Someone hisses, and Davis raises his hand to stop them.

"I do."

This isn't going to work. The Oath will know that I'm lying. They're all going to know—

Suddenly, pain lances through my arm. It's Nick, digging his fingers into my flesh deep enough to leave marks. I meet his eyes and he nods imperceptibly, urging me to focus on the blunt pressure of his nails. I chase the sensation down like a rabbit in the woods—and the ancient promise loosens its grip on my body.

Nick's quick thinking saved me. Maybe saved us both.

Across the altar, Nick's pulse leaps against his throat. It takes him two attempts to begin speaking.

"I, Nicholas Martin Davis . . ." Nick releases a harsh breath, as if drawing on a deep well for strength. "I . . ."

When he meets my gaze again, the look in his eyes fills my stomach with dread. There's pain, anger. Then, resignation.

When Nick's voice resonates through the Chapel, the Legendborn hold their breath.

"I, Nicholas Martin Davis, Scion and heir of King Arthur Pendragon of Britain, the son of Uther Pendragon, wielder of Caledfwlch, the blade Excalibur, and first-ranked of the Round Table in the Shadowborn holy war, accept your Oath on behalf of our ancient Order."

Nick watches the shock travel through me with sad, weary eyes.

I barely feel the aether Sel sends pulsing through Nick's hand and into mine. Our gazes are still locked, but everything else has changed.

King Arthur Pendragon of Britain.

Scion and heir.

"I welcome you to service. I grant you Sight, so that you may see the world illuminated for as long as your heart be true."

Why didn't you tell me? I send the question through my eyes. He flinches.

His words sit on my tongue while the flames swirl up my arms like silver-blue snakes. The mage flame washes over me without soaking into my skin.

You said you don't lie.

He sees the accusation on my face. Withdraws his hand. Stands, turning so his face is hidden in shadow.

Davis claps for attention. "Rise, siblings, as Oathed Pages of the Order of the Round Table and sworn servants of the Round Table!"

The night's sober tone finally breaks, and we are teenagers and students once again. There are whoops and cheers from the Pages behind us, and whistles from the Legendborn before us. I push to my feet on legs that are half-asleep, my stomach pulled into a knot.

No one notices that the Oath of Fealty didn't take or give me Sight. No one notices me at all.

Sel still kneels at the end of the altar, head bent over the stone, palms pressed to the surface. For a moment, I think he's been injured or overexerted by the Oath, but then those thoughts disappear.

Sel doesn't look pained—he looks intoxicated: eyes half-lidded, and unfocused, cheeks flushed, mouth parted and panting. He drags his tongue over his lower lip—and looks up to find me staring. I stiffen and turn away.

Whitty slaps a hand on my back in celebration, and I return his smile because I don't know what else to do.

Sel calling Nick the prodigal son. Felicity, staring speechless like he was the second coming. The shock on Sarah's face when I said his name. I'd been so focused on how I would uncover the Order's secrets that I hadn't stopped to really think about what all of those responses to Nick meant. I'd thought about what Nick represents to me but not what Nick represents to everyone else.

I look up to find Nick staring at me with a guarded expression, like he's waiting for me to arrive at the truth in my own way.

I suppose I have. . . .

He is King Arthur's descendant.

Davis calls us to order. "Let us close with the solemn pledge of our eternal Order."

The new Pages glance at one another. We don't know the pledge, but it seems we're expected to learn by example.

The chapter chants as one, and even though I can't hear his voice in the chorus, Nick joins them.

"When the shadows rise, so will the light, when blood is shed, blood will Call. By

the King's Table, for the Order's might, by our eternal Oaths, the Line is Law."

Davis turns to the stars in benediction. "By heaven's holy hand, the Line is—"

A bloodcurdling scream splits the night, and everyone freezes. The cry echoes against the trees, bounces off the stone beneath our feet. I pivot, searching for its source, and then the sound comes again, a shriek of pain that lifts the hair on the back of my neck.

At the back of the group, Felicity is on her knees with both hands clutching her temples. The crowd steps away just as Russ dashes to her side.

"Flick? Flick, answer me!" She screams again, the sound choking off on a sob. "Felicity?"

"What the hell?" Whitty breathes beside me. "What's happening to her?"

"Kingsmage!" Davis calls over his shoulder. "She needs aid."

"Felicity!" Russ cries again.

"Squire Copeland." Sel appears at his shoulder. Russ turns, his face a mixture of fear and worry. "It's her time. Step back."

Russ shakes his head. "No, no, it can't be—"

"Squire Copeland," Davis insists. Russ looks between the two of them desperately, then allows Sel to draw him away from the agonized girl on the ground.

Craig McMahon stands beside me. "This isn't possible. It's too soon."

"What isn't possible?" I ask.

In the center of the group, Felicity moans long and loud. Her head drops back, eyes blank, and a voice—deep, masculine, not hers—emerges from her throat.

"Though I may fall, I will not die, but call on blood to live."

She collapses forward in a crumpled heap.

Russ picks Felicity up and stands with her draped across his arms. "I'll get her back to the Lodge. She needs to rest."

Sel stops him. "I'm faster and stronger. Let me take her."

Russ hesitates for a moment, his jaw clenched. Then he nods once and gently passes Felicity's limp form to Sel, who lifts her easily. Without another word, Sel jogs through the trees and is gone.

As soon as he disappears, the crowd erupts—or at least the Pages do. The

Legendborn wear stony expressions, exchange worried glances. One of the third-years shakes her head, muttering, "She's fourth-ranked. This isn't right." One phrase rises above the chatter. "This is too soon."

Davis calls for calm, but it's his son's voice that quiets the Chapel.

"Why did he call her?"

The crowd parts around Nick.

Davis blinks in surprise. "You know as well as I do, Nicholas, that we don't control the Awakening of our knights. We are but instruments. They call us when there is need."

"When there is need, and in *command order*," Nick adds. "The first- through fifth-ranked knights haven't Called their Scions in decades. Felicity is fourth-ranked, which means the fifth must be Awake. When was the Scion of Kay Called?"

Murmurs from the others now. A nod of heads.

If Alice were here, she'd say it's too late. Now that I know the Scions are the descendants of the Round Table, called to power—violently—by their knights' spirits . . .

What have I done?

Renewed authority threads through Davis's voice. "This is not a chapter meeting. We should discuss these matters when we return to the Lodge."

"No." Nick raises his chin. "We should discuss it here. Why did Lamorak Call her, Dad? Why now?"

Davis's nostrils flare, but before he can respond, a low growl from the darkness answers Nick's question.

For a split second, no one moves. Frozen in disbelief, I think. A Shadowborn, here?

Another growl, this time followed by a high, nightmarish howl, one I'm now very familiar with.

Hellhound.

WHILE EVERYONE SPRINGS into action, I'm frozen, trembling. I thought they were rare. Thought, for some reason, that I wouldn't see another one. Not when I was with the Legendborn like this. Not while just looking for information. I thought this was a ritual. Initiation. Hazing, at best, not—

Davis fires off orders in rapid succession, and it's like a bomb goes off in the crowd. "Awakened Scions and Squires to the front! The rest in formation behind them. Pages, back to the Lodge!" Stillness explodes into action, and bodies scatter in several directions at once. Soldiers rushing to battle positions.

The next moments seem to pass in slow motion.

The Legendborn toss their robes off without hesitation and move with practiced, military precision into two defensive rows. Five stand at the back, pulling out weapons from harnesses, scabbards, and hidden straps: daggers, extendable quarterstaffs, and swords. Sarah and Tor string identical bows. Only three normal kids move to the front: the gentle-faced boy who saluted Nick in the foyer; Fitz; and a tall boy with red hair. I squint, trying to make out the red-haired boy's face, because something about him is familiar. When he turns his head, I realize it's because I know him. He's Evan Cooper, Charlotte's boyfriend.

The primitive part of my brain pleads with me to run to the Lodge with the others as fast as I can, but I can't look away from the three Legendborn boldly facing the darkness, empty hands thrust out at their sides. What are they thinking? Where are their weapons?

With the whooshing sound of a backdraft, mage flame appears in each of the three boys' palms. It circles in a smoky whirlpool, then climbs up their arms like iridescent snakes. In between one second and the next, the aether solidifies into weapons in their hands. Fitz and Evan hold identical shining swords. The gentle-faced boy holds two glowing daggers the length of my forearms. But the mage flame climbing their bodies isn't done. I watch, breathless, as it flows over their shoulders and legs, solidifying into gleaming plates of silver. Aether crawls up their throats and falls across their sternums until it becomes chainmail. On their arms, the smoke hardens into terrifying gauntlets.

Armor. Aether armor.

From the opposite direction, another howl rises. My blood runs cold. Not just one hellhound, but *two*?

"Split formation!" Davis yells. The boy with the daggers dashes to the other side of the Chapel, calling for three other Legendborn to follow.

"Bree!" Nick steps into my vision, blocking the armored boys from sight. "What are you still doing here? Get back to the Lodge! *Now!*" I pivot away from the clearing, but the other Pages have disappeared into the woods. I should have followed them. I have no idea how to get back. No idea which direction to run. Nick realizes this at the same time that I do and points his sword behind me. "That way. Run. Don't stop."

I sprint full speed into the forest, adrenaline shooting through my veins. I can barely see, but I keep going. I crash through brush. Briars scrape at my face and arms. I stumble.

Shouts echo behind me as the Legendborn take on the hounds.

Another howl.

Silence.

I turn. Did they kill the demons? Is it over?

Suddenly, the stench of mold and warm, stagnant water overtakes me. It clings to the back of my throat. The smell of rotten wood and dying things.

Things that haven't seen light in a long, long time. I cover my mouth.

A sound comes from my left, like a log breaking.

When I turn, two bottomless red orbs appear in the darkness a foot from my face. Glowing lanterns made of blood. One blinks, then the other.

Not lanterns.

Eyes.

I scream and stumble backward. Then, a voice. The nauseating sound of bones cracking, deep and sharp.

"You will help us."

Terror condenses to a sharp point. I pivot, but the eyes appear in front of me. A ten-foot-tall, hulking shape steps through the trees.

At first I think the shape is an enormous human, but the movements are all wrong. Their joints bend in the wrong places. In the sliver of light from above, I see a broad chest and thick limbs covered with moss. An iridescent, shiny green liquid pours out of open gashes on mottled skin. A face stretches across a bulbous, swollen head. Two long strips of rotting flesh connect gaping jaws. Their tongue lashes back and forth like a snake tasting the air. The demon hums in satisfaction. *"Yes. You will help us."*

I lunge to the side, but the demon moves too. Faster than I can track, so that they face me from the new angle, their held tilted to the side as if waiting for my response.

I think fast, heart hammering inside my chest. I can't outrun this demon, that much is clear. Which way would I go if I could? Wherever I am, I'm closer to the Legendborn than I am the Lodge. This demon doesn't seem to want to eat me like the hellhound did—yet.

I take a sliding step in the direction of the clearing but keep my eyes on the creature. Help your Are you—you sure I'm the best person for that?"

Lips pull back in a hungry smile, exposing two rows of black teeth that curl backward like scythes.

"Yes," they state, and lunge before I can make a sound.

The demon slings me over their shoulder like a sack of yams, jerking my body around so much my head spins. A squishy, hot arm wraps around the back of my knees, holding me in place. A scream builds in my throat, but I gag on the putrid stench steaming from their body.

There's a blur, then an abrupt stop that sends my chin crashing into the demon's wet spine. I gag again. Mildewed slop clings to my face.

Before I can orient myself, the demon pulls me down and around until I'm hanging like a doll, feet swinging off the ground. I struggle, but they only pull tighter, cutting off my breath in one sharp motion. I can't get enough air.

We're back at the Chapel, where the eight Legendborn and Lord Davis have cornered the second hellhound. Fitz and Nick have just speared it through when the demon holding me emits a hellish scream. *"Pendragon!"*

Everyone turns at once.

Nick's father shoots his son a silencing glare, and steps forward. Davis fingers the grip of a longsword in a scabbard at his side, a weapon that he'd hidden beneath his robe. "Why have you come, uchel?"

"Which of you is the Pendragon?"

Davis keeps his voice easy, calm. A Southern gentleman simply greeting a newcomer. "I am who you seek." His eyes flick to me. "You have one of our Pages. Let the girl go and we'll talk. Just you and me."

The demon's teeth clack against one another in a chittering pattern, like they are displeased. *Clackclackclack.* *"She will be easy to take apart, deceiver."* Razor-sharp nails drag a burning path down my cheek, slicing my skin open. I scream.

"Stop!" Nick shouts, already moving forward.

The hand at Davis's side clenches into a fist. It must be a signal, because the other Legendborn move in tight around Nick, locking him into place. Guarding him. Rage blooms across his face.

The demon points at Nick with one dripping claw. *"He is who we seek."*

"We?" Davis says, curious concern crossing his expression.

"Give him to us, Legendborn." The demon's hand tightens slowly around my chest, and black pain threatens to take over my vision. One of my ribs is bending, bending . . .

"I don't think so." Davis darts forward, pulling his blade as he runs, but he's nowhere near fast enough. There's another blur, and then the demon has the older man by the throat with one large hand, while still gripping me with the other. Davis's sword drops to the stone with a loud clatter.

"No!" Nick yells, pushing against Russ and Fitz both. His elbow flies into Fitz's nose, knocking the other boy down, but Evan takes Fitz's place before Nick can break out of the circle. Blood from an injury streams down Evan's forehead, but he stands firm.

The demon lifts Davis high in the air. Nick's father scrabbles at the demon's grip with both hands, wheezing for breath, eyes bulging. The color in his face goes red, redder.

"I will kill both of them while you watch, Pendragon," the demon snarls, squeezing Davis so much the man turns purple, *"and then I will take you."*

"You talk far too much."

I never thought I'd be happy to hear that voice. Sel drops onto the demon's back, wrapping his opponent in a headlock. The demon roars, dropping me to the ground and flinging Davis across the clearing. Nick's father hits a tree with a stomach-turning crunch and falls to the stone surface in a loose pile of limbs.

I scramble backward, just missing the stomp of one enormous foot. The demon grabs at Sel's back and hair, trying to dislodge him, but Sel hangs on tight, his face tucked away from their claws.

A pair of strong arms loop under my armpits and haul me up and away from the fray.

To my surprise, it's Sarah, the pixie girl. "Stay back," she urges once we're far enough. Then she runs over to where half of the group, Nick included, have gathered at Davis's side. Nick's father is not moving. *Oh God.*

The demon and Sel brawl in a blur of black and green. No one else dares to enter the fight, and why would they? No one else could keep up. When the two opponents lunge for each other, the force of their collision makes the earth shake. They twist and roll on the ground, fists connecting in deep thuds. After a few minutes, Sel's shirt is torn and darkened with slime and sweat.

The demon kicks at Sel's chest, and the Merlin goes flying.

Sel hits the ground with both feet in a sliding crouch. A feral grin crosses his face. He launches himself back at the creature like a bullet.

The sight turns my stomach. Nick's father could be dead, and Sel's *enjoying* himself.

"Hold him steady!"

Back at the tree, the boy who had daggers presses his hands over Davis's chest. A light film of silver liquid covers his fingers. As I watch, the liquid spreads down onto the man's shirt. A heartbeat later, Davis gasps awake. "Steady," the boy orders. "Not done . . ."

William, I think. *Their healer.*

William continues to work on Davis, but the relief around him is palpable. Nick's father is alive.

Everyone is so focused on Lord Davis that no one notices Nick until it's too late.

He bears down on the brawl, his father's sword in his hands.

Sel has the demon on the ground, one boot on the creature's chest, an aether blade at their throat.

"You nearly killed my father!" Nick shouts, fury turning his voice to iron.

The demon chitters eagerly. *"The boy approaches! Let him come, whelp! I—"* A squelching, hissing sound from the press of Sel's blade, and the creature is silenced.

"I have this, Nicholas." Sel keeps his eyes on his captive. "Back off. Let me do my job."

Nick ignores Sel's warning and swings, his blade arcing toward the demon's face—

With a sharp twist, the demon breaks Sel's ankle. Shoves the Merlin aside.

Nick's sword descends.

The demon meets it with one hand—the blade digging deep—and clenches Nick's throat with the other.

Nick pulls at the creature's fingers. Gurgling. Gasping.

The demon stands, snarling in a flash of triumph, lifting Nick high—then slams him into the silver stone. His body goes still.

I'm running.

I barrel into the demon just as Sel swings Nick's sword.

Together, we send the body in one direction, and the head in another.

14

NICK, HIS FATHER, and Evan aren't the only injured.

I stand in the corner of the Lodge's basement infirmary and watch two second-year Pages dash back and forth between five metal tables.

Nick's on the one closest to me. His father is next to him. Evan's in the middle, and Victoria lies at the end. I didn't even know that Tor had been hurt.

Her chest had been sliced open by a hound, and there's blood splattered across her blue dress and over her pale cheeks.

Still, she's in better shape than the Davis men. Lord Davis's spine is broken in two places.

Nick's skull is cracked.

I should have moved faster. Struggled harder against the uchel. Gotten to Nick before he went after the demon himself.

The infirmary is William's domain. He strides between the tables, his hands coated in silver aether so thick it looks like mercury. The bright, citrus smell of his aether signature fills the room.

There's a pattern. He starts with the life-threatening injuries first and spends a few minutes murmuring in a fluid, lyrical language that I don't understand. He stands over their bodies while aether drips down onto their wounds and disappears into their skin. Then he walks away and closes his eyes, murmuring another incantation that pulls aether from the air again. It coats his fingers, and the cycle starts over.

I look down at my own hands. They haven't stopped trembling.

When we returned to the Lodge, the group had dispersed. Most of the Pages were sent home. Russ went to check on Felicity. After confirming that she was still asleep—a common recovery from Awakening, I'm told—he came down to wait with me and offered me a sweatshirt. I put it on, because I didn't know what else to do. He asked me if I'd like to go upstairs to take a shower. I don't remember what I said, but he left me alone after that.

I look at the infirmary walls and wonder why they aren't green, like the small room at the hospital. Then, because my defenses are down, I'm at the hospital again. The nurse is there. And the Merlin. And my mother is gone before I could say goodbye. . . . I squeeze my eyes shut and count to ten until it is three months later. Until I'm back in the infirmary at the Lodge.

"Where is he?" Sel bursts through the door like an unholy angel in a long black coat, his eyes blazing like twin suns. If he notices the two Pages slipping out behind him with fear written all over their faces, he doesn't say anything.

William's voice is even but firm. "He's stable, but he's not awake. Sel—Sel!"

Sel strides over to Nick—and there's not even a hitch in his step. Did William heal his ankle already? Sel examines Nick where he lies. Nick's shirt is cut open, exposing his chest and stomach. His usually handsome, open face is pale and pinched. He hasn't opened his eyes since we arrived.

"You better not die, Davis," Sel orders. "Not now."

"Sel." William steps toward Sel, his silver-coated hands raised up like a doctor's. "Nick is stable," he repeats. "He will recover. Lord Davis, on the other hand, is not stable yet. I need to keep treating them both, and everyone here, and you're not helping with that."

Sel glances over to Evan's table, and the muscles in his jaw clench. "He can't die either. None of the Squires or the Scions."

"We know, Sel!" Russ runs his hand through his hair. "This is the ninth attack in what, two weeks?"

"And the first uchel spotted in years," Fitz says from where he leans against the doorway beside Sarah.

"That pack didn't come to feed or infuse themselves with aether. They came with a purpose," Sel retorts. "They *knew* we'd be gathered tonight, knew we'd scatter, and knew the Scion of Arthur would be there. How?"

Russ scoffs. "Shadowborn don't *know* anything. They're too brainless to think, much less plan."

"Did you not see the uchel, Copeland?" Sel sneers. The tips of his hair start to singe and smoke. "Only an uchel can command isel to work together, and that's exactly what happened tonight. You underestimate the greater demons at your peril. And at the peril of your Scion, whose life you will soon be Oathed to protect."

Russ winces and turns away.

Sel turns to go, but spots me and stops. When he speaks, his voice is precise. Dangerous. "What is *she* doing here?"

Sarah steps forward. "Bree was taken hostage by the uchel, Sel. She's covered in slime, frightened half to death. Take it easy, will you?" I'm surprised by her defense of me, someone she doesn't know. "She even tried to save Nick."

Sel's gaze hardens. "And we're to assume it was just a coincidence that the uchel came back with *her* in their arms?"

"I tried to help." I hate how small my voice sounds. Hate that it sounds like how I feel. "I tried to—"

"You tried to what, little girl?" Unlike everyone else's shoes on the hard white tile, Sel's feet make no sound as he advances on me. "Help? Help who? Nick or the uchel?"

I shake my head, though it does nothing but make me dizzy. "*Nick*. I—I—"

"Selwyn!" Sarah warns. "Leave her alone."

But he's already in front of me, standing so close his gaze rains down on my face like embers. The air between us starts to cook, forcing a gasp from my lips.

Fear flutters, collides with memories. I know this moment. I've been here before. Been in a hospital and wanted nothing else but to run away.

I didn't do it then. And I won't do it now.

Sel leans down until his mouth is by my ear. His breath billows against my cheeks, burnt cinnamon and smoke. "There's a lie about you, *Page Matthews*. If I find out that you were a part of this . . ."

"*I wasn't,*" I grit out.

He bares his teeth, then whirls away. "Where's Pete?"

"Patrolling with third- and fourth-year Pages," Russ answers. "Looking for more."

"No," Sel murmurs. "The Shadowborn have made their play tonight. There won't be more. Stay put, Copeland. I'll administer the Warrior's Oath between you and Felicity as soon as she wakes up." Sel pulls on the collar of his jacket with one hand and points at me with the other. "I want *her* gone. She doesn't belong here." He sweeps through the door and leaves the room in shaky silence.

"The worst part about that guy is that you're never sure if it's safe to talk shit about him behind his back," Russ remarks with a frustrated sigh. Sarah smacks his arm. "What? It's true!"

Sarah turns to me, her eyes equal parts worry and apology. "Sorry about Sel. He's . . . protective. You do belong here. You're one of us now."

I look away, because that's just the thing. I'm not one of them.

She frowns and moves closer to examine my cheek. "You'll get to Bree's face, won't you, William?"

"Of course," William mutters, his head bent low over Evan's forehead. "Let me triage, Squire Griffiths . . ." Even in chastisement, amusement colors the healer's words.

William stands up to Sel, who somehow listens to him, and teases Sarah, who stands up for me. I decide I like them both. Too bad a pang of guilt follows: Sel is wrong about me working with the Shadowborn, but he's not wrong about me lying.

Eager to get the attention off me, I change the subject. "What was that monster? I thought demons looked like animals, or—"

Sarah shakes her head. "If isels, the lesser demons, are strong enough to go full-corp, they look like animals or the creatures you see in the ancient texts. Imps with horns, tails. But the uchels are greater demons. Less mischief, more murder, and strong enough to go corp as soon as they cross over. They look"—she hesitates, shares a glance with William that I can't decipher—". . . more human."

Russ leans against a wall and crosses his arms. "If you believe the old tales, the most powerful uchel, the goruchel, can even pass for human. Walk hidden among us and all that."

A cold dagger of fear cuts through me. Sel had called *me* an uchel a few hours ago. He thinks I'm one of them, passing as human. Here to harm Nick and the rest of the chapter. Breath leaves my body in a silent exhale.

"Demons that pass for human." Fitz rolls his eyes. "Scary stories to tell kids at night. Legend and lore."

William tuts without looking up. "*We* are legend and lore, Scion Baldwin." Fitz makes a rude gesture in response.

"Why did they want Nick?" I whisper.

William pauses with his hands over Evan. The four Legendborn look at me, then one another.

Russ stands up straight. "Because he's our king, or he will be, formally. When he's Awakened."

"*If* he's Awakened," Sarah says.

Fitz scoffs, a red flush building at his collar. "You *really* think it's an 'if,' Sar? We're Called in order. Flick's Line is fourth, which means the Scion of Kay up at Northern musta been Called recently too, and Lord Davis didn't bother to tell us. Tor and the Line of Tristan'll be next. Then the kid at Western and the Line of Lancelot. Then number one, Nick. And boom, Camlann."

Russ shakes his head. "Come on, man, don't exaggerate."

"*Exaggerate*? You think I'm exaggerating?" Fitz's eyes fill with scorn. "The Scion of the Line of Lamorak—*your* Scion—has Awakened. Welcome to *our* reality, Squire Copeland. You high-ranked kids get to play around and pretend we're not actually at war, while the rest of us are Awakened and *dying* every other year." Fury contorts his features. "Camlann is *coming*, whether you want to believe it or not!"

No one says anything for a long moment.

In the silence, I ask, "What is Camlann?"

Fitz whistles, shaking his head. "I don't care if he *is* king, somebody's gonna have to give Nick Davis a talking-to. Bringing a Page forward without telling her shit is how Pages get dead. Y'all have fun with Legendborn 101. I'm out." His angry steps echo down the hallway.

"Nick's told me things," I say, barely keeping the defensiveness from my voice. I edge toward Nick's table to watch his chest rise in shallow, short breaths. "Just not . . . everything."

William's aether dissolves into Evan's forehead, and he stands with a sigh, speaking directly to me for the first time.

"Well, now is as good a time as any to catch you up."

15

AFTER DECLARING THAT his four patients are now stable and infused with enough healing aether to fully recover, William orders Sarah and Russ to watch over the room while he and I step out. Russ starts to complain, but William silences him with a single raised brow.

At the door, he beckons me to follow. I tell myself that I need to go because learning more about the Order is part of my mission, but a small voice inside whispers that the only reason I agree is the touch of rosy color finally returning to Nick's cheeks.

We step out into the long fluorescent-lit basement hallway and head toward the elevator. Staring at it brings back a brief, hazy memory of talking to Russ as he brought me down to the infirmary. "You have an elevator?" I'd asked.

He'd smiled wryly and replied with, "We've got a lot of things."

Once we're inside, William opens a panel in the wall that Russ hadn't used. He enters a code into a numeric keypad, then presses a square button that turns from black to orange. When the elevator lurches into motion, my stomach threatens to upend itself.

William regards me with unreadable gray eyes. "How're my arms?"

I blink, confused. "Your arms?"

He nods down at my forearms where I've wrapped them around my chest.

"I usually like to follow up with my patients, but you were taken away before I got a chance to."

Fear washes through me. Rule One means I can't tell him what I remember. "I . . . I'm not sure . . ."

He smirks. "No need for subterfuge. I'm a healer by inheritance and by nature. I genuinely want to know how your wounds are doing."

At a loss for words, I thrust both forearms out. He takes my wrists and traces one forefinger up the inner skin of one arm, then the other. "Good. You took aether well."

The elevator comes to a jerking stop. When I swallow down bile, William's shrewd eyes narrow minutely. The doors open onto an even lower level and a similar long hallway, but he punches the button to keep them open.

"May I?" He gestures at the sticky, aching spot on my right cheek. I nod. But instead of touching me again, he sticks one hand out into the hallway, then chuckles at the look on my face. "Aether is everywhere, but it's a bit like a cell signal. Hard to find in a metal box." He glances up at the elevator by way of explanation. I watch as mage flame swirls and gathers in his palm. It solidifies into a thick, silver sauce that bleeds out over his hand, coating his fingers and the green leather cuff around his wrist. He steps closer, making eye contact first, and hovers three shining fingers over my cheek. The bright citrus smell of his casting flows between us, filling my nose.

The aether is cold—and it reminds me a bit of the slop of the uchel on my skin. I flinch, and William hums. "Deep breaths." The cold spreads, soothing where it touches. There's an itchy sensation, a quiet hiss, and the ache disappears. "Done." A flick of his wrist, and the aether dissolves. "How do you feel? Dizzy?"

I take stock of my head, tilt it back and forth. "No. Not like last time."

"Acclimating fast for a Onceborn," he says thoughtfully.

"Thank you?"

He inclines his head in response and gestures to the hall. "Shall we?"

I step through, gnawing on my lower lip. He knows I was at the Lodge last night, but what else does he know?

William indicates a door at the far end of the hall. After a few seconds he speaks up, his voice casual. It feels like he's read my mind. "I know there's more to you than what you're sharing, Page Matthews." I begin to interject, but he holds up a hand, a soft smile on his lips. "I'm not Sel, so don't worry. I didn't bring you here to corner you. I don't know what you're hiding, and frankly, I don't need or want to."

I stop, completely stunned. "But—but aren't you worried that—"

"That you're an uchel?" He stops, too, and rolls his eyes. "Hardly. Sel is an incredible detective, the most powerful Merlin in a generation, but he's also . . ."

"An asshole?"

He suppresses a smile. "I was going to say *volatile*. I think he's wrong to antagonize you."

I shake my head, unable to believe even this tiny bit of generosity. "But—"

"I trust Nicholas. He is our king and, more than that, he is my friend. Whatever you two have decided is none of my business. And"—his eyes soften—"you brought him back to us. Something tells me he wouldn't be here if it weren't for you."

My breath catches. Nick *wouldn't* have been here tonight if it weren't for me.

The world spins. If I didn't know better, I'd say Sel was casting a mesmer, but this isn't him. He didn't do this.

Tonight was *my* choice, and it's too much. Everything. All of it. *Too much.* I'd chosen a ruse to find the truth about my mother's death. To find out the truth for myself. For my father. Maybe even to prove to Alice that I was right and she was wrong.

I *didn't* choose the smell of decay still clinging to the back of my tongue, to the inside of my mouth. I didn't choose the sound of Nick's father's spine shattering against the oak tree. The dull crack of Nick's skull splitting open on stone.

My stomach turns again—and an arm wraps around my shoulders. "This way." I stumble, and William pulls me tighter to his side as he pushes a door open. "Here we go."

A stall door, a toilet. Then I'm on my knees heaving, retching, heaving again until it feels like everything I've ever eaten has exited my body.

When I'm done, I lean back on my heels. His hand rubs soothing circles around my back. A cool palm rests against my forehead. We sit in the quiet until my breath slows.

After a while, William hands me a lime-colored cloth handkerchief. I stare down at it, puzzled at the alarmingly bright fabric. I hear the smile in his voice. "It was my father's. The Line of Gawain is what discerning people call 'ostentatious.'" I hold the cloth, hesitant to use it, but he counters before I can say a word. "Please. I have an embarrassingly large amount in an embarrassingly green chest somewhere."

I give a weak smile as I wipe my nose and mouth. When I'm done, he leads me to a cushioned bench near the bathroom's sinks.

"Thank you."

"No more of that." He pats my knee and watches my face with attentive eyes. "Our world is . . . a lot."

I inhale shakily. "Yes."

He tilts his head. "And you're sure you want to be in it?"

William's question takes me by surprise. *Am* I sure? After tonight, am I truly sure? I think of my father and our conversation on the library steps. I can hear his voice even now. ". . . This thing that's happening to us . . . I feel it too. I know it feels real bad." He feels this pain, and yet he goes to work every day. Lives in our house with the echo of my mother *every day*, when I could barely stand it. I think of my mother and the stubbornness—no, the *weakness*—that kept me from speaking to her after a foolish fight.

Our Brave Bree.

I inhale again, stronger this time. "Yes. I'm sure."

"Okay," he says, standing up. "If you're dead set on being here, then you definitely need that Legendborn crash course. But first, you need tea."

William wasn't kidding about the tea.

He makes me wait outside the bathroom for a few minutes while he goes down the hall to a kitchenette. When he comes back, he presses a steaming mug of lemon-ginger tea in between my palms and orders me to nurse it while we talk.

I'm beginning to understand why Sel didn't fight William's will. He's imperious without being arrogant, and has an uncanny knack for being right.

Plus, the tea is delicious.

He sweeps in front of me and leads us down the hall to a navy door at the far end, opposite the elevator. "How many basements does the Lodge have?" I ask.

"Two. The infirmary and training rooms are on the one above, plus some recovery rooms for seriously injured patients. Down here is all the other secret stuff we can't risk anyone seeing by accident. Artifacts and member documents"—he jerks a thumb at a door we've just passed—"are in a cold storage room where we have more control over the temperature and lighting conditions. Fortunately, the oldest items have been so infused with aether by Merlins over the years that we don't have to worry about them crumbling to pieces." He reaches the door and punches in another code on the keypad near the handle. "But this is what you really need to see."

I squeeze the mug between my hands. My heart gives a rowdy thump so loud I worry he can hear it. "No demons, right? You're not throwing me into a medieval fun house of horrors as some sort of hazing thing, are you?"

He laughs, loud and light. "No"—he opens the door and leans in, searching the interior wall for a light switch—"but 'Medieval Fun House of Horrors' would make a great band name."

I roll my eyes, but I'm grateful for his humor. Another sip of tea, and my stomach is almost calm.

He finds the light switch, illuminating not another room but the landing at the top of a wide spiral staircase.

We take the stairs down two more levels and he talks as we walk. "Legendborn parents explain the Order and Lines to their children when we're young. Vassals know enough to be dangerous, but with new Pages like you, the sponsors are usually the ones who fill in all the juicy details."

"Nick didn't really have the time," I mutter as I traipse down the stairs behind him. *I didn't really give him the time*, is what I think.

William remains unfazed. "I figured. That's all right—I kind of like doing the honors."

We reach a large, damp-smelling room that is empty save an old rug and a few sitting chairs. After he hits another set of overhead lights, he heads to the back. At the very far end is a wall covered by a black curtain that stretches as wide as the room. "After a Vassal swears to the Code of Secrecy and pledges to the Order, someone from their assigned Line explains the origin of the Order and its mission. If they want their kid to Page and have a chance of becoming a Squire, that child is sworn to the Code as well."

"And that *works?*"

"Yep." He unwraps a thick golden rope and grunts, drawing it down from a pulley. "Vassals don't expose us; most families have been aligned with the Order for centuries, and they have too much to gain socially and financially, even if their kids don't Squire in the end. Besides"—William grins—"rich people love secrets."

As he pulls, the curtain draws upward, revealing the entirety of the wall, or what I'd *thought* was a wall.

Taking up the whole of my vision is the largest single slab of silver I've ever seen. Even bigger than the Chapel. It must be three stories tall, reaching all the way up to the far wall of the first floor. Running down the slab are thousands of meticulously carved lines. Every few inches, the lines break for sparkling stars made of gems, then start again below them. The slab is so tall that I have to step back to see it in its entirety.

He crosses his arms and gazes up, up, up. "This is the Wall of Ages. The thirteen bloodlines of the Round Table, and their Scions."

At the very top of the Wall, embedded in silver, are thirteen fist-size stones. In the center is a white diamond, but the other gems glimmer in various shades of red and green and blue and yellow. Engraved in elegant script above the stones is one phrase: Y LLINACH YW'R DDEDDF.

"The Line is Law," William translates. "The Order and Vassal colonizers were a blended bunch: Welsh, English, Scots, Scotch-Irish, Germans. But sixth-century Wales is Arthur's birthplace, so Welsh was the Order's first language.

Some of the old incantations are still in Welsh, like the swyns I use in the infirmary."

Alice would love this, I think. *The history, the Wall, everything.* Then I feel a pang of guilt for wishing she was with me. I'd never want her to get hurt, and right now bodily injury seems like the price of admission.

"Potential Scion children are told the lore early and often. First by our parents, then by the Lieges—retired Scions and Squires—then by our parents again when we turn sixteen. That's the first year our knights may Call on us." His eyes lose focus as he returns to a story he's clearly heard many, many times. "At the Round Table's peak, Arthur had over one hundred and fifty knights at his command. But over time, the Shadowborn Wars, our fight with the Cysgodanedig, cut that number down until only the thirteen strongest knights remained. Merlin and Arthur feared what the world would become should the Table fall, and so Merlin devised the Spell of Eternity: a powerful casting to magnify the remaining knights' abilities and bind their spirits to their bloodline so that their heirs could forever stand against the darkness. So that the Table would live on, immortal." William's voice has dipped low with reverence, or perhaps he's echoing the reverence of those who told the story before. "When our knights Awaken, their spirit lives again. This is why we call those outside the Lines Unanedig. 'Onceborn.' And why we call ourselves Chwedlanedig. 'Legendborn.'"

To be able to trace one's family back that far is something I have never fathomed. My family only knows back to the generation after Emancipation. Suddenly, it's hard to stand here and take in the magnificence of the Wall and not feel an undeniable sense of ignorance and inadequacy. Then, a rush of frustration because someone probably wanted to record it all, but who could have written down my family's history as far back as this? Who would have been able to, been taught to, been allowed to? Where is *our* Wall? A Wall that doesn't make me feel lost, but found. A Wall that towers over anyone who lays eyes on it.

Instead of awe, I feel . . . *cheated.*

I take a deep breath and turn to William, my voice harsh. "You said sixth century? Wouldn't each knight's bloodline include thousands of living descendants by now?"

"Yes, but a Scion is more than a descendant—they're an heir. The knight's *inheritance*, their enhanced abilities and affinity for aether, lives in one person at a time. And that inheritance is only transmitted by an Awakened Scion, one who was Called to power like Felicity was tonight. Think the British monarchy and the line of succession: not every child is heir to the throne, only the eldest of the sovereign. If the heir apparent cannot take the throne, then it goes to their child, or their child's child, et cetera. If the heir has no child, power flows to their sibling, then their sibling's kids. And even then, whoever is in line must be eligible."

I frown. "You said something about being sixteen?"

He raises a brow. "You're quick. Good. A Scion must be between the ages of sixteen and twenty-two. I have to give it to Merlin, the Spell keeps things tidy. Here."

He places a finger onto a line second from last on the right. As soon as his fingertip touches stone, a rush of light streaks along the lineage lines flowing like blood in veins. Once the light reaches the top, a unique glowing engraving appears above each stone, while a larger symbol shines above them all.

Colors. Coins. Sigils.

I pull on Nick's necklace until the chain spills out of my shirt onto my palm—and see something I missed earlier. The coin is two-sided. On one side is the unifying symbol of the order, the circle with an embellished diamond in the center. On the other, a dragon rampant.

The Pendragon.

William steps closer, speaking with his back to me. "The Wall is enchanted to hide names in case an outsider finds their way to this room. The last sixty generations of Scion names are recorded here, all the way down to present day. The Order used to keep all the records in books. Still do, for convenience, of course, but the Southern Chapter founders started transferring records to the Wall once they decided to build the school."

My eyes widen. "The Order built Carolina?"

He winks. "Absolutely. The Shadowborn spread from Europe to the

Americas, maybe looking for fresh hunting grounds, and grew in number alongside the colonies. By the 1700s there was a high concentration of Gates on the East Coast. The founders opened the first Round Table chapter, built the Lodge, then added the school around it. Hell, Carolina was partially built as an excuse to gather and train eligible Scions. Early College was manufactured fairly recently to bring sixteen-year-old Scions to campus as early as possible, so they can live and train near the Gates with the chapter. The Lines are spread out along several historic schools, but our chapter's the oldest.

"The Lines follow the original Round Table's chain of command, and that rank determines the order in which we are Awakened." He points to a bloodline that descends from a green stone and ends in a small star. "This one is me. I'm the Scion of the Line of Sir Gawain, twelfth-ranked. In addition to enhanced healing, the Spell gave Gawain preternatural strength at midday and midnight." I gape and he shrugs. "Gawain was an odd guy, what can I say."

He shifts his finger to the next line on the Wall, one that descends from an orange stone: "Fitz is the Scion of Sir Bors, eleventh-ranked. In combat, he has agility like you've never seen. When we take a Squire, we're choosing a battle partner to join us in the Warrior's Oath. Someone who will share our bloodline's power. Fitz chose Evan as his Squire last year."

He moves over a handful to the line below a dark yellow gem: "Pete is new to us this year, a freshman. The Scion of Sir Owain, ranked seventh. Owain's Scions can call upon his lion familiar to join them in battle. Pete needs a Squire this year, just like I do."

Over a few, the red stone: "Felicity is the Scion of Lamorak's bloodline. Ranked fourth, as you know. She chose Russ as her Squire in last year's tournament. After tonight, she'll be strong enough to punch through a boulder—and when Sel Orders them, so will Russ."

Over one, blue. "Victoria is the Scion of the Line of Tristan, third-ranked, with Sarah as her Squire. When she Awakens, her name will go here. Marksmanship and speed."

He points to a final line, right down the center. "And this star is for Nick."

I look up. Arthur's pure white diamond leads down, down, down to a single shining star engraved in the wall at the same height as my hip.

My fingers reach out to touch it without my permission, and I yank them back. William's mouth quirks in a knowing smile.

"Under normal circumstances the Order operates just fine without an Awakened king. That's what the Regents are for. Shadowborn cross into our world to feed and terrorize, we kill them, and the peace is kept, relatively speaking. Low-ranked Scions like myself are Awakened frequently, and we're generally strong enough to keep the demons at bay. If you age out or expire, the next eligible Scion can be Called in your place, and the cycle continues."

"*Expire?* If you die, you mean?" I ask, horrified.

"The Scion in each bloodline and the nine potentially eligible descendants in the line of succession behind them begin training as soon as they can walk." He turns to me, his eyes assessing my expression. "We know the risks and prepare for them as best we can."

I remember what Fitz said earlier—and the orders Lord Davis had given to send the Awakened to the front lines against the hellhounds. "But if the lower-ranked Scions are Called all the time, then your Lines are—infantry. You're bearing the brunt of the war. The higher-ranked Scions—"

William cuts me off with a raised finger. "No, little Page, don't go down that road." He sighs. "Fitz's way—his entire family's way—is . . . dishonorable. We are Called first because fifteen hundred years ago, our knights were first to the field. It's like Lord Davis says, to serve is to elevate oneself. It is ennobling. Some carry the burden with resentment, but the truth is, none of us have a choice. Immortality has a price. In the end, there is evil in the world, and we are the ones equipped to fight it."

"Under normal circumstances, the Order is fine without an Awakened Arthur . . . but we're not 'under normal circumstances,' are we?"

"No, it seems not." William sighs heavily. "Nick was correct. A Scion ranked higher than sixth hasn't been Called in a very long time. And Sel was right too. Demons—isels especially—don't work together like they did tonight. And an uchel sighting is beyond rare." He studies me. "But why don't you ask the question that's really on your mind?"

"Just the one?" I quip.

His mouth twitches. "The big one."

"What is Camlann?"

He leads me over to a pair of sitting chairs, perfectly positioned for contemplating the Wall, or the Order's history and legacy, or both.

"It's written in the books that the magic holding Merlin's spell together—the engine behind the entire system—is preserved in the spirit of Arthur. As long as the king's spirit remains dormant, the spell is safe. This is why Arthur, the first knight, calls on his Scion last, and only when 'the demon scourge' becomes so powerful and so rampant, that the Round Table must be reunited under his leadership to fight it back. The threat must be great indeed, for Arthur to Awaken and enter the field, putting all of the Lines at risk."

William pauses, then recites the next words from memory: "'When thirteen Scions have Awakened and claimed Squires, the Scion of Arthur will lead the Round Table against the demon plague in a deadly battle.' This war is called Camlann, so named because, in legend, Camlann is where many of the final knights were killed. Camlann is the battlefield where Arthur fell. Camlann is where the original Round Table was broken—forever. If a fully Awakened Arthur is struck down by Shadowborn blood, the Legendborn Lines will be broken forever too."

I whisper, "And the humans, the Unanedig, will have no defenders."

"'And the Shadowborn will rule the earth.'"

The room falls into a tense silence. Somewhere behind the silver wall, I hear a dripping sound.

I remember Nick's warm smile on the walk through campus, then the terror branded on his face tonight in the woods. *I* brought that sequence of expressions to his face. Even if no one can control their knight's Call, I brought Nick closer to something he'll never wanted. Guilt settles heavy in my belly.

I look back up at Nick's star and think of him fighting, graceful like a dancer, feet light, body twisting. Swinging his sword with confidence and determination. Driving his blade through the hellhound. I can't think of him falling in battle. My brain can't imagine it.

"When was the last time Arthur Called his Scion?"

William cocks his head to the side. "Almost two hundred and fifty years ago? 1775, I think?"

"What? That's—"

"The Revolutionary War." One side of his mouth draws down in a tight frown. "Depends on who you ask, but in my opinion, that war would have happened anyway. And war is war, whether the Shadowborn incite it, prolong it, or use it as a feeding ground. People died by tens of thousands. Who cares what it's called."

I agree. My eyes are drawn to Nick's star again.

And I notice something beside it that I hadn't seen before. I stand and walk closer—yes, there's something there, connected to Nick's star by a shimmering dash.

"What is it?" William reaches my side, searching for what's grabbed my attention.

I point to the small, dark marble stuck in the slab directly beside Nick's name. It's so black it seems to absorb light. "That marble. What is that?"

"Ah." For the first time, he hesitates before he speaks. "Only the most powerful Merlin child in a generation is Selected to take the Kingsmage Oath. The child is taken from their family and bound here, in a formal ceremony before the chapter, to a child Scion of Arthur. For the rest of that Merlin's life, they are the Scion's sworn protector until death."

My stomach twists. *Taken from their family.* A child—and a childhood— sacrificed to protect another. "No child could possibly comprehend what it means to make an Oath like that."

"Like I said," he murmurs, "none of us have a choice."

My heart aches for both of them. Even for Sel, who is magically bound forever to a Scion who has never wanted his title. I may not like him and he sure seems to hate me, but I feel compelled to examine Sel's marble and read the script beside it:

Selwyn Emrys Kane.

William hums thoughtfully. "Ready to go back? I need to check on my patients."

I nod, ready to leave this place that feels more filled with death and loss than life.

Before I turn, my eyes drift up to the star above Nick's. Beside it, someone has carved "Martin Thomas Davis" into the stone. *Of course.* Lord Davis went to Carolina years ago, when he was the Scion of Arthur and before Nick was born. Then, something else catches my eye.

"What happened here?" I point to the marble linked to Lord Davis's star, representing his Kingsmage, an "Isaac Klaus Sorenson."

William squints. "Not sure. Maybe the archivist got sloppy?"

I don't follow right away, because what he said makes no sense. Every other line and stone and star has been meticulously carved, not a stroke out of place or an error in sight. But deep, angry slashes surround Isaac's marble on every side, like an animal has clawed it. And yet the marble itself looks just like Sel's: shiny, smooth, and perfectly round.

"Coming?"

"Yeah," I mumble, and follow him upstairs.

16

I PANIC WHEN we get back to the infirmary because Nick is gone and his table is cleared. Tor is gone too.

"Where are my patients?" William thunders at Russ and Sarah. The two wide-eyed Squires shrink backward. I don't blame them; the normally gentle-faced William looks murderous.

"They woke up! Nick went home," Russ says at the same time that Sarah blurts, "Tor's upstairs. She said she was hungry!"

My stomach drops. Nick just . . . left?

The raised voices elicit a low moan from Lord Davis, and William catches himself before he yells again. "And you let him?"

Russ recovers first. "He's the—the king?"

"In this infirmary," William hisses, advancing on him, "*I* am your king. Nick was *not* discharged! His head is still healing!"

"He left me?" I regret my question as soon as I say it out loud. It sounds so . . . *pathetic.* "I mean, just that he—not that I—" William's raised brow and Russ's confused expression don't help me out at all. "I just thought I'd get to check on him first."

Sarah takes pity. "We didn't know where you and Will went. Nick called your phone a bunch, said it went to voicemail. I think he thought you went home after . . . everything that happened in the woods."

I hear the words she doesn't say: he thinks I *gave up* after everything that happened in the woods. Ran home scared.

"Nick probably needs some space to catch his breath." Russ shrugs. "Think about it—he shows up to reclaim his title after years of being away, and boom! We're two Awakened Scions away from Arthur. I'd be freaking out too."

"Will?"

On the far table, Evan stirs. William is at his side in three steps, his fury gone and kind bedside manner in place. "Stay still, Ev. You took a claw to the head, my friend." Evan follows orders, but he blinks bleary eyes open and scans the room. It only takes him a second to find me. He tenses on the bed.

"Hey, Bree."

I give him an awkward wave. "Hey, Evan. And here I thought you were just a clueless frat boy."

His weak laugh ends in a cough. "Don't tell Char I got hurt, 'kay?"

Charlotte Simpson feels like a lifetime ago and a world away—a world that I have to return to tomorrow, like none of this happened. "I won't."

"Cool," he mutters, and relaxes on the bed.

William snorts. "If you're well enough to worry about your girlfriend, then you're well enough to recover in your own bed. Let me check you over before you go upstairs."

Someone tugs at my sleeve. It's Sarah. "Can I drive you home?"

I blink, surprised by her offer. "Do you want to check on Tor first?"

She seems pleased that I asked. "My girl's mad grouchy when she's hungry, but she's fine."

As we leave, William kicks Russ out of the infirmary too. I hear him mutter something about no peace in this house, and some Welsh that sounds a lot like curses.

Sarah isn't one of those people who has to fill a silent car with chatter. She turns the radio on, leaving me to spend the ride back to campus thinking about all I'd seen and done tonight. By the time she parks her car in one of the campus lots close to the dorms, all the thinking has given me a full-blown headache.

When we get out, I realize I'm still wearing the sweatshirt Russ gave me. I strip it off and offer it to her. "I think this is Russ's?"

She wrinkles her nose. "I'll get it to him."

I fold the shirt and hand it to her, then take a look at our ride for the first time. It's a Tesla. "Nice car."

She shrugs. "Not mine. The Order has a bunch we can use."

My eyes widen. "Wow. That's—"

"Pretentious."

I blink. "Are you allowed to say stuff like that?"

She rolls her eyes. "I mean, I wouldn't say it in front of the Regents, but . . ."

When I turn toward my dorm, she surprises me again by falling in step beside me. I try to figure out how to ask my question without being rude. "Aren't you a Vassal kid?"

"Aren't I rich, you mean?" I purse my lips, but she just smiles and wraps her sweater tighter around her narrow shoulders. "My mom comes from money, but my dad doesn't. She Paged at the Western Chapter in Virginia, but never Squired. That's where they met."

I turn this over a few times. My parents met after my mother graduated; Dad didn't go to college. I'd never thought about whether she'd met someone at school, dated. I'd always imagined her in a lab, but what did I really know about her life here? "Did your mother want to Squire?"

"At first. My grandparents *definitely* wanted her to, but then my parents got together and she realized she wanted a family." We turn down one of the walkways that Nick and I had taken two nights ago. "She'd never admit it, but I think she wanted the prestige, not the war."

"And your dad knew about the Order?"

Sarah shakes her head. "Nah. Not until later. He's a sworn and pledged Vassal—had to be before they could marry—but mostly what he knows is the dinner parties and the opera tickets and the formal galas. Not that he's particularly well received at any of them."

"Why's that?"

"He's Venezuelan. But I pass, so people don't realize I am too. Or they forget. They say racist crap around me sometimes."

"Then what?"

She shrugs. "Sometimes I check 'em. Sometimes I don't bother."

"Ah," I say, and neither one of us has to say anything else about that.

"Does he know how danger—" Sarah bumps my elbow so that I stop speaking. A pair of students—on the way to the twenty-four-hour library, by the looks of it—walk toward us on the path.

Right. This is what I signed up for. Following the Code of Secrecy means not talking about demon attacks within earshot of the general public.

Once they pass, she glances over her shoulder to watch them turn the corner. "Sorry. What were you asking? Does my dad know how dangerous all this is? He knows what we fight and why, but I don't think it *feels* dangerous to him. He can't See aether, and he's never seen a demon. He knows we have a healer and he knows that my Line hasn't been Called in decades, so he probably thinks I'm protected from the worst of it. Mom didn't want me to Squire unless I got Selected by a high-ranked Scion, since they're less likely to be Called. The Abatement, you know?"

"No, I don't. What's the Abatement?"

She curses low. "Fitz is an ass, but he's right. Nick should have educated you. You deserve to know the risks."

I stop. "Sar, what's the Abatement?"

She releases a heavy breath. "When a Scion is Awakened, all the power from their knight transfers to them. The Spell of Eternity is . . . serious casting, you know? But we're still human. The longer the Scions are Awake, the more it drains them. After they age out, most don't make it past thirty-five."

I struggle to breathe, to speak. William didn't say anything about that. I can't imagine him dying that young. "It *kills* them?"

Sarah hurries to correct me. "Only if they've been Awakened. It's . . . it's why the Legendborn are revered. Holy warriors and everything."

I think of Felicity. Six hours ago she thought she'd live till her eighties. But now . . . "Can't the Scions just *not* fight? Let some other relative take the inheritance?"

She kicks a pebble as we walk. "Scions can't opt out of their blood. And once Awakened, they feel this . . . this *need*. To fight. Directly from their knights. If Tor's Called, she'll feel it, and when we're bonded, so will I. Once I take some of Tristan's power through her, Abatement will come for me, too."

My chest is so tight I can barely get the words out. "Why would you *choose* this?"

"I can't answer for everyone, but service is how I was raised. And . . ." She shrugs, flushes. "I love her. I won't let her fight alone."

Before I can ask anything else about the bond of Scion and Squire, a shadow descends overhead. Sarah is in front of me in a blink, dropped into a fighter's crouch—hips angled, knees bent, one fist on guard, the other ready to strike.

"Page Matthews."

Sel takes three determined strides toward me before Sarah slides between us. Even though the Merlin is the superior opponent with a foot of height on her, the pint-size girl glares up at him poised for a fight. The steel in her eyes tells me she'd put up a good one.

"Back off, Sel. I'm taking Bree to her dorm."

"Not before I question her." It's only when he moves that we notice something's not right. He *stumbles*. Actually loses his footing.

I didn't think that was even possible.

Sarah stares in disbelief too. "What the—"

"She's not what she seems," he says imperiously. He dashes around her, but he's nowhere near as fast as he was earlier. When he comes to a stop, he towers over me—and brings a hot, oppressive cloud of smoke, charred cinnamon, and leather. The smell is so intense, I cover my nose in disgust and retreat.

"You're blitzed, buddy. Move." Sarah wriggles her arm between us and pushes him away from me. He bats at her hand—and misses. The economy of movement he'd always displayed is gone; every gesture imprecise, too big.

It's the most surreal thing I've ever seen, and after a night like tonight, that's saying a *lot*.

My question is muffled behind my fingers. "What's wrong with him?"

"He's aether-drunk," she says, as if that explains everything. She pushes against him with her full weight, but Sel sort of drapes his body over her. She grunts in frustration. "Must have just come from bonding Felicity and Russ. The Warrior's Oath is pretty hard-core, and on top of that, he Oathed y'all tonight too."

Oh. *Oh*.

That strange, intoxicated look on his face after the Oath of Fealty. His blood-shot eyes now. The dark pink of his parted lips, the angry flush on his cheeks.

"I am not!" Sel declares loudly. It'd be funny if I didn't know how lethal he was.

Sarah shoves him hard and Sel growls at her. Shockingly, she growls back. It's a small, silly-sounding imitation of his low rumble, but it *works*. He blinks at her and gives a confused grimace that is, somehow, the extreme opposite of intimidating.

"You are," she insists. "And I'm not leaving you alone with Bree when you're like this. Let's go."

"Tonight shouldn't have happened, Sar," he mutters. His dark brows draw together as if he's seeing it happen all over again. "Nothing like that . . . has ever happened before. When the Regents find out . . ."

Sarah's tone turns soothing. "It wasn't your fault."

"That's not what they'll say," Sel whispers, his hoarse voice almost lost to the wind. His eyes land on me and narrow accusingly.

"She's Nick's Page." Sarah shakes his shoulder. "The King's Wisdom, pal. Don't even think of laying a hand—"

Sel scoffs. "He's fucking *dormant*. No wisdom there. Head's so far up his own ass, he wouldn't notice Arthur's Call if it bit him there!"

His eyes find Nick's sigil on my chest and harden to golden flint. "If you harm him," he murmurs, his voice cold, hollow, "I'll kill you. Burn through you until your blood becomes dust." Sel watches the fear flood my body, and his mouth curls into a vicious grin. "You know I will, don't you? You know I can."

Sarah turns, pressing her back against Sel's chest to face me. "I've got him. Can you make it back on your own?"

My feet were already carrying me backward in the damp grass. Now I turn and sprint while Sel's laughter follows me across the quad.

My hands are shaking so badly it takes three attempts to get the key in the door. Once it opens, I fall through and shove it closed.

As if a door could stop Selwyn.

I lean against the wood, chest heaving. Waiting. Waiting.

Just in case.

"Bree?"

I jump. Hand pressed to my heart, I seek Alice out in the dim light.

She fumbles for her bedside lamp. "Do you have any idea what time it—" Her voice cuts off abruptly when the lamp light floods the room. "What the fuck?"

Alice *never* curses.

I shield my eyes against the light. "Sorry I'm late."

Alice leaps out of bed in her pajamas, snatching her glasses on the way. "What happened to you?"

I don't even know what lie to make up right now. What the fuck, indeed.

"I—I—"

"Bree?" I stop stammering at the tremor in her voice. She's right in front of me, her hands hovering inches from my shoulders, eyes roaming over my face, down my chest and legs. "*Oh my God.* You're hurt."

I blink. "What do you mean?"

Her voice is frantic now, panic making it soar. "You look like you've been *dragged*! Through mud!" She claps a hand over her nose. "You smell like a swamp. There are holes in your shirt. You're *filthy.* Your hair is . . . *God,* Matty. What the hell happened to you?"

17

MY MOUTH OPENS and closes like a fish. I want to lie to her, but where are the words? There just aren't any. No words to explain what happened to me tonight. What I *chose* tonight.

Horror dawns over Alice's face. "Did someone do this to you?"

I shake my head. No. No one did this to me. No one human, at least.

"You can tell me if something happened." She grabs both of my hands, tears welling up behind her glasses. "I'll believe you."

Alice has known me for half my life. We are sleepovers and skinned knees and first crushes and always making sure our lockers are side by side.

Her tears break me.

The sob I've been holding back since the woods finally bursts out.

"I can call someone. The campus cops, the—"

"No!" I shout, mind flashing to Norris, the dean. "It—it isn't like that. I promise."

"Okay," she says, her eyes darting back and forth as she processes. "If you okay."

Once I'm satisfied she won't call on a Vassal without realizing, my head thunks against the wood.

Alice rubs my forearms. "Let's get you cleaned up."

As with William, I let her guide me outside our room to the communal hall bathroom, my shower caddy tucked under her arm. When we enter, a girl washing her hands at one of the sinks gives us a funny look.

Once we're next to the row of empty showers, Alice tugs on the bottom of my shirt. "You'll feel better after a shower. Do you need help?"

She's speaking quietly and clearly, like you do when someone is so freaked out they can't handle complex sentences and you're trying to calm them down. I realize what she's doing, but I let her do it anyway. It's working.

"I got it," I mumble, and lift my T-shirt over my shoulders. She's right about the rips. Three thin cuts cross the fabric where the uchel's claws held me.

The door bangs open and closed, leaving us alone. Alice leans into one of the stall showers and turns the tap on. While she tests the water, I slip back to the other side to look at myself in the mirror.

No wonder she cursed.

I look *wrecked*.

My "cute bun" from earlier is long past cute. It's mostly intact, but ruined with the uchel's muck. Dark globs have plastered escaped curls to my forehead and the nape of my neck. Glossy eyes, puffy cheeks, bits of dirt on my nose. Most of the slime was on my shirt, but some of it's caked on my arms and caught in my inner elbow. A long red bruise follows the line of my rib cage. I tug my bra down to hide it. Nick's coin glints on my sternum. I take the necklace off and stuff it in my pocket.

"Water's ready, shower stuff's inside." Alice comes around to stare at me in the mirror. Opens her mouth to ask another question, but thinks better of it, whatever it was. "I'll be outside if you need anything."

Once she's gone, I undress as quickly as my rib will allow and step into the shower. The water pressure here is weak, but at least the stream's hot. Uchel stench wafts around me in a noxious steam until vanilla body wash chases it away.

My brain tries to piece together the next steps of a shower—and comes up blank.

This used to happen at home. In the weeks after my mom died, I'd manage the first step of some mundane task—get naked and into the shower, open the fridge and set out the deli meat, dump a load of laundry into the washing machine—and the next step would elude me. Like an old mill, my mind would wheel around and around until it picked up the next directive.

Hair. My hair is dirty. Yes. I can handle that.

I hadn't planned on even getting my hair wet for at least another week or so, but I can't avoid washing my curls tonight. Not when they smell like sick and swamp. They'll be clean and gorgeous tomorrow, but the unexpected added time makes me groan. That's another hour and a half *at least* before I can really climb into bed, even if I skip deep conditioning and styling and throw everything up into a wet pineapple.

Alice returns as I part my thick damp hair into sections.

"Okay in there?"

"Yeah. Just realized I need to wash my hair."

"Damn."

"Yeah."

Silence. She doesn't leave. I'm okay with that, because I want her company. Not just anyone's. Alice's.

She must be thinking the same thing, because from the other side of the shower curtain I hear her say, "Okay if I chill in here? You seem pretty rattled."

"I had the same idea."

"Jinx, then."

I rinse my hair out and start on conditioner, proud that I know the next step without having to think about it.

There's another step I need to take tonight too.

"Hey, Alice?"

"Yeah?"

"I'm sorry. About the Quarry. Our first Level, I know you'd go if I wanted to go and I guess I just decided that was okay. I know the dean called your parents, and I can't imagine what they said. I'm just . . . sorry for my part in it and sorry that I yelled at you and"—tears well up in my eyes, and my hands are too sudsy to wipe them, damnit—"said those things. That was unfair and wrong."

Alice sighs. "I'm sorry too. It was my decision to go to the Quarry, not yours. I shouldn't have jumped on you about your classes and about being here. I was just angry and worried." A pause. "Which is what I am right now, by the way. Worried on the way to terrified."

I dunk my head under the faucet. Pull water through my clumpy curls with shaking fingers. Section again, apply shampoo.

"You gonna tell me what happened tonight?"

I knew she'd ask, but the question still rocks me. I have to press both hands against the shower tile to stop the tremors. I'm clean, in the physical sense. But I still *feel* dirty.

"Bree?"

I squeeze my eyes shut, but the images I'd tried to bury flash by too quickly: the sharp rise of Nick's chest when William *pushed* aether into his body; Sel, in a dark, bitter rage, ripping the arms and legs off the dead uchel and throwing them into the woods; the way the hounds' bodies just . . . *dissolved* after a while. The memories threaten to suffocate me, just like the ones from the night my mother died.

"*I can't.*"

Another pause. The shampoo runs into my eyes. Stings.

"Trust me. Please?" I ask, so quietly I'm not sure she can hear it over the water. It gets harder to breathe. The hot tears of After-Bree burn behind my eyes.

"Fine." She doesn't sound angry, but she leaves without saying goodbye or good night.

The door clicks shut, and that *something* inside me breaks again. A rush of air leaves my lungs, like I've been holding my breath for hours and hours.

Then, my skin bursts into flames.

I slap my hands against the walls, the tile floor, but nothing stops the bloom of red climbing my fingers to my elbows. Bloodred fire ignites at the tips of my fingers and races to my elbows in a loud *whoosh*. Even under the water, the blaze grows brighter and wraps around my elbows like glowing vines.

The fire scalds my skin without burning, flickers over my nose like wild butterflies.

Spots in my vision bleed from tiny black dots into swirling obsidian pools. I fall to my knees, hand splayed across the tiles, heart pounding against my rib cage.

Mage flame.

That's what this is.

It's not silver-blue like Sel's or the Legendborns', or green like the hounds', but it's still mage flame.

Knowing what it is doesn't explain *why* it's here.

Why it's the sickening, raw color of a fresh wound.

Why the flame feels like it's coming from *inside* me.

The only beings I've seen leak flame from their bodies are demons. Sel already thinks I'm Shadowborn. If he sees me like this—

"*Oh God,*"I whimper.

There must be other explanations: It's my body's delayed reaction to the Oath. It's Sel's aether still lingering on my skin, turned sour from my resistance. It's something the uchel put *in* me when he opened me up. Any could be true, or none. The bottom line is the same: If I can't explain what's happening, then I have to find a way to control it, because if I can't control it . . .

You know I will, don't you? Kill you. And you know I can.

I squeeze my eyes shut. Find my barrier. Shape it into every image I've ever used to contain After-Bree and her explosive, dangerous rage—and then some.

A wall made of brick. Made of steel. With bolts the size of my fist.

A blockade a mile high.

Tall enough to contain a giant, strong enough to hold back a god.

A bank vault with two-foot-thick bulletproof doors.

Unbreakable metals, uncrackable surfaces, unscalable heights.

I push all of me behind all of them.

No fissures, no seams, no way in or out.

I shove and heave and cry until I'm safe behind my wall.

And when I open my eyes, the flames are gone.

18

WHEN I WAKE up, my head is clear. I'm tired, but I feel like myself.

I slip my satin scarf off and tug on a few damp curls. Let the shiny strands wrap around my fingers, then pop back into place.

My arms look normal again. Familiar. Ordinary.

Except what happened last night was not ordinary.

I review Nick's explanation in my head: Aether is an element in the air. Mage flame is the byproduct aether creates when it's called into a solid state. Awakened Scions and Merlins can call aether for various uses. These things I've witnessed. But I've been so busy learning about the Order and what they can do that I haven't really taken stock of what *I* can do.

Sight? Resisting mesmer? And as of last night, Oaths? The more I learn about Oaths and their role in the Order's structure, the more I agree with Nick that I shouldn't advertise that ability. But these are passive, quiet things. Easy to hide.

What happened last night was *not* a quiet thing. And if it happens again around the chapter, I don't know if I'll be able to hide it.

Rule Four. Never, ever let anyone see aether pouring out of my skin like burning blood.

My phone rings. I frown. It died at the Lodge and I don't remember plugging it in last night.

"I charged your phone for you." Alice is across the room, dressed and sitting at her desk. "Saw it was dead. Got you breakfast, too." She points her chin at a paper bag on my desk.

As soon as I see it, it's all I can smell. Biscuits. Still hot.

"You got me Bojangles?"

"Charlotte offered to pick it up."

We stare at each other in uneasy silence.

"Gonna answer that?"

"Yes." I reach for my phone and almost immediately wish she'd let it stay dead. "Hi, Dad."

"Briana Irene. Explain yourself."

I grab the Bojangles.

The thick scent wafting up from inside the paper makes my mouth water. *Buttermilk biscuit—Jesus, take the wheel.*

"I should have called you. I forgot. There's just been a ton going on."

It's not just any biscuit. It's a Bo-Berry Biscuit, thank you Lord. "Bless you," I mouth to Alice. She smiles and sits down at my desk chair looking very pleased with herself.

"Oh, really? Like what?"

"Started hanging with some kids."

"And how's that going?"

Every question leads me right to my doom, I just know it.

"Fine."

"Fine like getting sent to the dean's office fine? Like ending up in the back of a squad car fine?"

"It was just a warning . . ."

Alice raises a brow. Disapproval from two directions. I angle my phone away and whisper, "Don't you have a class to go to, or something?"

She smiles. "I'm free until ten."

My father continues in my ear: "You say you're gonna call me back, but you don't. Then I find out you were out late at some party?"

I sit back in alarm. "What party?"

Right. The fake party that Nick and/or Sel made up for my mesmer.

"Right, that party." I'm resigned to getting in trouble for things I *didn't* do because I have to hide the things I did. Wait, how did—

"Getting in late again last night?" *That* shocks me. The only way he'd know about that was if—

"Alice has been keeping me updated, and thank God for that. If I had to rely on you to tell me, who knows when I'd find out the truth."

I'm too shocked to respond to my father. All I can do is stare at my friend.

"You told him?"

A cold spear of resentment drives through me from head to toe, but it fades some when she throws her hands up and screeches, "You scared me!" at the same time my dad admonishes me with, "Don't get mad at Alice now! That's a good friend you got there."

Ganging up on me, the both of them. Now I know why she decided to sit through this call.

"What's gotten into you, damnit? You doing drugs?"

"What? *No,* I'm not doing drugs." I stare meaningfully at Alice, who has the grace to grimace.

My dad's done leading me to the edge. He sounds done, period. "Then what is going on, kiddo? Talk to me."

Alice must hear his request because her face goes expectant, just as I imagine his has. I sigh. This I can't deal with, on top of everything else. There's no way I'd tell either of them what I'm up to with the Order, not after last night. "I'm sorry. I've just . . . got a lot going on. I promise I'm okay."

Except not really. Mage flame pouring out of your skin isn't really okay in either of these two worlds I'm in.

"A lot like what?" My dad wasn't letting me off the hook.

Think, Bree. "Dean McKinnon hooked me up with this peer mentor, perfect student kid. He's supposed to check in with me all the time."

My dad grunts. "The dean did say he was going to see to it you'd get on the right track with some sort of model student type."

The best lies are a little close to the truth. "Nick's dad went here, so he's some sort of UNC royalty. He got me into one of those old invite-only student groups. Big house, rich kids. Like debutante, cotillion-type stuff, but for college students?"

Except instead of learning which fork to use, we'll learn to fight demon hordes.

Across from me, Alice raises a brow. My dad grunts again, but he doesn't pursue it. Instead, he shifts gears. "Bree, I've tried to give you space since Mom died, but I think that was a mistake. It's time I step in."

A ripple of anxiety runs down my spine. "Step in? Step in how?"

"You're going to counseling. I've set it up with Campus Health. They got you in quick, since you're a minor in the program."

My heartbeat picks up. "I'm not going to therapy."

I can tell by the surprise on Alice's face that she didn't know about the therapy part.

"Oh, you're going." His voice is as stern as I've ever heard it. "Or you're coming home." He lets that sit, then says, "Well? I'm waiting for an answer."

I search for an excuse, but none comes up.

"Fine."

"Twice a week."

My hands squeeze into fists. "Twice a week."

"Starting today."

"Starting *today*?" I shout. "I have classes, Dad. Homework."

He is unmoved. "Every Wednesday and every Friday, young lady. I sent Dr. Hartwood your class schedule. Get this: I was reading through the counselor profiles on the website and saw she got her undergrad degree right there at Carolina. Got her on the phone and asked about the timing and sure enough, she was there when your mom was."

I grip my cell phone tighter. "This doctor knew Mom?" Alice straightens, interest plain on her face.

My father's voice softens for the first time on the call. "Sure did, kiddo. Said they had a few classes together, believe it or not. Thought that was real nice, so that's why I picked her. That and she's a Black gal; not too many of us on that website."

"Wow," I murmur. My brain churns through the possibilities. Someone who knew my mother while she was here. Someone who may have a clue about how she got on the Order's radar . . .

He takes my silence for worry. "If you don't like her, we can switch—"

"No! I want to meet her," I say, and flash Alice a thumbs-up. She relaxes more than a little bit and gets up to gather her school binders and books. "It'll be good for me."

I wait until Alice waves goodbye to go through the deluge of notifications from last night.

Four calls and a voicemail from Nick. Eleven texts, also from Nick. I start in on the Bo-Berry Biscuit and listen to the voicemail: he sounds slightly out of breath. "B. Tonight was—I guess I just wanted to check in. I'm glad you're safe. I—I don't know where to start. Call me. Please. Or text. Whichever."

Not very specific, but maybe he was in the infirmary with listening ears nearby. The texts are more of the same.

He *had* tried to find me. He *had* been worried.

He'd called me "B."

I suddenly feel sheepish, like reading his words and letting them wash over me like this is . . . embarrassing. Alice is gone, but I'm sitting on my bed feeling exposed. And *warm*. Good. Fuzzy. For no reason at all.

Maybe that's why his last text, sent at 2:32 a.m., is so alarming: You need to forfeit. I've been away for too long and things are worse than I realized. I'll find out what happened to your mother. I swear it.

After all I've seen, I'm tempted to take him up on his offer. But then again, if his people are at war, where will my mission fall on the priority list, really? My fingers fly over the screen: I'm not quitting

I watch him type. Stop. Start again. Stop. Then:

Thought you might say that.

I grin.

He texts again. **The chapter's hosting dinner at the Lodge tonight at 6. They want all Pages there. Come by an hour early. There's a room where we can talk in private.**

That "no reason at all" heat swims through my chest.

Yeah, no problem

Sure, we need a private place in the secret society's semisecret house to talk about our supersecret infiltration and reconnaissance partnership.

Perfectly reasonable.

Patricia Hartwood texts me as soon as I arrive at my first class.

Hi, Bree! This is Dr. Hartwood. Your father arranged for us to meet regularly starting today. What do you think about meeting somewhere on campus? It's a beautiful day!

That sounds good. Where?

How about the Arboretum at 2pm after your Plants of the Piedmont class? Seems appropriate, the Arboretum after botany!

Adult texting humor is the *worst*.

Okay! is all I can muster, but inside I can't wait to meet her. What if she's the key to helping me unravel the mystery of my mother?

Alice was right. Plants of the Piedmont really is a slacker class. The TA sat in the corner and played around on his phone while we "watched" the fifty-five-minute-long, super-dated educational video he insisted would help prepare us for next week's test. Then he dismissed us early for no reason in particular, so I arrive at the Arboretum before our appointment time.

The Arboretum is much bigger than I'd realized. The herb garden sign says that it's home to more than five hundred species and cultivars. My mother would have loved it. As I walk, I imagine a younger version of her coming here for visits between classes, taking secret clippings and tucking them away in her purse. I turn a corner and stop daydreaming.

A black granite table sits in the middle of a quiet grotto, and underneath it leaks a steady stream of mage flame.

It's thinner than the thick ribbons that had coiled around my arms in the shower and much, much lighter. Pale yellow instead of rich crimson.

The table sits in the middle of a circle of dark brown and black soil and mulch. Underneath, bronze figurines reach their hands high to the thick granite tabletop as if holding its weight up in the air. The figurines are staggered in rows that disappear under the slab, giving the impression that there are more bodies lifting the table than the eye could ever see. Steady wisps of aether stream between their arms and legs and waft over the damp earth like golden mist.

"They put the table here for folks who want to read, study, or rest. And yet I find it difficult to sit here and do anything else but get sad."

The voice comes from a hidden corner of the grotto.

A stunning Black woman with graying locs sits on a stone bench, a late lunch spread out on the empty space beside her. A brightly patterned shawl with alternating burgundy and yellow tassels lining its edges drapes her shoulders. Her eyes are the color of warm, rich earth, and her oval face is a deep brown. She peers at me from behind a set of bright yellow horn-rimmed glasses. I can't tell how old she is, of course, because Black women are magical like that. She could be forty or sixty, or some number in between.

"Are you—"

"Dr. Patricia Hartwood." A wide smile spreads across her face. It makes me feel lighter, brighter. "You must be Bree."

I study this woman as if examining her face, really *leaning* into that simple act, could somehow bring me closer to my mother. Like maybe there's a new piece of her hidden in this woman's eyes. A crumb of life still preserved in someone who knew her in a way I didn't. I find I'm desperately, uncomfortably hungry for whatever she can give me.

She looks back calmly, as if she knows exactly what I'm thinking.

My eyes find the table again. "Why does this make you sad?"

"Take a closer look."

I walk between two of the stone seats until I'm less than a foot from the slab. When I crouch, mage flame billows into warm clouds around my ankles. The figurines aren't identical, like I'd assumed from far away, but they have several things in common: natural kinky hair. Broad, strong noses. Full lips.

Black folks.

They're all Black folks.

Black folks raising the round slab like hundreds of Atlases holding the world. Some of the men wear long shirts over pants. Others are bare-chested, their bronze muscles straining across stomachs and biceps. Women in skirts lift the impossibly heavy weight. Their feet are buried beneath the mud and mulch, and yet they push.

My voice is quiet and breathy. "What is this?"

"The Unsung Founders Memorial. Carolina's way of acknowledging the enslaved and the servants who built this place," she says, her voice wavering between pride and disdain. "We get this memorial, and it's something, I suppose. It was a class gift. Not unimportant. But how can I be at peace when I look down and see that they're still working? You know?"

I do know what she means. This type of knowing is an expensive toll to pay. I can't forget the knowledge just because the price is high. And yet, sometimes we have to tuck the reminders away today in order to grow power against them tomorrow.

Dr. Hartwood draws herself up on the bench. "But that is not what our session is about."

I stand, but it's difficult to disengage from the memorial, now that I know what—and who—it represents. It's hard to turn from its strange mage flame, too. Why would aether collect *here*? I make a mental note to ask Nick about it.

I finally tear my eyes away. "I'm guessing my dad told you all about me."

"He is very proud of you." Her smile reminds me of my mom's. Laugh lines at the edges. Lipstick that matches her shawl. "He told me you were bright and, more than that, wise,"

I snort. "Wise? I got in trouble my first night here. I'm not wise."

"Not a trait one can claim or dispose of themselves, I'm afraid."

"S'pose so." I'm surprised at the easy way my own drawl slips out. Talking to her feels familiar. Like home. Like reunions and fish fries and potato salad on picnic tables behind the church. I haven't felt like this, let my mouth move like this, since I came to Carolina.

I sit down, and she offers me her hand. When our palms touch, a low and steady hum of electricity courses up my arm to my elbow. It's nothing like Sel's gaze. It's warm like spiced cider on Christmas. Hot syrup over pancakes.

"Nice to meet you, Bree." She actually refrained from a platitude. An adult who definitely knows that my mother is dead. I'm stunned.

I stammer, "Uh . . . you, too, ma'am."

"Patricia, please. Dr. Hartwood, if you must, but I'm not one for the ma'ams." Patricia waves her hand dismissively. "Save that for the aunties who demand it."

I laugh, and she grins back. I haven't been around an auntie like that since my mother's funeral.

"So, you're my shrink?"

"Psychologist, counselor, therapist. I like those best. You've been living on campus for a few days now. How do you like it?"

Demons. Aether. Knights. Homework. A boy who makes me feel fuzzy.

"It's fine."

"Mm." Patricia's brown eyes seem to dig through my skull, like a drill covered in velvet. "Friends?"

"I came here with my friend Alice, but we had a bit of a rocky start."

Patricia nods sagely. "Common for students who room with friends from high school. Many find that the new environment challenges old relationships."

"That's an understatement. I've met a few people in classes and events."

Oh, you know, events like secret feudal rituals.

"Tell me about Alice."

How rude would it be to tell her the only reason I'm here is to find out what she knows?

"We've been best friends since we were little. We applied to EC together. We went off campus to this thing at the Eno Quarry, which I assume you know about, and we got in trouble. We fought about it. Did the silent treatment thing, but I think we made up last night. Mostly. I'm still kinda pissed that she called my dad, but I sort of get it."

Patricia's eyebrows have raised a fraction. "Were you aware it was against the rules to go to the Quarry?"

Something occurs to me, and I sit up straight. "Does my dad get reports on what we talk about here?"

She shakes her head. "Everything is confidential. Unless you express a desire to harm yourself or others, or describe abuse, either past or ongoing. In those cases, I'm required to file a report with university police."

"Hm," I say. "In that case, yeah. I knew it was against the rules."

"Did that give you pause?"

"Not at the time."

"You went anyway. Why is that, do you think?"

"I was upset. I just wanted to go somewhere. Do something."

"What type of something?"

Even though I don't want to answer, I think about the restlessness I'd felt at the cliffside before Sel found me. The pressure under my skin. The desire to explode.

"I don't know."

"Hm." Patricia doesn't believe me. She reminds me of my mother in that way. There was a reason I went behind her back to apply to Carolina. If I'd asked and she'd said no, she'd have read the defiance on my face. "Let's shift gears."

"Fine by me."

"I'd like to talk about your mother."

An eager sort of panic flutters in my stomach, at the back of my throat. "My dad said you knew her?"

"I did," she says warmly. "Not well. But I liked her very much."

Suddenly, swallowing is hard. I thought I'd wanted her to talk about my mother. Why does it feel bad now that she is? "Oh."

"Do you know why I asked to meet you here, Bree?"

Her question takes me by surprise. "No, not really. Is this a trick question?"

Apparently, my answer takes *Patricia* by surprise, because she blinks and sits back.

"These gardens are abundant with root energy. Are you not a Wildcrafter like your mother?"

19

SHOCK, FEAR, HOPE—EMOTIONS war in my belly. "What's a Wildcrafter?"

For the first time, Patricia looks rattled.

"Wildcraft is shorthand for the branch of Rootcraft she practiced. The type of energy she could manipulate is found in growing things—plants, herbs, trees. As a student, she spent hours here in the gardens and—" Her face folds into a sympathetic frown. "I'm so sorry, Bree . . . I thought this would be a comforting, familiar setting to you. I thought you knew about her."

I almost fall off the bench. How many times in a week can one have their world spun and fractured and put back together again? A dozen? Two dozen? After-Bree presses against the walls that restrain her. Against surprise and secrets and another moment of my life that breaks the world open a little further. My skin feels prickly and tight. I shut my eyes and shove it all back before panic steals my senses. "My mother . . . manipulated energy?"

"Yes."

Questions tumble against one another like dominoes. "What type of energy? What is Rootcraft?" Does *everyone* keep secrets here?

Patricia recovers her composure. She taps a polished nail on her lower lip, her eyes darting back and forth in thought. "I'm not sure that I should say any more."

Suddenly, I'm so impatient and indignant I could shake her until the answers fall out. Scream until she shares what she knows. I grit my teeth. "Why not?"

She hesitates, but meets my eyes. "I don't think it's my place."

"Why? Did she tell you to keep this from me?" A thought occurs to me. "Did my dad?"

She spreads her hands over her skirt. "I didn't know Faye very well, and we didn't keep up after graduation. I didn't even know she had a daughter until your father called me today, didn't even know she'd passed. And I doubt your father knows about any of this. Most often, the craft flows from mother to daughter."

"What?" I shoot to my feet.

"Bree, I'd like you to calm down."

"Why would I be calm about this? My mother had a secret life and she never told me. *Why didn't she tell me?*"

"I don't know why Faye made the decisions she did. When loved ones die, there are always questions like this, with answers we can only guess at."

Confusion and anger flood me in a hot rush. "And are those questions always about magic?"

"We don't call it magic."

"We?" My fists ball at my sides. "I just met you, and now it's 'we'? You and my mother?"

Patricia's lips thin.

"My mother was a botanist. A scientist. Five minutes ago, I thought any manipulation of plants she did happened in a—a pharmaceutical lab. And now you're telling me she *lied* to me."

A fine line appears between Patricia's brows. "Thank you for sharing how all of this is making you feel. You're right. I owe you more than what I've said. Please, sit."

Whiplash. "Just like that, you changed your mind?"

A smile tugs at her lips. "I find that, in my field, emotional agility comes with the territory."

My breath comes in shallow pants. My fists refuse to unclench. But I sit.

"Do you know what auras are?"

A vision of the red mage flame washes over me in a hot rush. Was *that* an aura? Was it not mage flame at all? Patricia's attention sharpens on my face, but before she can ask a follow-up, I wave a hand in a vague circle around my head. "Colors around people?"

"Mostly right. Auras are your personal energy, reflecting the state of your spirit."

"What do they look like?"

"From what I understand, they look like a faint sort of fog or thin mist."

That mage flame had *roared* up my skin, all fire and anger and blood. Not an aura, then.

"While an undergraduate here, I had a friend named Janice who was a Reader, someone whose branch of Rootcraft allowed her to see people's auras. Emotions, intentions, abilities. One day Janice saw me and your mother talking outside class and later, Janice told me that your mother knew the craft. So I asked your mother to practice and fellowship together. She was very polite, but she declined. She seemed so uncomfortable by my offer that I never mentioned it again. I wasn't offended. I thought maybe she had her own community. We tend to keep the craft private, but I thought, perhaps, she kept to a stricter code; rootcraft is taught within families, and different families have different approaches. Still, I am surprised that your mother never told you what she could do."

There's no air in my chest. Where is all the air? My mind is blanking, shutting down.

"Bree?" Patricia leans forward into my field of vision. "Take some deep breaths. Close your eyes and think of something or someone that made you feel safe in the last twenty-four hours."

I follow her instructions—and my mind travels to eyes, storm dark and blue.

It takes a few breaths before I open my eyes again. The panic is still there, but it has trouble taking hold.

I believe what Patricia's told me. After all that I've seen here, it would be foolish to think there's no more to learn. But of all the secrets I thought I'd uncover, I didn't think my mother's life—and the magic she wielded—would be one of them. Wildcrafting, plant energy manipulation. What danger would there be in sharing those abilities with others like her? Did she believe Patricia was dangerous? That seems unlikely—Patricia left her alone. The Order's militancy is more than enough reason to keep a low profile on this campus. But if that was her reasoning, then that means she knew about the Order and Merlins long before I was born. So, did a Merlin know about *her*? My instinct says yes. Why else would one be at her deathbed twenty-five years later?

Patricia stands up to wrap her shawl around her shoulders. "Traditionally, your mother would teach you all of this. For you not to know when your mother knew about her own abilities means she withheld this information for some reason. And that means, ethically, *I* need to consider what it means to tell you what your mother did not. Perhaps it's the therapist in me, but I would like to respect her wishes. I think we should stop for the day. We'll meet again on Friday and I'll give you my decision."

"No!" I'm on my feet, heart pounding. "I need you to tell me everything. I have to know—"

She pauses, frowns. "You have to know what?"

What can I say? Telling anyone that I suspect the Order was a part of my mother's death could put them in danger, much more so if they use aether. And if my mother hid parts of herself from Patricia, then should I hide my abilities too?

I choose the safest thing to share, and phrase it carefully. "I know about aether."

Patricia lets out a harsh breath, and I know immediately that I've said something wrong. "Where did you learn that word?"

"I—I can't say."

Patricia gives me a shrewd, measuring look. She knows I'm hiding something. *Like mother, like daughter,* I think.

"I respect and value confidentiality, and so I will not pry about what you know or how you know it. Instead, I will aim to earn your trust. But I must tell you that the . . . *practitioners*"—she says the word as if it tastes rancid in her mouth—"who use the word 'aether' are not your mother's people."

"Her people?" I ask.

"Her people. Our people. We are the descendants of those who developed the craft, and we do not call the invisible energy of the world 'aether.' We call it 'root.'"

"Now that we're best friends again, you wanna get dinner together? A girl from my Classics class wants to meet up." Alice wrinkles her nose. "It's 'Italian Night' at Lenoir, whatever that means."

After finishing classes for the day, we've been lounging on our respective beds, phones in hand. I'm not sure what Alice has been doing, but I've been opening my messaging app compulsively, as if Nick has texted me and the app is simply refusing to reveal it. Maybe this time. Maybe *this* time. Maybe *now*?

It's not embarrassing if no one sees me doing it, right?

I start no fewer than seven different texts but erase each one before sending, because what if I *do* text him and he doesn't text back?

More importantly, what would I say?

I decide not to mention my meeting with Patricia to Nick. Not until I know more. And even then, I'm not sure what I *should* share with him, or anyone.

If my mother knew about the Order, its claim on magic, and its tendency to put magic users on trial (or worse), it only makes sense that she'd have hid her abilities on campus, just as I'm doing now. If what Patricia said is true, then calling my father won't be of any use, because my mother kept this part of her life from him. So far, only Nick knows about me and what I can do, not counting the red flames. Maybe I should keep it that way?

Utterly confused, I toss my phone out of reach and flop back against my pillows to stare at the ceiling with a frustrated sigh.

Knowing that my mother was on Carolina's campus twenty-five years ago doing exactly what I'm doing now—keeping things secret, hiding parts of herself from other people—makes me feel closer to her and, simultaneously, like I never knew her at all.

Who was she, *really*?

"Bree?" Alice asks, pulling me away from my thoughts. "Italian Night?"

"You know what Italian Night means," I say, and sit up, snatching my phone again, because apparently I'm committed to being ridiculous. "Soggy, over-cooked cafeteria spaghetti and runny sauce. Sad lasagna that's been sitting under a warmer for two hours."

"It's either sad pasta or the food court. Which do you want?"

The dormer window of our top-floor room is cracked open. The whoops and cheers of the Wednesday night party crowd reach us from the sidewalk below. According to Charlotte, who'd stopped by our room on her way out, "Wednesday night is the new Thursday night and, by the way, nobody goes out on Fridays."

"I can't go anyways," I mutter, and my stomach twists on yet another lie. "That student group I mentioned? They're hosting dinner tonight at their house."

Across the room, Alice sits up. "What's this group called again?"

I'm ready for her question and keep my voice as calm as possible. "It's one of the secret societies."

Alice's eyes grow wide. "I've heard of those! Can you tell me which one?"

"No, sorry," I say. *I'm so sorry, Alice.*

She pouts. "I was hoping to get tapped by the Order of the Golden Fleece, but someone told me they don't go for EC kids. If that doesn't work, then DiPhi it is."

DiPhi is Carolina's student debate society. If Alice joins them, we'll both be in historic student orgs. The only difference is that she can list her membership on her resume.

Lying to Alice after last night and this morning makes me feel like a complete asshole. Maybe this is why Sel is the way he is? Angry and grumpy and accusatory. And maybe this is another reason why Nick doesn't want to be involved with the Order. All the lying, the strain of being on this campus and living two different lives. I sigh. "Nick says I've got to keep it secret, keep it safe."

"Did you just *Lord of the Rings* me?"

"Nope." I grin. "I just *Fellowship of the Ring*'d you."

Her face takes on a sly expression. "Why do you say his name like that?"

"Say whose name like what?"

The ends of her mouth lift. "Your voice got all funny when you said 'Nick.' It's the same exact way you used to say Scott Finley's name."

"I did not say Scott's name in any particular way." She did not have to do me like that. I was eleven when I had a crush on Scott Finley the baseball player.

Best friends and their deep cuts.

Alice points at me accusingly. "Lying liar who lies!" My heart clenches, even though I know she's joking. She rushes over to perch on the end of my bed. "What's Nick look like?"

We'd only started talking again—for-real talking, like best friends—since the morning, but the warmth spilling from her brown eyes fills my cup in a way I hadn't known I needed. With my mother's secrets—and lies—looming since the session with Patricia, and the memories of last night rising up like a nightmare every other hour, sitting with my best friend and talking about a cute boy is beyond refreshing. And, like nothing else in my life right now, it's easy.

Still, I can feel my cheeks burning. "Blond hair, blue eyes, and . . ."

"And?" Alice prompts, waving her hand for more. Laughter escapes me in a freeing rush. *God*, this feels good.

Words stream from my lips before I think about them too carefully. "And he looks like a gladiator. Like those oddly hot dudes on the sides of pottery from ancient Greece? Tall and athletic and"—Nick, pointing me to safety with his sword, his eyes hardened with both fear and focus—"heroic."

"Ahh!" Alice collapses onto her side. "See, that's the good stuff. Even if gladiators are Roman."

I poke her knees with my toe. "How about you? Any ladies catch your eye?"

She swats at my foot. "Nice try, but your deflections don't work on me. I'm immune. Let's talk about how you have a crush on your peer mentor. Like, the person who's supposed to be teaching you all about school? And tutoring you on how to achieve success after your brief descent into delinquency."

"'Crush' is the wrong word. I just met him."

"Bree." She grabs my ankles with both hands. With a face drawn in mock solemnity, she declares, "This is like a book. Or a TV show where everyone has great hair and is way too old to play a teenager. You are *literally* a walking rom-com right now."

"*Alice.*" I kick until she lets me go and hops up with a grin.

"I've got to go meet Teresa," she says, walking backward and pointing at me, "but when you get back tonight, you're telling me *everything*, Briana Matthews!"

I smile, even though I can't tell Alice everything. Not ever. Not if I want to keep her safe.

20

WHEN I KNOCK on the door to the Lodge that night, it's Evan who answers.

A grin splits the redhead's face. "There she is! The Page who *finally* brought our knight-errant out of the woodwork."

"Knight-errant?" He moves aside and I step through the door, shaking out my umbrella. It started drizzling on my way over.

"Yup," he says, taking my umbrella and dropping it into the bronze holder in the foyer. "That's old-timey for a knight who does their own thing and wanders around and stuff."

"And that's Nick?"

He smiles rakishly. "Not anymore."

"Evan, you're a frat boy by day and a Squire for an ancient order by night. How do you keep up with it all?"

"Magic," he says, and bows with a flourish.

I laugh, but then I think of Alice and my split life. "No, for real. How do you lie to Charlotte every day about who you are and what you do?"

He winks. "Lies are easy when you're fighting for the right cause."

"Hm." I consider my own lies and cause—and the person who's lying to Evan and the entire chapter on my behalf. "Do you know if the knight-errant is here?"

"Who's the knight-errant?" An amused voice interjects from the top of the stairs.

"There he is!"

Nick fixes Evan with a mock glare from where he's leaning on the balcony railing. "Quit harassing my Page, Ev."

Evan backs away, hands up. "Of course, my liege."

Nick groans. "Yeah, you can stop with that 'my liege' crap anytime you want. Come on up, Bree. Evan, stay put."

Evan closes the door with a loud laugh that echoes around the foyer.

Nick is waiting for me at the top of the stairs, and I absolutely blame Alice Chen for where my brain goes as I walk up to meet him, because all I can think is that he looks like a rom-com daydream come to life. His hands are stuffed in a pair of dark-wash jeans, and he's wearing a blue Henley that brings out his eyes. Eyes that roam over me, too, with a soft, unreadable expression.

When I reach the landing, he tilts his head to the left. "This way."

While the exterior is a castle and first floor interior a manor, the second floor, soaked in reds and browns and yellows, is truly the source for the Lodge's name. Restored pine floors hold notches and whorls from the original trees, and the heavy brocade fabric lining the walls in between the doors makes the floor feel warm and residential. Someone's music is bumping loud enough to make the sconces shake.

A door opens and Felicity and Russ emerge, their quiet giggles filling the hall. When the pair notices us approaching, Felicity's face flushes to match her hair.

"Oh! H-hi!" She waves with one hand while batting at a clingy Russ with the other. She looks adorably flustered, while Russ is openly beaming. I don't know whether to feel sympathy or laugh.

Nick doesn't miss a beat. "Felicity, how are you feeling?"

Russ leans in, nuzzling her neck. "Yeah, Flick, how are you feelin'?"

Her eyes grow wide as saucers and she shoves him away—a bit too hard. He flies back so high he hangs suspended in the air for a second before landing in a crouch on the other side of the hall.

While she gasps in horror and apologizes, Russ laughs uncontrollably, barely managing a response. "That enough answer for you, Nick?"

"I can answer for myself, thank you!" Felicity marches up to us with as much dignity as she can muster. "I'm fine, Nick, thank you for asking. Just not"—she glances back at her Squire, who's on his feet with a wide grin—"totally used to the strength yet."

"Me neither," Russ calls, striding over to us.

"And Lamorak had a temper, we've discovered," Felicity adds. "Not my favorite inheritance in the world."

"Are y'all okay?" Nick raises a brow. "Not fighting each other, are you?"

"No." Felicity blushes. "Not exactly . . ."

Nick opens his mouth, sees Russ's barely suppressed laughter, and his cheeks tinge pink. "We'll see you downstairs for dinner."

"Yep!" Russ loops an arm around his Scion's shoulder.

The two of them descend the stairs quickly and Nick gestures to keep walking. We stop at a room labeled 208, and he produces a key from his pocket. "I never use it, but my father keeps this room here for me."

"Why don't you use it?"

He shrugs, pushing the door inward. "Living here would send a certain message."

I begin to ask what he means, but the sight of his bedroom, and the realization that *that's* where he wants to talk, temporarily shorts my brain.

The room is large enough to comfortably fit a full bed, a dresser, a chest of drawers, and a trestle desk without sacrificing open floor space, which is more than I can say for my dorm. I wonder if all of the rooms in the Lodge have a similar layout, with similar furniture. The ones occupied by other members probably aren't decorated in sailor-themed blue-and-white stripes, with an anchor-shaped rug at the foot of the bed.

Lord Davis had definitely taken a trip to Bed Bath & Beyond.

Nick closes the door behind me. When I step farther inside, I realize our rooms have something in common: they're barely lived in. There's nothing about his room that feels like it belongs to anyone, much less Nick.

When I turn to say as much, I find myself engulfed in his arms, his fresh laundry–and–cedar scent folding around me in a warm cloud. His hands are so large they span the whole of my spine. Heat from his palms radiates out from where he clutches me. Face tucked into my neck, he mutters, "That thing was gonna kill you right in front of me. All I could think was that it was my fault for bringing you in." The worry and guilt in his muffled voice make tears prick at my eyes. Without my permission, my arms wrap around him, too.

"Funny story," I say, trying to lighten the mood. "I've been blaming myself for bringing *you* in."

When he laughs, the muscles in his back flex under my fingers. "Yeah, well, I said it first."

I grin into his shoulder. My "no reason at all" responses suddenly feel completely justified.

Nick lifts his head. His eyes roam over my face, my healed cheek, my torso. "Are you sure you're okay?" His left hand hovers over my side, fingers lightly touching the cotton material covering the now deep purple–and–black bruise on my ribs. Then, he seems to recognize how close his fingers are to other parts of me, so he steps back. Our arms fall awkwardly to our sides.

I'm floored that he knew to check for an injury there—that he'd been paying such close attention to where the uchel grabbed me. And I'm drawn to the two strawberry-colored thumbprints staining his cheeks.

"Bruised," I mumble, still warm and confused, "just bruised."

His voice comes out a tiny bit hoarse. "Good."

"Yes."

"Right."

I clear my throat. "How's your head?"

He rubs at the back of it. "Feels like I bumped it?"

"That is both an unbelievable and normal response, isn't it?"

"This is both an unbelievable and normal situation." His eyes twinkle.

We stare at each other, wrestling with this moment that feels both new and unfamiliar, both what we asked for and something we didn't expect. Nick's eyes are the waiting color of overcast skies.

I turn away first. "So, this is your room." *Why did I say that? We already covered that, Bree. Jesus.*

"I claim no responsibility for the decor."

I was wrong. The room isn't entirely lacking in Nick. There are a few personal items pinned on the corkboard mounted over his desk. When I move closer, I see one is a picture of an elementary-aged Nick in front of the red wolf habitat at the North Carolina Zoo. His hair is white-blond, and several teeth are missing from his smile. A junior high academic achievement award is pinned down below. The last item is a picture of Nick at eleven or twelve, Nick's father, and a smiling blond woman who must be his mother. The woman has his eyes and smile, even if Nick's grin is mostly metal braces in this photo. They're standing in front of a large hill under a clear blue sky.

"Arthur's Seat," Nick informs me. "Dad took us to Edinburgh for summer vacation. Couldn't resist the photo op with his Scion son."

"You look happy."

He tilts his head as if processing the idea. "We were. Then."

"You never talk about your mother."

His smile turns down on one end. "Another day."

He studies me like he did the first night we met. That feels like forever ago, but it's only been forty-eight hours. *And in another forty-eight hours I'll know more about my mother's magic, and maybe my own.*

"We need to talk."

I raise a brow. "About the fact that you're the descendant of King Arthur?"

"I'm not *the* descendant. I'm one of *many*."

"Why didn't you tell me?" I ask, irritation flaring.

Heat flashes through his eyes. "When could I have? When exactly, Bree? In the ten minutes before we walked into the Oath? In the two minutes before Sel attacked you?"

I cross my arms. "Yes."

He glares at me, his jaw ticking. Inhales, then breathes out through his nose. "They tell you about the Lines?"

"I saw the Wall."

"Who?"

"William."

"And what else did William tell you?"

"I know about Camlann."

His gaze hardens. "Then you know why I want you to forfeit."

"I already told you I'm not quitting." I blink, startled by the look on his face. "We made a deal!"

"And last night changed the deal. If Camlann is truly near, then becoming a Squire—mine, William's, Pete's—is too risky. You won't be able to just bounce afterward because we'll be at *war*." He grabs me by the arms, inclining his head to meet my eyes. "People *die* during Camlann, Bree."

Panic flutters in my chest like a caged bird. "No, this is the only way. This year. Right now."

"I never should have agreed to this, but I wanted to help you. I—" His fingers tighten where they hold me. "Becoming a Squire during peacetime is one thing. Once I reclaimed my title, I'd planned to step in, get you out before you're expected to take the Warrior's Oath. But now? The Order is on alert, and I *know* Sel. He could be ordered to bond you to your Scion right away and . . . and I can't let you do that."

I pull out of his grip. I can see the word in his eyes even if he doesn't say it: Abatement.

Nick doesn't want me to suffer the consequences of bonding. Doesn't want me to die before my time. The affection—and fear—on his face, all for me, makes my head swim. But there's determination there, plain in the sharp angles of his brow and jaw. Right now, he's giving me a choice to walk away. But now that I know who he is and what he could become, I know that choice could be taken from me.

I search his gaze, wondering. Would he do that? Have me thrown out? Would I let him?

Another tact first: "I can resist that Oath."

"Maybe you can, but your Scion will know, so Sel will know. He'll send you to the Regents."

"And you can order him not to. Or we'll find the information another way. Or maybe I take the Oath and just let it happen!" I throw up my hands. "I know about Abatement."

His eyes widen like I've uttered a word not spoken in polite company. "That's—"

"What I'm willing to risk to find the truth!" He begins to protest, but I cut him off again. The decision became clear as soon as I said it aloud. "She'd have done the same for me."

After a long, measuring look, he finally nods. "I don't like it, but I understand."

The tension in the room dissolves some, and I can breathe easier. "Maybe Camlann won't come after all. William said Arthur hasn't Called his Scion in two hundred and fifty years."

"He hasn't needed to, but that doesn't mean he won't." He runs a hand through his hair. "God, I wish things were different for you. Do you have any idea how many Scions and Squires wish they could just walk away?"

"Like you did?"

Nick's jaw tightens; then he visibly forces himself to relax. I realize I've been watching him do a version of the same progression since we've met: anger, restraint, resignation.

"No one, not even the Regents, thought I'd be Called. My renouncement was symbolic. Political. A child's protest. And it will take symbolic and political steps to restore the kingdom's, and the Table's, faith in me. To own the title in full."

Before last night, the odds had been in Nick's favor. Two hundred years since anyone in his Line had needed to step up to the plate, or had the power to. I see it now. The desperation in his face is for me, but it's for himself, too. The road ahead is long, and the bridges burned.

"What happens to you if . . . if . . ."

He sits on the room's window seat with a sigh. "If I am Called and Awakened,

I'll inherit Arthur's strength and wisdom. And I've been trained for that moment since I could walk. If the Shadowborn army is rising, I won't let my friends fight it alone."

"And the Abatement?"

His face turns grave. "My father says focus is death's most precious gift."

"Death doesn't give gifts."

"Tell that to a Scion."

I nudge his foot and he shifts over so that we can share the seat. "You don't want to lead."

He answers without meeting my eyes. "Never have."

"Don't want the glory?" I lean into him. "Don't want to be a king?"

He turns to me then, eyes serious. "Bree, if I get all of that, it means that Camlann is inevitable. I don't want the world to *need* a king."

21

TEN MINUTES LATER, we descend the stairs with a prickly sort of awareness bouncing between us. Yesterday we entered the great room in agreement,
but we each had limited information about the nature of our situation. Twenty-
four hours later, Nick's world is heading to war, and I'm preparing to unravel
my mother's history. As our paths continue, will we still find common ground?

When we reach the foyer, the sounds of dinner reach us from the vast dining
room around the corner. Clinking cutlery. Chairs scraping the floor. Voices.

I look back to find Nick watching me, my own uncertainty echoed on his
face. "We good, B?"

I nod. "We're good."

His mouth quirks. "I don't know why, but——"

Suddenly, the front doors open and humid, light rain sprays across the tiles.
Outside, three women stand deep in conversation, shaking their umbrellas on
the patio before entering. They're dressed head to toe in country club–chic:
blouses, cardigans, capris, spotless white tennis shoes. Their pale, perfectly con-
toured faces light up when they see Nick.

"As I live and breathe . . ." The woman on the left wears a neck scarf the deep
yellow of the Line of Owain.

"Is that——?"

"Nick Davis." The tallest woman, a brunette, speaks with a low rasp. The first woman elbows her, and she corrects herself. "Excuse me. Scion Davis."

Nick inclines his head, addressing them all in turn. "Rose members Hood, Edwards, and Schaefer. What brings you to the Lodge tonight?" He steps back to let them in. "The tournament trials are closed, as you know . . ."

It takes a second, but I recognize their last names and facial features. These three are mothers of chapter members: Pete Hood, Scion of Owain; Ainsley Edwards, a second-year Page; and Vaughn Schaefer, from my Page class.

Rose member Schaefer's eyes twinkle as she enters. She acknowledges me with a polite smile and a wave, then offers a sly glance to Nick. "We heard a rumor you returned."

"Elena, please." The Edwards woman waves a manicured hand adorned with nails the dark orange of Bors. "The Order of the Rose *always* supervises catering during the Trials." Still addressing Nick, she extends her umbrella toward me, handle first. "Take this and dry it? Now, tonight's meal—"

She stops speaking when I don't follow her instructions, and turns, fully looking at me for the first time.

"Did you not hear me?"

Indignation and rage burn through me like a furnace. "I heard you just fine," I mutter through clenched teeth.

She inhales sharply. "Where is your supervisor?"

"This is Briana Matthews, my Page." Nick takes the umbrella himself, hard steel under his placid tone. "She is not a servant, Virginia, nor will you treat her as such. Not in my presence or otherwise."

The other women detect Nick's quiet anger and say nothing.

But Virginia Edwards is not done. Her nostrils flare at Nick's admonishment. At a teenage boy's use of her given name, and the reminder of his authority. "Your . . . *Page?*" Her gaze darts from point to point as she processes this information, my face, hair, T-shirt, and jeans. How close I'm standing to Nick. "Scion Davis, I would expect you to select a Page from the Vassals to your Line, as is *tradition*."

"I value Page Matthews's abilities," Nick says, his face impassive, "and your *expectations* belong to you."

She stiffens. "What does your father think of this? Surely he must—"

"His father is thankful that he has returned." We turn to see Lord Davis entering the room using a wheelchair. Nick makes as if to assist him, but Davis waves him away. "And pleased that the Order of the Rose is here once again to support this year's tournament."

"Lord Davis." Vaughn's mother dips her head, as do the others. "My son shared that you'd been injured in battle."

"Don't you worry. I'll use braces by the weekend and walk without aid by Monday. Aether works fast, but we old folks just don't heal as quickly as the youth. Children"—Lord Davis turns to us, and gives me a wink—"why don't you join the chapter in the dining room. I'll guide our guests to the kitchen, where our *hired* catering staff dropped off the meal."

"The Order of the Rose?" I hiss as we walk, still fuming.

Nick grumbles, "A women's auxiliary founded centuries ago when they couldn't Page, Squire, or Scion. Mostly ceremonial now. A way for mothers or former Pages to support chapter events."

All I see are obstacles. Women who want their children in my spot. White women who assume a Black girl in the Lodge is a servant, not a member. Certainly not someone who outranks them. If Virginia treats me like that, how does she treat the caterers? My skin crawls. Then, something strikes me.

"Did you say women couldn't be Scions? I thought the Spell followed the bloodline, no matter who was eligible."

"It does." Nick's jaw tightens. "But for a long time, men didn't care what the Spell wanted. They'd eliminate daughters to force it to the next heir."

I stop walking and stare at him, my stomach twisting in horror.

He pauses at the dining room entrance. "Fifteen hundred years is a long time to operate. The Order was never above the world's brutality. It still isn't."

"That's . . . disgusting."

"That's what happens when you lead with fear and greed."

"Bree! Over here!" Greer waves me over, the Lamorak coin winking on their red bracelet. "Saved you a seat!"

Nick tilts his head. "That's our cue."

Still reeling from his revelation, I follow him into the room.

Nick makes his way to the Legendborn table where the Scions, Squires, and Sel sit. I slide into the open chair between Greer and Whitty at the Pages table, grateful to be between people I know.

Whitty digs into what looks like flank steak with fresh rosemary, while Greer passes me an enormous white stoneware dish of scalloped potatoes. "I was worried you dropped out."

"Nope. Not a quitter."

"A cheat, then?" Vaughn calls from across the table without looking up from his plate. As soon as the words leave his mouth, silence falls across the table.

The twist in my stomach tightens into a cold knot.

"Not a cheat, either."

Vaughn stabs a particularly bloody piece of beef and only sits back to look at me after he shoves it in his mouth. His eyes are the same brown color as his mother's, but where hers offered kindness, his deliver spite. "Then why'd you stay behind with the Legendborn last night even though we were given direct orders to return to the Lodge? What'd you think you'd do? Impress a Scion by showin' off during a fight?"

"That's not what happened, I . . ." Other Pages have fixed me with their own stares, some curious, some accusatory. "I froze. I tried to run back to the Lodge, but the uchel got to me first."

"Right," Vaughn sneers. "Then why are you spending time alone with the Scion of Arthur? Getting a pep talk? Giving him a *helping hand*?"

I freeze, stunned at his implication. Blood rushes in my ears like an angry ocean, but not loud enough to block out the snickers of the veteran Pages beside him. Ones I don't know—Ainsley, and the two third-year wrestling twins, Carson and Blake.

"You think I . . ." I can't even say it, what he thinks I'm doing to buy Nick's favor.

Vaughn points his knife at my chest. "I think you've let that coin around your neck go to your head."

"Put your knife down, Schaefer." Whitty's usually slow drawl is low with warning. "Nick can spend time talkin' to his Page. Ain't no harm there."

"His *Page*, not his Squire," Vaughn spits. "He brought her forth, but that doesn't mean she's gonna make it through the Trials. And even if she does, that doesn't mean she'll be Selected."

"I know that," I grit out, fingers digging into my thighs.

"Good." Vaughn gestures at the rest of the watching Pages as he speaks, his voice charged. "Because a lot of us here have waited and trained our *whole lives* to become a Legendborn Squire. And we're not gonna let some affirmative action *bullshit* fuck up our chances."

The table quiets as everyone waits for my response. Some of the Pages look away. Some stare me down. Others sit, jaws open and silent. Vaughn's smug mouth is half-twisted in a snarl.

I want to smash the damn scalloped potatoes into his face. I want to scream that preferential treatment for Vassals and rich kids is exactly how *they* got in the door. But Nick said I should disappear. Stay off the Vassals' radar. Keep my head down to make it through the tournament.

He was foolish to think that was ever possible. For bigots, it doesn't matter how or why I'm truly here; the fact that I'm here at all is wrong enough.

I'm *going* to make it through the tournament. I'll do what it takes to finish my mission.

But I'm not going to disappear. And I don't *want* to keep my head down.

Instead, I'm going to give Vaughn a glimpse of who I really am—and show him exactly who I'm not.

With my heart thundering through my chest and my throat tight, I answer him—and anyone else sitting at this table who thinks as he does.

"You're a bigot and a bully, Schaefer. You insult me because you think you know what I'm capable of, but you don't. I must make you nervous, though, for you to expose your insecurities about your odds of success in the tournament."

"My *insecurities?*" Vaughn growls, halfway to his feet.

"Yes," I bite out. "And your carelessness. You've just questioned, in public, the judgment of the Scion of Arthur himself by suggesting that he brought his Page forth without good reason." I grin and look Vaughn directly in the eye. "Our future king does not owe you an explanation, and behaving as though he does displays insubordination, disloyalty, and fear. Not power. Not strength. In fact, I *pity* the Scion who chooses *you* as their Squire. That is, if you get chosen at all."

A beat of silence—then Vaughn launches himself over the table. Carson catches him before he reaches me, just as I thought he would. Vaughn strains as Carson whispers in his ear. The curious gazes of his allies turn from me to him, as I'd hoped they would, and a dark flush consumes his features.

A heartbeat passes. Two. And Vaughn drops to his seat, violence in his eyes. "Not over, Matthews."

No, it's not. If Vaughn wasn't my enemy before, he is now.

But right now, I just can't bring myself to care.

Whitty breaks the silence, his voice casual as he asks, "Would ya pass the Brussels sprouts, Ainsley?"

Ainsley scowls and passes the bowl across my chest without saying "Excuse me." Conversation resumes around us, and dinner starts up again, but underneath the table my hands are trembling.

A light smattering of sparks falls across the bridge of my nose and cheeks. Across the room, no one at the bustling, loud, laughing Scion table has noticed what just occurred on our side of the room. No one except Selwyn Kane. The Kingsmage sits with his chin in hand, gazing at me with a contemplative expression. Like he'd been watching—and listening—to the entire exchange with Vaughn. Could he have heard us through all of the chatter and clinking silverware?

Greer surprises me by grabbing the steak tongs, then my plate. "Do you eat beef?"

"Yes." I nod, still dazed. "Why are you being so nice to me?"

They shrug. "If the world is simple, certain people will never be inconvenienced, never need to adapt. I disrupt those people, and you do too. You've been doing it since you walked in the door. I like disruptors and rhythm breakers. We should start a club."

I spear a slice of steak. "Are there T-shirts for this club?"

They laugh. Beside me, Whitty leans forward, and I realize he's still wearing that same comfortable, old-looking camo jacket. In a sea of button-downs and polos, he's disrupting a few rhythms himself. "I think we should get matchin' hats, y'all."

Greer looks at my hair and then gestures to theirs. Tonight it's thick double fishtail braids that extend from their crown to the bottom of each shoulder blade. "And cover up these gorgeous coifs? Get outta here with that trash idea, Whitlock."

"You see how they treat me, Bree?" He tsks. "Rude."

Just as people start drifting to the dessert table, Lord Davis enters the room. Nick stands at his father's side. All eyes turn to them.

"Hello, everyone. Thank you for your well wishes. Our healer, Scion Sitterson, believes I will be fully recovered before the weekend." All around me, members brush the pads of their fingers in circles for the *shhshhshh* of approval. "Unfortunately, it is premature for celebration. As I'm sure you all know by now, last night our fourth-ranked Scion, Felicity Caldwell, was Called to service by her knight, Sir Lamorak. And it is true that the fifth-ranked Scion of Kay was Called last week at our sister chapter in the North."

"Last week?" Fitz shouts. "Why didn't someone tell us?" Quiet nods of agreement.

"I understand your frustration," Davis says. "The Regents wished to keep this Awakening quiet, since it has been more than fifty years since a fifth-ranked Scion was Called. The truth is, there have been increased Shadowborn attacks at all chapter campuses. More Gates opening and more partial-corp crossings. Last night's fully corporeal uchel made it plain that the Shadowborn are gaining strength and may be coordinated. There is even talk of sightings of the Line of Morgaine."

There are a few whispers around the room. Beside me, Greer clenches their fist. Meanwhile, I'm blinking in confusion. What the hell is the Line of Morgaine?

"We must prepare for the callings of Tristan, Lancelot, and Arthur." He looks up at Nick, pride plain on his face. "'Yet some men say in many parts of England that King Arthur is not dead, but had by the will of our Lord Jesu into another place . . .'" He gestures for Nick to finish the quote.

Nick's brow knits at the performance, but he complies. "'And men say that he shall come again.'"

"'And men say that he shall come again,'" Davis repeats, the words like gospel. "*Le Morte d'Arthur*. Malory. A man who knew our cycles of war. Who knew of Camlann." He looks at the chapter and addresses us all once more. "The Regents have decided that in order to prepare the Round Table for the worst-case scenario, we need to accelerate this year's tournaments at all chapters. We cannot wait months for Scions of any rank to select a Squire if they have not done so already. With that in mind, we will proceed with the first trial after tonight's meal, and conclude the tournament with the Selection ceremony in six weeks' time. As soon as possible, all Squires and Scions will be accounted for and bonded."

A few chairs scoot on the hardwood, more nervous glances and low murmurs now. I make brief eye contact with Nick, who is already looking my way. Then I find William, leaning against the back wall. Pete, whom I don't know, looks nervous beside Evan. Could I really Oath myself to any of them?

"The Warrior's Oath is one of our most sacred vows, forever tying together Scion and Squire. Awakened pairs face death, be it on the battlefield or the Abatement. I tell you this, Pages, because this year's tournament and this year's Squire Selection are unlike any that this chapter has seen before." He pauses, templing his fingers. "What may come to pass in the months ahead is something our Order has not witnessed in two hundred and fifty years. I must ask all Pages to think deeply, right now, on your commitments here and elsewhere. I, for one, will not blame you should you decide to serve the mission in other ways. And so, please stand if you would like to forfeit your place in this year's tournament."

Uneasy murmurs in the room now. Some of the third-year Pages and the one fourth-year, the ones who have been around the longest, share nervous glances. Finally, the fourth-year boy, Craig, stands, shame and fear on his face. A third-year girl wearing a Gawain green necklace stands and forfeits. So does the small first-year boy, Lewis.

The number of competing Pages drops from fifteen to twelve.

Once they depart, the room is heavy with a single thought.

Camlann is coming.

22

NICK GUIDES ME through the forest behind the Lodge with a hand wrapped over each shoulder. Thankfully, the rain has stopped.

A thought strikes me a minute after we start walking that sends me into a quiet panic. "We don't have to take another Oath tonight, do we?" If the red flame comes back with everyone around . . .

"No. You're all done with Oaths as a Page."

I release a slow breath. "But why did Sel mesmer us again?"

"Last night was part ritual symbolism, part security—we can't allow the Unoathed to wander our grounds. But tonight is the first trial. Every competing Page is mesmered so no one will see the trial site and get an early advantage." He pinches my shoulder affectionately. "Slow, then a turn." Humidity hangs in the air from the rain, and my heels sink into the forest soil.

"Why mesmer the veteran Pages, though? Didn't they do this same thing last year?"

"Nope. The three aspects tested by the Trials are immutable, but the tests themselves change year to year. Slow, slow. Okay, easy, one foot in front of the other."

I wish I could see what he has me walking over. It feels bouncy and extremely unstable.

"What's the Line of Morgaine?"

"Caught that, did you?"

"I'm here to be sneaky and learn things."

"Uh-huh—whoa! Stop-stop-stop!" One of his arms loops tight around my middle, steadying us both on whatever unsteady surface we're standing on. The close smell of him—laundry, cedar, a slight tang of sweat—and the rocking sensation under our feet makes me dizzy. *Not good, Bree. Focus on the task at hand and not the nice boy who smells nice too.*

After a moment, the world stops tilting. "Okay, that's better." He gives my hip a squeeze. "You good?"

"Yep," I say in a voice that's about two octaves too high.

"'Kay"—he grasps each of my biceps—"one step at a time. Keep your right foot tucked in. Yep, like that. Where were we? Oh, right. The Line of Morgaine. Exodus 22:18. 'Thou shalt not suffer a witch to live.'"

"Okay . . ."

"That's essentially the Regents' take on the Line of Morgaine. After the Shadowborn, they're Order enemy number one. Sometime in the 1400s, things went downhill with a certain sect of Merlins. I don't know much, except that they didn't like the Regents' way of doing things. They also didn't want to wait around for a Scion of Arthur to be Called and risk that that Scion would rule the Order just as poorly. Some stories say they even started attacking Order members, using mesmers on Lieges to influence the Lines and Vassals. Eventually, that group of Merlins splintered off from the Order and rebranded. Called themselves the Line of Morgaine. A lot of things changed after that: how the Merlins are trained and Oathed, how the Regents manage their assignments. The Morgaines are the primary reason the Regents have a zero tolerance policy for anyone using aether outside their purview."

I mull on this. The Line of Morgaine are Merlins gone bad. There's something else bugging me about Nick's story, though, something much more immediate. "If the Regents found out about me, would they treat me like I'm from the Line of Morgaine?"

I feel him shrug. "Probably. There are tests they would do during your trial, but it doesn't really matter. All 'rogue' aether users are treated the same. Here, we're getting off the bridge—yes, it was a bridge, don't freak—and turning down the last path now."

I gulp. How high of a bridge? "What did the Morgaines do after they left?"

"After the splinter, they went underground, as far as I know. On their own, the Morgaines lost access to the training and ancient texts the Merlins use to develop their abilities. Without that, they weren't nearly as powerful as Merlins were, and couldn't be. They became a cautionary tale more than anything."

"Are the Morgaines organized enough to have their own missions out in the world, like the Merlins?"

"Damn." Nick knows where I'm headed. "The Merlin at the hospital could have been a Morgaine. I didn't even consider that until now."

"Is it possible?"

He blows out a puff of air. "It's not *im*possible. And you're sure you don't remember anything else that the cop may have erased?"

I chew on my lip. I've tried to remember more from that night dozens of times, but no other details ever appear. I don't even remember the officer's face, not really. Just the shape of his mouth, his eyes, and the sound of his casting. Nick and I discussed the possibility that I'm missing more than I know, but we just can't be sure. So far, I've recalled everything Sel tried to mesmer away.

"No. Nothing. How would I know if they were Merlin or Morgaine?"

"You wouldn't. We know they have the same abilities as Merlins, but when they stopped administering Oaths——" He stops short, starts again. "Without Oaths, the Order falls apart. Only a Merlin would be able to tell you whether that officer was a Morgaine or a Merlin, and even then they'd have to have been there. I'd say we could ask Sel, but——"

"He loathes me," I mutter, and think of Vaughn. "Along with everyone else on Team Anti-Bree."

Nick's fingers flex around my arms. "Someone bothering you?"

I think about whether I can stomach sharing what happened at dinner with Nick right now. If I could process his response *and* mine, go there again so soon. In the end, I say, "Nothing I can't handle. People think I'm gunning to be your Squire and, I guess, using my feminine wiles to try and convince you to select me."

Silence again.

"Nick?"

"Sorry, my brain shut down at 'feminine wiles.'"

"Nick!" I stop, which is a bad idea, because he runs right into me, and I can feel the press of him against my back, his shoulders shaking with laughter. He steps away after a second and I swat at where I think he is in the darkness—my hand hits air, hits air, then lands on his chest with a hard *thwack*. He's still laughing, but he traps my fingers between his and, before I can say a word, drops a soft kiss on my knuckles.

That kiss steals my breath. I don't think he even notices.

"First of all, are you saying you're *not* gunning to be my Squire? Insulted. And second—nope, sorry, this hand is mine now—I hate that other Pages are targeting you because of me. And third, I don't know what your *feminine wiles* are, *but* I'd be willing to assess them. To see if they could, indeed, seduce me enough to make me bond myself to you *forever*."

I freeze with my hand on his chest, clasped between his fingers, while my mind stumbles and trips over all that he's just uttered.

"Bree? I was just kid—"

"Do you . . . *want* me to try for your Squire?"

Nick squeezes my fingers and sighs. After a moment, his lips brush over my knuckles again, but this time his mouth lingers, moving against my skin as he speaks. "You need to decide that on your own." And then he releases me. When he speaks again, his voice is hoarse and low. "I'm gonna go check to see if they're ready for the Pages at the trial site. Be right back."

Then he's gone through the brush, each rhythmic footstep like a heartbeat in my sensitive ears until they fade away entirely.

I'm standing there alone in the woods for five minutes, maybe more, rubbing my fingers over the places that Nick's mouth touched, when I feel *his* eyes on my skin.

"I know you're there."

Sel's coat flaps in the night air, but I don't hear him land.

"Sense me, did you? Common trait of the Shadowborn to detect other aether users." His deep, smooth voice bounces around me. On my left, my right, ahead. "Nicholas's interest in you keeps you safe for now. However, you would do well to remember that getting closer to Nicholas also brings me closer to you. You'll either slip and expose yourself, or I will expose you."

I can smell his aether signature, whiskey sharp and a hint of burnt cinnamon that sends a shudder down my spine. He notices my response and chuckles from somewhere above me. I hate that I don't know how long he'd been nearby. Did he watch me and Nick? Listen to our conversation? Suddenly, I'm furious. First the racist shit at the Lodge and now this Merlin bully?

Words escape me in an angry stream. "You keep threatening me, but in the end you don't do *jack*. You can't touch me because I'm your king's Page, but you taunt me anyway because it makes you feel important. I can't imagine the beating your ego's taken, being ignored by the very Scion you swore your life to!"

Shocked silence. From both of us.

Then his voice is at my ear. "There it is. The self-righteous rage of demonkind. Pathetic."

"Not as pathetic as you."

"Mmm?"

I pause, just in case he tries to rush me or something, but he doesn't. I can't even tell if I'm still facing in the right direction. Undaunted, I keep going. "Let's say you go over Nick's head and report me to Lord Davis or the Regents. They'll put me on one of your trials. Ask you for proof of whatever it is you think I am, and that's the thing, Merlin. You have none."

Silence. Then, "Is that so?"

"Yeah, that's so." I'm bold now, and running with it. "My dad had a dog like you once, when he was little. His family lived out in the sticks and that dog raised hell over cars driving down the road, howled at every stray cat. Made it a useless guard dog, so his father gave it away. If you run your uchel hunch up the chain without evidence, the Regents will question your ability to do your job. And that's a risk you can't afford. You don't want to be that ole country dog, do you, Kingsmage?"

Silence. Then a low, slow laugh in the darkness.

"You have a silver tongue, mystery girl." A pause. "I feel a sudden urge to tear it out."

My pulse leaps in my throat.

"Lucky for you, I'm used to being baited." A whoosh of air, and then his voice finds me from overhead. "Maybe another time."

The moment he leaves, a fine tremor starts at my fingers. By the time Nick jogs back to me through the woods, both hands are shaking, my chest tight with fear.

"Okay, I think they're ready for you in the arena."

I nod, swallowing around a gigantic lump—and the tongue I'm still thankful to own.

"Hey, what's wrong?"

I give a wobbly smile. "Your Kingsmage stopped by for a little pre-game inspiration. He still thinks I'm a demon and threatened to out me, but this time I told him off. Now he wants to rip my tongue out of my head."

Nick makes a frustrated sound. "That's why I didn't feel him."

"You can *feel* Sel?"

"Lifelong perk of the Kingsmage Oath. He can feel when I'm in mortal danger, and I can feel his murderous intent. It's how I knew he was close before he attacked you last night."

I shiver, remembering the sensation of Sel gripping my ankle in the darkness. "Should I be *relieved* that you didn't feel his desire to murder me?"

An awkward pause. "Yes . . . ?"

"Wow."

"Yep." He takes my hand and tugs me forward.

"Wait, did you say *arena*?"

It's abundantly clear that Sydney *despises* me. As soon as Tor paired us together, she'd shot me a glare searing enough to cause third-degree burns.

Sydney doesn't seem to care much for Vaughn, so that's not it. To her credit, she'd turned to me, point-blank, and told me exactly why she doesn't like me: "I'm here to win this thing and I don't trust anyone here." Fair and direct. Can't fault her.

Unfortunately for her, she's going to have to trust me tonight. Because the only way either of us moves forward to the second trial is if we do it as a team.

If I fail tonight, so does she, and then she's out. Eliminated. We both are.

Which is why I'm not going to fail.

Sydney immediately took point at the top of the small ridge and ordered me to stay down in the ditch of our base, standing guard over our three Onceborn "victims."

"Any signal?" I whisper.

"Nothing yet," she bites out without looking at me, annoyed before anything has even happened.

I test the weight of the midsize stuffed mannequin. It must be 150 pounds at *least*. I pull it up over my shoulders, balancing on my heels, and stand up in a squat the way my father taught me. My knees shake and I get the mannequin up in the air without dropping it.

But could I *run* with it?

The "arena" is a flat strip of land that cuts through the forest behind the Lodge. At some point it'd been cleared to make way for those huge transmission power lines, but now it's just a grassy, open highway between two dense woods. A football field from one side to the other. There are Pages like us stationed fifty feet apart on either side, hidden by trees and bushes, tucked into ditches. And somewhere on a high ridge sit nine Scions and Squires with a clear view of the trial to come.

Lanterns give us just enough light to navigate the arena, illuminating the starting points for each team and, across the field, where we need to end up if we want to win.

Sydney taps her thigh nervously with one of her daggers. The shiny blade is as long as my forearm and razor-sharp. She'd come prepared tonight with two holsters already strapped to her thighs, so she hadn't needed to collect a weapon from the pile Russ and Evan had deposited in front of the twelve Pages. As soon as they'd given us our options, they'd left to join the rest of the Legendborn observing the trial. We'd been given free rein to choose from swords, daggers, long quarterstaffs, flails, even a bullwhip—but no hints as to which item would serve us best. I'm no weakling—I'm decently strong and have good stamina from Bentonville High track and field, but I'd never handled a weapon in my life. I was half-scared of chopping my own arm off, so I'd chosen the short, heavy wooden staff—what Whitty called a "cudgel"—and strapped it to my back with its leather harness.

We weren't given armor of any kind.

"There."

I let the stuffed mannequin fall to the ground with a heavy thud and crawl to Sydney. "Where?"

"Still mesmered, Matthews? Use your eyes! The Kingsmage is right there." She jabs a finger at one end of the arena. Selwyn, in all black, blends into the navy skyline, but I can just make him out by starlight, standing in the middle of the arena.

Without warning, Selwyn throws his arms out wide to either side of his body. His fingers curl up against the air, pulling aether out of the night sky in heavy, rhythmic waves. A small silver-blue mage flame tornado forms in one palm, then the other. They grow taller and taller until the open mouths of the funnels stretch ten feet over his head. We shield our eyes against the pulsing brightness. I look back just in time to watch him thrust both palms toward the other end of the arena, sending all that aether roaring straight down the middle. The sharp smell of charred cinnamon reaches my nose, enough to make me cough.

I knew Sel was strong, but nothing I've seen him do prepared me for this.

Flames snake through the air. Twist. Melt. Flow into six broad, snarling shapes. Shapes that grow short, stubby legs. Translucent fur rises up in a long ridge—spines. Aether solidifies into dark blue beady eyes. Extends into short snouts. Sharpens to crystalline points at the end of long, deadly tusks.

"Hellboars?" I whisper in horror.

"Hellboars the size of goddamn bison," Sydney mutters, her eyes narrowing on the glowing creature across from us. It kicks at the dirt, but unlike Sel, its hooves make tearing sounds, ripping up grass in great chunks.

Two Pages per team. Three teams run at a time. One goal: make it to the other side with all bodies—living and fake—in one piece.

In ten minutes or less.

"But they're not real."

"They'll gouge us just as badly as if they were. Us"—she twists around to assess our three rescue victims—"and them." I look at our weighted cargo and their stitched burlap skin with fresh anxiety. We're assigned to the second group of three, so maybe we can watch for strategies. And mistakes.

A whistle splits the air—and nothing happens.

A breeze snakes through the trees. My heartbeat hammers against my ribs. The arena is still.

Vaughn and Spencer leap from their base—and take off like rockets. Each boy carries a sword in one hand and a mannequin over a shoulder. Their hellboars squeal and thunder after them.

Whitty and Blake run next. Blake leads, twirling his quarterstaff with deadly precision. The spinning distracts both boars—and Whitty makes for the other side, mannequin in tow.

Down the field, Carson twirls a long-handled flail, keeping both boars at bay. Greer follows, the two lightest mannequins slung in a fireman's carry.

Sounds pierce the night: rotating weapons, whirring. Shouts. Squeals. Grunts. Each the sign of a potential victory or injury.

Vaughn and Spencer are closest—and I'd love nothing more than to watch Vaughn lose—so I study their attempt more than the others'.

The boars are still hot on their heels—until the boys zag sharply in opposite directions, nearly slipping in the wet grass. The constructs split up too, pivoting to follow—but their hooves slide in the dirt, kicking up mud and soil. They hit the ground hard and screaming.

The boars get to their feet. As if on cue, the boys heave their "Onceborn victims" off their shoulders. The mannequins hit the ground with a heavy *splat*.

At first, I think they've planned to fight the boars while their victims are out of harm's way, but Spencer doesn't draw his sword. Instead, he sprints back toward the base, his boar on his heels, and slides into the ditch to safety. Leaving Vaughn to face both boars alone.

"Coward!" Sydney hisses with disgust.

Spencer's boar reaches the lantern boundary, then turns back. It can't go any farther. It moves toward Vaughn, who has already used his sword to leave two gaping slashes in the sides of its companion. It's only when Spencer's boar has almost reached Vaughn that the boys' true strategy is revealed:

Spencer's head pops out of the bushes. He emerges carrying the smallest mannequin in a fireman's hold, then sprints straight across the arena.

"Not a coward," I whisper. "He's their runner."

I have to admit, it's smart: use Vaughn, the stronger fighter, to distract the two boars while Spencer, the faster of the two, completes the first third of the task.

Back on the field, Vaughn's slowing down. The boars have him pinned on both sides. He gets in quick slashes—one! two!—before darting back, barely escaping a snapping jaw.

Spencer's quick. He drops his mannequin in the far base without stopping, then runs back the way he'd come. He scoops up one of the heavier abandoned victims at the halfway mark, pivots to run it to the other side—

Vaughn shouts for help. Spencer's victim drops again. He runs to his partner's aid, grabbing his blade on the way.

Spencer leaps high, sword pulled back for a thrust. On the descent, he sinks his blade deep into one boar's spine. He yanks it free and jumps back in one motion.

The boar's guttural scream echoes up the ridge, crosses the field, makes my teeth grind.

Aether steams from its wound and turns to dust, like silver embers over a bonfire. The dying construct drops to its knees. Spencer charges again, this time spearing the beast between the eyes.

As Spencer runs to his partner, the boar melts into a silver puddle, then explodes into a sea of sparkling ashes.

Spencer and Vaughn make quick work of the remaining hellboar. In two minutes, it's on all four knees, keening pitifully. In unison, the boys spear it through the skull.

Cheers echo down the ridge as they gather the remaining two victims and run them to safety.

A whistle echoes from above. The first team has finished.

"Three minutes!" someone shouts. A warning to the others.

Greer and Carson are almost done. One boar is down. Greer has deposited both mannequins. They draw two daggers as they run back onto the field. Carson's flail twirls so fast all I can see are the spiked ends of the maces over the top of their final boar's head.

But Whitty and Blake are struggling. Somewhere between dropping off their first mannequin and their second, Whitty lost a dagger. They're surrounded, standing back to back. Blake's staff arcs up. Connects with the boar's skull. Sends it to its knees. It's a heavy blow, but not a killing one.

A chilling scream rips through the night, and I search for the source, panic fluttering in my chest. I fear the worst for my friend, but it's not Greer who's in trouble.

One of the boars has Carson pinned beneath it. He kicks and punches with all that he has, but his weapon is yards away.

Greer runs, leaps, and hovers in the air. They land on the second boar's back, spread their arms wide like a bird—and plunge a dagger into each lung. Carson scrambles backward just as the construct explodes and bright dust sprays his face. Some of it lands in his gasping mouth.

When I turn back, Blake and Whitty are just finishing off their second boar.

All three teams bring their final victim to safety. The first round is over.

And we're up next.

23

AINSLEY AND TUCKER are the first team that takes to the field holding only their weapons. They dart out before the rest of us, determination clear on their faces, and swords held high; they plan to take out both hellboars first, while unimpeded by mannequins.

It's a mistake.

There's a reason everyone else's strategy included distraction: the boars are big, heavy, easily confused beasts. They're unable to make quick pivots or turns.

But at a straight charge, they're nearly unstoppable.

We watch helplessly as the Pages go down in under sixty seconds.

At the last moment before impact, Ainsley shifts left. The weight of the sword takes her off-balance; she trips. She scramble to her feet—and the boar knocks her to the ground. She chokes out a bloodcurdling scream—am I going to watch her be devoured? Gouged to death?—and the boar explodes on top of her.

The second boar is a foot from goring Tucker through the middle—then it explodes mid-chase.

The arena freezes. The only sound is Ainsley crying on the ground as shiny particles rain down on her body.

"Page Edwards needs medical assistance," Sel says coolly. "She and Page Johnson are disqualified." Then, he turns to the rest of us and shouts: "The clock is still ticking!"

Sydney and I explode out of our ditch, and so do the other Pages, Celeste and Mina. How much time do we have? Eight minutes, maybe? Eight and a half?

I have to focus.

I have the heaviest mannequin over my shoulders, tucked against my weapon. My only thought is my agreed-upon goal—delivery. Behind me, one of Sydney's daggers whistles through the air. A deep *thunk*. The boar chasing me hits the ground. The earth shakes.

I don't look back; she planned to kill it in one strike, and I have no doubt she did.

The mannequin is heavy, but once I get momentum, I almost forget about it. And suddenly, I'm on the other side, heaving it up and over my head like a sack of potatoes.

I run wide back to our base, hoping to stay out of the other boar's sight. I know Sydney is saving her other dagger. We can't afford to make her use it on me.

Out of the corner of my eye, I see her dancing and weaving away from the monster. No, can't look. One goal: delivery.

I skid into our base and hoist the next-smallest mannequin, just like we'd planned.

Move the heaviest first, while I'm fresh. Save the lightest for last, when I'm spent.

I'm halfway across the field when I trip over Sydney's first dagger, abandoned in the grass. The mannequin and I go flying. It lands three feet in front of me—with a loud thud that draws our boar's attention.

Sydney's quick. She yells. Waves. Jumps to distract it, but—of course—our remaining boar has a scrap of focus.

Its beady eyes find me, and it charges.

I flash through my options: too far from the other side of the arena, can't stand my ground, can't use the mannequin in defense, can't carry it and outrun the boar.

I grab Sydney's knife and shoot to my feet, shouting at her, "Get it to safety!" I hope she knows what I mean.

I sprint back to our base, but arc wide so that the boar after me will curve too—and avoid trampling the lifeless mannequin on the ground.

Behind me, thundering hooves pound the earth. My thighs and lungs are on fire. Still, I push harder. I can hear its breathing—heavy grunts through a wet snout.

I veer left again to buy myself time, but the change in direction is too sharp, too fast. Something pulls painfully in my left knee. I keep running and fling myself into the ditch. My shoulder clips a pine tree, bark digs into my arm, but the frustrated squeal behind me lets me know I've made it. I'm safe.

When I twist back on my knees and look up, the boar is pawing at the ground and snorting in my direction. I hold my breath and watch as its heavy head begins swinging back and forth. Searching.

I'm less than six feet away, why is it—

It can't see me. Its eyes are weak.

A twig snaps beneath my right foot, and its ears flick forward, its snout lifting in a slow, searching pattern.

But it can hear me. It has a good sense of smell. Great.

Did Sydney do what I asked? Did she grab the mannequin and get it to the other side? I don't bother looking behind me; I know the smallest mannequin is there, still waiting to be rescued. How much time is left?

I hear shouting and pounding feet to my left. Celeste and Mina are still in the arena, still working.

My boar is pacing now, stubbornly waiting for me to come out so it can gore me. I've got to *do* something.

Okay. Think.

I have Sydney's dagger, but I don't have her throwing skills or aim. I have my cudgel still strapped to my back, but at this angle I don't have enough power for more than a hard poke to the chin. I look around, to my side, then up.

I shove Sydney's dagger handle into my mouth and start climbing the oak tree beside me before I decide whether it's a good idea or not. All I know is that I know trees. I've climbed them since I was a kid. Trees are good.

I step up onto the large burl overgrowths on either side of the oak, gripping their bulbous shapes as well as I can with sneakers, and wrap my hands around to find the next burl—hoist myself up. The boar's head lifts to follow me, but I'm gambling that it can't see me very well and just knows that I'm moving. The limbs are too far up to do me any good, but I stop about ten feet up with one arm in a death grip around the trunk, precariously balanced on a burl just wider than my shoe.

The boar has backed up now, just a few feet from the tree line. It's hard work getting the cudgel and its leather strap off with one hand, but I manage it quickly and hold the still-buckled weapon away from me and the tree, waving it a bit to get the boar's attention. It stops moving. Its beady eyes follow the motion eagerly.

This is a *bad* idea.

One. Two. *Three!*

I toss the cudgel off to my right and grab the dagger with my free hand while the creature does just what I hoped: it shifts its bulk toward the falling cudgel, away from me, its head dips down to inspect the staff—and I shove off from the tree, launching myself forward onto its back, dagger pointing down.

Gravity drives the sharp blade into the creature's shining neck, not me, but the blow works just the same.

The animal squeals and bucks, tossing me in the air like a rag doll. I hit the ground with a jarring thud and curl into a ball, ready for the heavy stomp of hooves—but it never comes.

My head pops up just in time to see the boar—my knife still lodged deep inside—crumble to the ground.

"Run!" Sydney screams. She's going for the mannequin. I scramble to my feet and sprint to the other side of the arena; we both have to get there in time.

Sydney slides down the ditch right behind me, mannequin over her shoulder, just as the whistle goes off.

We're the only team from our round to pass. Sometime during my flying squirrel impersonation, Celeste and Mina let two of their mannequins get gored.

When we emerge from our side of the arena, the Legendborn cheer from their observation spots in the woods. I feel dazed but exhilarated. Sydney doesn't smile at me, exactly, but she nods in my direction before she walks off to join Vaughn and Blake and the other four Pages who have passed. They stand together, congratulating one another.

The four who didn't are in varying levels of shock and devastation. Mina's wiping tears from her face while Ainsley rubs her back in slow circles. Celeste and Tucker are in a heated argument; from the snippets I hear, they both blame their partners for their eliminations.

I stand between them, unsure where I fit in.

When I glance his way, Sel is looking up the hill where the Legendborn have begun stomping their way through the trees to meet us. His brows are knitted together in concentration, his head cocked to the side as if listening for something.

"Nick! *Nick!*"

When Victoria shouts, Sel is already moving toward the sound. He flashes by me so quickly that I hear the wind crack around his body before he disappears into the tree line in a shadowy blur.

We're all running to follow.

The trees stand so thick up the slanted hill, it's hard to see what's happening, but we can hear it. *Something* is tumbling through the trees like an enormous bowling ball, cracking trunks in half like giant pins. That something is coming closer, the sounds are getting louder, and then it bursts through a pair of pine trees, sending bark and splinters in every direction, and spills out onto the arena floor, stopping us all short.

It's a massive, full-corp serpent, its scaled body as big and round as a tractor tire. It pulls half of its body up off the ground until it towers twenty feet above us, bloodred eyes the size of my fist blazing down on us. The glowing creature opens its jaws to release a shrill, nightmarish hiss that scrapes against my eardrums.

A hellsnake, my mind supplies. With a body wrapped tight in its glowing tail.

"Nick!" I scream for him, but it's no use. It only takes a second to see that

he's enveloped head to toe in a coil of muscle, only the pale hair at the top of his head visible in the hellsnake's grip.

The Awakened Legendborn gather aether as they run, forming glowing swords and daggers. I catch a glimpse of Felicity and Russ, casting armor on themselves as they dash forward, but the quick-shadow shape of Selwyn Kane speeds out of the trees and leaps onto the snake before anyone else has reached it.

While the serpent writhes, Sel scrabbles up its body, using its scales as handholds. He mounts its head as the creature thrashes back and forth, its forked tongue flicking out like a glowing whip. Sel had no time to form a weapon, but his entire body is wrapped in thin, swirling clouds of silver-blue aether. He pulls back with a roar and thrusts both of his arms into the snake's eyes, burying them into the sockets up to his elbow.

The creature screams loud enough to shatter glass. Its big body spasms so hard anyone else would have been thrown, but Sel holds tight and only pushes his arms in farther. Viscous fluid erupts in his face. After a final shudder, the hellsnake goes stiff and falls forward, releasing a gasping Nick right as its head hits the ground.

24

I STAND IN front of Nick's door for what feels like forever, but is probably only a few uncertain minutes.

I don't know why I'm hesitating. He could just be sleeping. He *should* just be sleeping. And if that's the case, I'll just go home and sleep too. See him in the morning.

No, I know why I'm hesitating. It's because it's late, the Lodge is quiet, and he might *not* be sleeping—and being alone with him has started to feel . . . intense.

I gaze hopefully down the hall as if someone might appear and rescue me from the Schrödinger's Cat of Conscious Boys scenario I find myself in, but it's empty and unhelpful. The only signs of life on the floor are the scattered few glowing lamps on some of the teak console tables between residents' doors.

On the other side of this door, Nick is recovering from yet another attack that could have killed him. That's what I should focus on. That's what I *need* to focus on.

I take a slow, deep breath and open his door, slipping inside and easing it closed behind me.

Nick is asleep on top of the comforter in loose clothing; flannel pants, a soft T-shirt. His arms lie straight down at his sides. The fine strands of his hair are partly matted on one side, partly strewn across the pillow like he's just been blasted by a gust of wind. He's flushed, too; each of his cheeks bears a slash of red.

I walk closer, my arms clutched tight across my middle.

He's recovered from the broken ribs that William treated. His steady breaths say he's out of danger and his lungs are fine, but the slight pull at the corners of his eyes says he could still be in pain. Did William give him something to make him sleep? I hope so.

I start to turn, to let him rest, but jump when Nick whispers behind me.

"Who's creepy now?"

I turn back to the bed, where Nick has started to push himself up his pillow. He winces but waves me off when I move to help him. "I'm okay, just stiff."

I look him over with a suspicious eye. "If I stay and talk to you, will William yell at me?"

Nick laughs, but the sound is cut short when his breath catches in pain. "William will yell at us both, probably." He rubs a hand over his chest and swallows thickly. Watching the motion sends my mind flying back to the arena.

I shift my weight from one foot to the other. "I heard Sel say to the others that he thinks this attack was planned too. Not a coincidence. That the Shadowborn sent a creature that would be able to subdue you quickly and take you away."

His eyes go distant as he nods. "My father said the same in the infirmary. The Regents have called a meeting. My dad is going to take another day to recover, then fly up to the Northern Chapter to speak with them and the other Viceroys." I watch him pick at the gold anchors embroidered on the comforter, almost like he needs to do something to keep his hands busy.

"Sel's in charge while he's gone, William said."

"Unfortunately."

After Nick had been recovered alive, but injured, Sel took him straight to the Lodge. The long walk back through the woods had given me a lot of time to think about my "mission" here, and the danger it was putting both me and Nick in. With every step, guilt dropped into my body, one heavy brick at a time.

Sel may be terrifying and cruel, but he's the only reason the Shadowborn's plan to kidnap Nick failed tonight. Sel's role as Kingsmage is more critical than ever right now, and his suspicions of me are taking his attention from his job. It's worse, too, because those suspicions are unfounded. He's wasting energy on me when, after tonight, there's no doubt that Nick's life is in danger. The Order is an army, and the Legendborn are its soldiers. Could I really keep going in the tournament and become William's or Pete's or even Nick's Squire if my only intention is to gain the title so that I can find out what happened to my mother?

This afternoon with Patricia, finding the truth had felt like the most important thing in the world. Important enough to lie to my father, lie to Alice, and lie to everyone at the Lodge every time I showed my face. My mission still feels important and necessary, because how can I rest knowing that someone may have taken my mother away from me? That it might not have been an accident at all.

But whether or not Camlann arrives, and whether or not someone in the Order killed my mother, Nick needs a *real* Squire, not a fraud.

For the first time, I wonder if maybe Sel's right and I *am* born of shadows. Or maybe those shadows aren't who I am, but I keep finding my way to them anyway.

Nick huffs. "Earth to Bree? You're just standing there, zoning out. It's making me anxious." He pats his bed, and his eyes hold a hint of their old mirth. "You can sit down, you know. I won't bite."

I stare at him then, *really* stare at him. Someone I care about is alive but hurt. Someone I like very much is right here in front of me, asking me to sit with him. It dawns on me that if I ignore that or forget how important that is, then I truly will make the shadows my home.

I take a deep breath and step forward, pulling off my shoes and climbing onto his bed, and just like that, the nearness of Nick pulls all of my focus: his warmth; the bright scent of William's aether mingling with the detergent smell of fresh clothes; his half-lidded eyes that follow me as I move toward him and watch me as I get settled. It's too much all of a sudden, and my entire body knows it. I lean back a tiny fraction.

Of course Nick notices. He presses his lips closed to fight a grin, and the expression somehow makes his already handsome face more endearing, more inviting. "You nervous, B?"

"No," I say, and raise my chin a fraction to feel—and appear—convincing. I'm not sure it works, because he makes a soft, curious sound.

"Do *I* make you nervous?" He tilts his head to the side in query, but it causes his matted hair to flare up comically. I cringe and laugh.

"You look like a rooster." It takes everything in me not to stretch up and press it down.

"A rooster?" He tilts his head the other way, sending his hair flopping again. I blow out a laugh, just like he wants me to, and he smiles.

I can't help it. I lean forward on my knees and smooth his hair down. Once the soft strands lay flat, I notice how carefully Nick watches me, how still he's gone. His eyes are slate blue with dashes of gray, his lashes fine strokes of paint against his skin.

I wonder if he's holding his breath too.

I start to pull back, but he catches my wrist with one hand and passes his thumb, calloused and warm, over the inside of my palm. The motion tingles and tickles, until his thumb presses down and sends an arrow of heat from my hand to my toes.

My heart beats so rapidly I'm sure he must see it, feel it through my palm.

"Thank you."

"For what?" I ask. This close, Nick's laundry-and-cedar scent is rich enough to make me dizzy. There are other smells that I pull in with a silent breath: green grass on a warm summer day, the slight bite of metal.

His eyes travel an unhurried route over my face, from my brows to my nose. They flicker to my mouth and back up to my eyes and, just like that, my breath is gone again.

"For still being here," he says, his expression a mixture of wonder and gratitude. "Even after the hellhound, and the uchel, and Felicity being Called, and now a sarff uffern. I never thought we'd be this close to Camlann, but I'm glad you're here with me." His eyes lower; he shakes his head. "When we first met, some part of me trusted you. I don't know why. I just did."

Despite my guilt, I think of how, in so many moments since I've met him, my own trust had risen inside to meet his, sure and steady.

Call and response.

Maybe Nick's thinking of that too, because he caresses my palm once more and takes a ragged breath.

"How about now?" he whispers, his voice rough.

"Now?" I breathe.

Something heady and dark pools in Nick's eyes. "Does *this* make you nervous?"

The last boy I kissed was Michael Gustin in ninth grade in the corner of the school dance. I remember being terrified and, after the too-wet, too-sloppy ick of it, disappointed. But that was ninth grade and Michael. This is now. And this is Nick.

I don't feel nervous. I feel desire batting against my ribs like a caged bird. I feel hesitation. I feel overwhelmed. Then, I feel mortification when I realize that Nick, with his sharp, perceptive eyes, has seen it all.

He smiles, small and secret, and brings his free hand up to cradle my jaw, sweeping his thumb over it. His eyes follow the movement thoughtfully before they rise to claim my gaze again. He squeezes my wrist, then lets me go.

I lurch backward on my knees, my cheeks heated, the ghosts of his hands on my skin.

I'm grateful that he's busy adjusting his pillows and not looking at me.

I have a feeling he's doing it on purpose, giving me a moment to collect myself.

Once he finishes, he settles back against the headboard and folds his hands in his lap. "Will you sit with me?" he asks pleasantly.

And just like that, the air between us feels lighter, easier. Like nothing unusual had happened at all.

I'm impressed, despite my still raging heartbeat. How does he do it? How does this boy navigate my emotions like a seasoned sailor, finding the clear skies and bringing them closer, when all I seem able to do is hold fast to the storms?

He waits patiently for me to decide, his eyes soft and open. Finally, I nod and crawl up to the headboard, making myself comfortable in the space beside him.

We sit like that for a long time, until our breaths rise and fall as one.

I must have dozed off, because I jump when I hear the Lodge's front door slam downstairs.

The room is black. For a moment I forget where I am.

Nick presses a hand to my knee and says in a groggy voice, "If it's bad, they'll come find us."

The digital clock above his door says it's close to one a.m. "I should go."

"If you leave now, Sel will know you're still here and yell at both of us," he says reasonably. "Stay."

I can't really argue with that. Plus, now that the adrenaline has fully left my body, I'm beyond exhausted.

Still, I pull out my phone and text Alice to let her know where I am and that I'm okay before putting my phone on silent. When the screen goes black, we sit in the darkness listening to the voices downstairs until the house becomes quiet again.

I start to wonder if I should find some pajamas and sneak into one of the spare rooms to go to bed for real. I reach up to my hair and tug on my bun. I'd hate to sleep without my satin pillowcase. Maybe Felicity has a scarf?

Before I can slip off the bed, Nick starts to speak, his voice low and disembodied in the pitch-black room.

"Most Scion parents can't wait until their child is old enough to begin training. I know my dad couldn't. My mother, though? When I look back, it was obvious that she was *terrified*."

"You don't have to talk about this now, if you don't want to."

"I do. Want to."

I reach for his hand in the darkness, and he squeezes my palm.

"My mother was raised in a Vassal family, and she Paged right away but never tried for a Squire title. Marrying a Scion of Arthur was the next best thing, her parents figured. My dad was never Called, but Scions of Arthur still hold . . . a lot of power. When I was growing up, she and my dad fought a lot. About my future, about my dad's training regimen. I couldn't go to regular school; he homeschooled me so he'd have more control over my studies. I was eight when Dad started bringing other Lieges around to train me. He told them not to go easy just because I was a kid. Because really, I wasn't a kid. I was their king. And they didn't. Go easy, that is. They . . ."

Nick pauses, and I can hear him swallow once, twice. I'm scared that he's crying and I don't know what to do. I press my shoulder into his and hope I can send my warmth and strength over to him. When he starts again, his voice is thick with memory.

"It's not the broken bones or the bruises, the black eyes or the concussions, that keep me up at night. Those were healed by a Scion of Gawain. It's the look in my mother's eyes when I'd come inside, like the sight of me was carving holes into her heart. They'd fight the most those days."

He takes a deep breath in the darkness, and I take one with him because I want him to know I'm here.

"One night she woke me up and told me to grab my things, that we were leaving. She'd had enough of watching her son get beaten. We made it about a mile out of town before these black cars surrounded us. Dad comes out of one of them and he's frightened and angry. More upset than I'd ever seen him. I think he was scared we'd *both* been kidnapped by the Shadowborn, and that's why he called the Regents for help. He'd never imagined his own wife would take his son from him. A Merlin I'd never met took my mother away without letting either of us say goodbye." His voice has gone cold with rage, quiet with sorrow. "Dad broke down in tears when they drove off, because he knew she'd be punished. I think he tried to stop it, but the Regents' word is final. The trainings stopped for a while. He started me at private school, stopped talking about my rank, our bloodline. The next . . . the next time I saw her was a few weeks later at a park near our neighborhood. My dad and I were getting ice cream. Mom walked by, and I ran up to her and gave her a hug, told her I was glad she was back. But she wasn't back. She smiled, but . . . then she held me at arm's length and asked who I was."

I choke on my next breath. Tears burn at the edges of my eyes.

"I spent years researching Merlins' mesmers. Trying to figure out how to break what they'd done. Extracting a mother's child from her psyche is mesmerwork only a Master Merlin could do. When we met and you told me you'd broken Sel's mesmer, I thought maybe I'd missed something . . ." His voice trails off into a heavy sigh.

That's what I'd seen in his eyes that first night at the Lodge. Hope. "I'm sorry," I murmur.

He squeezes my thigh. "Not your fault." He inhales sharply, returning to the memory. "Anyway, after we ran into her, Dad moved us out of town within the week. To protect me, I think. Not long after that, Sel came to live with us, and another Merlin brought us here to perform the Kingsmage Oath. Sel's a little kid, pledging his life to protect me, and all I could think was how much I *hated* the Merlins for being monsters and how I didn't want this strange boy in our house. I wanted my mother. I blamed my dad for calling the Regents that night, but, in the end, it was Arthur who drove my parents apart, and I'm . . . I'm so *angry* with him, Bree. Angry with a sixth-century ghost." He laughs bitterly. "I was so . . . so furious at *all of it* that I thought if I stopped training every day, stopped doing everything my dad wanted me to do, and stopped hanging around everyone here—William, Whitty, Sar, everyone—that I could make it so Arthur wouldn't even *want* to Call me. I left this world, the people, the politics, the rituals . . . so that maybe he'd think I was unworthy and leave me alone. And now that it might be real . . . ?" He huffs out another hollow laugh. "I've pushed it all away for so long that sometimes I'm not sure I'd even be able to hear Arthur if he did Call."

I wrap my arms around his chest and squeeze until he drops his cheek onto my head and squeezes back.

I don't mention Sel saying that same thing when he was aether-drunk, about Nick not being able to hear Arthur's Call.

I hate that Sel, in his own fit of fury, might have been right.

I wake up to the sound of Nick showering in the room's bathroom. My phone says it's seven thirty—early enough that I can still make my first class. I sit up, hands smoothing down my unwrapped, slept-on curls in apology, and notice a small basket of toiletries on the nightstand beside me. Soap, a washcloth, a comb I'll never be able to use, and a small toothbrush and tiny tube of toothpaste.

I can already hear Alice's squeal of delight when I tell her about Nick's efforts. I may not be able to tell my best friend everything, but I can at least tell her about sleeping in Nick's bed and waking up to a literal gift basket.

I grab the toiletries and head downstairs to one of the hall bathrooms, hoping against hope that no one saw me emerge from Nick's bedroom. Ten minutes later, Nick finds me and insists on walking me back to my dorm.

Dew and fog have settled over the grounds of the Lodge overnight, and the quiet of the morning falls thick and heavy around us.

Nick shakes his head, eyebrows drawn tight as soon as we step away from the building and toward the tree-lined gravel road and trail that leads back to campus.

"What?"

"Every time I come here, people look at me like I know what the hell I'm doing."

I cross my arms as we walk, and a memory comes to me. "My mom used to say, 'Fake it till you make it.' Maybe that's what you've got to do. Fake it till you make it."

He chuckles, and the warmth of it fills my chest. "Thanks, partner."

"Oh, I'm not your partner." I jerk a thumb over my shoulder, back toward the Lodge. "I think Vaughn wants that gig."

"Ugh, that dude." He rolls his eyes. "He keeps asking me to spar. It's all very . . . bro-y? Is that a word?" I giggle, imagining Vaughn the asshole chasing Nick down with sparring swords, begging him to practice. "I really don't want him as my Squire." Nick's eyes widen hopefully. "Any more thoughts about—"

I hold my hands up. "As we all saw last night, I don't have a clue how to hold a sword or a bow and arrow or . . . anything. I'd be horrible."

"We'd train you." Nick grins. "I've seen you move. You'd be *incredible*."

"Oh, really?" I cross my arms, narrowing my eyes.

"Yeah, really." His laugh is a soft rumble in the quiet morning air. "Maybe I like watching you move."

I open my mouth, but no actual words emerge, so I just shake my head and turn away.

He stops in the road, catches my wrist, and tugs until I have to angle toward him. "Don't do that," he chides.

"Do what?" Shadows play across his face as he draws me nearer. Like last night in his room, he presses his thumb into my palm, and just that bit of pressure ignites my insides, sets my heart racing.

"That thing you just did. That thing you do," he says, his eyes filled with humor—and a shadow of hurt. "Tell yourself I'm just teasing. It's okay to be nervous, but please don't dismiss the idea that I like you, B."

I make a strangled sort of indignant sound. "I'm not nervous. I'm just . . ."

He tilts his head. "Just what?"

I blink in shock, because he's really, really expecting an answer, isn't he? "I'm . . . a lot of things."

He hums in amused agreement, his lips tight in a suppressed smile. "You are. I agree."

"And . . . and . . . I'm not used to feeling this way."

"What way?"

I feel heat rise in my cheeks and look away just as Nick flashes a soft, knowing grin. He trails his fingers up my forearms to my inner elbows, making me shiver. His right hand skims past my elbow to my bicep, over my shoulder to rest on my collarbone, his thumb swiping along my jaw.

"I had a thought about what I said last night." His voice is quiet, almost meditative, as he watches his thumb on my cheek. "About being Arthur's Scion and how, on some level, I never thought I'd have to really deal with it, you know? Not really. My dad didn't. Granddad didn't. A dormant Scion has clout, but no real say in the Order. I never thought about how his powers might feel and what I might do with them, until . . ." His eyes flick to mine.

My breath hitches. "Until?"

"Until the uchel took you."

"Oh, sure," I joke, my voice trembling only slightly. His face is so close I can smell the shampoo he used this morning. See the fine lashes against his cheek. I'm scared to want him—but I want him anyway. My next words come out breathy and faint. "Damsel in distress activates your hero mode?"

The passion in his voice, the breathless force of it, is enough to make me shiver. "You're not a damsel to me, Bree. You're a warrior. You're strong and you're beautiful and you're brilliant and brave." He presses his forehead against mine, his eyes squeezed shut, and takes a slow, ragged breath. "And I'd *really* like to kiss you."

"Oh," I squeak, and immediately wish I'd thought of something more to say. *Anything* more.

He chuckles, his clean, minty breath already intimate against my mouth. "Oh, 'no'? Or oh, 'yes'?" He pulls back to meet my eyes, and there is affection and something more flickering in their heated depths. It's the something more that sends an arc of electricity through my body.

"The second o—" He tilts my chin and presses his mouth against mine, warm and soft.

I've read books, watched movies, whispered secret wishes to Alice in the darkness of bunk-bed sleepovers. I expect this kiss to feel an awkward sort of good.

I don't expect each gentle brush of Nick's lips to shift, grow insistent—and set me on fire.

The distant sounds of early morning birds fade away when Nick's fingers smooth up the column of my throat, angling my face so that our mouths connect more fully. My fingers clutch at his T-shirt, pulling closer until I am all feeling and no thought: my heart pounding with his, the heat of his chest against mine, the strength of his thigh pressing into my own. Someone gasps for air; then we find each other again. I make a sound in the back of my throat that should be embarrassing, but Nick consumes it with a low hum against my mouth, drawing me forward until we're flush. In that instant, I feel the two sides of our famil-iar dance. The call and response of trust and loyalty, intermingling until they become a melody. A beautiful truth that circles in the wind, swirling against my mind, growing louder until everyone, everyone must hear it too.

I don't know what our kiss is becoming—just as his lips ghost over my jaw, just as his fingers feather over my sternum, we hear someone's feet crunching down the gravel road behind us.

"Nick? That you?" Russ.

I instinctively freeze, but Nick lifts his head, a frustrated groan rising from his chest.

Another voice nearby. "Who's that—?" Oh God. Evan too. "Whoa!"

At some point, we'd rotated so that my back is toward the way we'd come, and Nick is facing Russ and Evan's disembodied voices. Thank the Lord, too, because I can duck my face into Nick's shoulder and catch my breath instead of die of mortification in front of frat boy *Evan Cooper*.

Evan crows. "Oh-kayyy, y'all! Sheeit . . . ! Get it!" He's wheezing with laughter.

"Is this a good morning kiss or a good night kiss?" Russ calls, the sound of a grin all over his voice. "Are we coming or going?"

"Kinda busy right now, guys." I can't help but feel a little thrill at the steel underneath Nick's hoarse voice.

"Oh, we can *see* that." Russ laughs at his own joke while Evan says, "Sorry to interrupt, my liege! Please, proceed with thy gentle tonguing!"

They both laugh a long time at that, and even I crack a grin into the soft fabric of Nick's shirt. They walk around us, whooping and cheering the entire way down the gravel road toward campus.

As soon as they get out of earshot, Nick sighs, pulling me tighter into the circle of his arms. "You okay?"

I nod into his chest and press my ear to it. We stand there in comfortable silence. After a few minutes, both our hearts slow from a rapid gallop to a steady thump. My lips still tingle and the fine hairs on my arms are alert with want, but I sigh into it all rather than act on it.

For the first time in a long while, I let myself enjoy a moment of warmth and safety without wondering if it's real.

25

"TONIGHT?" ALICE'S VOICE goes near supersonic in my ear.

"Yeahhhh," I say as I stroll through campus. It's a gorgeous day, and I navigate the brick pathways with a smile on my face. On Wednesday it was surreal to walk among thousands of Carolina students who had no idea what really went on at their school. Now it's Friday and that secret feels like nothing at all.

Reality sure does change after a kiss like that.

After he'd walked me home yesterday morning, Nick and I'd been texting each other constantly. I pretty much wore a perma-grin the entire day. This morning he sent a text asking me to go out with him and the other Legendborn tonight. I'd said yes, and then, like any good best friend, texted Alice. She'd called me back right away. I only have a few minutes to talk before I meet with Patricia, but I have to agree with Alice—melting on the phone with my best friend about any Nick-plus-lips topics is worth a quick phone call.

"Where?"

"Some bar downtown? A beer garden? I'm not sure."

She laughs. "You mean you don't care."

"Not really." I don't. I'm buzzing and eager to see Nick again.

"Okay, so is this a date?"

I turn down a narrow walkway while I think about her question. "Is it a date if there are like twenty other people around?"

"Wellll," Alice starts. In the background I can hear the murmur of voices and the *shhhhh* sound of wind; she's on her way to class somewhere near mid-campus. "I think it is if you act like it is. If it feels like it's just the two of you, then it's a date, no matter who else is around."

"Um, how are you this wise?"

"I read a lot of books. Next question: What are you gonna wear?"

"Um . . ." Patricia waves at me from where she's sitting against one of the campus's ubiquitous low stone walls. I wave back and hope she doesn't misinterpret the blanket of terror that has just taken over my expression. I hadn't even *thought* about what to wear on a date.

"Bree!" Alice cries.

I'm a few feet from Patricia now, and not a second too soon. "Gotta go, Alice."

"No! My parents are picking me up this afternoon, so I won't be there to be your glam squad. Do I need to call Charlotte? She's got cute clo—"

"Bye, Alice!" She grumbles but says goodbye. It's a bummer that she won't be around tonight. I make a mental note to at least text her a selfie before I go.

"Sorry about that," I say to Patricia, and tuck my phone into my messenger bag.

"No need to apologize." Patricia beams. Her burgundy lipstick matches today's shawl. "Thank you for meeting me here."

I look past her to take in our meeting location for the first time. I hadn't thought much of the cemetery during the campus tour; it was common for old towns in former colony states like North Carolina to have historic graveyards in the middle of a modern development. I certainly hadn't imagined I'd visit it during what was supposed to be a therapy appointment. "I did kinda wonder why you'd bring me here, not gonna lie."

"I'd be worried if you hadn't. No quizzes this time," she says, tugging her shawl tighter. "I brought you here because I've decided that I'd like to help you, and I believe this is the best place to start." Without waiting for my response, she starts toward the entrance of the cemetery, which is really just an open gap in the low wall.

"A graveyard?"

Her pace is surprisingly quick, considering how much shorter her legs are than mine. I have to take a few quick steps to catch up.

"Indeed."

The sky is a bright Carolina blue overhead, and the Old Chapel Hill Cemetery, part green lawn, part wooded preserve, is probably the most beautiful graveyard ever. It feels like a hidden park, a respite away from the throngs of students bent over their phones on the way to class, professors chatting on the way to the campus coffee shop.

Bits and pieces from the campus tour come back to me as we walk: When UNC was founded in the late eighteenth century, it began with one building—my dorm, Old East. Only a few years after it opened, a student died unexpectedly and was buried on an empty tract of land not far from the then center of the campus. As the campus expanded, the university marked the perimeter of the cemetery with informational placards and a low rock wall built sometime in the early 1800s to separate it from the rest of the grounds.

"So this is how you're going to help me understand my mother?"

Patricia huffs a bit as the path winds upward past an enormous crape myrtle. "I don't know very much about your mother, Bree, so understanding is a tall order. But I know about root."

"So the cemetery is where you'll teach me about root?"

"It's the starting point," she repeats enigmatically. "The root of root, if you will." She chuckles at her own joke, and I give up on pressing her.

The carved headstones we pass at the edge of the cemetery were made of polished, reflective granite. The engravings look freshly cut, even though they are ten, twenty, thirty years old. Some of them even have fresh flowers. Most grave markers are simple, flat stone squares with metal nameplates. Some are taller, solid rectangles atop stone slabs. There's even a courtyard of mausoleums, for some rich family, probably. But as we get closer to the middle, the markers are getting older, changing shapes. Mildew-stained obelisks, thinner tombstones with two and three sets of names on them. Long names, births and deaths in the early 1900s and late 1800s.

Patricia walks us past older gray headstones onto a narrow path that leads to another section of graves. "The cemetery is managed by the town, and everyone buried here was associated with the university or town in one way or another."

"Like deans and professors?"

"Mhm-hm," she hums. "Originally, it was used to bury students who died while enrolled, and faculty. That's the oldest section. The first was a young DiPhi boy buried in the late 1700s. Five more sections were added after that. A mix of faculty and staff, town philanthropists and donors, famous alumni and the like."

We come to a stop at an ancient-looking stone wall that runs the width of the cemetery.

"Notice anything?"

"I thought you said no quizzes." She tilts her head, her mouth folded in a secret smile, and it reminds me that Patricia holds all the cards here. And they're cards I want.

I scan the way we've come. We've been walking on dirt paths, pounded flat and hard and made smooth over time by many feet. They serve a dual purpose: they silently direct visitors to avoid walking directly on any of the graves, but they also separate sections of the cemetery. Beyond the boundaries of the cemetery, cars whoosh by toward the football stadium, but other than that, the only sounds are birds and wind. The Bell Tower erupts in Westminster Quarters. When it ends, a lone bell tells us it's two fifteen.

I stare at her, confused, but take another look at where we've stopped walking. On the other side over the stone wall is a grove. "There's only a few stone markers here." I point to a back corner, shaded by a low tree. "A few tombstones over there. It's barely filled."

"Oh, it's filled. This wall marks where the segregation begins. All the Black folks are buried in these two sections." She tips her head toward the grass beyond the wall.

My stomach twists at her words. This is not what I imagined therapy to be. This is not what anyone's therapy looks like, I'm fairly positive. She wraps her shoulders in the shawl and continues.

"Some were enslaved folk owned by faculty and kept on campus to help build and maintain the school. Some were servants or freed folk after slavery ended in this part of the Confederacy." She sighs, nodding her head at the grass over the wall. "That memorial over at the Arboretum is the pretty acknowledgment, the polite one. But the blood? The blood's buried here."

"Why aren't there any . . ." I swallow, suddenly wanting nothing else but to run from this place—this place that feels too close to home, too horrifying.

"Almost all are unmarked. People used fieldstones or wooden crosses, whatever someone could afford, or was deemed worthy. Some graves still have a bit of yucca or periwinkle, or a tree you can tell was planted deliberately," she says, pointing at plants scattered throughout the grass. "Families and community members did that, I suspect. In the eighties, folks used this section for football game parking, so who knows what was destroyed then. They did a preservation study not long ago using radar of some sort. Found almost five hundred unmarked graves in the ground in these two sections and the one on the other side of the wall, but a Medium could have told them that." She smiles, a bit of canny mischief sparking in her eyes. She walks through an opening in the wall and steps gingerly into the grass, turning when she realizes that I'm not following. I'm staring at the earth beneath our feet.

"Five hundred?"

"Yep."

I swallow. "Do I really have to walk on the grass? I could be walking right over someone's grave."

"You will be." Patricia turns away with a smile. "But we'll acknowledge them. Thank them."

I huff and let loose a long breath, then follow her footsteps, imagining that maybe she knows where the graves are and has avoided them for us both. We stop at an unmarked section of grass.

"This is where two of my ancestors are buried," Patricia says simply, as if she were just sharing where one could find a glass in a cupboard. *This is where the cups are. Here's where to find the mugs.* She sits down cross-legged in her long skirt.

I instinctively step back, but she regards me with a raised brow. "Sit."

I kneel carefully. The freshly mowed grass is warm and spiky on my bare legs.

I sit cross-legged in front of her as she opens the velvet pouch she'd been carrying and sets out a few stones on the ground between us: a bright green one shaped like a small, gnarled fist; a purple-and-white stone with a few rocky points—amethyst, I think; and a smoky quartz. To my surprise, Patricia arranges a few other items in front of us, items I'd never thought to bring to a grave: a smaller pouch with a bit of fruit in it, a plate with cornbread, and an empty mug that she fills with tea.

"I don't know who my ancestors are, past my great-grandmother anyway."

Patricia shrugs. "Lots of Black folks in the States don't know their people more than four, five generations back, don't know names before the late 1800s—and why would they? We didn't exactly inherit detailed family records when we were freed." She keeps arranging her offerings, not looking in my direction as she does.

I'm filled with a sour sense of betrayal, akin to the feeling I felt looking up at the Order's Wall. "I never even met my grandmother."

Patricia's head tilts toward me, her expression curious. "You never met your grandmother?"

I bristle. "No."

"She died before you were born?"

"Yes."

"No aunts on her side of the family? Great-aunts?"

"No." Frustration sparks in me, like a match has struck my insides, turned them to fire. Suddenly, my skin feels too tight all over my body. The fine hairs on the back of my neck lift. My vision blurs. I don't need to be reminded how alone I am. How lost.

"Bree, breathe." She speaks softly, but her order is firm. "Take slow breaths in through your nose." I hear Patricia speak, but her voice arrives from far away.

I do as she says until my heart slows down, but my throat is still the size of a straw. I have to clear it twice to get any words out. "So, what are we doing here?"

She smiles. "Do you trust me?"

I blink. "That's usually what someone says when they're about to do something weird to somebody else."

She grins. "I can handle weird if you can."

I think about all that's happened in the last week of my life. "I can handle real weird."

"Then we'll proceed." She draws herself up tall and folds her hands in her lap. "As you know, there is an invisible energy all around us, everywhere in the world, that only some people know about. Some of those people call it magic, some call it aether, some call it spirit, and we call it root. There is no single school of thought about this energy. Is it an element? A natural resource? I think it is both, but a practitioner in India or Nigeria or Ireland may not agree. The only universal truth about root is who—or what—can access it and how. The dead have the most access to root, and supernatural creatures have the next closest connection, but the living? The living must borrow, bargain for, or steal the ability to access and use this energy. Our people—Rootcrafters—borrow root temporarily, because we believe that energy is not for us to own." She waves a hand over her stones and food. "We make offerings to our ancestors so that they will share root with us for a time. And then, after it's returned, we thank them for being a bridge to its power. This is the unifying philosophy of our practice. Beyond that, families have their own variations, their own flavors, if you will. So it has always been, and so it is."

"You said you don't know how my family practiced."

"I don't. In your circumstance, it seems your family's way is gone. All I can do is introduce you to the craft as my family understands it, using my way of sharing its truths."

It makes sense, but . . . "What do you do with root?"

As Patricia looks at me, a soft, fuzzy warmth falls across my cheeks and nose, like sunlight uncovered. "Take my hands, and I'll show you."

Once I take her hands, there's a heartbeat of sensation—her skin is warm, dry, and soft—before the world around us twists, then disappears.

PART THREE

ROOTS

26

IT FEELS LIKE the hand of the universe has reached inside me and just . . . *pulled.*

The sensation of movement is so strong—I'm flying, expanding—then, just as suddenly, it stops.

I fall forward on my palms, dizzy and heaving large gulps of dusty air. Air that clings to the back of my throat and coats my mouth with the taste of copper.

"You're all right, Bree." Patricia's voice soothes from somewhere near my shoulder. She's standing beside me, her small, flat dress shoes right at my wrist. I open my eyes to find that my hands are spread wide on packed, crumbling clay that's been brushed and smoothed into an even surface. A floor. I'm *inside* a building. No, a cabin.

But we were just outside in the graveyard.

A woman moans nearby, a strangled sound of pain. My head snaps up to find the source, and I nearly fall forward again.

The small, rectangular space is lit only by a waist-high fireplace in the middle of the longest wall. The walls are made of rough-hewn wooden planks, and between every few boards are small scraps of cloth stuffed between gaps to shore up the openings against the night. Beside me on the dirt floor are two thin blankets, smudged brown, with tattered and uneven edges. Once I see the fireplace, the heat of it hits my face and I know then that this is not a dream, that this is real.

And so are the two figures in front of its hearth: a Black woman lying prone on an area of straw-covered ground whose body is mostly blocked from my sight, and the other, a middle-aged Black woman bent over her companion and wearing a long, plain dress and a white cotton cap.

The prone woman moans again, and the other soothes in a low, reassuring voice. "Hold tight, Abby, hold tight. Mary's coming."

Abby hisses in response, and it's the sound of sudden pain, so sharp it steals one's breath.

"Where are we?" My voice is barely a whisper and is almost lost to the sound of Abby's cries. I push up to my feet. Beside me, Patricia's face is pinched as she takes in the scene before us.

She speaks full-voiced, no whisper. "About twenty-five miles from where we sat down in the graveyard."

"How did—"

Patricia's face is a strange mixture of sorrow and pride. "The branch of my root allows me to work memories, understand their energy and power over our present day. I've taken you on a memory walk: a sort of time travel, if you will, into a memory of my ancestor, Louisa, whose grave we visited. It's a bit unorthodox for a memory worker to bring someone from outside the family along for a walk, but I'd hoped my intentions would be clear. With my offering, I asked Louisa to help me show you the world, and the people, that birthed our craft. And this is the memory Louisa chose." She inclines her head toward Abby, whose body I still cannot see clearly. I can just make out her head and shoulders. Her wide-set doe eyes are framed with the long lashes people pay to re-create, and her tight curls are thick and full around a heart-shaped bronze face. She can't be more than twenty.

"This is an example of the circumstances that strengthened the alliance of energy between our living and our dead, forming the tradition we call Rootcraft."

A chill runs through me, even with the fireplace cooking the room. "We're *inside* a memory?"

No one of the Order has ever mentioned anything like this. Sel is an illusionist and a caster, and he can manipulate memories with his mesmer, but traveling *into* them?

"Yes," Patricia affirms. "I know this one well, actually. This is early June, 1865. A couple months after the Battle of Appomattox, but before Juneteenth. We need to move closer. Mary is almost here." She takes a step forward, but I hang back, shaking my head, because I can guess the source of the suffocating, terrifying copper smell: blood. Lots of it.

When Patricia notices that I'm not behind her, she takes in my expression, and sympathy falls across her face. "It's all right to be scared, Bree. Like many true things, this is awful, and hard. If it helps, Abby endures, with the help of Mary. She lives a long life after this night."

It does help, some.

"Won't they see us?" I ask, watching as Louisa squeezes a wet cloth into a nearby bucket, worry etched across her brown face. Even in crisis, her hands are steady.

"No. Louisa's spirit brought us here, but what's past is past. We are observers only. She can't see or hear us, and neither can anyone else."

I gnaw on my cheek. "But why did she choose this memory?"

"You'll see. Come." Patricia offers me her hand, and I take it.

As we approach, the rickety door of the cabin swings inward and a young, dark-skinned woman wearing a deep beige dress sweeps into the room, focus pulling her elegant features tight. "What happened?"

Louisa exhales in relief, pushing herself to standing. The whole front of her dress is streaked with drying blood. "That rat-faced boy Carr got to her."

Louisa moves back as Mary steps forward. She has a bag made from cloth in one hand, and as she kneels, she starts working on the knot at the top. "What'd he say she do?"

A sneer mars Louisa's pretty features. "Same old mistruths. Gettin' uppity with some white woman on the street, talking back to her or some such nonsense."

Mary's got the bag open now and spreads it out over the dirt. Inside are bundled herbs, small green glass bottles of murky liquids, and some plants freshly pulled from the ground, moist soil still clinging to their spindly roots.

Her mouth twists in a grimace. "Bet you that boy's got a different story every time he tells it."

Louisa's so furious her fists shake at her sides. "Chloe said she ran to the garrison for help when I *told* this girl over and over that they ain't here to protect us, they here to keep us in line. Carr dragged her out." Louisa's eyes turn hard as flint. "Left her there on the ground, passed out from the whip. Me and Chloe carried her back here, and she woke up halfway. I been keeping her calm, but—"

"Mary?" Abby's voice is a reedy whisper.

"I'm here, Abby," Mary assures the other woman while her hands work at the materials on the floor.

Patricia has been pulling me forward slowly. We're at the hearth now, and I can finally see what's happened to Abby.

Her back is torn open like a great cat has used her spine for a scratching post. Long stripes of split flesh crisscross from shoulder to hip, some thin as a razor, others open wide enough to reveal folds of tissue in pinks and reds that I've only seen at the butcher. The whip took skin and cloth, leaving both her body and dress in shreds.

A human did this to another human. Some boy did *this* to Abby over some perceived slight. She ran for help and no one gave it to her. They handed her over to a boy who tore her body open and left her for dead.

Fury builds in me like venom. A sharp, dangerous feeling I've never felt about someone I haven't met. *"Carr."*

Patricia nods. "His monument is on the quad."

"His monument?" I turn to her, enraged that this monster is honored at Carolina or anywhere else.

She sighs heavily. "Everything has two histories. Especially in the South."

I search her features for the anger that I'm feeling, but her face is a tired mask. She must feel it. She *must*.

Patricia stares back as if she knows what I'm thinking. "Never forget. Be angry. And channel it." She reaches for my hand and grips it tight, and it's the only thing keeping me from swaying to the ground. "Watch. This is the heart of Rootcraft, Bree. Protection from those who would harm us, and, if they do, healing so that we can survive, resist, and thrive."

I watch Mary settle on her knees, palms facing up on her lap. I watch as she begins chanting beneath her breath, a low pulse that feels like warm drums beating in my feet, in my belly, my heart. Then, I watch as those drums become more than a feeling, as they take shape and become visible.

Light curls up from Mary's knuckles and coats her palms and wrists, as yellow flames grow and pulse along her skin.

"Mage flame," I whisper in awe. Patricia startles beside me, but somehow, that doesn't feel like it matters. Not when I see Mary lean forward over Abby's back until her glowing golden hands hover over the injuries and the wounds begin to slowly, slowly close. Not when Mary's breathing and Abby's ragged breaths come together until their chests rise and fall in the same rhythm, and the root knits muscle to muscle, muscle to fascia, skin to skin.

The smells of honey and blood mix together in my nose and mouth.

The two women breathe together for a long, long time, while the blood of Mary's ancestors comes forward to heal wounds wrought by a horse whip in the hands of an evil man.

Finally, Mary leans back, beads of sweat glistening on her forehead.

But Abby's wounds have not fully closed. "She's not done, is she?"

"She is."

"But Abby's still bleeding!"

"Look at the herbs."

Beside Mary's knees, the bundles of plants and herbs have turned withered and black. The moist roots have dried and curled into small, sooty fists. "I don't understand."

"Wildcrafters borrow power from their ancestors in order to use the energy of the plants. That power is finite, and so is the living energy of plants, as is Mary's ability to operate as a vessel, as with all crafters of her branch." Illustrating Patricia's words, Mary herself sways on her knees. Louisa rushes to her side to help steady her.

I shake my head. This is not what I've seen William do. He can close wounds fully, seal them up and heal them almost overnight. When I think of him and Sel and the other Awakened Scions, their power seems to have no limit. Why? Why not Mary's? "But Abby's still in pain."

"She's saved Abby from deadly infection. Abby's body will heal the rest of the way. Perhaps if another Wildcrafter were nearby, but even then, the ancestors may not allow a double treatment. We can't turn them on and off like a tap. They *allow* us to use their power, after all."

"Bless you, Mary," Abby whispers, her voice drowsy with exhaustion. "Bless you."

"Of course," Mary soothes as Louisa helps her to her feet. "Rest now."

"Mary, stay," Louisa says, gesturing over to the blankets I'd seen earlier. "You need rest too. The ancestors used you up, I expect."

Mary nods in agreement, her eyes half-lidded. "All right." Louisa guides her to the far end of the cabin, walking right past us, and helps lower Mary to the smooth clay floor.

"What did you say earlier?" Patricia tugs on my hand. "About Mary's power?"

I watch Mary settle under Lousia's blankets and feel an urge to give her my sweatshirt, my socks. Anything that could help her or Louisa or Abby feel warmer. "Mage flame. I saw her gather aether—root—into her palms before she healed Abby. It's the same color of aether surrounding the Unsung Founders Memorial."

She moves into my field of vision, eyes round. "You can see root?"

Her question catches me off guard. "You can't?"

A mixture of wonder and confusion transforms her face. "I *feel* it, but I don't see it. A Reader or a Medium or a Prophet could, perhaps, if she asked the ancestors to lend her their eyes. But never for more than a short time." Her expression shifts. "Who taught you these words, Bree?"

I don't want to lie. "The Order of the Round Table."

Dismay overtakes Patricia's features, and suddenly the air in the cabin runs cool. *"Bloodcrafters,"* she whispers, fear plain on her face.

"Is—is that another word for the Legendborn?" I stammer. "The way you call aether 'root'?"

"No, not just a word." She wraps her hands around mine, drawing them together between our bodies. The softness of her skin is only a sheath. Underneath, her hands are unyielding steel. "Bloodcrafters don't *borrow* power from their ancestors, they steal it. Bind it to their bodies for generations and generations."

"I—I know about the bloodlines," I sputter, a pool of dread forming in my stomach. "What they use their powers for, what they fight."

"Then you know their sins," Patricia says. "Bloodcraft is a curse brought to life."

Patricia's eyes hold every Legendborn horror I've heard of and witnessed, every evil I've imagined, and then some: the Merlin who stole my mother from me. The Merlin who took Nick's. Sel's ruthlessness. The Regents. Fitz's losses. The Lieges who abused a child they called king. "They're . . . It's—"

"Colonizer magic. Magic that *costs* and *takes*. Many practitioners face demons. Many of us face evil. But from the moment their founders arrived, from the moment they *stole* Native homelands, the Order themselves gave the demons plenty to feed on! They reap what their magic sows."

Suddenly, Louisa appears mere inches beside us. Patricia releases me, and we both stumble back. Then, without warning, Louisa turns her head, her eyes looking vaguely in my direction.

"I thought she couldn't see us?" I gasp.

Patricia's brows furrow as she watches her ancestor search the space where my head is. "She can't."

But Louisa's brown eyes fasten to mine like a button snapping into place, throwing sparks on my skin. "I see you," she whispers harshly.

Before I can say another word, Louisa wraps her hands around my elbow, and the world disappears again.

I open my eyes, gasping and choking on the tight clenching sensation around my spine. The feeling is less dizzying than the first memory walk, but I have to bend over, hands on knees to catch my breath before I can look at my surroundings.

I'm in another cabin like the first, but this one is smaller, brighter, and full of bustling Black women. Again, a woman's wail fills the space, a single torturous note drawn out, then ending. Voices of encouragement, another low moan.

"What was *that*?" I turn to ask Patricia. But Patricia is not with me. There is only Louisa.

The older woman stands beside me, still in her bloody dress, and stares across the cabin without answering me. Her eyes track two women who exit through a side door carrying a heavy metal pail held between them.

Seeing that she's not going to explain what she just did—or how she can see me at all—I try another question. "Where are we?"

Louisa answers without looking at me. "Not far from my home in the other memory. The better question is when, girl."

I stand up. "When are we?"

"Fifty years from my time, when my grandmother was young."

"1815. Why did you bring me here?"

Louisa regards me with shrewd eyes. "Because you need to see this."

"Where is Patricia?"

"So many questions!" Louisa snorts. "My descendant is back in her time. You'll return when we're done. Come." She grips me hard around the elbow and pulls without care that I'm stumbling behind her. The closer we get, the stronger the hot, copper smell of blood grows.

And then, the loud wail of a newborn.

Three women in long dresses kneel around a fourth, who has just given birth. The mother—a young girl who's maybe eighteen or nineteen—is propped up on blood-soaked blankets wrapped around a lumpy collection of straw and grass. Her skirts are bunched around her waist, her hands wrapped like vises around her bent knees. She's panting, exhausted, and sweaty, but the fierce determination on her warm golden-brown face makes her . . . striking. Gorgeous.

"It's Pearl that's just had the baby," Louisa says. She jerks her chin at the other three women, the youngest of whom looks Pearl's age and the others in their late twenties. "Cecilia, Betty, and Katherine."

"You know them?"

Louisa smirks and points out the youngest woman. "That's my mother's mother. She brought us here."

Cecilia wipes at Pearl's forehead while Betty works at the afterbirth. It's Katherine who holds the crying baby out of sight, wiping it down, I think, with one of the wet rags hanging over a pail of water. My eyes are drawn to a bloody blade on a wooden board beside her. It's hard to not think of the risks here—germs, infection, dirty water—even though I know women have done this for centuries with the same or less. "Why did she bring me here?"

Louisa tilts her head. "I don't know."

Katherine hisses, a sharp intake of air that turns everyone's heads. Pearl, a new mother on high alert, reaches for her child. "What is it, Kath? Is he all right?" Katherine turns around, and for the first time I can see the baby wrapped in her arms. He's still stained with blood, wrinkled and wet. His cries have gone quiet, replaced now with whimpers. Betty moves closer, and she and Katherine exchange glances. Pearl notices this too. "Betty? Something wrong?" Pearl asks cautiously, her eyes darting between the two other women. "Am I still bleeding bad?"

Betty shakes her head. "Seen worse. The bleeding's not the problem."

Pearl is frantic now. "Then give him to me!"

"Give him to her, Kath," Betty says quietly. Katherine obliges and passes the newborn to his mother. When Pearl reaches out, worry and love are written on her face. When she holds her baby close, a quiet horror takes over.

Over her shoulder, Cecilia gasps. "His eyes!"

A small curl of apprehension buzzes along my skin.

Maybe Cecilia has that feeling too, because she looks ready to bolt from Pearl's side.

Katherine shakes her head. "Told you not to mess with that red-eyed devil, but you did, didn't you? Ain't nothing good coming from a man you meet at the crossroads, Pearl. Nothing."

Pearl's eyes are filled with tears. She shakes her head twice, to deny Katherine or to deny what she's seeing, I don't know. "He's my son," she says with a trembling lip.

I speak to Louisa without looking, my feet already moving closer to the scene. "What's wrong with his eyes?"

"A crossroads child," Louisa says cryptically.

She doesn't stop me or call me back. I'm almost at Pearl's side, and my hands are shaking like my entire body already knows what's wrong with this baby. What—and who—he'll look like.

"He may look like a baby, but that is their disguise," Katherine says, sadness and chastisement equally strong in her voice. "They cannot be trusted because it is in their nature to lie. You *know* this, Pearl. Just like his father, he will turn on you one day."

I'm close enough to see the newborn now, standing between his mother and Cecilia. I lean forward, Pearl's desperate voice loud in my ear. "He is my child!" And I see what I dreaded I might.

Two amber eyes, glowing and bright, stare up at Pearl from the baby's soft brown face.

Then, defying Patricia's comprehension like Louisa before her, Cecilia grips my elbow. Her eyes blaze with awareness and lock firmly with mine. I try to turn away from their fire, their burning—but she holds fast. "This is not a child," she says fiercely. "It is a monster."

The world spins and disappears again.

After we land, Cecilia pulls me with her in a fast walk. I don't need to turn to know that Louisa is not with us. "This way."

We're back at Carolina, and it's the pitch black of the middle of the night. Cecilia drags me toward the center of the campus at a dizzying pace.

"Why did you show me that?"

"Because you needed to see it," Cecilia says breathlessly, echoing Louisa's earlier words.

"I needed to see that baby?" I gasp. "What was he?"

She explains without stopping. "A crossroads child, born of a crossroads man. The father walked among us and shared our form, but in truth he was a demon born of the shadows. The child is half-human."

I trip at Cecilia's cold, distant explanation. She yanks on my hand to pull me up.

Born of the shadows, but shaped like a man. A crossroads man. Is that what Rootcrafters call a goruchel? If I hadn't seen it with my own eyes, I'd never think such a union could be possible. "What happened to Pearl's baby?"

"They forced her to cast it away before it could grow large enough to do harm."

Cast away.

"We are close now. Pay attention."

I look around. I don't know when we are, but it must be somewhat recent, because I recognize the buildings, the trees, the walking paths. "Are you taking me back to Patricia?"

"No. It's Ruth that wanted you here."

"Who is Ruth?"

Cecilia doesn't answer, nor does she seem interested in talking. She stops us near a stone bench tucked under an old-growth poplar. Before I can ask another question, a familiar-looking woman walks past, hands tucked in her pockets, a modern messenger bag slung over her shoulder. She looks every bit a student.

"Ruth. Patricia's sister."

My eyes widen. Patricia's *sister*?

Cecilia pulls me along with her again until we're walking beside Ruth, who doesn't seem to see us. She has headphones in, the old wired kind with a metal band over her straight brown bob.

The three of us—an enslaved woman from the nineteenth century, a teenage girl from the twenty-first, and a college student from the twentieth—weave between Carolina students lingering in the low brick courtyard of the Pit. I don't know what will happen if I touch the undergrads nearby, and I don't want to find out. We descend the steps down to the street level behind the Stores, and Ruth leads us down South Road and through the crosswalk toward the very center of UNC's campus—the Bell Tower. Once we reach the edge of the Tower's shadow, Ruth freezes, then abruptly ducks down behind one of the Tower lawn's hedge borders and yanks her headphones from her ears.

"Why'd she stop?" I ask.

Cecilia points. "Because of them."

Together, the three of us peer into the shadows behind the brick patio at the base of the structure, where a hooded figure stands in a dark patch of grass on the far side of the lawn, nearly hidden from sight. Whoever they are, they have placed themselves strategically, pausing right where the imposing landmark shields them from late-night passersby and blocks the dull orange glow of campus lampposts. The sound of low, harsh chanting reaches my ears. It's not English. Not the Order's Welsh, either.

I sway on my feet while listening, momentarily captivated. I've taken a half step forward before I snap out of the sudden daze. I shudder. Something isn't right, here beneath the Tower's shadow.

Cecilia nudges me. "Go on. Get closer. They can't see you."

"Just like you and Louisa couldn't see me?" I hiss.

"Forces bigger than Patricia are at work with you," Cecilia says, narrowing her eyes. "Her original walk has been pulled into the current of our family's ancestral energy like a leaf in a river. The ancestors won't release you until they're done. Now, go." She shoves me hard until I move around the hedge onto the lawn.

As I approach, the chanting figure turns away so all I can see is their black hooded sweatshirt and jeans. They look over their shoulder, as if a noise has caught their attention—maybe Ruth—and I freeze, but they look right through me like I'm not even there.

Even two feet away, I can't make out their features. The hood is pulled low, but even their nose and mouth are shadowed shapes. Satisfied that they're alone, the figure turns back, fishing out a small item from their pocket. A vial of dark liquid. The figure unscrews the vial and pours it over a gloved hand. It's blood, I realize, and they coat their palms and fingers until the leather is glistening.

They walk slowly across the grass while swiping their bloodied glove in the air, palm out, leaving an arc of green mage flame in their wake. The flame hangs in the air like an emerald rainbow, then turns into liquid. Glowing aether flows down to the ground in thick trails. The figure backs away, chanting, and the aether spreads until it's a shining veil taller than a man and at least twenty feet across. There's a roaring sound, rising like a wave in my ears, and then a thick tear.

I feel the tug on my spine again, but just before the world disappears for the last time, I see dozens of partially corporeal clawed feet extend through the veil and land on the grass. A low howl begins out of sight, the garbled sound growing clearer, louder . . .

Hellhounds.

I come to with a gasp, sitting just as I was before Patricia's walk. There's a sound I can't quite parse. An "—ee" sound. I hear it again. "—ee?" A question. I blink and see Patricia on her knees, her hands trembling on my shoulders. Her mouth moves, and this time I hear it. "Bree?"

"Patricia."

"Oh, thank God." She pulls me in tight for a hug, then sits back. "You were here, but you weren't here. Breathing but unresponsive. Louisa wouldn't let me call on her again. I had a feeling I should wait, but—"

I shake my head to clear it of the fog, but the memories—my memories now—cling. Images paint the inside of my mind, pulsing through my consciousness like drums. Abby's back. Mary's hands. Bloodcrafters. The determined look on Pearl's face. The crossroads child and his golden-orange gaze. The Shadowborn Gate.

A pack of hellhounds crossing to our world.

My eyes find Patricia's. "You have a sister named Ruth."

She blinks. "I did. She passed a few years ago."

"Oh," I whisper. "I didn't realize."

Patricia smiles like she knows what I'm thinking. "I've walked with her. I miss her, and yet I see her when I need to. Why do you ask?"

"Because I walked with her too. When she went to school here. When was she enrolled?"

"She graduated maybe twenty-five years ago. Why?"

It feels like she's just punched me in the gut. My mother was at Carolina twenty-five years ago, maybe living in a dorm not far from where Ruth was that night.

Then, I remember what Louisa showed me—Pearl's baby that was cast away, the red-eyed man who was its father—and dread in my stomach grows until it chills me through. "I have to go."

"Go where?" Patricia blinks. "What did you see?"

"They showed me those memories on purpose," I murmur, scrambling to my feet. "I'm sorry, I've got to go."

"Bree! What happened?"

"I'm sorry!" I'm already pulling my phone out of my pocket as I run.

Nick doesn't answer my call, but it doesn't deter me. I have every intention of sprinting through campus and straight on to the Lodge, until I realize I have to stop somewhere first.

Because as urgent as my new missions are, I have to see it.

When I reach the statue, it's like I'm looking at it for the first time.

Carr stands in full Civil War uniform with a long-barreled rifle grasped in both hands. The sculptor, whoever he was, made sure that Carr's spine was straight, his shoulders back, and his chin up. A soldier proudly standing for a war that wasn't won.

That venomous rage returns.

Heart pounding for too many reasons to count, I think back on the Wall of Ages and its Lines and the mixture of disconnection and frustration I'd felt staring at it. Then, from the monument's place of honor at the top of Carolina's campus, I look back on the school's buildings and manicured lawns and brick walkways. I let my gaze draw lines here, too, from building to building, from tree to tree, from buried lives to beaten ones, from blood stolen to blood hidden. I map this terrain's sins, the invisible and the many, and hold them close. Because even if the pain of those sins takes my breath away, that pain feels like belonging, and ignoring it after all I've just witnessed would be loss.

I stand at that statue and claim the bodies whose names the world wants to forget. I claim those bodies whose names *I* was taught to forget. And I claim the unsung bloodlines that soak the ground beneath my feet, because I know, I just *know*, that if they could, they would claim me.

I don't know why I do it, really, but before I go, I turn around to face that statue, press both palms against it, and *push*. I imagine all of the hands that built Carolina and suffered on its grounds pushing through my palms too, and while the statue doesn't budge, it feels like I've sent it a message.

Maybe it's my imagination, but I feel stronger. Taller. Like I might have the roots to grow just what I need.

And then, with fire in my veins, I turn on my heel and run.

27

SARAH AND TOR are talking in the foyer when I come hurtling through the front door.

"Bree? Are you all right?" Sarah asks, taking in my disheveled appearance.

"Where's Nick?"

Tor frowns. "Driving his dad to the airport."

Damnit. I'd completely forgotten. Lord Davis is flying to the Northern Chapter to meet with the Regents. "When will he be back?"

"He's meeting us at the Tap Rail tonight in an hour, newbie," Tor says, crossing her arms. "Why?"

The bar. God, I'd forgotten that, too. Which means I can't talk about the Gate and the mysterious figure until later. *One crisis at a time, Matthews.* If Nick and Lord Davis are both gone . . .

"I need William."

Sarah's brows shoot up. "Are you injured?"

"No." I start for the hallway that leads to the elevator, but Tor steps into my path.

"Then why do you need him?"

I glare at her, too tired to play nice. Sarah steps in. "He's downstairs in the infirmary."

"Pages don't go down there unless they're told," Tor protests. "Listen, Matthews, you can't run around doing whatever you want—"

"Torrrrr," Sarah groans. "Bree, go ahead." The look Sarah gives Tor is the look you give someone who tries your very last nerve, even when you love them more than you can stand. It suddenly becomes clear who's really calling the shots between the Scion and her Squire.

Down in the infirmary, I find William alone, sitting in a back corner behind a desk, typing on a silver laptop. He looks up when I enter, but the smile on his face disappears when he sees me. "Are you okay?" he asks, standing up, eyes already searching me for injury.

"I'm fine," I say. "Well, no, I'm not fine."

His face goes from relief to a wary curiosity. "What's going on?"

A nameless red-eyed man rises up behind my eyes, followed by his amber-eyed son. "Sel isn't human."

William's gray eyes widen a fraction. "Sel's our Merlin and Kingsmage."

"I don't mean his *titles*, William!"

A muscle in his jaw twitches. "What's this about?"

I pace as I talk. "Lord Davis made it sound like Merlins are humans who are just naturally magical. But that's not true for Sel, is it?" When I look up, I see the subtle flex of William's fingers, the minute jump of the pulse in his neck. My jaw clenches; I know what secrets look like by now. "You know, don't you?"

"Know what?" he says blithely, reaching for some paperwork.

"That Sel is Shadowborn."

"Close the door," William orders, his voice sterner than I've ever heard.

How many more secrets are there? "I—"

"Please." His lips press into a line.

I follow my friend's command because of the "please," but I feel my trust in him bleeding away with every step I take back to his desk.

William runs a hand through his light hair and releases a long sigh. "I apologize for my tone. This is not information that Pages generally have access to. Hard to sell someone on the war against the evil demon hordes when you have one living under your roof." He smiles stiffly. "Yes. Selwyn is, technically, Shadowborn."

I knew the truth before I walked in the room, but to hear it from William, to have it confirmed . . . "He's a demon. How *could* you—"

"He's *part* demon." William sits back in his chair with his hands folded on his lap.

"How can you trust him? How can *anyone* trust him to—"

He cuts me off. "All Merlins are part demon, Bree. They always have been."

This is not the conversation I thought I was going to have with him. The memory walk is fresh. Behind my eyes, I can still see Pearl's face contorted in fear of her own child. I can still see the midwife backing away from the infant as if it were cursed. *He may look like a baby, but that is their disguise. They cannot be trusted because it is in their nature to lie. You know this, Pearl. Just like his father, he will turn on you one day. . . . This is not a child. It is a monster.* "How can the Order use monsters? Nick's life is in danger. All of these attacks—"

William sighs heavily. "There are protections in place—"

"Protections?" How can he be so *calm* about this? I sputter, "But if he's half demon . . . half uchel—"

"Sel's mother was a Merlin and his father is human. You've heard of incubi and succubi, yes?"

I blink, head spun by the turns in this conversation. "*Sex* demons?"

His mouth widens into a full, amused smile. "Did you just whisper the word 'sex'?"

"No," I retort, flushing around my collar. "I emphasized it."

"Sure, we'll say that," he says, leaning over his desk to pull out a notebook. He grabs a pen and starts sketching a diagram, starting with two circles labeled *MM* and *I*.

I open my mouth, but he stops me again. "I need you to listen. Not talk."

"Willia—"

"*Listen*, Pageling." He points his pen at me. "Give me five minutes."

I take a deep breath. "Fine."

"Thank you," he says primly, and taps the first circle. "Way back in the sixth century, Merlin's mother was a human woman who fell into bed with a powerful goruchel incubus. A little bump, a little grind, and you get a cambion. A child who is part human and part demon." He draws a line between the two circles and a perpendicular line down to another circle, *M*. "Aether affinity in demon blood is dominant. Like, break your Punnett square dominant. Which means that all of Merlin's descendants are cambions too. The people we have come to call Merlins can draw on and use aether almost as well as Merlin himself could, even with only a single drop of his demon blood—no Legendborn Awakening spell needed."

I stare blankly. "All Merlins are part sex demon."

He smirks. "Technically, yes, but at this level of genetic distance, their seductive traits are . . . passive." He waves his hand dismissively. "Nothing that normal human genes couldn't produce, eye color aside. Unnatural beauty, distinctive voice, et cetera. Passive, but still effective. One minute you're taking bloodwork, the next you're wondering if the infirmary bed will hold two people. Don't believe me?" His eyes sparkle as he leans in close. "Just ask Tor."

My stomach flips a bit at his teased revelation. Tor and Sel dated? Or, if not dated, they'd . . . I push it from my mind. "So, he's not . . . *evil?*"

"Volatile, like I said, but not evil." William scratches his chin in thought. "From both a medical and military perspective, Merlins are perfect warriors: hearts like long-distance runners, pumping a leisurely thirty beats per minute; core temps a toasty one hundred and ten degrees Fahrenheit— hot enough to cook a human brain like chicken fried steak, but it means they burn away any human viruses or bugs. Enhanced metabolism, speed, strength, vision—"

"*And hearing!*" The door slams open behind us and Sel sweeps in, yellow eyes blazing.

William bolts out of his chair, hands up. "Sel, calm down!"

I back away as Sel bears down on me, the tips of his hair smoking. "Snooping about me now, are you? Looking for information you can use against me?"

Even though the details of Sel's physiology are still echoing in my ears, after all I've experienced today, I can't stand the idea of letting even Sel, with his superhuman physiology, make me cower. "This is getting real old, Kingsmage. You need new tricks."

Before Sel can respond, William steps in between us in a way I've only ever seen Nick do. "You need to cool down. Bree wasn't snooping. If you're going to get angry at anyone, get angry at me for telling her."

"Oh, I am," Sel growls. His golden eyes rain hot sparks all over me.

"Throwing a temper tantrum, *crossroads child?*" I spit. Both of Sel's dark brows fly up to his hairline, and red spots appear on his cheeks. *Direct hit.*

"Stop it! Both of you!" William orders. He presses his back against me, crowding me into the wall. "If you're going to hurt Bree, you'll have to go through me to do it, which your Oath of Service won't allow. So instead of making a fool of yourself, just walk." He jerks his head toward the door. "Shoo."

Sel glances between the two of us a final time, then leaves the room in an angry blur. In the distance, another door slams, marking his exit.

"Oath of Service?" *How many Oaths are there? And how many has Sel sworn?*

William sighs, still facing the open door and hallway. "Sel's primary Oath is to Nick. His second is to the Legendborn." He turns around to wag a finger in my face. "But he's right about one thing. You're trouble, aren't you?"

At this point, I can't say I disagree.

It's way too easy to convince the bouncer at Tap Rail that I am a twenty-one-year-old Black woman named Monica Staten. I blink down at the NC driver's license in my hand, stunned.

"I can't believe that worked," I say.

Greer winks. "Got it off my roommate, Les. She got it off a girl who graduated last year. When Whitty came by my room earlier and said we were going out, I remembered you're only sixteen. I figure Les uses it all the time, so it was worth a shot."

"Yeah, but this is *really* bad," I say, shaking my head. "It says right here that Monica Staten is like six inches shorter than I am! And she wears glasses."

"What can I say?" They shrug. "White folks' face-blindness for different races is a thing!"

The only thing Monica Staten and I have in common is our taste in fashion;

I'd sent Alice a selfie of my red halter top and jeans, and she'd approved, so that's what I'm wearing.

The chapter has commandeered the entire back wooden porch of Tap Rail, the streetcar turned biergarten on the far end of Franklin Street, Chapel Hill's downtown drag. Two long wooden tables have been pushed together to seat all of us. Nick's last text said he'd be here soon. William had other plans. Sel's nowhere to be found.

I check my phone while I wait. Patricia's called me eight times. I'd sent her a text on the way over saying that I needed to take care of something, and that I'd explain later. Her warnings echo in my mind—Bloodcrafters, curses come to life. I don't doubt that there's truth to what she said. Abatement is evidence enough. But right now I need to talk to Nick and tell him about the Gate.

At the bar inside, Greer chooses a local craft beer right away but changes their mind when Felicity points out that the bar makes a mean Cheerwine and bourbon. The surly bartender mixes a shot of bourbon with soda until it's a deep red-purple and smells like spiked candy.

Felicity hands me a gin and tonic. "Tastes kinda like Sprite."

I almost refuse, but then I think of the conversation I need to have with Nick and suddenly alcohol sounds like a good idea. I take a sip and cough at the burn. "Sprite's a stretch," I say hoarsely.

She shrugs. "I could take it off your hands. How 'bout a whiskey and Coke?"

I choke, mind spinning with thoughts of the occasional scent I pick up in Sel's castings. "No! No whiskey."

Felicity laughs and leans a hip against the bar. "So what are y'all wearing to the Selection Gala?"

I hold up a hand. "Say what now?"

"Oh no." Felicity sets her drink down. "Did no one tell you? I'm so sorry. I guess I thought everyone knew . . ."

Greer grimaces. "Sorry."

I purse my lips. "It's fine."

Felicity is quick to fill me in. "The gala is a big formal event at one of the campus clubs. Dinner, dancing, champagne everywhere. Every year, Vassal families come and schmooze with Page and Legendborn families to celebrate the end of the tournament. After dinner, the Scions who need Squires announce which Page they've chosen. But shopping for dresses is the best part! The Order of the Rose even sends professional hair stylists . . ."

Felicity's voice fades away. I can't wrap my head around a formal dinner party. Or formal wear. Or dancing. Maybe it's the alcohol, but suddenly all I can think of is Nick, standing in front of everyone and announcing his chosen Squire who isn't me.

Felicity's voice returns. "I like an updo, but I think Bree should wear her hair loose. I mean, *look* at these curls!"

Someone—no, *two* someones—tug gently at my hair.

I yank my head away. "What the *hell?*" Both Greer and Felicity have their hands up, surprise clear on their faces. "Don't touch my hair."

Greer looks chagrined. Felicity stammers, "I—I was just telling Greer about the stylist that comes to the Lodge, and *your* hair—"

"Is different than yours?" I snap. "Is curly? Big? Sure, but that doesn't mean you get to touch it whenever you want. I'm not a petting zoo."

"Sorry, Bree," Greer says, flushing.

Felicity blinks, almost starts speaking again, then stops herself. Nods. "Sorry. I didn't realize . . ."

"Yeah." I take a deep breath, nodding. "Well, now you do."

Back at the porch, the group has split into two. The raucous crowd at the table is working on second and third rounds. Someone ordered pitchers. From the lawn comes the irregular *thunk, ga-thunk, thunk* of cornhole. To any outside observer, they're all just a table of college students out for drinks. Not descendants of ancient bloodlines, not healers, or speedsters, or strong women, or warriors. Just kids. To any outside observer, I'm one of them.

Pete is just starting a story about his father hunting a demon on the Appalachian Trail when Nick and Sel walk out onto the porch. It looks like the Kingsmage is taking his job as Nick's personal guard more seriously after Wednesday night's attack. It's the first time I've ever seen them arrive some-where together, or even stand next to each other without fighting. Sel's in dour black, as always, but Nick's in a comfortable-looking *X-Men* tee and a pair of old jeans. After the day I've had, it takes everything in me not to run into his arms, but Russ jumps up instead, clapping Nick on the back and shoving a drink into his hand.

After a few hellos, Nick spots me and makes a beeline toward the end of the table. He drops down on my other side, laundry and cedar on max, and shoves a red-and-white checkered paper basket of bacon-cheddar tater tots in front of me. "Hey."

"Hey." I try not to focus on the way Nick sits so close to me. Or how, after he settles, he doesn't move his body away from mine. Or how warm his bicep and hip are through his clothing. But it's difficult. Suddenly, my low halter-top back feels *too* low. My skin *too* exposed. I'd just spent the last twenty-four hours obsessing over every text, every emoji, but now I'm so attuned to him that his very *closeness* makes me want to run far, far away? *What the hell, Matthews? Get it together.*

Sel takes a spot across from us, tucked back under the overhang, and bal-ances against the wall on the back legs of a chair. He seems plenty happy to keep his eyes on me and doesn't look interested in budging. After our con-frontation and the revelation about his heritage, half of me is screaming to look away, and the other half wants to keep an eye on *him*. The left side of his mouth curls upward in a smirk, like he knows what I'm thinking and finds it amusing.

Ass.

Beside me, Nick tilts his head with a frown, eyes drawn to my mouth. "No smile. Everything okay?"

"Not exactly." How do I talk about what I saw on the memory walk? I witnessed something no one I know has ever seen. How would I even *begin* to talk about it with a blond-haired, blue-eyed boy who would have never been on the receiving end of Carr's whip? Would Cecilia and Ruth even *want* me to share their memories? They hadn't shown them to Patricia.

I don't know how to carry the borrowed images that still feel alive and raw in my body. How does Patricia do it?

"You said you wanted to talk?"

I gesture off to the side of the porch where we can have some privacy. He catches my drift and shoves up from the table, grabbing a tot on the way. Before we can untangle our legs from the picnic table, Vaughn strolls by. Without preamble, he asks, "So, is the Table being reunited or what?"

A beat of silence.

Nick regards the other boy quietly before he answers. "If you're asking if Arthur has Called me yet . . ." He looks down the table at the other listening faces. "If any of you are wondering that, the answer is no. Not yet."

"I got a friend up at Western." Whitty shoves his hands in his pockets beside Evan. "Said they've seen six Shadowborn up there in the last week."

Nick sighs so quietly that only I can hear it. He drops his half-eaten tater tot into the basket and wipes his fingertips. "My dad is talking it over with the Regents tonight and tomorrow. If Tor is Called"—he looks down the table where Sar is perched on Tor's lap—"the plan may change, but for now, we're to sit tight, keep training, and keep our eyes open."

"Here, here!" Evan calls, and those with drinks raise their glasses. Some of the Legendborn toast to their Lines or the Order itself.

Nick and I take the opportunity to slip away and head down the steps to the empty lawn and abandoned cornhole tables. Once we reach the bottom of the stairs, he tugs me into the dark nook underneath the porch and leans down to my ear. "You look great tonight."

I shiver even though the night is hot and muggy. "Thank you."

He laces our fingers together and flashes a small, secret smile. "So, about yesterday morning . . ."

"What about yesterday morning?" I ask, the fresh thrill of being in his orbit returning in a single rush.

That smile stretches into a grin as he shakes his head. "You forget already, B?" He slides one palm up my shoulder to my neck, caresses my collarbone with his thumb. Draws me in until our foreheads touch. "Must have been an awful kiss," he murmurs.

"Terrible," I breathe, and the coiled tension of the day releases by a thread.

"I knew it," he says, then angles his mouth to meet mine—and the sound of a throat clearing beside us breaks us apart.

Sel stands at Nick's elbow. "The drive to the airport was one thing, but now that you're back, I need you to stay in sight."

Nick sighs and releases me. "We need to talk in private for a few minutes, Sel. We aren't leaving." He moves to step around Sel, but Sel follows, stopping us.

The Kingsmage's eyes flick down to our joined hands. "This is a bad idea."

I can't tell if he means our leaving the porch or our holding hands, and Nick's stormy expression says he notices the ambiguity too, and doesn't appreciate it. I didn't realize I'd started to pull away until Nick's hand tightens around mine. "Leave us."

Sel's eyes slide to the crowd over Nick's shoulder, then back. "Is that an order?"

"It is."

Sel's mouth curves into a sardonic smile. "Cute. But your father left me in charge while he's gone, and you're staying here. The Shadowborn want you, and I'm not going to make their job easier."

Nick is so incensed I can hear his teeth grinding together. "Sel . . ."

"Don't make a scene, Nicholas."

I chance a quick look over my shoulder. Tor's watching our exchange, and so are a few others. Sarah, Russ, Vaughn, Fitz. I tug on Nick's hand, and his eyes drop to mine. I try to communicate with my eyes that I don't want an audience. The look on his face says he understands, but he's still not happy. He lets me lead him back to the tables. He sits close again, so that our shoulders and hips are snug, but this time I can feel his entire body shaking in impotent rage.

Back in my room, I miss Alice already, but I also feel a guilty sort of relief that she's gone; all of this lying and hiding is wearing me thin.

"How did you find this out again?" Nick asks, the confusion in his voice clear over the phone. I'd spent the last twenty minutes pacing the length of our room, filling him in on the mysterious figure on campus who opened a Gate twenty-five years ago.

"Are you sure Sel can't hear you?"

"I told you, he's on patrol with Tor and Sar and ordered me to stay inside the Lodge's wards." I remember the aether shield I'd touched that first time I visited the Lodge and how it ripples against my skin whenever I walk through it. Sarah had explained that the wards will keep out anyone—or anything—who hasn't been invited. I hate to say it, but I agree with Sel; Nick should stay inside for now.

"Bree?" Nick prompts, then repeats, "Who told you about this other Gate opening?"

"I don't know if I can say," I say with a sigh.

He chuckles. "Okay . . ."

I plop down on my comforter. "I don't want to betray this person's trust or put them at risk. You're the one who told me that the Regents are severely anti–aether users they don't control."

"I did. So this person is an aether user? On campus?"

I hesitate. But this is Nick. I can tell him at least that much. "Yes."

"An aether user you found? Or one that found you?"

"A bit of both?"

"Are they safe?" The concern in his voice is clear.

"Yes. They want to help me. And they were here when my mom was here, although they didn't know her well. They . . . keep a low profile."

He takes this news surprisingly well. "Probably best I don't know who they are, then. Are they like you?"

I fall back on my pillow. "I don't think so."

"Ah. But you believe them?"

I gnaw on my lip, trying to think of the phrasing that will keep Rootcraft and memory walks and Patricia out of the conversation. "I believe what they showed me. Why? You don't believe me?"

He sighs, and I imagine him in his room, lying back on his bed too. The thought—and the memory of sleeping there with him—makes something warm curl up in a ball in my belly. "Oh, I believe you, but I've never heard of anything like that happening. Dad's never said anything about it and neither has Sel, and as Kingsmage for this chapter he has access to all the records of Shadowborn Gate crossings, appearances, and attacks. I don't think even the *eighth*-ranked Scion was Called back then, so it was peacetime as far as Camlann is concerned. As far as I know, only demon blood can open Gates, so maybe it was an uchel in human form?"

I chew on my cheek, parsing through all that I've seen and learned today. "Or a Merlin?"

"They're bound by Oaths."

"What about a human holding a vial of demon blood?"

"Where'd you get that idea?"

"Something William said earlier about taking Sel's bloodwork."

"Sel's—" A pause. A sigh. "He told you about Sel?"

I scrunch up my face. "I guessed."

"Why am I not surprised?"

"Because I'm clever."

"That you are." Affection and pride bloom in his voice. "Well, Sel's a cambion, so theoretically even his blood could work. But that's still casting beyond anything I've ever heard of. Dark casting."

The chanting *sounded* dark. "The Line of Morgaine?"

"Possibly. And this person just so happened to open this Gate and release partial-corp hellhounds at the time you think your mother was enrolled?"

"I'm positive it's when she was here. It's too much of a coincidence. The question is, if the Regents found out about the Gate opening, would they have kept it secret?"

"Partial-corp hounds aren't visible to Onceborns. The Merlin would have detected the pack and sent the chapter to kill them. No need to involve the Regents."

"But if the demons consumed enough aether to go full-corp?"

A pause.

"If Onceborns witnessed and were attacked by a corporeal pack, the Regents would do everything in their power to bury it. Work with the Vassals or former Pages in the university's administration to keep it quiet on campus. Facilitate bribes to any outsiders in the town's government to keep it off the news. Pay off any Onceborn families if their children were injured or killed. Mesmer them if they had to."

"What about sending a Merlin to chase down a Onceborn witness?" I ask. "Even if it's almost three decades later?"

"Without question." He blows out a long, low stream of air. "I don't trust the Order to always use the best methods, but the mission is protecting Onceborns, not murdering them."

"Yes, but maybe the mesmer didn't take and they found out she was like me."

We both sit in silence for a moment. I can hear the gears turning in his head. His voice is wary, low. "If you accuse the High Council of Regents of murdering your mother, then you'll expose yourself in the process. It won't matter if you're right or wrong."

For the second time today, it feels like I've been punched by someone's words. "Of *course* it matters if I'm right!"

"I'm sorry. I didn't mean that." He sighs. "I just—I don't want anything to happen to you. I of all people know how it feels to want to go after the Regents for their sins, but I can't protect you from them and the Merlins. Not on this. No one can, not even my dad. The only way . . ."

I grip the phone tight. "The only way what?"

When Nick speaks again, the familiar heaviness is threaded through his voice. "The only way I could stand between you and the Regents is if Arthur Calls me and I'm fully Awakened. As king, I'd control the whole of the Order, the Regents included. But if Arthur Calls me . . ."

"Camlann."

"Camlann."

"So we just let them get away with this?"

"No, we keep looking for proof, and when we find it, I bring it to my father. He never got over what they did to my mom. I think he'd help with this. And who knows, the way things are going, I might be king in a few weeks. Having proof in hand will only make it easier for me to find out who's responsible."

"And punish them for what they did?"

A long pause.

"Punish them how, Bree? What would you have me do?"

I don't respond, but it's not because I don't know the answer.

28

"WELCOME TO THE second trial, Pagelings."

Sel stands like a drill sergeant on the Lodge's front lawn, feet planted wide and hands behind his back. He's dressed in black, as always, but his long coat is gone. His tattoos are on full display below sleeves rolled at the elbow. They wind down his forearms and wrists, and I can't help but study them. I wonder how far up they go and how many he has before I remember that I detest him and shouldn't care about his tattoos at all.

The only people who don't appear to be intimidated by him are Whitty and Vaughn. Neither one of them even looks tired; they bounce on the balls of their feet. Ready. The rest of us are barely awake, dragging, and fighting yawns.

Evan, Fitz, and Tor had gone from dorm to dorm to wake us all up in the middle of the night. They'd banged on my door dressed in black tactical gear, faces covered in black and green grease, and yelled at me to get dressed in less than two minutes—or forfeit the tournament entirely. I'd gotten maybe three hours of sleep after getting off the phone with Nick.

"Tonight's event is a scavenger hunt." From the way Sel's gaze pauses on us, one at a time, I get the feeling he can definitely see better in the dark than we can. "We provide each of you with a list of aether-formed objects, and you all scurry around campus collecting them. The six Pages with the highest number of objects in their possession at the end of the night will progress to the third and final trial."

I glance down the row of Pages to my left. There are eight of us remaining. Greer, Whitty, Spencer, Vaughn, Sydney, Carson, and Blake.

"How does a scavenger hunt . . ." Spencer yawns, a hand covering his mouth. "Test our strategic abilities?"

"Look alive, Monroe." Tor strides between Spencer and Vaughn, smacking her Page on the back of the head. Spencer steps forward with the force of it, indignation flashing on his face and delight rippling across Vaughn's. "Sel left out the juiciest part. The more aether objects you collect, the more Sel's aether hellhounds will be drawn to you. If you get cornered or injured, you automatically fail."

Tor and the rest of the Legendborn, eight Scions and Squires altogether, have emerged from the Lodge and joined Sel, lining up in a row across from us.

Each sponsor moves to stand across from their Page, except for Evan. He'd sponsored Ainsley. I hadn't seen her since she was disqualified, but I assume she only comes around the Lodge as needed now. I heard the eliminated Pages are still welcome for meals and events, even though they can't compete.

When Nick stands in front of me, my stomach leaps up somewhere near my lungs. Even covered in paint, even ten feet away, his face sends a wave of relief through me. If Nick's here, I'll be all right. The thought rings in my mind, clear and bright as a bell.

Nick's eyes take me in, flitting rapidly across my face. He mouths, "You okay?" I respond yes with a subtle dip of my chin. From the look on his face, he's not happy that he'd been forced to keep tonight's trial a surprise. Who knows? Maybe he himself only found out an hour or so before I did. He looks tired. And pissed.

My cheeks prickle, and Sel clears his throat. Aside from his eyes flicking sharply away from me, the rest of his body has gone still with tension. "Lest anyone has forgotten, your sponsor cannot aid you during the Trials. Violations of this rule will result in elimination."

Tor produces a folder of papers and hands them to the Legendborn to her left and right. She also passes out drawstring bags to each Page. "Tonight's hunt will pair each Page with a Scion or Squire who is *not* their sponsor, for monitoring purposes only. They will record your progress, report your final score, and dispatch a hound if you find yourself in trouble."

Tor pairs us off. Felicity is paired with Spencer. Russ pairs with Whitty. Victoria and Sarah split Carson and Blake, taking one each. William takes Greer, who seems pleased with this. I curse under my breath. If I couldn't have Felicity, Evan, or Russ by my side, I'd want William. Greer shoots me a look of genuine apology, and I send a weak smile back; I could be disappointed, but it's not their fault.

That leaves Nick and Pete, the Scion of Owain. And Fitz. A needle of fear spears my insides. I silently beg Tor not to torture me with Fitz. I don't know Pete at all, but I know he's new, and kind.

"Pete, you'll go with Vaughn." Tor taps her bottom lip, staring at me and Sydney. We're the only two Pages left.

If I can't be paired with Nick, that leaves me with Fitz.

Fitz lands on this outcome a heartbeat after I do, and his lips pull back in an eager grin. He starts walking toward me when Sel intervenes.

"I'll take Briana. Fitz, you pair with Sydney. Nicholas, you'll stay in the Lodge behind the wards."

The murmuring behind us goes silent. Nick looks like he's just eaten an icicle. "Everyone else has a Scion or Squire."

Sel tucks his hands in his pockets and strides through the grass, holding me still with his electric stare. Tiny pinpricks across my cheeks. "You heard me. I'll keep track of Briana." From this distance I can see he's swapped his pea-shaped black earplugs for silver ones. He speaks to Nick without releasing me from his gaze. "The three skills and abilities tested by the Trials are fixed, but the format of those trials is left up to the chapter leadership in place during the tournament." He shrugs and the gesture speaks for him. "And I've changed my mind."

It only takes two steps for Nick to reach Sel's side. He towers over the sorcerer by several inches. "Well, I don't agree."

Sel turns slowly, deliberately to Nick. "You haven't taken up Excalibur yet, Davis, and your father named me the current leader. Further, as your Kingsmage, it's my responsibility to keep you safe." His low voice carries to the rest of the group in the quiet, reaching every ear over the rhythmic trill of crickets. I catch a faint gust of cinnamon and whiskey between the scents of night-blooming jasmine and crushed grass. "Until that sword is in your hands, you will stand down."

Nick's face is unreadable, his eyes a deep, cold blue. He stalks back into the Lodge without another word.

Sel tilts his gaze to the sky. He tracks the moon for a few seconds, then quickly scans the sky and stars around it. His eyes drop to the group.

"It is now one thirty a.m. You have three hours."

There are forty objects on the list, but any relief I feel disappears when I read the first three clues and see how they're written.

Eighty-eight keys and not a lock in sight.

Microfiche, carrels, stacks abound, and yet on this floor, there's not a book to be found.

"Riddles?" I exclaim.

Sel's lips quirk as we walk toward campus through the Battle Park forest. A handful of pairs have run ahead, but the rest, like me, are reviewing the clues before they dash off.

I point to one of the clues farther down with the light of my phone. "'Silver and red, white and yellow, find me flashing where the stoners mellow'?! How am I supposed to know where 'the stoners mellow'?"

"Maybe you'd know if you got high," Sel says dryly.

I suppress the urge to smack him. I'm pretty sure I don't want to touch him, but maybe a kick will do. I inhale and turn back to the page, trying to ignore the prickling sensation of his gaze. "The first one is easy. That's a piano, and the music building isn't far."

"Ah," Sel says in a noncommittal tone. I ignore him and start jogging west, thankful that I'd thrown on exercise leggings and sneakers. He keeps up with me easily, his feet practically floating over the ground, silent as the dead.

After a few minutes, I fold. "Why?" My breath comes out in short puffs.

"Why what, Briana?" His voice is so even, he could be standing still.

"You know what."

"I told you, I'm keeping an eye on you, mystery girl."

"Because you think I'm a demon?"

"Are you saying you're not?"

His response pulls a frustrated sound from my chest. "Isn't that the pot calling the kettle black? Aren't you the Shadowborn here?"

His hand moves faster than my eyes can follow. He grabs my arm with hot, strong fingers, jerking me to a halt. "I don't know what you think you know or what you've been taught. But I am not born of shadows." Sel's cheek twitches. "Planting an uchel demon in our ranks disguised as a naive Onceborn is a perfect way to sow discord, but it won't work with me."

I pull my arm from his grasp. "Why bother planting an uchel when your paranoia sows discord just fine on its own?" I stomp away from him, tamping down my frustration before it turns into something I can't control.

I reach the music building, Hill Hall, a few minutes later and find it empty. I'm surprised there aren't other Pages surrounding it; it was an easy riddle. Low-hanging fruit, really. I can't tell if I should feel pleased with myself or worried.

Sel steps up beside me as my fingers wrap around the door handle, and I leap at least a foot in the air. I hadn't heard him move at all.

"Jesus!" I screech.

His eyes cut to mine, annoyance flashing across his brow, quick like a shooting star. "Why so jumpy, Briana? Nervous about something?"

"Nervous" feels like Nick's and my word now. Our inside joke. My temper flares. "You *have* threatened to kill me! Also, why are you so damn quiet?"

"It's not in my control"—he narrows his eyes—"as you now know."

Oh. "Right. Demon feet." A thought occurs to me. "You know *my* feet make sound, don't you?"

He studies me languidly. "Goruchels are said to be a consummate mimics, when it facilitates their human ruse."

I roll my eyes. The door creaks long and loud when I open it, and slams shut behind us when we step into the building's rotunda. I hold up my phone, flashlight app on, and shine it on the directory on the wall beside us. "Piano rooms, basement level."

My footsteps echo on the wood floor, and the blue-white of my flashlight swings back and forth to find the stairs. "Why aren't these buildings locked at night?"

Sel answers from just a foot behind me. "Administration is aware of tonight's event."

"They just let the Legendborn get away with everything, don't they?"

Sel draws up beside me. "How do you know they aren't Order members themselves?"

Down the stairs in the basement, there's a long hallway of identical piano rooms, each holding an upright and a chair. "Don't suppose you could use, like, a secret hand signal or something and point me to which room I need?"

"I only created the objects. The others hid them. I have no idea which room you need." He flashes a satisfied smile. I glower back.

We go through four rooms in silence. I lift up the lids of the pianos, bend down to search under them and their matching benches. In each, the air is stale, and Sel stands much too close for comfort. Sel's presence, even in the expansive hallway, makes every space feel too small, too tight.

In the very last room on the left, I see it. A plain stone mug shimmers sea-foam blue in the darkness underneath the back leg of a piano. I don't bother hiding the joyous sound that escapes me when I rush to grab it. Sel leans on the doorjamb, watching me.

I examine the mug in my hand. Its light pulses in a slow rhythm. "Why does it go in and out like that?"

"Aether is an active element. I'm holding its shape in place." He turns and walks down the hall. "You've spent twenty minutes looking for one object. Better hurry if you don't want to end up in the bottom two."

I stuff the mug in my bag and jog to catch up to him, curious in spite of myself. "You're holding all forty objects together? Right now?"

Sel rakes his fingers through his hair and sighs impatiently. "I created them all at once, but I can sense them at a distance and reinforce them if this lasts more than a couple of hours."

"Wait, what?" I stop in the hallway. "You can cast aether remotely?"

"Yes." He pivots on his heel. "Are you coming?"

I shake my head, trying to imagine the effort of keeping up with forty anythings, much less forty castings—and that's not even mentioning his hellhounds. I don't know what it feels like to cast, but what he's done tonight sounds impressive. Impossible. Both.

"You're burning moonlight." He stares at me incredulously. "Or do you want to interrogate me and forfeit instead?"

I catch up with him again, and we run through the building for the exit.

I work through five more items on the list without much trouble—and without any sight of a hound. The only one that catches me off guard is the one about the books. To reach the "floor with no books in sight," I'd had to find the extremely well-hidden door to the roof on the eighth floor of the library.

I'm not particularly fond of heights.

And it took me twenty minutes to find the jewelry box inside a vent pipe.

Sel, on the other hand, had kept himself occupied by walking on the four-inch-wide raised brick perimeter of the roof, perfectly balanced. While whistling.

I keep waiting for him to jump, grab, or try to kill me again, but he seems content to watch me struggle with riddles and run from one end of the campus to the other. It's unnerving. I've never spent any amount of time with him that wasn't filled with threats, mesmers, or intimidation.

Once we're back outside, I check my bag: the jewelry box; the mug from the piano; a flashlight from the fountain in front of the graduate school building; a very hard-to-spot tiny metal key that had been wedged between a pair of bricks on the journalism building; and a candle that had been tucked in the crook of a statue's arms.

I look up to find Sel studying me again, as if he's waiting for me to turn demon by accident.

"Where are the hounds?" I ask, and he shrugs.

"I created them, but I gave them a little push to make them more independent. I felt one earlier near the Campus Y, but it didn't catch your scent."

"Oh, lovely," I drawl. "Were you going to warn me a bloodthirsty hellhound was nearby?"

He scoffs. "Why would I do that?"

I groan and look down at the list for another clue. "'I was the first and my rest is the oldest, let there be no debate.'" I pull my cheek between my teeth.

Sel, perched on one of the many low stone walls around campus, watches me with hooded eyes as I puzzle through the riddle. I'm certain he's been figuring out the riddles before I do and enjoying not telling me the answers.

I check my watch. I have an hour left, we're in the middle of the campus, and there's no use walking until I figure out where to go.

I pace back and forth and Sel's eyes, glittering in the darkness, follow my steps. "'I was the first and my rest is the oldest, let there be no debate.' Just my luck this is some sort of uber obscure medieval crap."

A hoarse bark of laughter escapes Sel, and we both blink in shock at the genuine, uncontrolled sound. The sound of someone who's not used to laughing. I don't think I've ever heard him express anything other than carefully aimed barbs, seething irritation, or dry sarcasm. He must see the thought on my face, because his expression goes stony in a heartbeat. Like he's flipped a switch inside.

I walk to the edge of the wall down a few feet from Sel and look out over the campus. I start at my left, my eyes following the line of buildings in front of us: the low dining hall, the towering library breaking the skyline, and the Bell Tower striking three thirty.

My eyes track back to the left of the Bell Tower. "'I was the first and my rest is the oldest, let there be no debate.'"

"While it's quite poetic, it's not a cantrip, Matthews." Sel saunters over, shadows clinging to his gliding shape. "Repetition will not make its meaning clearer."

"Shut up." His left eye twitches in silent reproach.

I have a feeling I know where the next object is, but I'm not quite ready to go there. It feels too soon. But what choice do I have?

I sigh and gesture for him to follow. "Come on."

The first was a young DiPhi boy buried in the late 1700s.

That's what Patricia said. And, thanks to Alice, I know DiPhi is the very old campus debating society. I desperately wish I'd asked Patricia to point out the grave marker during the day, because searching for it at night is like looking for a certain shade of blue in the ocean.

The graveyard is poorly lit by intermittent lampposts, and the wide hedges and hills make it slow going. As apprehensive as I thought I might be, the grave-yard actually feels . . . familiar to me now.

Each time I check over my shoulder, Sel is there, a silent figure blending into the shadows in one moment, limned by golden light in the next. I think I hear him chuckle, but the sound is carried away on a gust that whips dirt and twigs into my face.

"You've never seen me harm Nick, so why do you still think I'm Shadowborn?" I don't know why I ask. Maybe because with me in the lead, I don't have to look him in the face.

"You're immune to mesmer."

"Not true," I retort, hiking up a particularly long hill.

"Lies." He doesn't miss a beat. "You wield the Sight too easily for someone who has only recently received it. You Saw the isel at the Quarry." That surprises me, but I don't show it. He strides up the hill with frustrating ease, and when he reaches the top to look down at me and Nick's coin on my chest, there's casual contempt in his eyes. "And you have enthralled Nicholas."

I sputter, heat filling my cheeks, and tuck the necklace away. "What? Enthralled?! I—no—he—he . . . That's . . ." Sel raises a black brow. A curious hawk, watching a frantic mouse skitter back and forth.

He makes a soft, dismissive sound in the back of his throat. Not wanting to hear any more about Nick or any sort of *thralling*, I turn and walk down the hill to the next section of graves.

"In addition, the timing of your appearance," he begins, following behind me, "is too convenient. Demons are crossing through Gates at increasing rates at not only our chapter but also the others embedded in schools up the coast. It's all but inevitable that the Table will be gathered, but Nicholas is vulnerable. Symbolic. If anything happens to him before Arthur calls and he claims his rightful title, the Order will go to chaos."

I walk the aisles, looking for the marker on the ground in the oldest section. "I thought you hated Nick."

Sel falls in step beside me. "Nicholas's petty childhood concerns and daddy issues have never been of greater importance than the Order's mission. He should have been preparing himself for the Call instead of whining about his duty."

I stop walking at that. "I don't think his mother getting mesmered so severely that she doesn't remember her own child is a 'petty childhood concern.' She only wanted to protect him."

"She tried to *kidnap* him." He stares at me, his tone even and eyes opaque. "And the Line is Law."

I shake my head in disgust. "Unbelievable."

I step around him and continue down the aisle. I'm grateful that Sel at least stops talking, leaving me to look for the marker in silence. A flap of heavy wings interrupts my crunching steps as I walk over leaves and yellowed fescue, long dead from the heat of summer. I turn to point out the grave section to Sel, but he's gone. The aisle behind me is empty.

"Sel?" Stillness and wind are the only replies. Doubt drops into my stomach.

A low growl behind me breaks the silence.

I don't turn back. I don't need to.

I run.

29

I'M AT A full-on sprint in seconds. Sel's hellhound is fast; I can hear its heavy breaths behind me, closer and louder with every step. Hear its claws scraping over stone markers. I reach the section with the headstones, and I zig and zag around them, hoping that I'm nimbler than it is.

I've never run this fast in my life, and it still doesn't feel fast enough.

"Reveal yourself, Briana!" Sel's voice, taunting and amused, calls down from somewhere above me. I leap over a wall and a gravestone, then another headstone, racing toward the mausoleum section.

I'm almost there. I can see the three low buildings facing inward and the courtyard in the middle. If I can get inside one of them . . . I push faster, will my legs to stretch farther. Sel's voice keeps pace. He shouts down from a tree just over my shoulder. "Give up the ruse!"

Just after I leap over a low stone wall, just when the courtyard is within reach, the hound decides it's time to act. I hear a grunt, as if it's launched its whole body into the air. I change course, trip over a low marker, and fly forward, skidding across the courtyard bricks on stomach and hands. The hound lands headfirst against a mausoleum. Its skull cracks against the marble wall.

By the time I scramble breathlessly to my feet, the hound has recovered, so that when I turn, I see it for the first time.

Sel's hound looks the same as the first hound I'd laid eyes on, but his is far, far bigger, and fully corporeal. It throws glowing silver aether off in waves. Details I'd missed before are clearer now, even in the dim light: its long snout with nostrils flared and tipped like a bat's. Sel's given it the Shadowborn's heart-blood eyes, dark and impossibly red. I can't look away; I can barely move for terror that when I do, it will strike.

I edge one foot back, and my heel hits something hard, vertical, smooth. Another mausoleum. I know without looking that the door is out of reach. The only escape routes are between the corners of the buildings and the fourth, open side I've just come through—the side that the hound is now closing off with its massive body.

It snarls and snaps its saliva-drenched jaws, in delight or fury, I don't know. It lowers itself into a crouch, ears flicked forward. My heart accelerates into a full gallop, blood pounding in my ears. "Call it off, Sel!"

Sel drops down silently beside his construct, landing in a crouch and rising with a satisfied smile. "Just as I thought. A coward and a liar both."

Sel's hellhound pants at me, its mouth wide and open in a doglike grin. "Call it off!" I press my back into the wall.

Sel crosses his arms over his chest, pleasure painted all over his face. "Once a true hellhound has the scent, it never gives up its prey. The only way to stop it is to kill it. As much as I despise those Shadowborn beasts, I find I'm much the same way. So I decided to give you two final options: reveal your true form, or kill me."

"You set me up!" Adrenaline and rage surge through my veins. "You planned to corner me here."

He groans, as if correcting a dense student. "*Of course*. I must admit, I was inspired by what you said yesterday in William's infirmary. You were right—all of this cat and mouse *is getting old.*"

I risk a step forward, but the hound snaps. I fall backward onto the bricks. "Why are you doing this?"

"Because I'm *tired*, Briana, of your Shadowborn lies and the fun you must be having at our expense. Planting your brethren at our Oath, sending the serpent to take Nicholas under my nose, taking part in our trials." With every slow step forward, his features turn more menacing and his eyes wilder until he looks more like his hellhound construct than himself. Looks more demon than human. "We both know you don't care about our mission. I can see it in your face!"

"That's not true!" I scream.

Sel's expression is pained, annoyed. "More lies? Even now?" He kneels in front of me, his upper lip curling into a sneer. "I know you Saw the isel before taking the Oath. We *both* know the First Oath never took, that you sloughed off our sacred commitment like it was nothing. Like it was worthless to you, less valuable than dirt."

I tremble. *How did he know? Did he see—*

He chuckles low at my confusion. "You think I don't recognize my own casting or sense its absence?" He leans close to whisper in my ear. "I can *feel* them, Briana. The Oaths I've cast." His eyes drift across my face and throat. "And I don't feel any of me . . . on you."

"Get away from me!" I shove him hard with shaking hands, and he laughs, rocking back on his heels. I scramble to my feet, but his hound is right there, its slobbering jaws at my shoulder.

Sel rises. "Nicholas needs to know who you are before he is called to the throne and you make a fool of him. William, Felicity, Russ, Sarah . . . They all seem to think you might *actually* belong with us, when we both know you don't belong anywhere."

I feel myself shaking. And not just because of what Sel says about Nick or the others, but because of his last words.

You don't belong anywhere.

After everything that's happened to me, everything I've done to make it this far, to get this close to the truth of my mother's murder, those words snap something inside me.

My hands begin to flex at my sides, clenching and unclenching. The tips of my fingers feel like they could pop, like there's a balloon beneath my skin that just wants to expand outward and explode. I look at Sel's hound and think of breathing fire in the monster's face and watching it burn, burn, burn. Laughing at its pain, because it's so small next to mine. I see Sel. See his confidence in his ancient mission and his hunger to take me down.

I may not know my own ancestors, but after seeing Mary and Louisa and Cecilia, all I want is to show him that he's not the only one with power in his veins.

"Nick was right," I say in a low voice I barely recognize. "Merlins *are* monsters. *You* are a monster."

His eyes widen, and his lips press into a thin, angry line—but I don't find out what horrid thing he might spout next because he doesn't get a chance to respond at all.

A crashing in the woods pulls our attention. A low howl. A high, piercing bark, then another that echoes against the closed-in courtyard.

Sel scowls. "What did you do? Call in reinforcements?"

I hiss, "I didn't do anything, you asshole!" Like him, my eyes are glued to the graveyard.

We don't have to wait long.

Three nightmares appear out of the woods and jump onto the stone wall. Three enormous foxes, green aether drifting up like steam off their scaly backs.

These are true Shadowborn. No construct. No illusion.

Sel's hound dissolves until it's nothing but silver dust.

"*Cedny uffern!*" Sel hisses. He slides backward into a fighting stance. "Call them off, uchel! If you kill me, you'll never get close to Nicholas. All your efforts will be for naught."

"They're not *mine*!" I snap.

The partial-corp creatures leap down to the courtyard as one, covering the ten-foot distance easily. The foxes yip and snarl, chittering as they stalk toward us on long legs, their hairless, ratlike tails whipping behind them.

"I said *call them off*!"

"I didn't *do* this!"

"Briana—"

"*Please,* Sel!"

His jaw clenches as he stares me down, fresh doubt at my plea warring with the fury in his eyes. A flash of blue-white aether, and then Sel is murmuring while aether streams rapidly into his hands. It collects into spinning globes in his palms. Then the globes expand and elongate until they form two long staffs that harden into shimmering crystalline weapons, dense and heavy.

Instead of retreating, the foxes snap their jaws eagerly at the sight.

"What are they doing?" I breathe, but Sel's eyes are only for the demons.

Suddenly, all three hellfoxes release bloodcurdling screams, the sound bouncing in the courtyard and droning on and on until I cover my ears in pain. Then I see that it's not a scream at all.

It's a call.

I know the Shadowborn use aether to grow solid, but I've never seen it happen before now. The aether from Sel's weapons unravels and flows in the air toward their open mouths like a stream spilling into a lake. He gasps, squeezing each staff in a fist, but it's no use. His weapons dissolve before our eyes until he's holding nothing but air between his fingers. The foxes flicker, but the silver-blue aether he called turns green when it reaches them. Sel is already calling another batch of aether, but the foxes scream once more and take it before he can form anything in his palms. He roars, cursing as they take his power from him, siphoning it as fast as he can call it.

The sharp burn of his casting fills the air. The foxes take it all and use it to grow larger, stronger. Aether swells from within their bodies, bloating them outward until there's the sound of splitting skin. Dark green, foul-smelling ichor oozes out of the openings, turning my stomach. Sel begins calling a third batch of aether to make a weapon against them—but they'll be corporeal soon, and visible to any passing Onceborn.

"Stop!" I shout. "They're just using it to go corp!"

I didn't need to yell; he'd figured it out too, and realized his efforts would be futile. His face turns feral with frustration, and he growls at the creatures with canines bared.

In my vision, the world trembles, but it's not the world that is shaking, boiling, rising. It's me.

Time slows, and I see the prowling foxes with new eyes. Their outstretched claws and rows of teeth, their eyes gleaming with bloodlust. Everything about my perception of them—sight, smell, sound—is suddenly crisper, brighter. Their cracked-lava skin is in high definition, every shift and ripple of their muscles clear beneath the surface. I can taste their sour, rotten aether bodies, the smell thick at the back of my throat. A rumbling growl is coming from one, I know, because I hear the air building to produce it, deep in its chest.

"What the hell is that?" Sel's voice breaks my focus, and the world speeds back up.

I blink and look down. I've taken two steps toward the foxes without even realizing I've moved. My hands are outstretched at my sides—and bright crimson flames stream from my fingertips. A short scream escapes me, then a whimper. I shake my hands to try to toss the flames away. "I don't, I don't—"

The hellfoxes don't wait for me to explain. The one on the far left is already moving, dashing for me at breakneck speed. I dodge at the last minute, and it collides into the wall. While it recovers, another screeches, braces for a leap—

Strong arms grab me around the waist and pull both my feet off the ground. The graveyard, the ground, the trees fly by in a dizzying blur of colors, and then I'm released. The world goes hazy, dark . . .

"Datgelaf, dadrithiaf . . . datgelaf, dadrithiaf . . ."

The ground beneath my face comes into focus. My stomach feels like it's somewhere up near my lungs. My fingers curl in the dirt—the red mage flame is gone. "Ughh . . . ," I moan, rising to my knees. I couldn't have been out for more than a minute.

"You're welcome," Sel grumbles, before returning to his chant. "Datgelaf, dadrithiaf . . ." He stands beside me, his fingers and hands contorting in the air over the massive roots of an oak tree. I look up to find that we're on McCulhlu Place, the northernmost quad. Maybe a ten-minute walk from the graveyard. "Datgelaf—"

A hellfox scream rends the night air.

"Oh God." I use the tree to stand. "They're coming."

"I'm aware."

Another scream, louder this time. "They're getting closer!"

"I have ears!"

"We've got to run." I take a halting step, but the world is still adjusting itself after Sel's snatch-and-grab.

"No," he says, "we've got to hide." There's a whoosh of air, and low, translucent double doors appear over the tree's roots. Sel yanks his hand backward, and one of the doors opens, revealing a dark bottomless pit below. "Get in."

"I'm not going down there!"

Without a word, he wraps an arm around my middle and lifts me up, tossing me down into the gloom. I land ass-first, pain shooting up my spine. At least the dirt floor is six or seven feet below ground level instead of the unfathomable descent into nothingness I'd imagined. Sel drops down beside me and lands like a cat—silent and light. He yanks down again, and the door slams shut, plunging us into darkness.

30

"WHAT THE F—"

"Shut up."

"Why—"

One of Sel's hands shoves me back against a dirt wall and the other claps down over my mouth. *Hard.* When I make a muffled noise, that hand presses even harder. *"Shh!"*

A loud snuffling noise reaches us from no more than two feet above my head. I suck in a breath, heart pounding so loud that I'm certain Sel can hear it. The question is, can the hellfox above us? I pray that it can't, because if Sel has chosen to hide rather than fight, it means he doesn't think he can beat these creatures. The other two foxes join the first. We freeze in the darkness while the three demons try to sniff us out. Their paws are silent, but the weight of their aether bodies sends soil showering down over my hair, down the back of my T-shirt. I shut my eyes and let the pebbles rain over my cheeks and Sel's fingers, still covering my mouth. What if they start digging? My mind races, questions coming faster. Do they know the hidden door is here? Can they sense the aether that hid it, just like Sel can sense the aether that makes them solid? Wait. Why didn't Sel notice the foxes approaching in the first place?

I must make some sound, or maybe my breathing changes against his knuckles, because he leans against me as if in warning. My eyes snap open—and meet his glowing yellow ones in the dark. Definitely a warning. One I can read clear as day: *Don't. Move.*

After a minute, the sounds of their snouts grow distant as the hellfoxes move on. Sel waits a beat for good measure, then a second, and releases me. He snaps his fingers, and a small blue flame appears over his palm, illuminating the cave he's put us in. No, not a cave. A tunnel.

"Let's move." He walks forward, the blue mage flame casting eerie shadows against wide exposed roots, crumbling dirt walls, and ancient beams holding the earth up above us.

"Did you just cast a tunnel?"

He doesn't wait for me to follow, so I have to clamber after him to keep up.

"I *revealed* a tunnel. The tree trunk is the illusion, and an old one. The founders knew that the university would need to be a public front, so they dug tunnels for easy movement and caves for storage before the campus was built."

"They dug all these to get around more easily?"

"These are fail-safes. Escape routes. The original Merlins warded them to mask aether so that Shadowborn cannot follow, even above ground."

I tug my phone out of my pocket, but there's no cell signal. The battery's half-dead, so I could use the flashlight, but why drain it when Sel's lighting the way plenty himself? "Why are we here and not the Lodge? You could have run us back there—"

He stops and fixes me with a glare. "I don't know why those things attacked us or where they came from, and neither, it seems, do you. I'm not going to lead them right to Nicholas, even with the Lodge's wards in place. If they're anything like the hounds, they've caught our scent and will be on the hunt for us and no one else. I'd like to keep it that way."

"Why didn't you sense them?"

His eyes drop and he keeps walking, pulling the only light source with him. "I'm not sure." Something in his voice sounds off, like he's holding back an answer he doesn't want to say out loud.

"How did they steal your aether?"

"I don't know."

"Does that mean you've never seen a hellfox before?"

He turns around abruptly, and I almost stumble into him. "What are you?"

"I—"

"The truth," he demands. "How did you generate that aether at your fingertips?"

I blink. "I didn't generate anything—"

He regards me through narrow eyes. "This explains why you distracted me that night at the Quarry when I was hunting the isel. I detected a flare of your aether, then incorrectly assumed my senses had led me astray." He leans closer with his flame fingers and points at my chest with his other hand. "But just a few minutes ago you were cooking aether like a furnace, right *here*."

"Back off!" I push his hand away and cross my arms over my chest. The scent of even Sel's small casting is filling the tunnel and clinging to my nose.

"You don't know how to navigate these tunnels, and even if you could, you can't open any of the doors to the surface," he says, raising a brow, "so you may as well be honest. How did you do that?"

I want desperately to stomp off, but he's right. I have no idea where to go. He watches me come to this conclusion as if dealing with a small, stubborn child who wants to protest their way out of bedtime. I resent everything about his face, from his ridiculous hair to his cambion eyes to the irritating smirk tugging at the side of his goddamn mouth. *"I don't know."* I can hear the petulance in my own voice, and I hate that, too.

Sel narrows his golden eyes to calculating slits while he inspects my face. A beat passes. "You're telling the truth, at least about what you are and where your power comes from."

"Yes! I am!" That much *is* true. I don't know what I am and neither does Patricia. That I know about root, that my mother was a practitioner—I'll never tell him those things.

His face takes on a considering expression. "My mother was a Merlin and an aether scholar. She studied demonology, Gate aether, runes, ancient texts, you name it. I was a precocious child, so I often snuck into her office to read her gramarye and those of Merlins before us."

I grit my teeth, unnerved that he has brought up his own mother. Can he see that I was thinking about mine? "Is this story going somewhere?"

Sel ignores me. "With that upbringing, I, more than most, understand that our magic, if you will, is at its core and in its very fundamentals, a type of physics." He extends his arm in the dim light. The tattoo claiming most of his forearm is a bold black circle divided by five lines into five equal segments. "Earth, air, water, fire, and aether, or what medieval alchemists called 'quintessence.' Every Merlin is taught that aether cannot be created or destroyed, only infused into a body or manipulated into temporary mass. So"—he looks directly into my eyes—"how is it that you, Briana Matthews, defy every law of aether that thousands of Merlins have followed for the past fifteen centuries?"

I stare back, scared of what he's saying but refusing to show him that. "Maybe the Order doesn't know everything about magic in the world."

He hums and steps back. "There are a lot of things the Order does not know." He walks ahead again without adding a word to *that* enigmatic comment, and I have no choice but to follow.

The deeper we go, the more the scent of rotting things overwhelms me. I tug my T-shirt up over my nose for relief, then pull it down again because it's freezing here.

After a while I ask him the question that needs to be asked. "Are you going to turn me over to the Regents?"

He answers without looking back. "I haven't decided. Why are you really joining our Order?"

He's a Merlin. I can't trust him with the real answer, and doing so would go against everything Nick's specifically warned me about.

"You must be thinking up a lie," he muses, "because you're taking too long for the truth." He stops again and gives me an expectant look.

I pull together the best possible, truest answer I can and look him right in the eyes while I say it. "I asked Nick to help me join because I need to understand the things I've seen, and I need to know why I see them."

"What does Nicholas think of your ability to generate aether?"

"I . . . he doesn't know about that. It's only happened once before. Randomly, the night of the initiation. I thought it might be a reaction to the Oath. I didn't know . . ."

He searches my face for a moment; then his lips curl back in disgust. "You *truly* have no idea what you are, and Nicholas, ever the hero, offered to help you find out by bringing you into an ancient secret society for which you had no background knowledge or training?"

I shift under his gaze. "Well, no, I sort of . . . pushed him to sponsor me. It was more my idea than his."

He looks completely appalled. "You're both fools, then." He grimaces. "And so am I for believing you could be anything other than a silly little Unanedig girl." He whirls away and stalks down the dirt corridor, muttering under his breath.

My jaw drops. "I thought you just said I defy 'every law of aether'!"

"I did"—he sneers over his shoulder—"but I've been watching you closely all week, and apparently you can defy our laws while still being a silly little Unanedig girl. Congratulations."

It's our first meeting at the Quarry cliffside all over again—as soon as he'd found the isel, he'd dismissed me wholesale, because if you're not Sel's prey, you're not worth his time. "Aren't you supposed to . . . to . . . investigate anomalies?" I say, hurrying behind him, half-indignant and half-relieved.

"I investigate *threats*. Whatever aether ability you have, you can't control it. You can barely kill a hellboar construct without the assistance of the planet's gravity." He huffs a low laugh, like he's been laughing at me about that trial ever since it happened.

I'm so confused by Sel's comments—and by how much he's actually *talking* to me—that I stop walking right then and there. Had I misjudged him? Had Nick? Or is Sel operating just as he always has—treating any and everyone as a threat until his own eyes and facts prove otherwise? Up until an hour ago I qualified, but now . . . I don't? I don't expect to be so insulted, but after all this time and all those menacing glares suggesting bodily harm, I absolutely am. I'm insulted *and* annoyed. *How dare he*—

"Are you going to stand there gawking in the dark?" Sel snaps his left fingers to produce a new mage flame, and rotates his other wrist to extinguish the first so he can use that hand to steady himself against a low support beam. I follow his gaze ahead where there's a rise of dirt that we'll need to climb over to pass. "Or is there something else you'd like to add?"

"But—but what about all that talk of enthralling Nick?" I sputter. "And me making a fool of him? And . . . and . . . how I don't belong? Were you just saying all of that to be an ass?"

"Oh no, I meant every word. Because I thought you were Shadowborn, I hoped to provoke you into an emotional response—the more negative the better, as that's what demons are drawn to, even within themselves. It worked, in a way, albeit not how I'd imagined." He sighs and turns around, a bored expression on his face. "As for Nicholas, if you cause a problem or distract him from his path to the throne, I won't hesitate to turn you in to the Regents and tell their Merlins exactly how to trigger you so they can throw you in a lab somewhere and investigate you for themselves."

A chill runs through me at his words. Is that what would happen? Nick never said—

"If you continue through initiation as you are, you'll undoubtedly fail the combat trial, which means I only need to wait a few weeks to be rid of you. Something tells me that with Nicholas's *obnoxiously* earnest assistance, you'll find some loophole out of your Page status *and* the chapter as a whole. Maybe he'll use your non-Vassal background to call for an exception to lifelong membership, claiming you were a failed experiment. Or perhaps he'll call in a favor with his father, who will grant it out of guilt and appreciation that his son has *finally* accepted his birthright. Then, when you leave us, you won't break the Code of Secrecy to expose the Order since you genuinely care for Nicholas, and doing so would make our once and future king's life that much harder, hindering our mission. Do I have the right of it?"

My jaw almost hits the dirt floor.

"Thought as much. In short, right now I have far greater concerns than the 'mystery of you,' not the least of which is the likely imminence of Camlann. Such concerns also include the truly *active* threats to both Nicholas's life and the chapter I am Oathbound to protect." *The type of threats that I will be punished for—painfully—if I don't pursue them.* He doesn't add that next bit, but I hear it anyway, remembering what Lord Davis said about Sel's Kingsmage Oath burning a hole through his throat.

"I'm sorry," I say, shaking my head, "I just can't get over the fact that you have definitely, *definitely* made violent threats on my life and now you're just . . . not."

"Don't think for a second that I didn't mean those violent threats, because I absolutely did. Still do, to be quite honest, should you force my hand. At the moment, however, I'm reconsidering how I described you," he murmurs, climbing gracefully over the small hill. "I should have called you both silly *and* self-centered."

I'm fuming, but I follow behind him in silence. I don't want to give him any more verbal ammunition.

Sel seems to know where he's going, because we stop at a small round cave about ten minutes later and he points up at an opening between the petrified beams. "This door will bring us to the surface on the far side of campus. There's an illusioned lockbox of metal weapons in the woods if the foxes have found us somehow, but they'd have to possess more than the average demon's sense of smell to track us here. I'll go first, give the clear, and then I'll pull you up."

I nod and watch as he begins murmuring again. The Welsh sounds similar to the sounds of the swyns William says when he's healing. Sel's fingers create shapes in the air above our heads; then, in a reverse of the last time, he punches up with an open palm. A door above bangs open.

Sel crouches, leaps the vertical equivalent of twice his own height, and then lands on the grass beside the door. After a moment, he whispers that we're clear and reaches down to pull me to the surface.

We emerge right where Sel said we would: a low stone wall marking the campus perimeter and beyond that, the thick forests that belong to the town of Chapel Hill. Sel's back is turned to the base of the wide oak we've emerged from, twisting his palms to hide its aether door again, when the hairs on the nape of my neck rise in warning.

When Sel shouts, "Get down!" my body doesn't argue. I throw myself to the ground in time to see a hellfox sailing overhead, its skull colliding with the side of the mighty oak with a loud, ground-shaking crack.

While it recovers, a second fox screeches, tackling Sel. It's heavy paws and weight knock him to the ground. Like with the uchel, Sel and the fox are tumbling, rolling on the grass in a blur of black clothes and smoky-green scales.

Sel must glance my way, because he shouts in warning just as the third fox lunges toward where I've landed on the ground. His warning gives me just enough time to roll. Jaws snap by my right ear—where my face had been a split second earlier.

There's an awful tearing sound, and a high-pitched yowl cuts the air.

Sel tore something off his opponent.

The fox beside me runs to its brethren's aid, and then Sel is screaming, trying to wrestle both at once without calling any aether.

He needs weapons.

I scramble to my feet, jump over the wall, and sprint toward the woods and the illusioned lockbox. Between one blink and the next, a hellfox appears in front of me. Its head is split open in the middle, glowing-green aether oozing from the jagged crack: the fox that hit the tree.

I stumble. Trip over my own feet. My back hits the ground. Hard. The breath is knocked out of me.

I'm writhing in the grass, choking for air, my brain screaming for it, but I can't scream. Not even when the hellfox lowers its head, pinning me with beady black eyes—and leaps.

It's going to land claws out. Right on top of me.

I'm going to die.

I squeeze my eyes shut, waiting for its heavy weight and razor-sharp teeth. In a desperate, untrained move, I swing one fist up in a wild punch.

There's a howling scream, a deep squelching sound, a hot, burning weight on my chest, then blackness swells up to take me.

Something hot and thick is pulsing rapidly against my fingers.

I open my eyes, but I can't comprehend what I'm seeing or feeling. My brain spins up, knits images together bit by bit:

I am alive.

The fox is on top of me.

My face is not between its teeth, because its jaws hang slack.

Its front two legs are limp in the dirt on either side of my body.

My left arm is a mess of green ooze. It runs in thick rivers down my skin and into the grass.

My right shoulder is twisted painfully. Because my fist and forearm have disappeared up to the elbow inside the fox's chest.

And that arm is covered in red flames.

There are screams. Mine.

My vision swims. I yank my hand back, but something catches my wrist—a sharp-ended broken rib. Vomit rises, burns at the back of my throat. The screams start again. I'm wailing as I try to extract my fist from another creature's body. Green, viscous ichor spills down its stomach. I pull too hard, and that's worse. Its wound pours onto my chest, putrid and rotting, while its tongue lolls to the side.

Angry chittering, and a hellfox scream rends the air, but I'm on my back, and the dead demon on my chest is so very heavy. I watch upside down as another fox runs toward me with frightening speed. I push at the carcass, grunting and panting.

But before it can reach me, the sharp, pointy end of a black metal spear pierces its throat.

The fox makes a gurgling sound and hits the ground. Sel appears at its side and pulls the spear out, then uses all his strength to slam his weapon through the creature's skull. It stops moving. Sel leans heavily on the end of the staff, breathing hard.

My eyes burn. The carcass is steaming aether now. A raspy groan escapes me, and Sel's head jerks up. He's at my side in half a second, his hands going to the creature's shoulders.

"The other one—" I say, searching frantically.

"Dead. Hold on." His dark eyebrows draw together as he assesses the dead fox and me. "It can't dust with something living inside it. I need to pull it off you."

My eyes are watering now, and I can't tell if it's from the aether or tears. I think it's both. I have to cough twice before I can speak, and even then my voice is hoarse from screaming. "I can't get my hand out . . . I can't . . ."

He kneels low until his head is level with mine, pushing up at the shoulder so he can see where I'm connected to the fox. This close I can see he's bleeding from a deep bite to his collarbone, barely visible under the black T-shirt now sticking to the wound. His magic—cinnamon-whiskey-smoke—flows over my face. I am so thankful for his scent that I moan, inhaling again so that it masks the hellfox's stench.

"The hole is the exact size of your fist. You've got to close your hand," Sel murmurs. He heaves upward until the creature's chest lifts off me, and I gasp at the immediate relief. "Close your hand."

I don't move. I want to, but I just . . . don't. I whimper and shake my head.

Sel's golden eyes find mine. "Close your hand, Bree." His voice is shockingly soft. "I'll do the rest."

I hold his gaze for a moment. Whether it's because of his oddly kind tone or the fact that he called me "Bree" for the first time, I nod and close my right hand, crying out as my fingernails scrape past the still-warm heart. Sel stands and pulls the fox by the shoulders until my flaming fist emerges from the steaming hole between its ribs. When my hand comes free, there's a wet, sucking sound and a fresh blob of dark green ichor falls down between my legs. I crabwalk backward, bringing my shaking left hand to my mouth.

Sel drops the carcass, and a second after it hits the ground, it explodes with a ripping sound into a fox-shaped cloud of green dust. Behind me, the other fox explodes too, like the aether has torn it open from the inside out.

The world is shaking again, and again I realize it's me. Just me. I'm trembling uncontrollably. My pulse won't slow down. My chest feels like it's going to explode right along with the foxes.

I wrench over onto my hands and knees and vomit, heaving until burning bile eats at my throat and tongue.

Sel drops to his knees beside me. "You're okay. They're gone."

They're gone.

But I'm not okay.

I crawl away from the sick until I can twist to a seated position, resting my arms on bent knees. While I wipe my mouth with a clean bit of T-shirt, I watch Sel watching me.

His eyes trail over my head, my shoulders, my arms. "It's fading." I look down, and he's right. The crimson light on my forearm and fist are dimming. The ichor caked on my knuckles breaks apart, cracking and crumbling between my fingers. After a moment, only a few black specks remain. "It . . . it's acting like a shield," Sel begins, his voice more filled with wonder than I've ever heard before. "Burning off the hellfox blood."

He's right. When the red glow goes, so does the rest of the liquid. I shake my head, disbelieving everything, everything that just happened to me.

Sel is in much the same boat, it seems. He stands up, his expression too confused to be accusatory. "What are you?" We stare at each other until we hear the shouts.

"Bree!"

"Sel!"

"Bree! Sel!"

I recognize the voices. Evan. Tor. "I found them!" Evan shouts.

I turn from my seated position to see the Squire jump over the wall and jog over to where we're huddled together. A blond-haired figure streaks past him faster than the eye can track, and suddenly Tor is standing beside us.

Sel notices her speed too. "Are you—?"

"Awakened?" Evan finishes. "Yep. Tor went down about an hour ago. We took her back to the Lodge and called everyone in, but you two never showed up."

"And you're up and running already?"

"Accelerated metabolism, William thinks." Tor grins, but then she notices what's on the ground around us, sees me sitting there. "What the hell happened here?"

Evan notices the fading green piles too. "Is that Shadowborn dust?"

A new voice shouts to us from beyond the wall. "Did you find them?"

At the sound of Nick's voice, Sel takes a step back, retreating. My eyes follow the movement, and Sel and I lock gazes. I watch his face shutter in real time from wonder and something I can only interpret as concern, to the grim neutrality of a soldier at war. And just like that, the Selwyn Kane from a few moments ago is buried under stone like a secret gone to the grave.

"Hey!" Nick jumps the wall and runs toward us, relief for both me and Sel plain on his face. Sarah follows close behind him. "Are you both okay? We didn't know where the hell you were. Then Tor was Called, and—" Nick slows when he sees my bloodied arm. "No . . ." He's at my side in a heartbeat. He reaches with gentle fingers for my left hand. When he rotates it, he hisses at the sight. The cuts are long and deep, running from elbow to wrist, and dirt and pebbles are sticking where my arm had pressed into the earth. I hadn't noticed.

Tor curses under her breath, and she and Sarah share a brief look. I move to stand, but my knees aren't cooperating. My entire body feels slow, heavy.

"I'm okay," I rasp. Nick's hand goes to my brow, his fingers pressing against my forehead, trailing down my neck and shoulder like touching me will give him the answers I can't say out loud.

Evan toes at a pile of powder where one of the hellfoxes had dissolved. "There are three green piles. Sel's hounds are blue."

Nick leans around me to look at the pile himself. His blue eyes sharpen, and his jaw goes tight. "What happened here?"

No one looks at me. Everyone looks at Sel.

Selwyn Kane is an annoyed, slightly bored sorcerer for all that anyone can see. But I can see beneath that now. He's nervous. Rattled. "Hellfoxes. Almost fully materialized." He nods at the piles. "They stole the aether from my weapons. We went to ground, took the tunnels, but they found us somehow."

Evan walks toward us, shaking his head. "But three? Working together in the same location at the same time? No Gate is big enough for three to pass at once. Where'd they come from?"

"They ambushed us at the graveyard."

"Three Shadowborn ambushed *you*?" Evan frowns. "You can sense a non-corp imp half a mile away. How did these demons catch you off guard?"

There's a crack in Sel's facade. When he doesn't answer right away, I feel Nick tense beside me. "How did they surprise you, Sel?" he asks his Kingsmage.

Sel meets Nick's eyes, and I know then why he didn't fully answer my question in the tunnels. "I was . . . distracted."

Tor's anxious glance between Sel and Nick, Evan's uncharacteristic silence, and the subtle clench of the fingers holding mine are all the warning we get.

Nick stands to face his Kingsmage. "Distracted? By what?"

Sel swipes his tongue over his lower lip, a nervous gesture that looks unnatural on his face. "We haven't seen a Shadowborn uprising in two hundred years. If you were planning one, what would you do? Use a scout to disable us first? Knock us off-balance? What better time to disrupt our ranks than initiation? What better opportunity to break the Table before it's gathered than to take out our king before he is Called?"

"Thinking like a demon now, Sel?"

Sel growls in frustration. "It's my *job* to think like a demon."

Nick's brow furrows as he makes the connections. "What does this have to do with Bree?"

Sel meets his gaze head-on. "That first uchel wanted *you*, Nick. It called for the Pendragon. How did it know where to find you? A goruchel need simply to pose as a Page—act as a mole—to uncover that information, and it's only a matter of time before a mole exposes themselves." Sel swallows, and a shadow passes through his eyes, but he doesn't look away from his future king. I give him points for that. "I decided to accelerate the process."

Nick takes a step toward his Kingsmage. When he speaks, his voice is deadly quiet. "What did you do?"

The muscle in Sel's jaw twitches, but he holds Nick's gaze.

Another step. "*What* did you do?"

Sel lifts his chin. "I could have called the hound off her at any moment—"

Using the momentum of his next step, Nick throws a fast, hard punch to Sel's jaw. The hit knocks the sorcerer back into the same oak that stunned the fox. Nick must have put real power into his swing, because my ears ring with the *crack* of bone meeting bone. It all happens so fast—had to, to catch Sel off guard—that it takes a second for anyone else to react. Sarah yelps and Evan curses, but no one moves to step between them.

Sel is against the tree trunk, utterly still, his stunned expression warring with a visible urge to retaliate.

"Well, that wasn't entirely fair, Nicholas," he finally mutters. He pushes to standing and spits bright red blood onto the grass before dragging the back of his hand over his mouth. It leaves a crimson streak across his pale knuckles. "You know I can't strike you in return."

In a voice made of iron, Nick says, "Precisely."

Sel's eyes flash. His lips curl over bloodied teeth, then smooth over in the same breath. Fury, barely bottled.

My eyes dart between the two of them, king-to-be and his sworn protector. When they'd battled in the woods that first night, Sel had aimed for me, not Nick. The Kingsmage Oath means he can never *intend* to injure Nick without risking his own destruction, but it does nothing to prevent Nick from harming Sel. They'd grown up together with this power imbalance, but I'd never expect Nick to exploit it. Not like this . . .

Sel shrugs, like Nick's violence is no matter, but tension radiates from his shoulders, the raised veins of his neck. He chuckles—then winces, bringing a hand to his chin. "Hm. You don't have Arthur's strength yet, but I think you almost broke my jaw. Imagine the damage you'll do once you're Awakened."

"Is this why you wanted to be with Bree tonight? To threaten my Page with your constructs?" Nick's fists shake at his sides. "To defy me?"

The Kingsmage scowls and looks away, and I see where the anger is truly directed: at himself. He slipped up and his abilities failed him—just like Lord Davis suggested that night in the woods. And here is Lord Davis's son, bearing witness to that failure and punishing him for it.

I feel the urge to stand and defend him, but what would I say? I'm not a mole. I'm not an uchel. I don't know what I am, but I'm not a threat to Nick. And yet . . . there's something in me that recognizes something in him.

"Stay away from her," Nick orders, his voice low. "Excalibur or not, Called or not, if you try anything like this again . . ." He doesn't finish the sentence, but consequences hang in the air where we can all imagine them. Nick raises his chin. "Do you understand me, *Kingsmage?*"

"Yes." Sel's eyes darken until they go flat and unreadable. "My liege."

Nick turns without another word and walks back to me. Everything about him is vibrating, with adrenaline or anger, I'm not sure, but when his eyes meet mine, they soften into the ocean I know. "Can you stand? We need to get you to William."

I nod, but wave his hand away when he reaches to pick me up. "I can walk." Still, he takes most of my weight easily with one arm wrapped about my ribs, and we turn in the direction of the Lodge. Tor and Sarah fall in on one side, and Evan on the other. Flanking us, I realize. For protection.

When we walk down the path, I'm the only one who looks back.

The Kingsmage and I lock eyes once more just as the three piles of Shadowborn dust swirl up in the air around him, then spark out of existence.

31

"IT ITCHES."

"I didn't take you as a complainer," William murmurs, his hands hovering over my forearms.

"I'm not a complainer."

"Mhm-hmm." William leans down to watch as the last bit of skin closes up over a fresh scar. He makes a twisting gesture with his wrist, and the silver aether coating his fingers and my arm disappears with a quiet pop. "That'll do. You'll wake up without scars. Try to keep my arms in good shape next time?"

I've been leaning over a silver hospital tray for ten minutes as he worked. It feels good to finally lie back in bed under blankets, but then the rest of the aches immediately become more apparent. I grunt when my head hits the pillow. William makes a soft, displeased sound. "I can use aether to heal those bruises."

Heat floods my cheeks. "The ones all over my ass and back? I'm good."

He rolls his eyes. "I'm a medical professional, or I will be soon. Pre-med, in addition to being the Scion of Gawain, remember?" He wiggles his fingers. "Double healer."

"So"—I puff up the pillows around my head—"you're saying that I should feel comfortable getting down to my skivvies with you."

"I'd never tell someone what they need to be comfortable with," William

says, his gray eyes thoughtful. "I was just offering context. If it helps, I'm happily
in love and not at all interested."

I grin, despite my fatigue. "Oh yeah? Who's the lucky person?"

"He's not Legendborn, that's for sure." William laughs warmly. "Dating
inside the Order is nothing but trouble."

I perk up. "Why's that?"

"Bloodlines, oaths, inheritances? Pick one." William pulls the table away
and leans back against the other bed. "Pages can date Pages, easy. Squires dating Squires is fine, but tricky. A Squire's job is to protect their Scion, and that
bond is unbreakable, sacred. In battle a Squire can't prioritize their partner's
well-being over their Scion, and the Warrior's Oath is forever, even after the
eligibility period ends and the inheritances disappear. Who wants to be with
someone who's already emotionally and magically bonded to someone else—
for life?"

I grimace. "That sounds awful."

"It is." He whistles low. "You should hear the jealous snark that comes out
of people's mouths at the Selection Gala. It's all Order grudges and gossip and
drama. But even that's just . . . awkward and inconvenient." He shakes his head.
"Dating Scions is a whole different ball game."

I push up on one elbow, eager to learn more. "Why?"

"Sixty generations, give or take, of managing the bloodlines . . . It gets
complicated. The Regents had to step in and lay down rules at some point.
Order law forbids crossing the bloodlines, so no hanky-panky between anyone
who could become a Scion or whose kids could become a Scion in the line of
succession. If they didn't prohibit it, there'd be babies with two, three, four
lineages running around. It'd be chaos trying to track who'll be Called next and
how the bloodline will be preserved. It's easier for couples where pregnancy
is one hundred percent impossible. But for couples who could get pregnant?
They're *screwed*. In the not-fun way."

"That's . . ."

"Awful, I know. Though it's sort of a modern *fin'amor*. The medieval ideal of
courtly, ennobling love that can never be consummated. Very romantic concept

back then. But today? There were rumors of a Scion couple at another chapter who hid their relationship, but the Regents have spies everywhere. They were caught. And punished." He furrows his brow at that last word.

I know that, if I asked, William would tell me what the Regents do to the couples they catch, but the shudder that passes through his shoulders tells me I might not want the answer. The more I hear about the Regents and the more I hear about how much they meddle in both Onceborn and Legendborn lives, the more I hate them. No one in the chapter has spoken of the Regents without a touch of fear, or at least deference, in their voices. Not Nick, not Sel. Not even Lord Davis. Who are these all-powerful figures who keep the Order's records, control its bloodlines, and send Merlins out in the world like demonic assassins and hypnotists?

I change the subject. "So . . . what about a Scion dating their own Squire?"

"Like Russ and Felicity? Or Tor and Sar?" William makes an iffy motion with his head. "Scions dating their Squires *can* work—but imagine breaking up and then being bonded to your ex *forever*. I don't know about you, but I'd rather eat my own aether sword."

"Ah," is all I can manage.

"'Ah,' she says,"—William lifts a mocking eyebrow—"as if this is just idle conversation and has nothing *at all* to do with her relationship to one Scion in particular."

"Shush."

William laughs again. I like his laughter. It brings small crow's-feet to the corners of his gray eyes.

"So"—he wiggles his eyebrows playfully—"shall I heal your ass, or are you still worried I'm gonna check it out?"

I sigh and reach down to tug my jeans off. "You can check me out if you want. I'm not *not* cute."

"Ha!" he says. "I knew I liked you."

Once I'm in my undies and on my stomach, William begins. The aether feels like heaven over my tender skin. I stifle a moan.

"You know," William says thoughtfully, "while you're not as banged up as one could be from facing multiple demons, your vitals were all over the place when they brought you in."

Apparently somewhere between the graveyard and the Lodge, I'd passed out. Nick had carried me the rest of the way and then down the elevator to the infirmary. I'd woken up to Nick and William bickering over whether the would-be king could stay in the room during my treatment. Once I opened my eyes, Nick had grumbled and left William to finish his examination in peace. William sponged off the muck, disinfected the wounds, and got to work.

"I'd guessed at first that you would be in shock, but that didn't quite fit. High blood pressure, increased oxygen levels, shallow breaths, dilated pupils. Typical signs of an adrenaline rush after a demon fight. I see 'em all the time. Fight-or-flight responses are inherently draining, and after an hour or so, vitals return to standard ranges. But your numbers were subnormal: pupils constricted, slow breaths, sluggish heart rate, low body temp."

I chew on my bottom lip, remembering the shining red flames around my fingers and what Sel said about generating my own aether. "Is that bad?"

"'Bad' is a subjective term around here." William hovers over a particularly painful spot on my lower back. "But it's not typical. It was like your system had fired so intensely that instead of simply leveling out, it put you into hibernation."

Firing intensely seems like the right way to put it. The very first time in the shower after the Oath, I'd been . . . terrified, overwhelmed, sad, but I'd been able to put it all behind a wall. Tonight I'd been angry in the graveyard, and terrified for my life with the hound, and the flames had faded away on their own. Sel's right, I truly have no idea how this works, and I don't have a lot of options for help. Sel has no interest in trying to help me understand, nor would I want to experiment with him to figure it out. I could tell Nick, but he was pissed beyond belief tonight. And scared, after Tor's Awakening. He and everyone else in the building are on edge. I don't know if it's a good idea to spring another surprise on him. Maybe Patricia—

The door opens, and Nick walks in. "Hey, Will, is—"

I screech and twist into a ball, pulling the thin blanket up over my entire body. It's not fast enough. Nick's face has gone summer-strawberry red. He definitely saw my butt. And my back. And my bra straps. And maybe some side boob.

He chokes out a strangled, "Um, sorry!" and disappears into the hall, slamming the door behind him.

"Ugh!" I pull the sheet up higher so my face can hide too.

William taps on the fabric like it's a door. "Pardon me?"

I yank it down so that only my eyes are visible. "What?"

His eyes twinkle. "In past centuries, *some* courtiers wanted nothing more than for an eligible king to 'accidentally' see them naked."

"Shut *up*, William!"

When I'm fully healed, all I feel is tired. I just want my own bed. I thank William, and he walks me to the elevator. Nick greets us upstairs. His cheeks are still flushed, but they're less summer strawberry, more peach.

William squeezes my arm. When he steps back into the elevator to ride up to the residence level, he gives a wink before the doors close. "Call me if you need anything, *courtier Matthews*."

Nick's confused expression bounces between the elevator and me, but I wave it away. "William being William."

I'm relieved when he decides not to mention any accidental sightings of my flesh. Instead he wraps me in his arms and presses a kiss to my forehead. It's meant to be comforting, but his lips on my skin make me shiver, send goose bumps down my spine. "You're sure you're okay?"

I nod and lean against his chest. Right now I just want to enjoy the feeling of being folded into him, breathe the clean smell of his new shirt. "I could sleep for a full day, but I'm okay."

He pulls back to examine my face, runs a thumb over my lower lip. "I never should have let you go off with Sel alone. It was my Rule Three, and I broke it."

"He challenged you in front of everyone," I counter.

"It won't happen again. I swear it." He pulls me in for a soft, lingering kiss to seal the vow.

This boy makes my chest ache.

"Let's get you home."

Early morning light streams through cracks between clouds, diffusing the open, quiet foyer with sleepy sun. We only make it a handful of steps before two figures sitting on a bench in one of the foyer's recessed alcoves stand up to greet us. I drop Nick's arm before the figures move out of the shadows, and the small *hrmn* sound of disappointment he emits fills me with warm, fizzy bubbles.

"Bree!" Greer rushes forward with Whitty beside them, worry etched across their face. They wrap me in their arms, then pull back to look me over. *"Hellfoxes?"*

"Sar said they took Sel's aether?" Whitty asks. "Right outta his weapons?"

Greer punches him lightly in the arm. "We're worried about Bree right now, Whitlock."

Whitty flushes. "Sorry. Ya all right there, Matthews?"

"I'm okay, really." I rub my healing, itching arms and look around at the dimly lit foyer. All the other Pages have gone back to their dorms, and the Legendborn are in bed in the two floors above us. "Y'all didn't have to wait up for me."

"You and Sel were missing for over an hour," Greer says, not standing close enough to Nick to clock the tension that their words are causing, "and neither of you were answering your phone. No one knew if the trial was over, still going, or what. Then Tor collapsed right out front while we were waiting, everyone started freaking out—"

Whitty notices Nick's expression and bumps Greer in the shoulder to cut them off.

I turn their words over in my mind, speechless for a moment. I'd completely forgotten how the night started. The scavenger hunt, the trial, the tournament. Right.

Nick fills me in while I'm still recalibrating. "You, Vaughn, and Whitty found far and away the most objects on the list, followed by Sydney, Greer, and Blake. Carson only found two objects, and Spencer"—a line appears between his brows—"got pinned by one of Sel's hounds. They're both out."

Down in the infirmary, William said that the Kingsmage hadn't come home yet. I wonder if he's off somewhere licking his wounds after the fight with Nick.

"It's only the combat trial left now," Whitty says, stifling a yawn. "I heard that's Thursday, with everythin' headin' the way it is."

"Thursday?" I croak. When Lord Davis announced the accelerated tournament schedule, six weeks had sounded like enough time to at least learn how to fight *decently* with one weapon. Maybe the cudgel. But today is Saturday. What could I learn in five days? "What happened to six weeks?"

Nick stiffens beside me. "That was before Tor was Called."

"Sorry, Bree," Greer mutters, shifting their weight from one foot to the next. Whitty winces, his expression sympathetic. They both know what I know, which is that there's almost no chance I'll do well in the final trial. Greer and Whitty say their goodbyes and head out the front door. I watch them go, my heart sinking.

"I may as well quit now."

"Only if you want to," Nick says with a sigh, looping our fingers together. I send him a questioning look, and he shrugs. "I made a few calls while you were downstairs. I requested that one of the Lieges who trained me—one of the good ones—lead the training sessions for the group. Gillian's solid. I trust her."

"Is she a miracle worker?"

The side of his mouth lifts. "Better. The former Scion of Kay. You don't need to win every match on Thursday. You just need to lose *well*."

I sigh and shake my head. "Losing well sounds a lot like regular losing."

"They aren't the same thing," he murmurs, his thumb passing over my knuckles. "Believe me."

We pause in the middle of the foyer and stare up at the windows as the sun creeps forth and early morning birds start their day. I glance at Nick beside me, his head tilted back and eyes closed, his blond hair turned gold in the light. His face appears illuminated from within. I try to imagine him as a king in a painting, noble and stern. I can almost see it. Especially after tonight. Maybe I should try to tell him. Explain what happened to me.

"Nick?"

"Hm?"

"What Sel did was wrong . . ." Nick tenses, but drops his head to stare at me. The mix of anger and fierce protectiveness in his eyes takes my breath away. My heart, slow as William said it was, wakes up like the sun, *ba-dumps* in my chest. I ignore it, just to get this out. "But I *am* lying to people. I'm not here for the same reasons as everyone else, and we both know it . . ."

Nick's eyes are twin blue moons, shining bright. "What are you saying?"

What *am* I saying? "That he has a point. I don't belong here. I'm a . . . a distraction." The words feel true as soon as I say them out loud.

Nick's head jerks back like I'd slapped him, and his eyes flash. "Sel used his powers to directly *threaten* a member of this chapter! If you were Legendborn, his Oath of Service would have burned him alive. Do you have any *idea* what my father would do to him if he were here?"

I blink, startled by his vehemence. "Yes, but he thought I was here to hurt you, Nick! He was just doing his job. You've said it yourself, I'm an anomaly. The things I can do—"

He presses a finger to my mouth. "Not here."

He's right. The echoing foyer isn't exactly soundproof if someone above opens a door. I lower my voice. "Sel didn't hurt me."

"He's the reason you got hurt!" he insists in a rough whisper.

"No, he's not," I counter.

He laughs, incredulous, and releases me to tunnel both hands through his hair. "How are you defending him right now?!"

"I'm not." I groan. "Sel shouldn't have sent his hound after me, but he's not wrong to be vigilant. You didn't see those hellfoxes, Nick. They'll eat the Legendborn's weapons and armor, steal it away. Leave all of you *helpless*—"

"Which is why I need to be able to *trust* my Kingsmage," he fires back. "And right now, *I don't trust him.* I don't!"

"But—"

He grasps my hands, his eyes turning pleading in the dim light. "If Camlann is coming, and I become king, I'm going to have to make hard decisions, Bree. But they will never be the kind of decisions that make it okay for us to turn on our own or behave as badly as Shadowborn. I won't be the leader that allows our opponents to turn us into reckless monsters, and that's exactly what Sel let happen tonight. He allowed his anger and fear to twist his perception of facts and turn him into his worst self. If he succumbs to—" He stops short. Grips my fingers, turning them so that he can press his lips to the back of my hand. "That's not the type of warrior we can afford to take into battle."

The words rattle around in my chest. "What do you mean? What are you going to do? Are you . . . can you . . ."

He rests his forehead against mine and takes a deep breath. "I don't know what I'm going to do, B. The only thing I know right now is that we both need rest. We've been up all night. You need to heal. Your trainer will be here in twelve hours, I've got to call my dad by lunch . . ." He presses another soft kiss to my cheek. "Let me drive you home?"

I nod weakly because Nick's right. We're both exhausted, and maybe right now isn't the best time to have serious discussions about leading a kingdom or punishing a Kingsmage, or what makes a person a monster.

But nothing about how I feel—how *everything* feels—seems right at all.

32

THANK GOD FOR Saturdays.

I sleep until noon, and even then I only drag myself out of bed because my bladder and growling stomach begin protesting with alternating pangs of discomfort. I glance at my image in the mirror of the bathroom and shudder.

William may have healed my injuries, but I still *look* like someone who's been fighting hellcreatures. I guess even aether can't fix that. Between the tangled, sweat-matted curls under my scarf, the bags under my eyes, and the morning breath, I *feel* like a hellcreature.

A hot shower, brushing my teeth, and a bit of water and leave-in conditioner on my hair do wonders. I'm still in my towel, water dripping down my neck, when I get a group text from a number I don't recognize.

This is Tor, Pagelings. Dinner's at five, and the training rooms open at six. Liege Roberts and Liege Hanover will be joining us. Dress appropriately. Don't be late. Don't embarrass us.

As I walk through the drowsy campus toward the dining hall, I'm filled with quiet awe at how, with all that's happened to me in the past week, the world keeps spinning. It's three weeks until fall starts, technically, but the oppressive roar of late summer heat has already dissipated. The sky is a calm blue with few clouds, and it's cool enough that I might need a sweater tonight. Somewhere in the distance, the Tar Heels marching band is rehearsing for the home game tomorrow. I pass by kids I don't know who are handing out flyers for their student group. A steady stream of students wind their way through the lawn toward the libraries to study, because no matter what's happened to me, classes are still running. There's a quiz I haven't studied for in English on Tuesday. A trial I'm not ready for on Thursday. Nick—my boyfriend? Partner in crime? Co-conspirator who I want to kiss again?—is one Scion away from being called to the throne of a modern-day kingdom. A part-demon mage claims I can create mystic energy inside myself, and he might be right, but even if he is, I have no idea what I am. All of this and yet . . . the planet still spins.

My phone buzzes in my hand. It's Patricia, texting to ask if we could meet for a special session at the Arboretum this afternoon at one. I'm on campus already, so I accept.

I decided during my shower that even if I don't know Patricia well, I do trust her. Sel said my red flames break the laws of aether as the Merlins understand it. Well, Patricia operates outside the Order's rules and uses root in ways that probably fall outside their laws, too. She may not like the Order—and that's fair, honestly—but she's shown me more about my mother's secret life than the Order ever could. Understanding my magic could be the key to understanding my mother's own magic—and from there, how she might have gotten involved with the Order in the first place.

Nick texts too. Just getting up. How about u?

Same. Heading to the dining hall for lunch. Want to meet?

Sorry, can't. My dad's calling soon to get the full update about last night. Not gonna be pretty.

I grimace. I can't imagine what Lord Davis will say. I wonder if Nick's going to tell his father everything that happened with Sel, or withhold some of the details. Or wait until he gets back into town. I'm almost at the dining hall doors before it dawns on me that, out of the two of us, *I'm* the only one who has a reason to hide some of what transpired last night. Nick doesn't know about the red mage flames, so he has no reason to censor his report. It bugs me that even though I know he'd protect my secret, I don't feel ready to share it with him. But at least this way, he doesn't have to lie for me. He's doing enough of that already.

Stomach full of two burgers and a large serving of cheesy fries, I head toward the Arboretum to meet Patricia.

When I get there, I'm surprised to see her sitting with a young Black woman just a few years older than me. She has large, dark eyes behind round glasses, red-brown skin, and hair that runs slick and tight against her scalp before it blooms into a wide, soft puff at her crown.

"Bree." Patricia stands, and so does the younger woman. "This is Mariah, a junior here and a fellow practitioner."

I stare at this girl, and envy and curiosity bite at my insides, opening up old wounds. She knows root because her mother taught her.

I could have been her.

"Isn't therapy supposed to be confidential?"

Patricia inclines her head. "This won't be a . . . normal session. After what happened yesterday at the graveyard, I realized we might need some assistance to get to the bottom of your mother's story, and your own. I asked Mariah if she would join us today to explore some of what you experienced during our walk. She will keep anything you say in confidence. I am sorry for catching you off guard." Her apology seems genuine. "I wasn't sure Mariah would be able to join us on such short notice. We can meet alone, if you prefer?"

There's no deception in her face, not a hint of manipulation. She means it. And Mariah, for her part, nods in agreement. I could send her away if I wanted. But if I do, I won't get answers.

"It's fine," I mutter.

Mariah smiles, steps forward, and extends a palm. "Hi, Bree." When I shake her hand, the black of her pupils blows wide. "Wow. Death knows you *well*," she declares, her voice breathy and low.

I yank my hand from hers, a shiver rippling up my palm to my recently healed elbow. "Nice to meet you, too?"

"My bad," she says apologetically, shaking her hand like she'd just gotten it wet. "I'm a Medium. Didn't mean to freak you out."

My eyes widen. "You can talk to dead people?"

"Why don't we sit first?" Patricia intervenes and indicates the blanket near the bench, where there's three cafeteria to-go boxes.

Mariah follows Patricia's suggestion without argument, so it seems like I'm expected to as well. Patricia kneels daintily and draws her legs and skirt to one side while Mariah settles into a cross-legged position. The blanket is soft and worn, and the grass and ground underneath holds heat from the afternoon sun.

After I decline their offer for lunch, Mariah reaches for one of the boxes. "You a member of BSM?"

"BSM?"

She smiles pleasantly. "Black Student Movement. We meet up for meals and events, and we've got a room in the Union, a magazine, performance groups, committees. It's pretty dope. Lots of ways in."

"I didn't realize there was a BSM," I murmur, shifting on the blanket. Another group, another place to belong, except this time it's not a secret. I can hear my father now. *You need a community, Bree.*

Reading my face, Patricia assures me. "It's only the first week of school, Bree. No need to beat yourself up if you haven't found everything and everyone."

The gentle grace and warmth in their faces gets me by the throat, and my face contorts into a grateful expression that's out of my control. I take a deep breath, then give Patricia a wobbly smile. Mariah tells me more about BSM and invites me to a meeting next week, and I ask about her major, because that's the question everyone on campus seems to ask first.

"Art history," she says around bites of roast beef. "My parents weren't thrilled when I declared, but I studied abroad in Paris this summer and got a curation and archival internship at the Musée d'Orsay. That helped."

"I bet." I hadn't considered studying abroad at all. EC students couldn't apply through Carolina, but exchange programs were out there for high school students.

"How 'bout you?"

"I'm Early College, so we don't really declare a major. We take a lot of liberal arts classes and pre-reqs."

Mariah leans forward to inspect my face, concern pulling at her mouth and eyes. "You're so young! I didn't realize."

I shrug. "I'm tall."

"No," she says, pausing with her sandwich halfway down, "that's not what I meant. I mean you're so young to be so acquainted with death."

I hadn't heard anyone say something like that since the funeral. I look between the two of them again and see it—the pity. My wall is up before I reply, "I'm sorry, how are you supposed to help me again?"

Patricia sets her own sandwich aside. "Bree, several things became clear to me during our walk yesterday. The first is that you yourself have a branch of root, one that gives you the ability to see root in its raw form. The second is what you revealed to me in Louisa's memory—that you are acquainted with the Order of the Round Table. If that's true, then it follows that the only reason you're sitting here right now is because the Order is not aware of what you can do. Am I correct?"

I fidget under her gaze, but nod.

"I'm relieved," Patricia says with a sigh. "Our people have learned the hard way to hide our abilities from them, even when we were working in their homes and caring for their babies."

I hadn't considered this and feel foolish for not asking about it earlier. How *did* the Rootcrafters hide all they could do, all the time, from the Scions, Squires, Pages . . . or anyone who took the First Oath and was granted Sight? Patricia reads my expression.

"We can be plenty invisible when they want us to be," she says dryly. "Rootcraft knows of their origins, their mission, and how they use their 'aether' to fight the crossroads creatures. We also know from experience what they do to outsiders who use power. How they take them away, lock them up, or worse."

"I didn't tell anyone in the Order about you," I say quickly, "if that's what you're worried about."

She places a hand over mine. "I didn't think you would. But you're still in danger every time you go near them."

"I know," I murmur.

"Then why do it?" Mariah asks, confusion written on her face. "Hiding what you are on top of hanging out with the good ole boys club? Twisting yourself all up into a shape that's convenient for them?" She wrinkles her nose. "Sounds *exhausting*."

I swallow around an unexpected lump, because she's right. The looks Vaughn still gives me. Tor's words the night of my Oath. The look I get from a few of the eliminated Pages that hang around the Lodge. How much energy I spend wondering if they're thinking the same thing Vaughn is about why I'm Nick's Page—that it's sex, or race, or both. Between Nick's rules and the ones I already carry around with me every day, it *is* exhausting. I could argue that the Order's not all white, that Sarah's there, but then I remember what she said about her dad and the dinner parties and get tired all over again. They're both doing a version of the same contortionist act that I'm doing: figuring out how to survive in water that you *know* has sharks, because you have to.

I don't feel any of that here with Mariah and Patricia. Alice is my safe space, my home, and that would never change. But it's been *months* since I've held space with only Black women and it's not just safe, it's . . . a release.

Lying to them right now feels like the straw that will break my back. And I can't afford for my back to break. Not now.

"I don't believe my mother's death was an accident," I begin, and their eyes grow wide. "Last week I recovered a . . . memory. The night she died, one of their casters—a Merlin—erased my and my father's memories at the hospital, and I don't know why. I believe the Order may have killed her, that something happened while she was enrolled here that made her a target. I've become one of their initiates to find out the truth, but I'm not *with* them. I'm against them."

In the moment of silence after I finish, the wind picks up Patricia's scarf and Mariah's and my curls. It says something about the Order's reputation that neither one of them denies my suspicion, or even questions it. The same emotion passes over both of their expressions, too quick for me to name.

It's Patricia who speaks first. "And do you have proof?"

"I have Ruth's memories of something that happened on campus when my mother was here. If I pass their Trials, I gain a title in their world, and they'll trust me. I can ask more questions, get answers, and then I'll *get* proof."

"You seek revenge?"

My eyelids flutter. That specific word had never fallen from my mouth. But it didn't need to, did it? It's always been there, in a way. Revenge, retaliation, justice. But even those words aren't enough, a small voice whispers. They don't feel deep enough. Big enough.

What did I say to Nick? *Punish them for what they did.* "Punish" feels better. Punish feels . . . right.

"Bree? Is that what you want?"

"I want to find who's responsible"—the words come fast, from the quiet thoughts I've buried deep—"use my root abilities, the title I'll gain, and the contacts I have to bring to justice anyone who was involved."

Patricia regards me closely. "You said you can resist their hypnosis?"

"Yes, if I want to." Patricia and Mariah exchange a worried glance. "What is it?"

Patricia's frown lines deepen. "What else can you do, Bree?"

I tell her everything. How it's not just the Sight or the mesmer resistance. How I can smell castings. How I can feel Sel's gaze on my skin. And last, I tell them about the red mage flames.

Mariah's jaw has long since dropped, but the mage flames bit must have tipped her over. "Holy shit."

"Language," Patricia chastises, but her face looks pretty "holy shit" too. She covers trembling fingers with her burgundy shawl, to hide them from me, I think. "And you've never called on an ancestor for any of these abilities?"

"No."

"If you aren't asking to borrow these powers, then they've been bound to you somehow."

"Bound to me—" I stutter, shaking my head. "No. I mean, bound by who?" Her warning about the Order and their powers comes back to me all in a rush. "You think I'm a Bloodcrafter? No, I've never—"

"I know," Patricia says. "This is why I've asked Mariah here today. To get answers."

Mariah nods to Patricia. "I definitely get it now," she says, then points a finger at me. "You need to talk to your ancestors."

I look between the two of them. "You're serious, aren't you?"

The corner of Mariah's mouth twitches. "On the other side, they have access to more knowledge than we do. When Doc Hartwood called me this morning, I set out offerings for my grandma to pass the gift to me today. Sometimes, if I'm lucky, I can help other people talk to their ancestors too."

My throat closes tight, my stomach clenches, and my fingers grip the earth beside my knees. Could I really see my mother? Talk to her like I did Louisa? Ask her what *happened* that night?

"You . . . can help me talk to my mom? See her again?"

Mariah's face folds, and I can tell she expected my question. "I can help you call for your people, but I don't control who answers."

I nod and blink stinging tears away. My chest is full of the sharp pang of loss and an unexpected feeling of relief. When I imagine seeing my mother again—something I never thought possible—it feels like there are a thousand words that want to come out of my mouth at once. So very many that I cannot speak at all.

Like she's read my mind, Patricia leans forward to touch my knee. "Love is a powerful thing, more powerful than blood, although both run through us like a river. She may answer you, but if she does not, she still loves you."

I nod, but my emotions are swirling inside me like a hurricane. "How does it work?"

Mariah folds her hands in her lap. "I amplify the connection between family members, and then make the request. Sort of like sonar. The ancestor who responds might be your mother, it might be a grandparent or great-grandparent, or even further back. If the signal's strong enough. I can help you speak to them."

I nibble on my lower lip and wonder if my mother might not want to answer my call. Would she still be angry with me, like she was the night before she died? Would she be proud of what I'm doing? Would she want me to stop? Would I stop if she asked me to?

"Okay," I say quietly.

Mariah gestures for me to face her until our crossed legs touch, knee to knee. She takes my hands in hers and closes her eyes. Patricia nods reassuringly, and I close mine, too.

"We'll start slow, Bree," Patricia says. "You'll just focus on your love for your mother."

I pull an image of my mother up from memory and, right away, there's pain. I see her in her favorite summer housedress, drifting through our home to open up the windows. She's humming a melody-less tune. I'm reading a book on our living room couch, and when she reaches over my head to open the window, she looks down with a broad, toothy smile against copper-brown skin. Behind her glasses, love, pride, and affection live in the corners of her eyes. I smile, sending my love back, but it twists and sharpens into something else.

"Steady," Patricia whispers. "Focus on your love for her. Now, imagine the love stretching back to your grandparents, then back further, like a strong thread connecting the generations. That's what Mariah will follow."

Like a Line.

I do my best to follow her instructions, imagine my grandmother as my mother described her, but as soon as I do, grief slices through me.

Patricia must sense my pain, like she always does. "Bree, it's all right. Take slow breaths. We're right here; you're not alone."

I don't listen. All I can think of is *loss*. My loss of my mother, my mother's loss of hers. And what I didn't tell Patricia: that my great-grandmother died before my mom was born too. None of us met our grandmothers.

Mariah makes a low, whining sound. "There are wells of life, deep ones but they're all separated. Tied off from one another."

Because death breaks *our connection!* I want to scream. Death is not a thread. It is the sharp cut that severs us. Death separates us from one another, and yet it holds us close. As deeply as we hate it, it loves us more.

My heart pounds to its rhythm.

One mother, two mothers, three mothers. Gone.

Gone.

Gone.

Gone.

Mariah gasps and releases my hands. My eyes open to find her eyes wide, her chest rising with rapid breaths. "Something terrible happened in your family . . . didn't it?"

I scramble to my feet, panting and dizzy. "Bree?" Patricia reaches for me, but I can't look at her. Or Mariah. Patricia calls my name again and again, but her voice sounds farther and farther away—and no wonder, because I'm running from her. Again.

I feel like a coward, but I don't stop.

33

AFTER THE MEETING with Patricia and Mariah, several hours ignoring their calls, and a fitful nap that left me more tired than rested, I arrive at the Lodge completely uninterested in sitting at a table and making small talk. Nick is nowhere to be found. **Busy**, he'd texted. That's fine; I don't feel like talking.

The dinner display is massive: shrimp cocktails on the rim of mini wine goblets filled with red cocktail sauce; vegetable crudités on two-tiered silver serving dishes; seasonal flowers in red and white nestling between baskets of warm rolls, crostinis, and olive-oil soaked baguettes. Layers of grilled pineapple sticks sit by chocolate-covered melon on a white serving platter.

Right now, none of it is appealing.

I keep thinking about how Mariah and Patricia looked at me when I told them that the Order killed my mother. I can still see their eyes: they may believe my story, and they're sorry if it's true, but they think it's something I need to accept.

Their branches of root bring both of them closer to death, and so maybe acceptance is possible for them, but I'm not them.

I'm a daughter whose mother was taken from her.

Acceptance, I decide, is for people whose parents just died with no reason. True accidents or illness. Acceptance is not possible for murder.

Whatever Mariah did sent cracks through all of my old walls and brought

After-Bree, raw and spiteful, clawing to the surface. I don't bother to repair them. I just let myself *feel*. More deeply than ever before, I feel the presence of death in my chest. My mother's, my grandmother's, my great-grandmother's. Now that I hold all of that death, how can I just accept it?

If there's one thing the Order has taught me, it's that I'm *my* family's Scion. I have a duty to fight for them.

I'd been in the infirmary in the Lodge basement so many times, I'd started thinking of the entire floor as "William's." I'd completely forgotten it houses the Order's training rooms too.

Even underground, the biggest room's ceiling is twelve feet overhead. It can easily fit every chapter member and probably another twenty on top of that. Tonight, however, it's just the six Pages that remain in the tournament, spread out while we wait for our coaches.

In the center are three concentric circles painted on a large square mat. The smallest circle in the middle is outlined in white, the next-largest blue, and the one after—almost fifty feet in diameter—is red.

On the far wall, lined up on a rack, is an assortment of metal weapons. Long wooden staffs banded with silver rings, four sets of silver bows with a quiver of silver arrows beneath each, maces, swords, and daggers.

I remind myself that I don't need to *win* win. I just need to lose *well*.

The door bangs open. In walk a man and a woman in their late thirties. The man is tall and broad-shouldered with closely cropped blond hair. The woman is taller than Nick, and her black hair is cut into a short, severe bob. They're both dressed in expensive athletic gear and wearing soft, worn shoes that make little sound as they walk.

"Line up," the man barks at us, pointing to one side of the mat. We scurry over while he watches. If the eyes are windows, then this man's are boarded shut with no clear view into what goes on within. "My name is Liege Owen Roberts, Squire of a Fallen Scion of Bors. This is Gillian Hanover, a Liege of Kay."

Fallen Scion. What would it feel like to lose one's Scion in battle? Suddenly, the man's hardened appearance takes on new meaning.

And Gillian, Nick's former trainer, was never Awakened at fifth-ranked, but nothing about her looks weak or incapable. Nick said she'd been in the field since she was fifteen, deployed by the Regents to fight Shadowborn worldwide, just like the Merlins.

In other words, they're both plenty deadly.

"We are here for the next five nights to oversee your preparation for the combat trial, and assist with skill acquisition as necessary." The last bit Gillian says with an eye on me, and it takes everything in me not to look away in embarrassment. Somewhere to my left, Vaughn snickers. "We will also referee the trial so that the members of this chapter, and the three Scions in need of Squires, may evaluate your bouts from the audience."

When Gillian takes a step forward, the weight on her left side lands differently: she wears a prosthesis. It's possible she's always used it, and equally possible she'd been injured in battle.

"All Scions must become proficient in the use of a longsword, but not every Scion will inherit one from their knight. As a Squire, you will need to demonstrate proficiency in the weapon your Scion uses, as you'll be generating that same weapon from aether once the two of you are bonded. Who here can explain the inherited weapons of the Lines of Arthur, Owain, and Gawain?"

Vaughn recites the details as if reading from a book. "Scions in the Line of Arthur inherit enhanced strength and intuition for battle strategy, and the ability to wield Excalibur. As such, Scion Davis uses a longsword. Scions of Owain inherit the Knight of the Lion's aether construct familiar and use the quarterstaff. Scions of Gawain, healing, strength at noon and midnight, dual daggers."

"Very good." Gillian nods, her eyes assessing Vaughn quickly. "Over the next three nights, we will begin the evening with a demonstration, modeling the bouts you will undertake on Thursday evening. These bouts will be Page against Page, and structured so that each of you has an opportunity to demonstrate your skill—or weakness—with each form of combat."

I wait for Gillian and Owen to step into the sparring circle, but instead the door slams open and Sel strides into the room in loose pants and a black tank.

The Kingsmage pulls everyone's attention like a magnet, but he passes the Pages without a word, his face a blank mask. As he walks toward the smallest ring, he calls swirling blue aether into one palm and draws it out with the other until it stretches and solidifies into a shining quarterstaff. In the white ring, he pivots to face the coaches and twirls the crystalline weapon from one hand to the next, behind his back and across his chest.

I haven't seen him since the fight between him and Nick. To anyone else he looks like his normal broody, stoic self, but I can tell it's just a front; his casting smells acrid and sharp in my nose.

Sel is *furious*.

I take slow, deep breaths in through my mouth to block out the scent of his rage. I add duct tape and glue and spackle and plaster to my walls, because inside me, After-Bree is responding to him. She wants to be furious too.

"Selwyn and I will demonstrate quarterstaff combat," Owen says. "Pages aiming for the Line of Owain, please pay close attention. Watch our demo for speed of attacks and for techniques to defend against a Shadowborn opponent, which Selwyn here will mimic for educational purposes."

The coaches know for a fact that Sel is part demon, but no one else here does. No one except me. Distantly, I wonder if I should warn Owen. Yell that he should reschedule, stop the match now before it starts. Sel's far too angry. Another, freshly cruel part of me says, why bother? If Owen knew who I was, he'd probably turn me in without a second thought. Let Sel beat him. Let me watch.

They start slow with measured footwork, one opponent rotating around the other. Then, at some cue, Owen advances, and the fight begins.

I can't take my eyes off Sel. His movements are everything that I know mine won't be: arcs that glide through the air, quick strikes that send his staff whistling toward Owen's. Where Nick is powerful and arena-ready, Sel is lean and built for agility and speed. He doesn't move like a human at all, and it baffles me that I ever thought he was one.

Loud clacks fill the room; the weapons meet again and again.

Owen's staff whips low at Sel's legs. Sel leaps—into a perfect one-handed back-flip. The wood never meets its mark. Owen scowls. Sel straightens with a grin.

Owen shifts tactics, lunging for an overhead strike. Sel evades fluidly, under and around Owen's attack, then twists his staff for a wicked blow to Owen's ribs. Owen grunts, recovers, and moves into a flurry of attacks.

Sel meets each downward smash, sweep, thrust, and lunge with preternatural speed. He uses the full length of his staff—the top, the middle, the butt end—and even blocks one of Owen's blows with a bare forearm.

Eventually Owen lands a blow. He clips Sel on the shoulder. It doesn't even faze him. Instead, the Kingsmage grins and sweeps low, swiping at Owen's shins. The Liege blocks—barely—with a downward stab to the mat.

Still smiling, Sel presses Owen toward the edge of the circle, corralling the older man like prey with rapid-fire attacks. Owen can barely keep up.

Finally, one sharp crack to the head sends Owen to a knee. He raises a hand to concede, and the fight is finished.

The room claps as Owen stands with a grimace, his chest still heaving.

With Gillian's help, the Liege makes his way slowly to the door, and William's infirmary.

Back at the circle, Sel watches, unwinded, as they depart. He spins his staff idly, his face unreadable. After a moment, he holds the weapon out with one hand and clenches his fist until it dusts.

He passes by, close enough to touch, but doesn't spare me a single glance and leaves without a word.

When Gillian returns, she instructs each of us to take quarterstaffs and pair up if we wish. Everyone except me, that is.

As the others spread around the room, Gillian paces toward me, her arms behind her back. I swear, with every step she grows an inch in height. "You're the Onceborn outsider Nick sponsored."

"Yes."

"I won't go easy on you."

"I didn't ask you to," I snap, unable to stop myself.

She assesses me, green eyes taking in my arms and hands, my shoulders and stature. Then she heads to the back wall and the rack of weapons. She comes back holding two wooden practice staffs, banded with silver, tucked under one firm bicep. I grunt a little when she drops one into my hands.

"No matter what you do, engage your core."

Over the next hour, while everyone else is in practice bouts with each other, Gillian works with me. She shows me how to charge, bringing the staff down toward my opponent's head, and how to block by raising the staff with both hands over my own. Her heavy strikes send jarring tremors down into my elbows. I'm tall enough that my strikes make her stretch for each block, but that's my only advantage. She wipes the floor with me, and I end up on my ass more often than not.

When Gillian calls time, my wrists and shoulders are aching. "Now I'll show you how to move to maximize each strike or block. The correct position of your feet provides stability and agility so that you can move quickly into the next movement, be it offensive or defensive. Think of it as a dance."

I lean against my staff, wincing from a stitch in my side. "Shouldn't I have learned footwork first, then?"

"How do your ankles feel?"

I rotate a foot. "They hurt."

"Good."

I furrow my brow in confusion. She grins, all teeth and cruelty. "Babies learn to walk faster on tile than on carpet. Now you have incentive to get the footwork right."

I envision slapping her, but the Gillian in my mind has me on my back before I can lift a hand. Her mouth quirks like she knows exactly what I'm thinking.

After showing me how to balance my weight with the staff in various positions, she teaches me how to move forward and backward without tripping or falling. Different holds make movement easier or harder.

By the time Nick pokes his head in, every joint in my body is both painful and unmanageable. My stomach is sore. My glutes are on fire. The webbing between my hands feels like it might tear if I stretch my fingers too far. I collapse to the floor in a heap and look up at the clock; three hours have passed and it's close to ten.

"How's it going, Gill?" Nick asks.

Gillian looks me over for a moment. "She's about as good as you were . . . when you were eight."

Nick winces. "It's her first night."

The older woman shrugs and plucks the staff from my hand.

Nick helps me to standing, taking my weight when I hop up on sore feet. "At times like these, there are only two words I can offer."

"Yeah, what are they?" I mutter.

"William's waiting."

On the car ride home, I fall into an exhausted, aether-drugged sleep. Nick offers to help me upstairs twice before I wave him away.

The images I dream of melt and bleed into one another like oil over water.

I see my mother, hunched over her desk, writing. When she looks down and smiles, I know I am a child, and this is a memory.

Her face slips into familiar blue-and-white smoke.

I wear shining aether armor. Metal gleams over my arms and chest. Nameless, faceless Regents kneel on the ground before me.

Men in robes playing god.

I level my crystal blade at their throats.

Beside me, Nick gasps. My armor matches his. I am his Squire. But his sword is sheathed. When I reach for his arm, he pulls away like I am a stranger.

I am on my hands and knees in the graveyard, bent over earth and stone with hands smeared in blood.

The graveyard falls into never-ending darkness, black and silent and suffocating.

I sleep until after noon again on Sunday. Nick texted while I was asleep:

Gotta deal with some Order issues. Will try to text later. Have a good session tonight!

Just as I'm leaving for lunch, Patricia texts to ask if we can meet, and I tell her I can't, that I have to study for my English quiz, which is true. It feels like I haven't touched a textbook in days.

I fully expect Patricia to keep calling or texting me after I'd run out on yesterday's therapy session.

I didn't expect her to show up at my dorm.

I'm so focused on getting out the door to head to the library that I don't notice her until she calls my name. She has her phone out like she's about to call me to come down and meet her.

I sigh and walk over. "I didn't know you made house calls."

She smiles. "I don't, usually." I let her guide me to the grass beyond the sidewalk. Today her glasses are Carolina blue, and her shawl is cerulean and gold paisley.

"Let me guess. You're here to tell me not to run away from my feelings?"

"I actually just came to check on you after yesterday. Are you all right?"

"I'm fine." I hike my bag up on my shoulders.

She looks like she has more to say, but decides not to. Instead, she wraps her bare arms more tightly in the shawl. "I realize our sessions together have been very unorthodox."

I raise a brow. "You think?"

"You're suffering right now, Bree. More than I realized."

I look up at the sky. "Isn't that what grief is?"

"I think you are suffering from traumatic grief now, and if you continue as you are over time, you'll likely develop a condition called Persistent Complex Bereavement Disorder. Panic attacks, or something like them. Your anger, your distrust of new people, your obsession with the circumstances of her death, and your inability to truly live *forward*? These are all classic symptoms of PCBD."

My laugh is hollow and derisive. "Sure. Fine."

She presses on. "Therapy is only beneficial if the patient wants help with the ghosts that haunt them. And I think that during yesterday's session, we touched on your ghost."

"My ghost?" I repeat, bewildered.

"An emotional ghost is a moment, an event, even a person, that hovers over us no matter how far we run to escape it or them."

"Sure," I say reasonably. "I already know the answer to this quiz. It's the moment that I found out my mom died. There, easy."

"Not so fast," she says with warm amusement. "Do you want to know how I locate a patient's ghost, Bree?" An early morning breeze lifts up the edge of her shawl, blowing the material over her cheek in a soft billow.

I don't, in fact, want to know.

Patricia presses forward anyway. "I listen for what they *don't* talk about. Ghosts are invisible, after all."

"Okay."

"And you don't talk about your mother."

I open my mouth to say, *Yes, I do. I just spoke about her. Right now*—but Patricia raises a palm.

"You might talk about her death, but you don't talk about her life. This is a symptom of the type of grief you're experiencing too: an inability to process that a person is more than their absence. That love is about more than loss."

"She isn't lost," I snap. "She didn't just wander off and get lost somewhere. I hate it when people say that."

"Well, what happened to her?"

"What do you mean what happened to her? She died! And someone is responsible for that!"

Her lips go thin. Behind her glasses, Patricia's brown eyes have iron in them now. "Rootcraft is used for healing, protection, and self-knowledge. The same can be said for therapy. But you don't want those things, do you, Bree?"

I don't know what to say to that, so I turn away.

She speaks calmly, but her words are weighted stones dropping one after another, dragging my limbs down, pulling me into unknown depths. "Even if you succeed in your goal and find proof, revenge won't bring her back.

Why someone dies is not the same question as why they are gone."

After-Bree simmers just below the surface of my skin. "I know that," I say through gritted teeth, "but it *will* make me feel better."

"Why is that exactly?"

I blink. "Isn't it self-explanatory?"

Patricia narrows her eyes. "No. It's not." She turns toward the open quad and tugs her shawl tighter. "I'm going to go now. I apologize for surprising you here today."

"That's it?" I follow her as she descends down the steps. "You're just going?"

"I'll call your father next week to give him a referral to another therapist, someone who specializes in your condition."

"What?" I sputter. "You're just . . . getting rid of me? Why?"

She turns then, eyes more somber than I've ever seen them. "I thought that I could help ease you through grief by connecting you to your mother and our community, but I made a mistake. I brought the craft into our sessions when perhaps I shouldn't have, particularly as your mother never brought you into the fold herself."

"So you're just abandoning me?" I say, my voice cracking with sudden emotion.

She sighs heavily. "There comes a time when even passive support turns to endorsement, and I won't endorse what you're doing with the Order. I can't."

My hands ball into fists. "And you won't help me figure out what I am?"

When she speaks again, her voice is thick with sorrow. "I want you to figure out who you are. We all deserve that answer, and the journey it takes to find it. But I fear for you, Bree, and the path you have assigned yourself. I know that the Order, for what they're worth, has worked for centuries to rid our plane of the creatures who cross over and take material form. They may fight monsters, but they aren't protectors."

"Because they're Bloodcrafters and they've stolen their root," I say.

"We borrow root because keeping it in our living bodies creates an imbalance of energy. We call Bloodcraft a curse because power taken and not returned incurs a debt, and the universe and the dead will always come to collect, one way or another. The Order has tied power to their bloodlines for *hundreds* of years. Tell me, Bree, how large do you think their debt is? Do you know how they pay it? The only currency that Bloodcraft accepts is suffering and death."

My stomach bottoms out in horror. *"Fifteen centuries."* That's what Sel said in the tunnels. All of the lives and Oaths and heavy prices paid. And the Abatement. Hundreds of life spans, taken. Cut short.

Patricia reaches for my hand and gives it a final, brief squeeze before she leaves me standing in the grass behind her.

34

PATRICIA'S WARNING HAUNTS me for the rest of the day.

But it dissolves as soon as I walk into the training room, where excitement ripples through the five Pages waiting for Gillian and Owen. Something's happened, but I don't know what.

Greer and Whitty pull me aside to fill me in:

Yesterday afternoon William barred Sel from performing the Warrior's Oath to bond Sar and Tor until he calmed down—which only made Sel even angrier. After that, Nick, Sel, and Lord Davis were overheard on a tense phone call that lasted late into the night. There'd been shouting. Even a scuffle. It ended with Sel smashing a chair and storming out the front door. No one's seen Nick since.

Gillian walks in right as they finish talking, so I don't get a chance to text Nick for answers. Between the sour taste in my mouth from my "breakup" with Patricia and my worry about Nick, the rest of the evening goes miserably.

Sel and Gillian demo the longsword, and face off to a draw. Again, Sel doesn't speak to anyone and leaves as soon as they're done.

Owen and Gillian introduce us to hard, custom-designed polypropylene practice swords. For me, it's an utter disaster—even against the heavy wooden dummies we start with for the first hour.

On the second hour, they pair us up and that's much, much worse.

Gillian drops her head into her hands every time Whitty disarms me. "It's an extension of your arm, Matthews!" When I raise a hand to ask Whitty for a break three times in ten minutes, out of breath and hands clutching my knees, Gillian groans. "You have no stamina, Matthews! What if your Scion needed you? Do you think you can call time with a gwyllgi on your heels?" I want to scream at her that I have no idea what a gwyllgi is, but instead I stagger to standing, my heart thudding in my chest like a hammer, and start again.

When it's over, I call Nick's cell twice, but he doesn't pick up.

Alice is studying when I get home. She notices my workout gear right away, and I'm ready with a lie: "Scavenger hunts and obstacle courses and team-building crap. Nothing dangerous, just ridiculous initiation stuff." It takes everything in me to stay awake as we catch up. I tell her an abridged version of the "date" with Nick at the bar, and she gives me news about classmates from back home.

Nick texts right as I drift off in bed:

Hey, my dad sent a plane for me. Said I needed to join him at Northern and show face at the other chapters. Things are getting worse up here, just like there. Gates opening where we haven't seen them before. I'll be back for Thursday's trial. Gillian's good—trust her. You can do this, B.

Monday with the daggers is far worse than Sunday with the longsword.

I lose every match with Greer. They have years of training on their side and use their long arms and legs to every advantage.

After, they help me walk to William's with a sore tailbone and a smattering of bruises from one side of my rib cage to the other, and from sternum to belly button.

According to Gillian's calculations, if the blades were real, I'd have been gutted thirty times.

When I get home, I force myself to walk normally in front of Alice.

On Tuesday, there is no demo, but Sel shows up anyway. To watch, it seems.

He's not the only one. Vaughn and Blake, and even Sydney now, watch my drills and smile smugly in the corner of the room.

I don't need to hear them say it. Their eyes and laughter communicate clearly enough: no Scion would ever select me.

Each night there's a cycle: I tell myself I don't care what they think. Then, because I'm not used to losing, frustration wells inside, spilling into my limbs and burning muscles, and I push myself to get better, train harder. Later, while William heals my wounds—three broken fingers, a broken elbow, a bruised kidney and ribs—I remember that I'm not planning to stay. That this isn't truly my life. And the cycle begins again.

Only Whitty and Greer seem to take pity, but any kindness they show me during our sparring matches is immediately caught by our trainers, who deal out punishment to us all in the form of laps or push-ups or tire flips.

Wednesday night goes horribly.

"Sydney, you're up. Pick the weapon."

Sydney walks to the rack and pulls the quarterstaff. By now I know that she and Blake are in a silent battle to become Pete's squire, so I'm not surprised she picked the staff. We'd never be friends, but after the hellboar trial she'd at least treated me with respect.

I already know Owen's going to call my name. I feel it in my gut.

"Bree."

At the end of the line, Vaughn's laughter is a deep, mocking rumble.

"Can it, Schaefer," Gill warns.

Greer uses the distraction to lean close. "You're taller than her and have a longer reach, but she knows that and will go for the sweep."

I nod a silent thanks and make my way to the rack. When I turn back to the ring, I see Sel slip through the open door and take a seat on a bench near the wall.

Owen lays out the rules of engagement. "A match is won when your opponent yields or when they take a step outside the line."

We step inside the blue ring and stand in starting positions, staffs at an angle across our bodies, one grip facing down, the other up. Owen gives the signal.

Sydney whips up; I block before it hits my ribs.

She dances back. I surge forward for a strike to her shoulder. She blocks. Counters with a low swing. Wood cracks against my shin, and pain blazes up to my knees.

Satisfaction glows in her eyes. She'd been waiting for that opening, and I'd walked right into it.

I stand—her staff flies toward my neck—and duck.

She throws her weight into a thrust at my solar plexus. I block, pushing her weapon to the left of my waist. It forces her off-balance, and I lean right so she falls forward. She plants her staff hard just before the blue line, halting her momentum before she tumbles out of the ring.

I should have used that opportunity to drop her to the mat.

She pushes off, pivots on a heel, and twirls her staff to strike at my temple. I panic and lean back too far. Miss the attack, but fall hard on my ass—

Her staff is at my throat.

"Yield," she pants.

Everything happened so fast. Too fast. My throat bobs against her weapon.

Sydney presses lightly against my neck.

"I yield!" I snarl, knocking her staff to the side.

A few days ago she would have helped me up, if begrudgingly.

Now she smirks and walks away. The other Pages clap lightly at her performance.

I curse and roll to standing. When I recover my staff, I find Sel's eyes on me from the bench where he's leaned forward on his knees, chin on his palm. I'd forgotten he was here. Heat spreads over my throat and chest when I realize he'd watched me fall horribly, and with his personal weapon of choice.

Greer manages to best Blake with the practice sword, disarming him in a few minutes. Vaughn uses his weight and size to press Whitty out of the ring before they exchange more than a few blows. Whitty curses and throws his blade down, the maddest I've ever seen him.

Gill calls it a night. Her eyes linger on mine when she reminds the group we can use the rooms any time we want to practice before tomorrow's trial.

Right as I meet Greer at the door, I feel Sel's gaze on my back. I haven't spoken to him all week, but there's an expectant weight in the sensation of his eyes.

I sigh. "You know what? I'm gonna stay for a bit. You go on ahead."

Greer raises a brow. They look over my shoulder at Sel sitting on the bench, then back at me. "You sure?"

"Yeah, it's fine."

He waits until their footsteps disappear down the hall.

"Do you want to be a Squire?" His voice is inches behind me, and I yelp even though I should expect his silent approach at this point.

I frown, not sure how to answer. Do I want to achieve the title? Yes, so that I'll be powerful enough in the hierarchy to demand an audience—and the truth—from the Regents. Do I want to fight in this war as a Squire?

"It's a yes or no question."

"I do, yes."

He hums. Then turns, shucking his jacket and tossing it onto the bench behind him as he moves to the center ring. Then he stands there in his usual black tank and loose pants, rotating his wrists and stretching until corded muscles stand out on his forearms and biceps.

"What are you doing?"

"I've decided that watching you fail this spectacularly is too painful to bear. Get over here."

"What?"

He rolls his eyes. "I'm offering to train you, silly thing."

"What happened to 'Briana'? I like that better than 'silly thing.'"

"Stop stalling."

I toss my towel into the linen basket by the door. "There's no way I'd let you train me."

"Why?"

"Why do you want to in the first place? You can't want me to succeed."

He bends to stretch one arm to an ankle, but I can still see the upturned edges of his smile. "Let's just say that I am not particularly fond of bullies at the moment, and the way they attack others' weaknesses. It would please me to watch yours fall tomorrow."

I jut my chin out. "I don't believe you."

"Obstinate creature," he huffs under his breath. "Come here. I am serious. I swear it."

I swear it. A vow Nick utters too. For all their differences, there are still echoes.

I pace slowly to the ring, step over the white line, and come to stop in front of him.

He crosses his arms over his chest and fixes me with a stern gaze. "Do you know why you keep getting taken down in the ring?"

"Because the other Pages have years of experience fighting and I don't."

"No. It's because the other Pages fight with singular focus. You don't, because you're here for more than one reason. The other reason is that they know their strengths well and use them. I've seen you punch a hole through a hellfox. The fact that you're bumbling around this week tells me you still can't control your gifts. Or aren't trying to." He scoffs. "If I could produce aether from my body, cook it up the way you can, I'd spend every waking moment trying to do it again."

"We have different priorities."

"An understatement."

"Bye." I turn to leave.

"Wait." He catches my arm. When I look down at his fingers, he releases me. "I can still assist you, aether furnace or not."

"You're going to help me win a match?"

He snorts. "Oh no, you're nowhere near skilled enough to win anything. I'm going to help you lose less terribly."

"Wow. You're a peach."

"No," he retorts, pulling a spinning ball of blue aether into his palm. "I'm part demon."

THE NEXT NIGHT, the chapter mills around the great room. The competing Pages are too nervous to eat, but other people are enjoying satay chicken skewers and peanut sauce. I'm trying my best to stay calm, even with my heart pounding in my chest.

Tonight's the combat trial and, while I still feel unprepared, the session with Sel last night at least gave me hope. We never reproduced the red mage flame—and we both agreed that was a good thing, in the public setting of the trial—but he'd shown me how to use my height and limited abilities in new ways.

Nick enters and finds me right away, pulling me to the balcony windows. It feels like I haven't seen him in ages.

"I'm so sorry I had to leave without notice. My dad just wanted me close, and the other chapters are asking questions about the Table, and . . . it's bad. Really bad. Can you forgive me?" He leans back and frowns. "You look scared, B." His eyes widen. "Did Sel get to you again?"

"Not like that," I say vaguely. "He . . . gave me some combat tips yesterday."

"What?" Nick's jaw clenches. "I *ordered* him to stay away, not to look at you, talk to you—"

"It's fine." I squeeze his arm. "It was good. He genuinely helped."

He looks skeptical, but some of the strain leaves his shoulders. "Still, Rule Three is in full effect. Even more so after he performs Tor and Sar's Oath ceremony tonight." His eyes are slate and storm, worry and tension. "Did something else happen?"

Every time I think of Patricia, I get both angry and sad. "Remember that person on campus who I thought could help me? The one I trusted?"

"Yeah?"

Our moment of privacy is coming to a close. Heads are turning our way. "I was wrong. They can't help me."

I can tell he's genuinely disappointed. "I'm sorry, B. It's gonna be okay, though. We can—" The lights flicker, cutting him off.

Time to head down to the trial.

The room empties around us, and Nick leans against the window, my hand in his still hidden from view. He watches the others file out while I try to find some semblance of reason. As soon as the last person leaves and the door clicks shut, he wraps me in his arms and buries his face in my hair. I resist for a moment, not ready to let him in, but as soon as he holds me, I feel warmer, stronger, safer. Nick's heart beats and mine answers, call and response. I could sob with relief.

"You're hurting, and I don't know what to do. Please tell me what to do."

"I don't think there's anything you can do."

"Deep breaths, okay? It'll help you stay calm."

Irritation flares inside me. *Deep breaths. Stay calm.* The same things Patricia says to me when I get upset. When the memories come, the anger and the sadness wash over me in waves, each one bigger than the last, and she has no idea how much they hurt. "Don't tell me to be *calm.*"

"I'm sorry," he soothes, pressing a kiss to my forehead, then my temple. "I won't say it again."

"I'm really tired of people telling me to be calm and take fuoking *deep breaths.*"

"Okay." He nods against my forehead. "Then let me just be there for you tonight." He reaches his hand into his back pocket and presses a key into my hand.

I look down, wiping my tears away with a sleeve. "What's this?"

He smirks, but there's hesitation there, mixed with pleasure. "My room key."

"And why are you giving this to me?"

"I have to go pick up my dad from the airport after the trial. It's a four-hour round trip. After the bouts, why don't you go upstairs and wait for me in my room. When I get back, we can talk about whatever's going on. Or not talk."

"Not talk?" I lift both brows. Red rushes up to his cheekbones.

"That's *not* what I meant," he says hurriedly, then pauses, reconsiders. "Unless that's what *you* meant? The version of not talking that means we're doing other things?"

I press my lips together to keep from laughing. "I didn't actually say any words just now, Davis. That was all you." The look on his face is an adorable blend of hope and uncertainty. "Tell you what," I say, closing my hand around the bronze key. "I'll take this and wait upstairs in your room after Gillian kicks my ass, as long as you let me use your shower while you're gone."

"Deal."

We smile at each other, and the moment feels like it's ours. Secret. Butterflies swarm in my stomach because while we've exchanged a few pecks, nothing has been as heated or intense as that first kiss. Taking him up on his invite means we'll be alone in his room for the first time since the second trial. Nick gazes down at me, that same awareness mirrored in his eyes. He tugs on my belt until we're standing flush and presses a warm thumb into my palm like a promise.

It takes another flicker of the lights to break us apart and send us in our separate directions, but I head down to the prep area with at least one thing to look forward to.

The arena for the combat trial is not far from the silver Chapel in the woods. There's a single drawn circle in the densely padded dirt about the size of the middle ring inside the training room. Chairs and stools surround the circle where our audience will sit. Owen and Gill are posted at opposite sides of the arena with a clear view of the center. I don't know where Sel is, but I feel his gaze from above. A tree, maybe. It's not quite dark yet.

The six competing Pages wear fitted pants for maximum mobility, and tunics in the color of our sponsor's Line, adorned with their sigil in the center.

I am the only Page who wears the gold of the Line of Arthur.

Sel said I had too many reasons to be here. Fractured goals.

Tonight I have only one focus, and I fight for only one family: my own.

The matches are set up so that each Page goes in the ring three times, for a total of nine matches. When the first pair goes up, Nick makes eye contact with me and winks. He's never seen me in the arena, and his easy confidence in my abilities triples my nerves.

Sydney easily beats Greer with the quarterstaff but loses to Blake when it comes to the longsword.

Whitty knocks Blake out of the ring with rapid stabs and swipes of his dagger. Then, to everyone's surprise, manages to beat Vaughn into submission with the staff. Vaughn smacks Whitty's staff away and leaves the ring, face as red as his tunic. It's been obvious since warm-ups that he'd planned to get through the night three for three, winning each match with each weapon. He launches his staff against the trees, splitting it down the middle. Fitz walks over to his Page to pat his back encouragingly and murmur in the other boy's ear. Even though Fitz doesn't need a Squire—he's got Evan—it seems he's still invested in his Page's success.

The other Pages, Squires, and Scions cheer or groan, and chat between rounds. Only Nick sits hunched over, silently watching the bouts with a neutral expression.

Each time Pages enter the ring with the hard, black practice swords, all eyes go to him. Everyone wants to know what the Scion of Arthur is thinking.

My first match is against Sydney, with the dagger.

Greer claps me on the back and nods when I go up. "You got this."

Sydney, in an orange tunic, smiles back and struts to the ring. I'd never seen the Line of Bors's sigil up close—three bands across a circle. She doesn't seem to be at all concerned about the outcome of our fight. I shake my shoulders to loosen them up, and force the fingers of my right hand to stretch wide before grasping the handle of the rubber dagger. Sydney and I take our stances: balanced over bent knees, body and vital organs behind the knife, blade up and forward in a hammer grip.

Gillian signals the start.

We dance—Sydney attacking, me dodging—long enough for sweat to build on our brows. I manage to avoid every attack, but I only get in one of my own: a swipe that she blocks, with effort. She lunges underneath our elbows, and I leap back—only to hear a whistle.

"Out of bounds, Matthews. Round to Page Hall." Gillian claps. Match over.

Damnit!

I'm angry about losing to a simple misstep, but the fury in Sydney's eyes almost makes up for it. She'd never expected me to last even that long in a match and, from the looks on a few of the others' faces—including Gillian's—neither had anyone else.

When I take the bench, Nick and I lock eyes. He wiggles his shoulders as if to say, *Shake it off.*

I get one round to rest before my next match. Had Vaughn's dagger been real, Greer would have been fully disemboweled.

When Gillian calls his name, Blake stands. He flexes his broad shoulders, pulling against his tunic, the dark yellow of Owain. Then she calls mine.

Right away Blake presses his advantages—strength and height—with a powerful overhead strike. I block, but it's clear that if we stay on his terms, the win will be about sheer force more than speed or fancy footwork.

I'm faster than he is. I know I am.

I have to keep moving.

His arm and weapon rain down again and again, each crack echoing in my ears like a thunderclap. Every block sends a teeth-jarring reverberation into my elbows. Three minutes in, my thighs *burn*. Countering him takes every muscle in my body just to remain upright.

"Everyone leaves an opening. Find it, then throw everything into it."

Blake pauses to pace around the ring. "Give up, Matthews." I've been up close and personal to Sel's snarl; Blake's watered-down version would make me laugh if my lungs weren't on fire. Our breaths come in hard, labored pants. "You can't block forever."

He lunges.

I snap my staff up longways to block his two-handed midbody strike, but it takes everything I have to keep the weapon in my shaking hands. My fingers spasm around the wood, barely keeping it in a grip.

He retreats.

His brown hair is black under a river of sweat. He's running out of steam too, and catching his breath.

Blake swings high to my left, and it's like he's moving in slow motion. My eyes track each shift of his muscles, every movement from his shoulder to his arm.

I have plenty of time to duck, so I do. I keep my eyes on Blake's broad chest—there!

I launch myself forward, ramming the end of my staff into his solar plexus. For a moment, he seems to hang in the air. His staff flies out of his hand and over my right shoulder.

Time accelerates.

Blake's back hits the mat.

Gillian's whistle splits the air.

"Weapon out of bounds. Match to Matthews." She sounds just as surprised as I am.

Applause reaches me, but I barely register it. Blake rolls over with a groan and pushes to all fours before standing. His face is a blistering red grimace. I stand stunned in the middle of the ring until Gillian steps in front of me and waves a hand. A small smile plays over the older woman's face. "Earth to Matthews."

"Matty," I correct. "Earth to Matty." Alice would be proud.

I head to the benches, but not before I see Sel. Up in the trees, he tips his head in a silent salute that fills me with an embarrassing amount of pride. Great, overflowing buckets of the stuff.

Whitty offers a fist bump before he and Greer go to the ring together. Thanks to their fencing experience, Greer handily defeats Whitty with the sword. I'm gently massaging my sore shoulders when I hear my name again.

I should have known that my last match would be with Vaughn.

Vaughn leaps off the bench without hesitation. He throws a towel from his shoulders and struts to the rack, pulling his black, heavy polypropylene practice sword.

A few of the Scions murmur to one another. Apparently news of our rivalry has spread.

Greer and Whitty say something encouraging to me, but I don't hear it over the sound of the blood pounding in my ears. Nick sits up as I pass the viewing area to pick my own sword. I look away from his worried expression before it becomes all I can think about.

Vaughn prowls back and forth in the center of the ring, waiting for me.

When I step onto the mat, Gillian calls for a clean match. She looks at me. "Match is over when one opponent yields or steps—or loses a weapon— outside the ring." She looks at Vaughn. "No headshots."

A short, high whistle signals the start.

Vaughn sways in a wide opening stance, tossing his blade from hand to hand. Every time he catches the hilt under the crossguard, the hard muscles on his shoulders and biceps roll and flex. His mouth parts in a taunting grin. "No shame in yielding now, Matthews."

"Don't listen to him, Bree!" Greer cheers.

I don't want to listen to him, but I can't help but hear his low, mocking laugh. Can't help but notice his eyes meandering up my body, starting at my legs and lingering over my hips and chest. "Fine, stay." He mutters, so that only I can hear him, "I don't mind the view."

Anger floods me, but I won't give him the satisfaction of an emotional, undisciplined attack. He shrugs as if to say, *Have it your way*—and lunges.

He strikes so quickly, the black blade whistles when it swings. I parry, catching the broad side of his sword against the hardest part of my own—the forte—and leap back.

Vaughn spins his sword once with a smile, as if to remind me what his weapon can do. The Order's practice swords aren't steel, but they're plenty heavy and wide. Strong enough to break a bone with a well-aimed hit.

He surges forward. Brings his blade down in an overhead strike. I raise my sword to block it, but he stalls—then leans back and kicks me hard in the stomach.

I stumble, my midsection a dizzying cocktail of nausea and pain.

Vaughn sweeps in—I just barely turn my sword to meet the low hack at my legs.

Then he charges again, swinging, and it's a basic drill, just a twist of my wrist to deflect.

Too easy.

I cough, and blood—iron rich and salty—fills my mouth. Feral humor glitters in Vaughn's eyes. Understanding dawns.

That kick was well aimed. Strategic.

Every movement, every twist and stretch and pivot, is ten times harder with internal bleeding.

He's toying with me.

Everything—Vaughn's face, the trees, the ring—blurs under the veil of white-hot fury.

I shift my grip, preparing for a two-handed blow to his ribs, when Sel's last lesson echoes in my ears.

"Typical anger can hinder or help. But the kind that burns in your gut? That's fury. And fury is meant to be used."

I strafe, twisting left, then pivot. The flat of my blade smacks his fingers hard, breaking his grip. Both swords drop to the ground.

Vaughn looks up, shock crossing his features, and lunges for me, but I'm already in the air.

His momentum carries him forward—right into my flying knee.

His head snaps back.

His spine hits the mat, and blood streams across his nose and mouth.

For a second, the woods are completely silent.

Then Russ jumps to his feet and whoops, triggering a wave of shouts and applause.

Vaughn rocks slightly, his hands covering his face. But he doesn't get up.

"Match to Matthews!" Gillian calls, an astonished smile lighting her face.

At some point, Nick had gotten up from his chair and approached the outer ring. He stands there, feet just touching the red paint, wearing the most beautiful smile I've ever seen. I take a stumbling step forward. Triumph fizzes in my chest; I could burst with it.

Nick's gaze locks into mine, his eyes widening and smile falling. He roars my name.

Vaughn's blade swings down in my peripheral vision.

I hear the deep crack in my collarbone before I feel it.

When the pain comes, darkness follows. There's shouting, then silence.

36

I WAKE UP once before William's done healing me. I must have done something I shouldn't—tried to sit up, tried to talk—because firm hands hold me down.

I slide back into a murky, aether-induced sleep.

When I open my eyes again, I'm in an empty, windowless room lit only by a small lamp. The digital clock on the wall reads 10:17 p.m.

My left fingers fly to my right collarbone, where there's a steady, pulsing ache. Stiff paper crinkles when I touch it. I pull it away, expecting a bandage but instead find two yellow sticky notes.

> Clean, oblique fracture to the
> r. clavicle. Hit you hard with swyns.
> Will heal in a few days.
> Wear the sling.
> Min. healing time w/o aether? =
> 8 wks, + physical therapy.
> You're welcome.
> William

P.S. Mod. intra-abdominal bleeding.
Healed, but STAY PUT.
P.P.S. Nick wanted to stay.
I told him to go on to the airport
since you'd just be sleeping.
GO BACK TO SLEEP!

"Sorry, William," I whisper. "Got a boy to see."

It's only after I'm in the elevator that I realize I'm going to have to walk down the very public upstairs hallway of the second floor of the Lodge in order to get to Nick's room. This realization takes me so off guard that I accidentally get off on the first floor and run right into Sarah.

"Bree!" A wide grin spans her face and she bounces on her heels under her skirt. "What are you still doing here? Do you need a ride home? I could drive you back to your dorm, no problem, easy peasy!"

I narrow my eyes. "Are you talking faster than normal?"

She flushes pink and bites her lip. "I think so?"

Realization hits me then. Everything about Sarah is brighter, and I swear I can actually see her vibrating. "You're bonded to Tor now. You have Tristan's speed."

She tilts her head back and forth. "Technically, I have Tor's speed. *She* has Tristan's speed. But yes! Wait." She frowns, and the cogs in her mind turn faster than ever. Her eyes grow wide. "You're waiting for Nick, aren't you?"

Voices reach us from the dining room and the living room. "What if I am?"

"Oh, I think you two are a cute couple. Do you want something to drink while you wait?" She's already walking down the hall under the staircase toward the kitchen, so I follow.

The Lodge's bright chef's kitchen is empty when we walk in. I've never actually been in here before, since most of the meals are catered in, and very few of the Legendborn seem to cook for themselves. It's a large, square room with white cabinets, two stainless steel fridges, a gas stove on a center island, and gleaming gray-and-white quartz countertops. Sarah pulls out two glasses and fills them with water while she talks.

"People are such gossips around here, but honestly, it's not a big deal that you're hooking up with Nick. There are some Pages who might be jealous. Ainsley, for one. Sydney. Spencer too."

I settle into a bar stool, cradling my shoulder in its sling. "Wonderful."

"Nick *lost it* on Vaughn, by the way. Kicked him out of the tournament. Said there's no place for vengeance at the Table." She shakes her head. "Vaughn thought that being the best combatant made him the best Squire for Nick, but it doesn't work like that. It's not just the fighting. It's the match."

The way she says that last word, the emphasis she puts on it, reminds me that she's got more than Tor's speed now. She has access to her emotions. She'll always know when she's in danger. They're in sync now and forever.

And her life span has just been capped. I can't think of a polite way to ask how she feels about the Abatement, so I ask another question instead.

"What does it feel like? To be bonded?"

She considers my question. "Tor and I were already bonded in a way. We're in love, so I thought this would feel like more of the same, but it's not. It's deeper. More intimate. I don't know how it feels to other people. Maybe it depends on how long they've been bonded or how well they already knew each other."

"How long have you and Tor been together?"

"Couple of years. Before that she was with Sel, and I was still in high school."

I hadn't forgotten William's revelation, but now that it's out in the open . . . "About that . . . I'm having a little trouble imagining it."

Sarah laughs. "Yeah, that was Tor's rebellious phase. I think she did it just to piss her parents off."

"Dating Sel pissed her parents off?"

"Dating a *Merlin* would piss any Legendborn parent off." She rolls her eyes and tips her glass back.

That surprises me. Sure, Sel is a jerk, but does that mean all Merlins are? "Why?"

Her nose wrinkles. "It's just not done."

"But—"

Boom! A thunderous sound reaches us from the woods behind the Lodge. I'm on my feet in a second.

"Speaking of . . ." She doesn't even budge from her chair, just rolls her eyes and finishes her glass of water. "You want a refill?"

"What was that?" I gape at her nonchalance, then jolt again when a large *crack* echoes in the forest, followed by the sound of a flock of nearby birds fleeing into the night sky.

"That"—Sarah raises an unimpressed brow—"is Selwyn, aether-drunk from our Oath," she says as if that explains everything. "Except he's been pissed off all week, so it's worse than normal." She takes my glass and brings both over to the dishwasher. "I wouldn't go in the woods tonight, if I were you. He'll be out there for a while throwing a tantrum. When he cools off, he'll come back in, slam a bunch of doors, and hole himself up in his tower for the rest of the night. It's a whole thing."

Sarah walks me back to the elevator, spilling gossip at a rapid-fire pace. I can barely keep up with her new speed, and right now I'm only half listening. I wait until she takes the elevator to her and Tor's room on the third floor, then move as quietly as I can to the stairwell and out the back exit.

The sounds of destruction grow louder as soon as I step into the woods.

Using my phone as a flashlight, I take the path Nick guided me down the first night—I know it must be the same because it's the only one I see. This close to Selwyn's epicenter, each crash and boom and crack sends reverberations through the ground beneath my feet. Whatever he's doing, it's violent. I must be the only living thing in a mile radius that hasn't taken shelter from his rage.

I don't quite know why I'm walking into the storm instead of waiting it out like Sarah suggested. I could be upstairs in Nick's shower, using the much-stronger water pressure in the Lodge to release the tension from my back and arm muscles. Then, rooting around in his drawers for pajamas that smell like him.

But I'm not.

Maybe I'm seeking Sel out tonight because last night *he* stayed behind to help *me*. Nick told him to stay away. Sarah told me to stay away. And yet there he was, and here I am. We keep crossing paths in all the wrong ways.

As if compelled by a force out of my control, I follow the sounds of Sel's anger, through the curve where I first met Lord Davis, down the rocking bridge that Nick guided me over, and past the hint of silver on the forest floor that marks the ceremony site.

I end up climbing a slope. The deep cracking sounds are further and further apart now, but each time they come, they're loud enough to set my teeth on edge and send adrenaline spiking. I pause to catch my breath against a tree trunk and get my bearings. I've walked half a mile or so, some of it uphill. The Lodge's balcony lights are barely visible through the dense trees, and beyond that is the misty haze of light marking the tops of campus buildings, the nearby hospital, and the rest of downtown. I direct my flashlight up the hill again and gasp.

Starting about twenty feet away are half a dozen broken tree trunks. Jagged, pale yellow spikes and splinters the size of my forearm stretch up from raw stumps about the height of my knee. They look like fresh wounds. Beside them are long fallen trunks, laid out like Lincoln Logs on the forest floor.

Right on cue, I hear another tree being torn apart. I follow the sound.

This close I can catch all the details of Sel's efforts: the initial popping sound of a wide trunk protesting against his muscles; the ripping sound of bark tearing away; a slow, deep whine and a final *crack* when the trunk is severed from its base.

Just as I reach the ridge, I see him about fifty feet away, hefting a long pine trunk between his hands. He inhales deep and heaves it over the side. There's a second where all I can hear are his panting breaths amidst silence, and then a mighty boom shakes the ground as the tree splits into pieces on the earth below. In the waning moonlight, I can make out a dozen trees just like it, spread out across the grass like broken chopsticks as tall as a house.

I realize where I am—this is the ridge above the arena from the first trial. This is where the Legendborn watched us fight Sel's boars and where Nick was taken out from under Sel's nose by a hellsnake.

"What are you doing here?"

My head jerks around at Sel's voice. In the second I'd taken to peer down into the arena, he'd turned to face me. His gaze feels like sparks, but they're scattered. Unfocused.

The last time we spoke, he'd made a joke about his lineage. Taught me how to follow through on a lunge.

Now it feels like he wants to burn me to ash.

I stumble on a response but stop when I see his expression. Sarah was right, he's aether-drunk, and it's worse than before. Even though he's on his feet, he's swaying gently, his normally stern eyes blurry and red-rimmed. He glances down at my injured arm, briefly.

"Well?"

"Why are you so angry?"

His laugh is a hollow, dry bark. "Learn that shit from your therapist?"

I swear I see red. "*What* did you just say to me?"

He smirks. "I saw your little outdoor therapy session with that campus doctor."

"You *spied* on me?" *Which session? How much did he hear?*

Sel rolls his eyes to the sky. "*Of course* I spied on you. The day after the Oath, I followed you from your dorm to the gardens, listened in while you and she had a heart-to-heart about your abilities." He bends down and picks up a rock, then chucks it across the arena so hard it makes a loud *pop!* against a tree on the other side.

"How dare you—that was private!" I shout.

He scoffs. "Put your self-righteousness away, mystery girl. I followed you that day to see if you were meeting an uchel coconspirator, and I thought you two were speaking in code about your demon lineage. Looking back, I'd given you *far* too much credit. I don't care about your family drama, and I sure as fuck don't care about someone whose dead mother used aether to grow prettier *flowers*—"

"*Don't* talk about my mother," I growl.

"All of that effort"——he shakes his head and gives a mirthless laugh——"and look where it got me. What a waste of time."

Fury and panic are rushing through my blood, and I don't know which one to act on. I'm still reeling from the revelation that Sel followed me, my mind searching through that first conversation with Patricia to remember what he could have learned.

"God, *look* at you!" Sel chuckles incredulously. "You're trying to remember what I overheard that day and how much I know about your boring, basic Onceborn life."

He prowls toward me on slightly unsteady legs, his glowing eyes tracing my features. A tiny memory from the back of my mind reminds me that running from a predator only invites them to chase you, so I freeze where I am.

And I thought I could be what? His friend?

Sel's low voice dips and slurs as he talks, and I can't tell if his words are for me or for himself. "How could I have risked so much for a lost little girl who probably needs as much therapy as I do?" He tilts his head, eyes going unfocused. "Well, that's not possible." He laughs again, but this time it's so self-deprecating it feels like my anger has nowhere else to go. "No one needs as much therapy as I do."

"Is that why you're out here chucking trees over a cliff?" I snarl.

His head snaps up. "Why are you here again?"

"I have no idea," I say, and turn to leave.

"I do." Even intoxicated, he's far faster than I am. He's in front of me the second I turn. "Guilt."

"Get out of the way."

He leans back against a tree in my path and regards me under half-lidded eyes. "I bet you heard I was out here throwing a fit and that I'd been 'monstrous, angry Sel' all weekend. I bet Nicholas told you we fought again and that Lord Davis put me in my place yesterday. And now you feel bad because you still haven't told Nicholas that you can generate aether, and you think if you had, maybe he'd realize my instincts were right, and I wouldn't be out here crushing trees and feeling sorry for myself."

I sputter, but I can't deny the ring of truth in Sel's words. Is *that* what brought me here through the woods to him? Guilt?

"Move." I take a step, but he matches me again. His eyes gleam, mocking the thoughts he'd deduced from me like a demonic Sherlock Holmes.

"Well, don't bother feeling guilty," Sel purrs. "For our once and *future king*, the ends will never justify the means. He's a good person like that. And further, Nicholas doesn't care about what you can *do*, he only cares about *you*. A fact now fully impressed upon the recently disgraced Page Schaefer. As a matter of fact, how do you think he'd feel if he heard you sought me out in the woods while I was drunk on aether?" His gaze hits me all over—sharp pricks across my face, down my throat, and over my bare arms.

Face hot, I flounder for words. "I——I have no idea."

He snorts. "Liar. Nicholas would draw and quarter me and you know it."

"That's a little dramatic."

He unhitches himself from the tree and stands up, shaking his head. "Do you honestly not realize what he feels for you?"

He's turning everything around so quickly. I feel a wave of confusing emotions: fury at him still for following me, pleasure at hearing about the strength of Nick's feelings for me, guilt for being here against Nick's wishes and our agreed-upon rule, and bewilderment that I'm having *boy talk* with Sel.

"You don't." Sel glares at me, and this close I can see the fine tremor in his mouth, his shoulders, all the way down to his fists. He steps closer, crowding me. "Not fully."

I back away, but it's a mistake. There's only a foot between me, the edge of the ridge, and a steep drop down to the valley and the arena floor below. It's much too much like our first meeting. And this time I know exactly who Sel is and what he's capable of.

"Sel, stop it! I'm gonna fall!"

He shrugs. "Only if you move."

"Let me pass."

"No. You're going to stand right here and listen to me explain something to you."

I glance over my shoulder. He's right; I'm safe——if I don't move again. "Explain what?"

"Do you know why Merlins serve the Legendborn?"

That catches me off guard. "No."

"*Guess.*"

His tone is so sharp, I speak slowly to avoid being cut. "To fight the Shadowborn?"

"Adorable." He rolls his eyes. "The Shadowborn *are* evil, but don't think for one second that every Merlin serves the Order wholly out of the goodness of their heart. You called me a crossroads child once, but you don't fully understand what that means. You can't."

He takes another step forward, not enough to push me over but close enough that I can smell lingering spice from the Oath on his skin and feel the warmth rolling off him. A memory of his heated fingers that first night at the Lodge flashes through my mind, and I wonder, just briefly, if the rest of him runs just as hot.

"Merlin children are, for all intents and purposes, fully human at birth. But when we turn seven, the changes begin—the strength, the speed, the senses—and with those changes comes a type of . . . countdown. Every year after that we gain power and our connection to aether deepens, and every year we lose a bit more of our humanity. We call it 'succumbing to the blood.'" Sel shudders, eyes focusing on me again. "When Merlin created the Legendborn spell for Arthur and his knights, he designed a similar spell for himself. One that would allow all of his descendants to inherit the unique mage abilities he'd honed over time—mesmer, constructs, an affinity for aether." The tiny tips of his white canines gleam as he speaks. "But Merlin knew his own nature. He knew that demons only care for themselves and chaos, and powerful but uncontrollable part demons would never be compatible servants to the eternal Order he and Arthur envisioned. So, in *his* spell, Merlin folded in a bit of *insurance*."

My chest is suddenly tight. "What kind of insurance?"

Bitterness turns his features sharp in the shadows. "Do you remember when I told you that the hellfox couldn't dust with a part of you still inside it? That's because the darkness of the underworld and the light of the living shouldn't exist in one body. My blood is fighting itself every day. The older I get, the stronger the demon essence becomes, but my commitments to this Order and its members keep me from going over."

I return his stare, horror and understanding washing over me in a wave. "The Oaths . . ."

"The Oaths." His eyes are suddenly bright. Fierce. "They are Merlin's insurance that his descendants would never abandon his mission. Performing them, fulfilling them, no matter how large or how small the task. It's the Oaths that bind the two sides of a Merlin together. As long as we are in service, we are in control of our own souls. It's why they Oath us early, before we're old enough for our blood to gain a foothold."

Cecilia's voice comes back to me, and what she said about the infant in Pearl's arms. *Cast it away before it could grow large enough to do harm.*

Sel's not done yet. His eyes dart back and forth across my face, cataloging my responses to his words. "There. You understand now. You can see how, for any Merlin—even a weak one—raised as a human among humans, the greatest punishment would be to cast us out of the Order's service. Force us to witness our own regression. To strip a Merlin powerful enough to earn the title of Kingsmage of that same title would mean taking them away from their charge. Cutting them off from the immense connective power of that Oath. It's a penalty so severe that it's never been done before."

The burning heat rolling off him and the poison in his eyes scare me more than his temper ever has.

"But we are two Called Scions away from Camlann. So, after Nicholas told his father what I did to you, Lord Davis threatened to replace me. Take my title, cast me out. Leave me to self-destruction." He huffs. "Bullies, like I said."

Air leaves my lungs in a rush, like I've been tossed over the cliff myself. "No, that . . . that sounds like torture. Nick wouldn't let that happen—"

"Oh, it *is* torture. But if the Order thinks I'm growing unstable, that is *exactly* what Nicholas will be forced to do." His face turns sour. "These are the choices kings make, mystery girl."

"I'll talk to him. I'll tell him—"

I don't get to finish my sentence, because Sel spins me in a blur of speed, pushing me to the path. "Too late. Go away."

"Sel—" I smell the crackle of Sel's casting and turn to see him standing at the edge of the cliff, his hair swaying gently in the early stages of mage flame, his eyes shining like stoked coals.

"Nicholas thinks I'm losing my humanity. Maybe I am. But I have *not* lost my dignity," he sneers. "I don't need your help."

Before I can say another word, he steps over the cliff and drops out of sight, landing without a sound far below.

37

THE MOON LIGHTS my sprint to the Lodge, but by the time I reach the back lawn, clouds have folded in, solid and thick like a sheet cake.

I slip in the side door. There are a few night-owl members still awake in the great room. I climb the stairs to avoid their attention. When I finally reach Nick's room and slip inside, the adrenaline that carried me through the woods slips out of my body, and I collapse in a heap on his bed, turning Sel's words over and over in my mind.

I did this, I think. *Just by being here.*

I've gone from being hunted by Sel to being the reason his title, his humanity, his very soul, is at risk. And what's worse, the hot fury I'd grown used to seeing in him has turned into something darker. The desolation in his eyes, the self-hatred . . .

I pull out my phone, but there's a reason to skip every one of my recent contacts. I texted Alice earlier to say I wouldn't be home tonight, and what could I say to her anyway? Where would I have to start and stop? I'd been texting my father with updates that "everything is going well with Patricia," so how do I tell him that she let me go? He'll find out soon enough when she calls him, and I don't have the energy to think that far ahead. Nick is driving to pick up his father, and I'd have to wait until he gets home to tell him about the red flames I can't control.

In the end, every conversation would require an explanation first, because no one in my life knows all of the threads that have led me here.

I squeeze my eyes shut, but the tears come anyway, dropping onto the cheery blue-and-white comforter until there's an ugly stain.

I must have fallen asleep on Nick's bed, because a loud slam jerks me awake. I rub at the damp skin of my cheek where the wrinkled fabric of the comforter has pressed it into misshapen creases. A moment later, there's another loud slam, this time overhead.

Sel.

Sarah said that when he was done, he came home and slammed doors, then shut himself in his room. I imagine him there, drained from destroying half the forest, maybe still recovering from aether's effects. I check the clock.

It'll be hours still before Nick comes back. I already know I'll tell him everything that's happened. I'll even break Patricia's trust and tell him about Rootcraft. But I know that Sel is right; it won't change how Nick feels about his Kingsmage, the boy he's been bonded to most of his life.

The Wall of Ages stretches up in my memory. Their names, carved side by side for years. *Nicholas Martin Davis. Selwyn Emrys Kane.*

If Lord Davis takes Sel's title, will he remove his name from the Wall? Sand the silver until it's smooth, like Sel was never there? Dig his ceremonial marble out, replace it with another—

I sit straight up on the bed, a realization striking me like lightning.

The tower rooms are at the far end of the top floor's residence halls. The dim hallway ends in a T shape, with a nameplate that points left for the north wing and right for the south. Faint music, slow and bass-heavy, reaches me through a door on my right.

I stop in front of a plain wooden door with a brass plate bearing the initials *S.K.*

Half a second after I knock, I remind myself that it's useless to listen for his footsteps. Half a second after that, I'm struck thoughtless—because Sel flings the door open wearing nothing but a deeply annoyed expression and a pair of low-slung jeans.

I can't help but follow the path of banded muscles from his abdomen to his chest. Intricate black and gray tattoos encircle his arms, cover his shoulders, and connect in a Celtic knot on his breastbone. I should look away, but instead I notice the droplets of water that fall from his thick black hair and the tiny transparent beads still clinging to his lashes.

His eyes widen before he trains his features into an annoyed glare. "I told you to go away."

I raise my chin. "I need to talk to you. Can I come in?"

I take a step forward, but he shoots a toned arm out across the doorway to block my path. "'Go away' is a complete sentence."

"What you said earlier about the Order never stripping a Kingsmage of their title? It's not true."

I've never seen Sel look so shocked, or confused. As still as a painting. He's so stunned by my words that I'm able to duck under his arm before he can stop me.

His room is circular, following the cylindrical shape of the tower itself, with windows curving along the exterior wall. A bed extends into the center of the room from a curved wall; on one side is a desk piled high with books, some modern, some old, and a laptop. On the other there's a small rug and what looks like an altar of candles. Fragrant, clean-smelling steam drifts out of a door left ajar, leading to an en suite. He's just taken a shower.

The door closes behind me, and Sel leans against it, annoyed glare restored. "Nicholas will be home in a couple of hours, and if he knows you're here, he'll either punch me again or take my title, or both, so if you have something to share, do it now and quickly." He wipes a hand down his face. To my dismay, it does extremely distracting things to his stomach muscles. Things I don't *want* to notice.

I look away, a spike of guilt making my throat tight. "Can you please put a shirt on so we can have a serious conversation?"

He looks at me between his fingers. "Don't tell me you're prudish?" He laughs self-deprecatingly. "How did I *ever* think you were Shadowborn? Now

I'm truly embarrassed. Mortified, really. Perhaps I *should* resign from my post."

"I'm trying to help you." I grit my teeth.

"Poorly, I imagine." He strolls to a chest of drawers, and I get a glimpse of charcoal-and-obsidian feathers—another, larger tattoo that I can't see in its entirety. Whatever it is, it stretches across his ribs and spans his back and sends heat from my chest to my toes. When he pulls a black T-shirt out, I breathe a slight sigh of relief. *Clothes are good*, I think. *In general. On people. On Sel, especially.* But then he shrugs the tee on, and it fits him like a second skin—a marginal improvement at *best*.

He snatches a towel off a hook on his door and scrubs at his hair as he steps around me to drop into his desk chair. "All right, I am curious, I admit. Tell me what you think you know."

"Are you going to listen?"

Head bent under his towel, he lifts a shoulder in a half shrug. All the answer I'll get.

"It might take a while to explain." His tawny eyes flick to the bed, the only other sitting surface in the room. I sit down begrudgingly and take a deep breath.

"You weren't the first Merlin I've met, and your mesmer wasn't the first one I've resisted."

That gets his attention. He tosses his towel, shoves his hair back from his face, and fixes me with a stare. "Talk."

And then I tell him. I tell him about the night at the hospital and the night I met Nick. I tell him about how and why I forced Nick's hand and got him to name me his Page. I tell him about needing to find the truth, not just about my mother's death but about my own abilities and how they might be connected to hers. I don't tell him Patricia's name, or her ancestors', but I tell him about the facts of Ruth's memory. And then I tell him about the memory that drove me to his room—the Wall of Ages with the marble representing Lord Davis's Kingsmage, and how the silver surface had been scratched.

Like someone had carved one marble out and replaced it with another.

"What if you were wrong about a mole but right about the attacks being organized by someone close to the chapter? What if it was a previous *Kingsmage* who opened that Gate twenty-five years ago, and the Order punished them by removing them from their post? If this Kingsmage became unstable away from their Oaths, then what would stop them from taking revenge on the Order and anyone else who led to their being caught? Maybe this Merlin-gone-bad went after my mother because she was a witness that night. And then they came here to hurt the Order by opening Gates again and kidnapping the most valuable Scion. After the attempts to take Nick didn't work, they sent hellfoxes after the current Kingsmage to take you out of the picture. If these attacks are all connected, I can find my mom's killer and you can prove your hunches were right!"

When I finish, he sits back in his chair and studies me for a long, silent while. He stands up to pace to the end of the room and back. Stops, stares down at me, then paces again.

"Say something."

"Something."

I roll my eyes. "You can go down to the Wall. Check for yourself if you don't believe me."

He waves a hand. "I know what your lies look like. This isn't one of them." He pauses, shakes his head. "Is this what you and Nicholas are truly up to? Looking for the truth about your mother?"

I release a slow breath. "Yes."

His eyes are unreadable. I brace for a challenge about my and Nick's plan or a derisive jab at Nick for not claiming his title for the right reasons. Neither comes.

"Say you're right and this Kingsmage opened a Gate. There's no way the Regents would let that Merlin run free. They lock up Merlins who succumb to their blood. The second we begin to turn, they put us in a warded prison under guard." His brows furrow. "And before you ask, I've seen the prisons. Escape is impossible."

"But who would be more interested in vengeance than a formerly incarcerated, more-demon-than-human, unstable Merlin? If not the Kingsmage, could it be the Line of Morgaine?"

He frowns. "Too many things don't add up. I am the Sergeant-at-Arms of this chapter, trained to take this exact post since I was a *child*. If someone opened a Gate on campus *on purpose* twenty-five years ago and hellhounds in that number attacked Onceborns, why has that history never been shared with me? *Especially* if it was a Morgaine? Why would Lord Davis and the Master Merlins tell me that a Kingsmage had never been removed if it had, in fact, happened right here? And to Davis's own Kingsmage at that?"

"Maybe it's a cover-up."

He considers this, looks for the holes in my logic, then sighs. "Lots of leaps here, but I'd buy that. If that attack was initiated by one of our own, that would explain why all of this was buried and why I was never told about it. And taking me out *would* be the best way to get to Nicholas." He scratches his chin. "What I don't get is the timing. If we go with your Kingsmage theory, why would they go after your mother almost three decades later? *She* wasn't the reason this Merlin was stripped of their title, and she wasn't connected to the chapter in any way. Further, why bother showing up and mesmering you? If they killed your mother, they shouldn't have needed to meet you at all."

My shoulders drop. It feels like we have all the pieces to the puzzle, but the picture doesn't make any sense. Which means we can't have all the pieces. We're missing something.

Sel glances at his watch. "We have time," he murmurs. "If we hurry."

He speeds to his closet, pulling his boots on in a blur. Before I can say anything, he walks over to the window, unlatches it, and pushes it open to the night air. He leans both hands on the windowsill and looks at me over his shoulder. "Come here."

I stand and walk over. "Why?"

"Reasons." He grabs me around the waist in the blink of an eye and tosses me over his shoulder until I'm draped over his back, facing his room. I squirm, but before I can protest further, he wraps an iron forearm around my thighs, pressing them to his chest. Everywhere our skin touches leaves a trail of sparks.

"Please tell me you're not jumping out of this window right now!"

"I'm not jumping out of this window right now," he says. Then he promptly climbs up—and jumps.

38

HE LANDS LIKE a Merlin—light-footed, cushioning the impact with his knees—but his shoulder digs into my hips, and my stomach threatens to upend all over his spine. My right collarbone burns with a deep ache.

"Put me down!"

He calls over his shoulder, "Do you want answers or not?"

"Of course I want answers!"

"Then we need to hurry."

"You're not carrying me like this!" I sputter, gesturing to my sling. "Just— just tossed over your back like a sack of potatoes—"

He bends and drops me onto my feet, not helping me *at all* when I stumble back and nearly fall, disoriented. Instead he releases a slow, frustrated stream of air through his nostrils. "How would you *like* me to carry you? What would please you, Page Matthews?"

I huff and circle him, evaluating my options and ignoring his long-suffering stare. "Piggyback."

"Excuse me?"

"You heard me."

"Like that movie—"

"Shut up."

"Churlish."

"Arrogant."

He swoops in, turning and pulling my uninjured arm at the same time until I'm draped piggyback like I asked. I cling instinctively, and he makes a gargled noise, pulling at my forearm where I've crushed it against his Adam's apple. "I do need to breathe," he mutters, before his voice turns sardonic. "I'm not actually a vampire."

I loosen my grip slightly and will his hands away from my skin where the electric sensation is zipping up my arms. He shifts until he has his hands under my thighs, moving me like I weigh about as much as paper.

"Hold on"—a pause—"and keep your mouth closed."

"Why do I need to keep my mouth closed?"

He chuckles, hefts me up a little higher. "Bugs." That's the only warning I get before he starts running.

The last time Sel ran me across campus, I'd been half out of my own mind with fear from hellfoxes and mage flames. All I remember is a blur. This time, it feels completely different. This time, it's *exhilarating*.

He's fast, all right. Not as fast as the uchel, but far faster than any human being.

I wonder if he makes an extra attempt to keep the ride smooth, because my shoulder barely jostles.

The gravel road, trees, and streetlights all pass in a smear of colors, and then he turns up a paved road that winds through one of the historic neighborhoods where the professors live. I see just a glimpse of a two-story brick manor at the end of a cul-de-sac and a second later we're in its backyard. Sel releases my legs, and I slide down, wobbling only slightly this time.

"Whose house is this?" I ask as he strides forward to bend down at the back door.

"This"—he lifts up a weathered rubber mat, feels under it for a moment, and produces a spare key—"is where Nicholas and I grew up."

I stare up at the house with new eyes. And a slow, dawning horror. "I can't go in there."

He scoffs. "Why?"

"Because it's trespassing."

He rolls his eyes. "I was raised here. The Davises took me in when I was ten."

"But——" I stammer, trying to put my hesitation into words. "Why don't we just wait until Nick and his dad get back from the airport and ask Lord Davis in person?"

"Because I don't trust Lord Davis to speak the truth," he says simply. Nothing in his tone holds rancor or spite. It's a simple statement of fact.

"Why not? Didn't he raise you?"

"The two are not mutually exclusive. And the reason I don't trust him is because that man is Oathed to the hilt, just like I am. He is sworn to do the Regents' bidding by an Oath of Service, the same way I am sworn to the Legendborn. We could ask him what he knows, but if your theories are true, his Oaths would force him to lie to keep their secrets."

"But *why* are we at their house?"

"This is *Lord Davis's* house. Nicholas doesn't live here any longer. We're here because his father is the Viceroy of the Southern chapter, and because I have excellent hearing and old paper smells different than new. I happen to know that Lord Davis keeps historic chapter records and archives locked away in his personal study."

"Why didn't Nick bring me here before?"

"Nicholas rejected the Order's history, so he didn't know to look. The truth about your mother's history with the chapter might be here. Why are you hesitating, Matthews?"

Because Nick and I are supposed to do this together, I think. Sel watches me, waiting for an answer. "It just doesn't feel right."

Sel sighs and looks up at the sky. "We have an hour at most before they get back. It'll go faster if you help me look, but if *morals* are getting in the way, you can tell Nicholas I brought you here against your will and stay out here in the yard." He gestures behind me. "There's an old swing set there. Watch out for splinters." He turns back toward the door with the key.

I hate the offhand way he dismisses me, but I do want answers. And if Lord Davis can't be trusted . . . ? When would I get another opportunity like this? Nick will understand, won't he, if I tell him right away? I shift from one foot to the other in indecision while Sel opens the door and disappears inside.

It doesn't escape my notice that he's left the door cracked open behind him. With a quiet curse, I follow him in.

I trip twice walking up the basement stairs and stumble into Sel's back when we get to the main level. As I follow him into the foyer, he mutters, "I can't believe I thought you were a creature of the night," under his breath. I scowl at his shoulders.

He moves through the house easily, with both the familiarity of long residence and Merlin night vision on his side. I stare at the dark shape of Sel's back as he walks to the interior stairs at a human pace—for my sake more than anything, I'm sure. "Why can't we turn on the lights?"

"Because the neighbors are nosy."

Light filters in from a window on the second-floor landing, so I can see a little now, enough to make out the framed pictures of both boys hanging alongside us in the stairwell. Nick in a PeeWee football uniform, grinning wide. Sel at a violin recital, looking thin and dour even as a small child. I'm torn between a deep curiosity and the feeling that I'm violating Nick's privacy.

Right as I get to the top of the stairwell, the LED-bright headlights of a luxury car flare through the large picture window. Sel grabs my hand, yanking me down as the car approaches. His fingers are five sizzling points that sear into my bones, and I cry out, yanking my hand away. He blinks down at me in confusion. My heart thuds against my chest so loud his sensitive ears must hear it. The car passes. A garage door lifts—but it's the house next door. We exhale in unison.

I move to stand, but he presses me back with the flat of his palm on my uninjured shoulder. "Wait until they go inside."

Once the garage door descends, he looks down at where I've started rubbing my wrist with my other hand. "I didn't touch your wounded arm, or grab you that hard. Why did you scream?"

"I don't know," I say truthfully. "It felt like an electrical current. Like static, but worse."

Several questions flash across his face before he decides on one. "You never answered me that night at the Quarry. Do you feel something when I look at you?"

I stand up to put distance between us, suddenly hesitant to talk about this part of my abilities. I haven't mentioned how his gaze affects me, or any of the other more sensory parts of what I can do. "Yes."

He stands. Looks at me like he's trying to see inside my brain and assess its contents. "Explain."

"It's going to sound weird."

"Weird is relative."

Understatement of the year. "When you look at me, it feels . . . prickly. When you're mad, your eyes feel like sparks."

His eyebrows raise in the middle. A strange sort of tension runs through his shoulders—like anger, but not quite. He looks like he wants to press the issue, but instead he turns down the hallway. "We need to hurry."

I follow behind him until a familiar smell reaches my nose halfway down the hall. I stop. To my right is an open door, and suddenly I realize *why* the smell is familiar. This room belongs to Nick. The color scheme is similar to his room at the Lodge—blues and whites on the twin bed in the corner and in the checkered curtains. There's a small desk and two large bookcases.

"We don't have time for you to snoop around your boyfriend's childhood room." Sel sounds utterly annoyed.

I scowl at him in the darkness, knowing full well he can see it, but catch up to where he's standing at the very end of the hall. I join him in front of a wide wooden door.

"I probably should have thought about doing this before," he says with a hint of chagrin. He takes the two finely engraved silver rings off his left hand and adds them to the empty fingers on his right, so that all four fingers have rings on them.

"You should have thought about your jewelry?"

He side-eyes me. "No, breaking into Lord Davis's records. And, for your information, silver conducts aether best." He calls a tiny, bright sphere of aether into his palm, letting it rotate and build until it becomes a small spinning planet with white clouds swirling across the surface.

His brows knit together. The spinning ball changes shape, stretching into a very thin, translucent blade. As I watch, it hardens in layers, growing denser with every passing second, until it forms into a razor-sharp point, with the base still swirling in a ball in Sel's hand. He wraps his fingers around the handle and draws the blade down the seam of the door until the latch releases. The door unhitches with a quiet click.

Sel says we have about an hour before Nick and his father come home. I ask him again if we can just wait, ask Nick to help us, and he glares at me before pointing to the other side of Lord Davis's office where there are at least four sets of filing cabinets up against a wall.

"What are we looking for exactly?"

"Records, membership details, witness accounts, anything someone might have documented about the attacks."

We divide and conquer, with Sel taking one side of the room and me taking the other. I go slow with one injured arm, but can use my right fingers to hold single pages. After ten minutes, Sel speaks up.

"You're good for him, you know."

We both know exactly who he's talking about.

He pulls another drawer open. "He's always been self-righteous, but now he has focus. Before you showed up, he defied his father to prove to himself that he doesn't care what the man thinks. Now he's actually considering the legacy he used to shove aside."

It's my turn to scoff. "Nick *doesn't* care what his father thinks. He did that to avoid Arthur."

He chuckles. "I'm sure that's what he believes, but I've known him since we were in diapers. He resents his father and hated his upbringing. After his wife departed, Davis doted on his son in every way possible. Gave in to his tantrums and fantasies. Allowed our future king to turn his back on the rest of us."

"But—"

"Take it from me, Bree." Sel sighs. "No matter what a partially abandoned child says, in the end, there is one truth: one parent left, and the other stayed."

"His mother didn't leave him. She was taken."

"His mother made a choice. She knew the risks." A pause. "And she made her choice anyway."

I pause. My mother is gone, but she'd never have chosen to leave me, or run the risk of us being parted. That's my own truth, and one I hadn't considered.

I put back the folder in my hand and move on to another. "Well, if the two of you are so similar, why does he hate you so much? I know how he feels about Merlins in general, but you were a child when his mother was mesmered. You had nothing to do with it."

Sel grabs a thick folder and drops down to the floor with it, speaking without looking up. "When I was young, my mother was killed by an uchel while on a mission. After that, my human father fell into a liquor bottle and never came out."

I blink, stunned at both the matter-of-fact tone of his story and how familiar that tone sounds. Sometimes, you say the awful thing quickly and without taking a breath because lingering is too painful.

If an uchel killed Sel's mother, then no wonder he'd threatened to murder me. Frankly, I'm surprised at his restraint.

"The Regents moved me to a school for Merlins in the mountains, but when I was Oathed to Nicholas, his father took me in. While my own parents were absent, Davis was kind and generous. Not long after I showed up, Nicholas began to see his father's praise and attention as a zero-sum game. And since I was obedient, I was getting those things." He shrugs. "Over time, jealousy became anger, anger became resentment."

I mull this over for a moment. "For both of you?"

Sel exhales and looks at me, thinking. "Perhaps."

We sit silently for a moment before he continues, his voice heavy with memory. "I thought Nicholas was amazing. He was everything I wasn't: bright, open, popular. Heroic. He made it all look so easy. Still does. I wanted to be close to that." He sighs softly. "Probably why I fell in love with him."

Oh.

"I didn't realize. You—does he—"

"I was thirteen. I'm well over it." Sel lets out a loose, wry chuckle, head still bent over a filing cabinet. "And everyone falls in love with Nicholas, Bree—it's part of his insufferable charm."

I want to know more, despite the complicated feelings this conversation is giving me, and Sel answers before I can ask.

"There's so much baggage between Nicholas and me; there was never going to be room enough for anything else to grow." Sel gives the paperwork in his hands a tight scowl. "When I think about that crush now, I remember how much of my life I sacrificed to protect a spoiled brat who didn't even want his crown—and feel *entirely* grateful I moved on to more mature people."

"Like Tor?" I reply without thinking.

Sel turns to me, raises a brow. "Among others."

A confusing mixture of jealousy and curiosity and *want* swirls in my stomach.

Sel turns back to his work. "Any more personal questions or shall we get back to looking for a rogue, murderous mage?"

I open my mouth to shoot back another retort when he goes completely stiff. "What?"

"This is it," he whispers, pulling a thick green hanging folder stuffed with paper out of the cabinet. "Stamped confidential with the Regents' seal. 'Documentation and affidavits about a spate of demon attacks on campus.' Dated twenty-five years ago. Let's go."

The trip back to the Lodge goes just as quickly, but this time I'm on Sel's back as he leaps up to the second-floor trellis, then yanks on a ledge to propel us the rest of the way to his open window.

Once we're inside, he drops down on the floor and spreads the folder open, laying out stacks of paper in a row. His casual way of sitting and the deliberate movements of his hands catch me off guard, but then I remember that even though Sel is a Kingsmage, he's still an eighteen-year-old junior in college. He has to study and do homework and write papers just like the rest of us.

Someone slams a door down the hall, and I hear voices. It's almost dawn.

I kneel down across from him. *This is it*, I think. *This is the moment when I find out what happened to my mother, and why. And who is responsible.* I reach for the top stack of papers with a shaking hand, but Sel has already found what we need: a slightly yellowed affidavit, three pages long and handwritten in a formal script.

He looks up at me with a question in his eyes. I nod, and Sel reads aloud:

"*April 9th, 1995*
Confidential and Classified

Attn: Honored Lieges and Mage Seneschals of the High Council of Regents of the Order of the Round Table

I will begin this affidavit without equivocation of any kind. The Southern Chapter of the Order of the Round Table has failed in its duties. As requested, this personal report details in linear fashion and from my perspective the events that transpired starting last week and up to today. I write this with the understanding that the facts herein will be filed for the record in the Order archives.

On Friday, March 31, our Merlin alerted the Scions of Gawain and Bors to a partially materialized sarff uffern. The two Scions successfully dispatched the serpent, as recorded in our logs, and we assumed we would have respite from another crossing.

Four days later, unbeknownst to us, a large Gate opened near the mouth of ogof y ddraig. A dozen partially materialized cŵn uffern emerged. Within minutes, our Merlin alerted us to their presence, and we dispatched all six Scions, each with a well-trained Squire, and our Merlin. We were certain we were capable of destroying the creatures; our hubris was our mistake.

Before we arrived, six Unanedig had already been eviscerated. The Cysgodanedig—the Shadowborn—were coordinated, and split up into three groups when they detected us, affording them time to grow fully corporeal. In the course of chasing these three groups, eight more Unanedig were killed. In all cases, we dispatched the beasts and sent their bodies to dust, but could not do so with discretion. We worked with the Vassal network on campus and off to hide the true nature of the deaths and framed the losses as an accident due to a gas explosion. All families have been paid a settlement from Order coffers via the University legal department.

There were fifteen surviving Unanedig witnesses. Our Merlin mesmered them with false memories, and we held them here at the Lodge, but as you know, mesmered memories must be of equal weight to the originals. The shock and graphic nature of these attacks prevented the mesmer from taking hold. Too late, we realized we needed the Regents' assistance.

With the help of the Regents' attending Merlins, the witnesses were successfully mesmered and released. Each witness has a file, attached here, with further details regarding their management.

As tragic as this account is, I'm afraid that I must add further unsavory details to complete the record. The Regents members and Merlins, in their wisdom and due right, proceeded immediately with an investigation into the incident, its origins, and the chapter's responses. Our actions and failings as described here were recorded by the committee. However, in the course of the subsequent investigation, new information has come to light and devastated our chapter.

It was discovered that our Merlin and Kingsmage, Na—"

Sel stops reading abruptly, his face stricken.

"What is it?"

His eyes scan the letter again, darting back and forth as the blood drains from his face.

"Sel? Selwyn?"

I reach for the paper, and he doesn't resist when I slip it from his slack fingers. The mixture of horror and shock contorting his face, marring his beautiful, precise features, sends a cold blade into my heart.

"Read it." His usually sonorous voice scrapes the quiet of the room.

"Maybe—"

"Read it, Bree," he repeats, a fierce command threaded through his words.

I do. I read the story of his mother.

"It was discovered that our Merlin and Kingsmage, Natasia Kane, opened the Gates herself using an arcane ritual and Cysgodanedig blood she procured specifically because of its strength and ability to open Gates of that size. Kingsmage Kane gave no reason for her abominable behavior and denied the investigation's findings at every turn. In hindsight, perhaps we should have considered the possibility of Natasia's involvement the moment the first Gate was found; it is well documented that the more power Merlins command, the more they succumb to their unnatural, demonic nature. Natasia is the product of careful Merlin bloodline curation, and she's the most powerful sorceress in a generation. But we were swayed by her gifts and did not expect her corruption to manifest so early. In the weeks leading up to the attack, Natasia had been consumed by an obsession with the Cysgodanedig. She'd been so certain that a goruchel had crossed over that she became paranoid, unreasonable, even suspicious of our own chapter members.

The usual sentence for treason of this magnitude and

intentional exposure resulting in death(s) is forcible elimination. In truth, even the Regents are not certain that elimination is possible due to Natasia's unusually strong affinity for aether. As such, Natasia has been secured in one of the Regents' most heavily warded prisons.

Regent Ross has informed me that the loss of her bloodline would be a blow to our efforts against the Cysgodanedig, so in the event that her stability returns under rehabilitation, the Regents will consider offering temporary probation so that she may bear an heir. Any child she produces will need to be Oathed early and raised under close supervision.

On a personal note, I would like to state for the record that I have known Natasia most of my life. I am not sure what it says that I, her charge, did not sense her intentions. Perhaps she hid them from me to protect me as best she could. I offer this possibility and perspective in hopes that it will support her fair treatment while in Order custody.

The Regents requested that I write this report so that it may serve as a reminder to others of the Line. They have asked me to state for the record that while the Merlins' aether abilities hold the keys to our Order's mission, their cambion blood affliction requires constant vigilance.

Merlin Isaac Sorenson has agreed to take on our open Kingsmage post. The Regents have advised that all records of Natasia Kane be expunged. They have also agreed, by our request, that the other chapters remain ignorant of the culprit behind these incidents, lest the report generate strife and distrust within our Order.

Yours in the Lines,
Martin Davis, Scion of Arthur

Addendum I: 5 years from incident
Natasia Kane has exhibited several years of stability. She will be released under probation and monitoring.

Addendum II: 12 years from incident
Natasia Kane has exhibited a relapse of blood symptoms. The High Council of Regents has taken action to remove her from service and return her to containment. Her young son will be admitted to a residential Merlin academy in Asheville, North Carolina, and monitored by the Masters on faculty. There is some hope that, under their close supervision, he can be groomed as the next Kingsmage for the Line of Arthur, and bonded to my own son, Nicholas."

I look up to see Sel clenching and unclenching his fists where they rest on his knees. His breath is a rattling, choking sound, like a man drowning on land.

Of all the horrible, possible truths, this is one I could have never, ever imagined.

39

I'D NEVER CONSIDERED that the loss of someone else's mother would be so connected to losing my own. Or that that loss would go hand in hand with death, destruction, and a horrifying fate. Nick's mother, Sel's, mine. How many mothers has the Order taken?

I want to say something, offer *something* to Sel, but the tension in his body and the thunder building in his unseeing gaze are all screaming at me to run. Run away before the bomb goes off, before the building explodes.

Suddenly, Sel is on his feet. He paces to the end of the room, the back of his hand pressed hard against his mouth like he doesn't trust what could come out of himself. It takes everything in me to stay seated when he kicks his closet door and the wood splinters into a boot-shaped hole.

I realize then that I'm watching grief like mine come crashing down on Sel, all at once. The sudden, sharp, all-consuming pain of loss is tearing into him right in front of me. I remember how that felt. I remember how much it hurts. The pages fall from my hand.

I don't remember standing up. I don't remember walking to him. I just know that my arm is around his middle. His entire body turns to stone as soon as I touch him, and his smoke-and-whiskey scent swirls around us, heavy and burning, but I don't let go. "I'm sorry," I whisper into his spine. He doesn't answer, but his muscles release the tiniest fraction. I wonder how long it's been since someone touched him. We stay like that until his breathing slows.

When he finally speaks, his voice is pitched low. "You called me a monster once."

My arm drops and I pull away, my voice colored with despair. "I was angry. I—I didn't mean that."

He turns, and his red-rimmed eyes sweep across my features. After a moment, a shadow crosses his face, and his mouth folds into a small, rueful smile, like he wants to admonish me and call me a liar. I look for tears, but he hasn't shed them. His eyes take on a faraway, haunted expression. "Maybe you were right. It looks like I came from one."

I've never heard Sel speak this way. So dazed, like he's not really here in the room with me at all. I want to comfort him, but it feels like it's not my place to offer comfort in the face of his family history. And yet I'm the reason he knows that history in the first place. I'm the reason he's standing there, hollow and fractured.

The guilt is enough to choke me.

"'So that she may bear an heir . . . ,'" he whispers, his eyes turned inward. I flinch at the cold language. The hope and expectation that his mother would produce a child—a weapon—for the Order fills me with nauseous horror.

He shudders, and his eyelashes flutter, as if he's just remembered that I'm standing in front of him. He inhales deeply through his nose and looks over my shoulder at the pile of paperwork behind me. When he exhales, the cold, calculating, distant Sel is back, his analysis curt. "It appears I was lied to, likely for my protection. Which means there was no uchel, no mission. They released her for a time and took her away when she relapsed. I suppose I was too young to see that she was losing herself, or too admiring of her abilities . . ."

Watching him Holmes his way through his own devastation is almost more than I can take. I open my mouth, but he cuts me off.

"At any rate, she's alive." His voice breaks on the revelation. Then he sucks in another breath. "But locked away, has been for years, so she's not our culprit. And, it seems, I inherited her penchant for paranoia, so perhaps there is no mole at all and never was. As for your quest, your mother may be one of the witnesses."

I'd already thought of that, of course, but . . . "Sel—"

He brushes past me. "We should find out what happened to your mother," he says flatly. He crouches down and pushes the affidavit aside, flipping through the file's other papers.

I kneel beside him and place a hand on his forearm, ignoring the small sizzle between our skin. He freezes without looking at me, muscles hard beneath my fingers. "Sel."

His voice drops into a register meant to scare and intimidate. "Don't." But I hear the restrained desperation in his voice. A pause. Then, quietly: "Please."

I recognize that sound. It's the sound of holding on to a cliff by the edge of your nails. The sound of barely containing a pain so immense that to look at it, to raise your own flesh and examine what's beneath, is to risk falling into a darkness you know you'll never escape.

It hits me then, that I'd come all this way for my mother and for the truth, but the pain of existing without her, the deep searing wound in my own chest, hasn't gotten any better. It has only changed shape.

Wordlessly, I slip my hand from his arm. His shoulders sag, as if he's just released a heavy weight, and he reaches for the papers again.

"Here." He taps a stack of papers clipped together. "These are the witnesses who were mesmered. All students. Looks like alphabetical order."

The first few witnesses in my pile are all white. Psychology student. Football player. Theater kid. Then I flip the page and everything stops when I see her face.

Sel notices my shaking hands. "Did you find her?"

The words don't come because there are no words.

Her student picture must have been taken when she'd just arrived to campus as an undergraduate, because her features are relaxed and bright with the promise of adventure. The creases at her cheeks and the edges of her eyes, the ones from laughter and time, have yet to form. Her sharp brown eyes stare at the camera as if challenging it in a contest she knew she'd win. Hair permed straight and curled at the ends. Nothing like the short, cropped coils she'd adopted when I was ten.

"I'd almost forgotten what she looked like," I whisper.

Sel's voice is gentle. "What does the file say?"

I release a wavering breath and flip to the one-page summary. "'Witness Eleven. Faye Ayeola Carter, age nineteen. Sophomore. Biology major, chemistry minor.'"

Sel lets out a low whistle. "Bio major, chem minor? That sounds painful."

I hear the quiet pride in my own voice. "That's a scientist."

"What else does it say?"

I keep reading. "'The Scion of Owain and Squire Harris found Ms. Carter and two other Onceborns (see file names Mitchell and Howard) near the ogof y . . . ddraig'? What is that?"

"*Ogov uh thrah-eeg,*" he corrects my pronunciation. "The Welsh 'dd' is the soft 'th' in 'leather.' It means 'cave of the dragon.' The cave is at the center of the tunnel network. Keep reading."

"'. . . near the ogof y ddraig, cornered by a hound. Once the creature was killed, the three Onceborns were taken into custody—'"

Sel sighs in frustration. "I'm sure they came willingly, too, after the shock of seeing a full-corp hellhound. Probably had to knock them out first." I glare at him, and he shrugs. "It's protocol."

I release a steadying breath. "'. . . taken into custody and brought back to the Lodge. Once their memories were altered, Ms. Carter and the others were monitored in chapter custody for one day to assure the mesmer had taken, and released. As with the other witnesses, Ms. Carter will be monitored during her time on campus by Order members and assigned a field Merlin when she graduates.'"

"What's the rest?" Sel points to a table under the written summary.

I realize what the table is almost immediately. "Check-ins. They're all dated like a log, with columns for date, time, location, and a short section for notes." I point to one of the early rows. "'May 1, 1995. 10:31 a.m. Undergraduate library, UNC-CH. Working with Ms. Carter on a group project final for our LING 207 class. Have spent several hours with her this week. Even with some gentle probing about campus events, she does not mention or recall last month's attack.'"

Sel hums. "They didn't just watch her, they tested her. How many entries are there?"

I flip the page. And flip again. And flip again. "There must be dozens of pages here. At least one entry every week for the first year, then once a month after graduation . . . They kept tabs on her for *years*."

"Witness protection," he murmurs. "Sort of." He clears his throat and takes the stack from me, thumbing to the very back. "Let's see what the last entry says."

I swallow around the lump in my throat. "Okay."

Sel pauses, his finger resting on the final slip of paper in the back, and dips his head to catch my eye. "This is the last page," he says, but I hear the meaning behind the words. I know what he's really asking me: *Are you ready?*

My heart pounds in my chest, and blood rushes in my ears like an ocean. Am I ready? I'd started this whole mission worried about finding the truth and convinced that nothing could be worse than not knowing. But now?

Sel's eyes are patient but wary, and no wonder; he'd just learned his own horrible truth.

"Read it."

"'May 13, 2020. 9:18 a.m. Bentonville County Hospital, Bentonville, North Carolina. Ms. Carter was killed in a hit-and-run near her home at 8:47 p.m. last night, May twelfth. I was alerted to her death by a Vassal working in the local police department. In order to confirm Ms. Carter's death, I assumed the identity of an officer. She leaves behind a husband, Edwin Matthews, and a teenage daughter. As recorded in the enclosed logs, Ms. Carter has never shown any evidence of her memory returning or knowledge of the incidents. As such, she has not, in the past or currently, given cause to pursue containment steps. This is the final entry in Witness Eleven's file.'"

Sel passes me the paper, but I wave it away. I can't touch it.

I can't breathe.

"Is this the Merlin you saw?"

I drag my eyes back to a small photo clipped to the back of the file. In a single rushing moment, I'm back at the hospital with new details filling in the blanks.

Thin mouth, bushy brows, blue eyes. His badge flickering in the light.

Everything inside me pinches and recoils, twists and tightens, until it feels like my entire body is a knot made of lead, heavy and poisonous. A low, pained whine escapes me, ending in a choking sob. I can only nod in answer.

Sel reaches for me, but I squeeze my eyes shut. After that, he doesn't try to touch me again. "I'm sorry, Bree."

"That's it," I say wearily, a strange numbness flooding my body. A humorless laugh leaves me in a low huff, and I open my eyes. "Now I know."

I thought that once I had the truth, it would get better. That things would feel right. But they don't. Everything's just as wrong, all over again.

I stand and start toward the door.

"Bree, wait." Sel follows me. "You can sense aether, you can see it, feel it, but you also resist illusion. If mesmer doesn't work on you, maybe it didn't work on your mother, either."

"Yeah." My throat is tight. "Already thought of that."

"And?"

"And?" I whip around, fighting back tears. "Don't you get it? She did the *smart* thing. The thing *I* should have done in the first place. She hid. She hid every time one of those Scions or Squires pretended to be her friend and 'tested' her. She hid what she knew from *everyone* for twenty-five years, so this medieval boys' club, this feudalist fever dream, this whole . . . fucked-up world of yours could never find her!"

Sel looks like he wants to say something but thinks better of it. Good. Nothing he could say could make this moment better.

My chest feels like it's imploding. "She hid it from me. Or she tried to. But it didn't work, because I'm a selfish daughter and I *had* to come here and dig."

"Bree, you're not—" Sel starts, but I don't let him finish.

The words spill out of my mouth in an angry, sobbing rush. "She didn't want me to find the Order"—I turn, snarling at Sel—"because she didn't want me to become your target, but I did anyway." He flinches, but I don't care. I tug my shirt down to the still-healing purple bruise on my collarbone from tonight's trial. "Didn't want me to get hurt, but I did anyway. I had to barge in with the barest shadow of a plan and no clue what I was doing——" My voice breaks off.

I see words of comfort and repair hovering uselessly on his lips. He wants to help me, but he doesn't know how.

I do.

The idea unfurls in my mind like a matted, frayed rope thrown down a well. I know, logically, that climbing that rope is a mistake, but in this moment, anything is better than staying here. Anything.

The words fall from my mouth in a desperate whisper. "Take her away."

Sel looks bewildered. "Who?"

I step toward him. "I don't want this anymore." I take another. "I don't want to feel this anymore."

Understanding floods his features, and after it a pained, sickened expression. "Bree, no."

I plead with him, "You can do it. Please. I won't break the mesmer. I'll——I'll let it happen."

When I reach him, his lips curl in something like disgust. "Don't ask me that."

"If I can't have her, I don't want to remember her."

"You don't *mean* that," he hisses.

"Yes, I do!" My eyes swim with tears.

He takes a deep breath, holds his ground. "Even if I wanted to——" He shakes his head. "I'm not powerful enough. The older or more traumatic the memory, the stronger the replacement has to be. Like for like. 'Memories of equal weight.'"

Memories of equal weight. There *are* no memories that could equal this weight. And the last hour has just made them heavier.

I break then. Snap. The tears run hot down my cheeks, and my breathing comes in ragged sobs. Sel watches me with a sad, helpless expression. Almost like he's worried for me, hurting for me . . . but if that's true, it's another truth I can't handle.

I open the door and run into the hallway, letting the door slam shut behind me. Sel lets me go at first. I make it all the way to the foyer and front door before he catches up. I can feel his gaze along the back of my neck. "Leave me alone, Sel."

He grasps my left shoulder. "You aren't in any shape to walk home alone."

I jerk back, but we both know the only reason he lets me go is because he chooses to.

He stands there in the grand foyer, a shadow with searching eyes, and suddenly it all becomes so clear. He was born to this world, for better or for worse. And Nick and the Scions and the Squires and the Pages . . . they grew up living inside the Order's legends. Suddenly, all I can see is the hundreds of years of history that don't belong to me. A war that doesn't belong to me.

"I never should have come here."

"Bree—" He reaches for me again right as I open the front door—and come face-to-face with Nick.

40

IT ONLY TAKES a second for Nick's eyes to take in my tearstained face, Sel's hand on my shoulder, and Sel standing behind me. Russ and Felicity peer around Nick with wary expressions just as Sel's hand falls away.

"What the hell is going on here?" Nick demands.

My breath falters at the look in Nick's eyes. In them is the small beginning of some strong, sharp emotion, straining outward like a blade against cloth. "I need to go home." I make as if to move around him, and he catches me around my good elbow before I take two steps.

"What—why?" He looks between me and Sel's stoic expression, directs the blade of his anger at his Kingsmage. "What did you do to her?"

"I didn't do this," Sel says wearily. "Not that you'll believe me."

"He didn't—didn't do anything," I confirm, and slip out of Nick's grip. I push between him and Russ and move down the stairs.

Nick follows me. "Then why are you *crying?*"

I whirl around. "I need to go home. I can't be here right now." I catch Felicity's eye. "Can you please drive me home, Felicity?"

"I can drive you home," Nick insists.

I can't look at him. "Felicity? Please?"

She glances between Nick and me, back to Sel, then to Russ. "Russy, can you get my car?" Russ doesn't hesitate. He jogs down the stone steps toward the Lodge garage.

"Bree!"

"Let her go, Nick," Sel says from the doorway, and Nick and I both freeze. *"Nick."* Not Nicholas. Sel's eyes find mine. Our eyes meet—for half a heartbeat, so quick—but Nick catches it. In that split second, he sees something new between me and his Kingsmage. Something I can't explain right now, not even to myself. When Nick turns back to me, the raw confusion and hurt in his eyes crushes my heart.

I stammer, try to start several sentences, but none of them take hold in my mouth. The words are caught in a jumble, and I don't know where to start. I stare at him without an answer. Finally, I utter the only thing that could make him understand, my voice cracking on every word.

"It was just an accident."

It's the wrong thing to say.

Nick takes a step closer, his voice soft and pained. "What was just an accident, B?" He doesn't know I mean my mother. He thinks I mean the something with Sel.

Oh God. No. That's not—

There's movement inside the Lodge. Behind Sel, I see Tor and Sar, both in pajamas. A crowd is gathering. They'll all know. They'll all see me like this.

I tear my eyes away and back to Nick, take a shaky breath, and try again, because he needs to understand. "The car," I whisper, fresh tears burning at my eyes. "That night. The hospital. No one . . . just . . . an accident."

As understanding passes through him, the blood drains from his face. The devastation I see there is all for me, all for my pain. But if I accept it, if it touches me, I'll shatter. I know I will. He reaches for me, but I raise both palms, and his hand falls. That simple gesture—pushing him away—looks like it breaks him as much as it breaks me.

"How? How did you—" He stops. Turns again to the Lodge door may whom Sel is watching us, his face unreadable. This time when Nick faces me, his eyes hold stony accusation. "With *him?*"

"I'm sorry," I whisper, walking backward on the lawn. "This was all a mistake."

Tires over gravel. Russ pulling up behind me in Felicity's Jeep. Nick shaking his head *no.*

The car idles, loud enough that the Legendborn in the foyer can't hear me. But Nick can . . . and so can Sel. "I can't be here anymore."

The air leaves Nick's chest in a broken rush. He knows I don't mean tonight. He knows I mean forever.

"No, wait!" He shakes his head, desperation making his eyes bright. "Please. I need you. You have to know I'd choose you. I want *you*, Bree. If Camlann is coming, I want you."

The lead in my stomach turns hot, melting into all of my limbs. The words feel heavy and thick at the back of my throat, but I say them anyway.

"No. You don't."

I climb into the car and leave him behind, standing alone in the gravel as we drive away.

PART FOUR

SPLINTER

MY PHONE DINGS so many times that day and the next, that, after a while, I just block Nick's number.

Then Sar tries. William. Greer. Whitty. I block all of them, one at a time. It hurts, but the pain feels right. Necessary. Like I deserve it for wasting their time.

I'd taken Nick's necklace off as soon as I got home and buried the chain and coin under some socks in my drawer.

I'd thought myself brave for facing the Order. For chasing down the truth. But every time I close my eyes, all I see are the faces of the people I've lied to in order to find it.

My mother didn't pursue the Order and its war.

My mother didn't share her Rootcraft. Not with me and not with anyone else.

The least I can do, after defying her in so many ways, is finally follow in her footsteps.

The next days pass in a blur because I force them to. I focus only on what's in front of me.

Classes, studying in the library, meals with Alice, sleepless nights. Repeat.

I take the sling off in public, so no one asks questions. Alice asks questions anyway. I tell her I fell during initiation.

Patricia made good on her promise to call my father and tell him we weren't a good fit, that she wishes me well. I know she said that last part because he calls me to ask if I'd like to talk about it. I say no.

I walk the campus half expecting Nick or Greer or even Sel to jump out at me from behind a line of students or a tree. Not that they ever have; I think it's a Legendborn rule to avoid one another on campus. But they could find me . . . if they wanted. It makes it much easier on me that they don't.

I can do what my mother did, I think. Live oblivious in the world the way that everyone else does. Maybe our paths were different, but my mother and I came to the same conclusion.

I have to forget them, because remembering is too dangerous.

". . . Maybe after class?"

"Mm." I chew absentmindedly on my blueberry jam–smothered biscuit as I read the *DTH*. I didn't even know until this week that Carolina *had* a school newspaper.

"Bree."

"Yeah?"

"You're making a mess."

"What?"

Alice points at my lap where three warm pools of butter have expanded into lakes that stretch from the horoscope section to an article on student body elections. A biscuit crumb falls from my hand into the center of a butter lake and promptly drowns. "Damn." I push the paper away while she covers a laugh behind her coffee cup.

I'd let Alice drag me out of bed earlier than was strictly necessary, at least by my own standards. "So we can actually eat breakfast" is the type of reasoning that only sounds reasonable if you're Alice. Alice, whose parents get her up at six thirty a.m. even on *weekends*.

"Did you hear anything I just said?"

"No . . . ?"

She puts her cup down and gives me a long stare. A *clunk-clunk-c-c-clunk* reaches us from across the dining hall, where students are dumping used and empty food trays onto a conveyor belt with varying degrees of care. "You've been weird all week."

I poke at my bowl of cheesy grits and shrug. "Just focusing on school stuff. I got a C minus on that English test, so it's clearly warranted. What were you saying?"

"A C minus? Matty, you've never gotten anything below an A in English in your life. What's going on?" Alice tilts her head and fixes me with a stare. I stare back. After a moment of silence she sighs, wrinkling her mouth and nose together. "I said I know you don't have a dress for the gala thing this weekend. We should go shopping after class. There are a ton of boutiques downtown, and I saw some sales."

I look away and gnaw at the inside of my cheek. "Yeah, about that. I'm not going."

Alice rears back, gawking at me like I've grown scales. "I'm sorry, *what* did you just say?"

I blink. "I decided not to go through with that group. So, I'm not going—"

"Hi, yes, hello. I regret to inform you that you've had a temporary lapse in judgment. These things happen, and I'm going to try not to make you feel too badly about it. But you're going to that gala."

I groan. "Alice, I don't want to go."

"You are going to that gala, Matty, even if I have to force you into one of Charlotte's dresses!" Alice says, her eyes gone flinty behind her frames.

I sigh and fold up the greasy newspaper as neatly as I can, then toss it onto my tray. "You don't understand."

Alice crosses her arms over her chest. I understand you've suddenly stopped talking to a hottie-hot boy who adores you, and you won't explain why, and it sounds like he did nothing wrong. I understand you have an invitation to a black-tie event that you seem to want to toss in the trash. And I understand that I begged my parents to let me stay on campus this weekend just so I could help you get ready, and honestly, Bree, we were way too nerdy in high school for me to let you throw this opportunity away!"

I gape at her. "What's gotten into you?"

"Sixteen years of Disney movies that I know you watched just as much as I did, so what's really going on here?"

"I don't want to go!" I'm loud enough that Alice flinches, and the two girls sitting beside us turn their heads in our direction. I pull my bag out from underneath the table and start zipping it up. "And I need to get to class."

Alice watches me, shaking her head. "This ain't it, Matty."

"What's not it?"

"This." She waves her hand at me. "A couple weeks ago you were all over this group, texting this Nick kid all the time, going to therapy, staying out late. And this week all of that's gone? You get back to the room earlier than I do? Spend more time studying than *I* do? Read the school newspaper? And I *know* you're not sleeping." She shakes her head again. "This ain't it."

"You get mad at me for not taking school seriously enough, and now I'm taking it too seriously?" I scoff. "A couple weeks ago I came home crying, too. Is that what you want?"

"Of course not. But . . .This week you're a zombie. You know what you need?"

I stand up and sigh. "You gonna say Jesus?"

"No." She points at me. "You need homeostasis."

"Did you just . . . biology me?"

"Sure did."

I falter, no comeback in sight. In the end, I give up. "I gotta go," I mutter. I pick up my tray and leave, ignoring the look of disappointment on Alice's face.

That night I lie in bed with the window open, twisting my hair and listening to the shouts and conversations on the busy sidewalk below. Old East is close to the north perimeter, so I suppose every week we'll be able to hear the undergrads leaving the campus grounds and heading to the main drag for the bars and clubs. For a moment, I wonder if I'll hear the Legendborn.

Maybe they'll go back to the biergarten to celebrate the end of the Trials.

I make myself imagine the gala, even though it hurts. A grand room, hundreds of people in formal wear. A stage. When I imagine Nick in a tuxedo and bow tie, I curl into a tight ball of want on my bed. I lean into the vision to remind myself of the loss. I see him. Tall, handsome, and—for a short while, a quick moment, a heartbeat—mine.

On the other side of the room, Alice's snores are light and even. I know she's right. I don't have homeostasis. I don't have equilibrium, no matter the stimuli. Patricia knew it, saw it, and wanted nothing of it.

My agony has a hunger, I've discovered. It doesn't want the truth. Not really. It just wants to feed itself sorrow until no other emotion is left.

My father calls before eight on Friday morning. He knows I don't have an early class on Fridays, but he rarely calls me before noon, especially this close to the weekend when his shop is busiest.

"Dad?" I say, holding my phone to my ear as I pull on a pair of jeans.

"Hey, kiddo." I half expect to hear the heavy clink of a dropped tool on concrete and the high-pitched whirr-whine of a pneumatic wrench, but there's nothing like that. "You busy?"

"Nope. My first class is at ten. What's up?"

"Come have breakfast with me. My treat."

I chuckle. "If only."

"Naw, kid. Meet me downstairs and bring your books."

I freeze. "You're here?"

"Yep. Sittin' in the lot."

"... why are you here?"

"Oh, just in the area."

It's a four-hour drive, and if he's here, that means he took off work. No "in the area" about it. I close my eyes and sigh. "Alice."

"Is a good friend," he finishes with a warm laugh. "Better hurry before one of these meter cops gives me a ticket."

***

My father has worked with cars his entire life. Starting in the shop before moving up to manager ten years ago. He still gets into a repair every now and then; it shows in the ever-present gray-black line of grime under his short nails and the faint grease fingerprints on the upholstery of his car door. He's my height and stocky, and if he's not in the shop polo and khakis, he's in a tracksuit and a cap. His skin is a deep, earthy brown the color of fallen pine needles. When I open the passenger side door, he smiles, and his entire face rises until his eyes tilt up at his temples.

"Seat belt." His eyes flick down to my waist and then to his side mirror as we pull out of the drive. Black and blue striped tracksuit today. White cap with a blue Tar Heel.

His car smells like home. I expect to feel the twinge of pain in my chest, and I do, but it's chased by warmth.

The Waffle House is thick with the smell of processed syrup and stale coffee. Mostly empty booths line the wall to our left, and a mottled gray counter runs down the right. The quiet murmurs, the sizzle of the griddle in the kitchen, and the low jukebox music remind me that there's life outside UNC. The woman behind the counter barely glances up when we enter.

Dad leads us to the empty booth that looks the least sticky. The red cushion backs hiss and sigh when we slide in, and there's a constellation of crumbs strewn across the creaky table.

A waitress strolls over, one hand deep in her black apron and the other clutching a pair of stained menus. "I'm Sheryl. I'll be takin' care of you today. Here's a menu. Can I start y'all off with some drinks?" She tugs a notepad out and waits, watching us from underneath a black visor.

Dad flips his menu over once, then hands it back to her. "Coffee, please. Black. And I'll have a waffle with city ham and smothered and covered hashbrowns, large."

"How 'bout you, sweetie?"

I hand mine back too. "A large orange juice. Pecan waffle with regular hash-browns, smothered, covered, and peppered, please."

Dad waits until Sheryl's on the other side of counter before he sits back and looks me full in the eye. The silence is interminable. The kind that makes everything said afterward a thousand times louder.

I avoid his eyes and inspect the condiment collection at the edge of the table. It's the usual suspects: A1, Heinz ketchup and mustard, salt, pepper, and a glass sugar dispenser heavy enough to double as a free weight. I wrinkle my nose at the Tabasco bottle; Texas Pete or nothing. Thank goodness there's a small bottle of it at the back.

"You gonna make me pull it out of you?" My father's voice is low and measured, slower in person than on the phone. It releases that part of me that I'm always holding tight at school, even if what he's saying makes me shift uncomfortably in my chair.

"You bribin' me with hashbrowns so you don't have to?"

"Yep."

"That ain't right."

"Life ain't fair." His tone sharpens. "You gonna make me ask again?"

I swallow, hard. "No, sir."

He sniffs, nodding a thank-you to Sheryl when she drops off our drinks. My lower lip trembles. My chest tightens. I don't want to lie again. I can't. But I can't put him at risk by telling the truth. The hands of the Order—and my mistakes—are still clenched tight around my neck, squeezing when they want to, suffocating me. The tears I'd held back since I'd heard his voice on the phone fill my eyes now, and I look down at my orange juice to hide them.

"Bree," he says softly. He reaches a weathered hand out to me, across the table. I shake my head, refusing to look at him. "Look at me, kiddo. You can come home if you want. I'll move you out today, but it better not be because that dean got you scared."

I stare at him, gobsmacked, while Sheryl deposits our food. "What?"

"Alice says you been going hard with school, not acting like yourself. I didn't send you here so you could run yourself into the ground. I heard the better-than-you in that man's voice. Just don't want you doing all this because of him." By the time he finishes, Dad is smearing butter into his waffle's squares in angry, hard strokes.

My father has never gone to college himself. He'd never gotten the chance to, not really. But now I wondered if he wished he had, or if he'd tried—and met his own Dean McKinnon.

"That's not it," I mutter. "I can handle classes, and the last time I heard from the dean was the day he called you."

"Well, what's got you down, then? Was it therapy? Cuz we can find you someone new." He cuts a bite of waffle and sticks it together with a piece of city ham. Before he puts it in his mouth, he gestures at my plate with his fork. "Eat your food 'fore it gets cold."

I pick up the Texas Pete and sprinkle it on my hashbrowns while I think. Then, a question comes. "Did Mom ever talk to you about Grandma?"

My father's gray-flecked bushy eyebrows rise, and he sighs heavily, sitting back in the worn booth. "Not much. Your grandmother died when she was young. Eighteen or so, I think? So she was gone by the time your mom and I met." He looks out the window, eyes going distant. "I could tell her mother's death weighed heavy on her, you know? Real heavy."

That surprises me. I knew the facts about my grandmother: she did hair in a salon in Texas, where my mother was raised. She didn't have any siblings her-self. She died from cancer. I knew about the woman, but I rarely saw my own mother's pain from losing her. "She never said anything."

He smirks as he reaches for the Texas Pete. "It didn't come out like that. Came out in how she raised you." He chuckles, tapping the Texas Pete bottle until it half empties onto his hashbrowns. "I didn't notice it at first, but she had these nerves that started up when you were, what, ten? Eleven? You'd do a sloppy job cleaning your room or forget to take out the trash—didn't matter, what it was, she just got on you for it. You remember."

"That's just . . . parents, though?"

He shrugs. "Black parents been pushin' their kids hard for decades. My parents did it. I know your grandmother did it too, but your mom took it to another level. She tried to control it around you, but in private?" He whistled. "Anxious, rattled. Sometimes even straight-up scared. Had nightmares about you getting hurt or kidnapped. A few years ago it started taking longer and longer for her to calm down. One week when you were thirteen, you left the milk out on the counter overnight, remember that? It took three days for her to let it go. That's when I finally told her, I said, 'Faye, she's a kid! She's gonna mess up!' She'd say she just wanted to get you ready, make sure you could handle yourself if we weren't around."

My chest tightens. *Did she know?*

My father reads my expression. "I think she was scared she'd leave you early, just like her mom left her." He inhales sharply and draws his shoulders back, and I know we're both thinking the same thing.

That she was right.

My hands wipe at the tears traveling in quiet streams down my cheeks. *She knew what this is like.*

He stares out the window, voice heavy with grief and regret. "We weren't raised with therapy and all that. Not somethin' Black folks did or talked about. If you said anything, you got sent to the church—" He sighs, shaking his head. "Anyway, when you applied to Carolina, it was like the dam she had inside . . . just broke. And all of it, every fight, every worry, came out on you."

"Because she never wanted me to come here."

"Or maybe she just wasn't ready to let you go and got mad at you for forcing her hand. But that fight wasn't your fault, Bree. And it wasn't hers, either. All of that stuff your mom was holding back, hiding . . . It's why I wanted to make sure you started seeing somebody soon. So you could get some peace, maybe head all of that suffering off at the pass."

While my father takes a sip of his cold coffee and grimaces, then signals for Sheryl, I look at him with new eyes. He'd done all of this thinking and planning and hoping for *me*, because of the pain he'd witnessed in my mother. Her death had sent him on his own mission to save our family, and I'd never noticed.

I'd never taken the *time* to notice.

After Sheryl refills his cup and moves on, I ask, "Why didn't she move us away from here? Then I'd never even know about this school."

"In some ways, I think your mother couldn't stand Carolina, but she loved it something fierce, too. Said no matter how she felt about that school, she never could get it out of her system." He shrugs. "You woulda found out about her graduating from here eventually. Maybe applied anyway, just because she did."

I take one of the too-small waxy napkins from the metal dispenser. "I think she was right, anyway," I whisper, and wipe my nose.

He looks up from blowing on his coffee, startled. "What now?"

"About me not being ready," I explain.

His eyes sharpen, and he clunks his coffee down. "You got that wrong. All wrong. And I thought you were smart. You're wrong, cuz she was wrong. It was never about you not being ready, kiddo. It was always about her."

I set my jaw stubbornly. "Stop trying to make me feel better."

He fixes me with a stern glare. "That's the truth. *She* wasn't ready to let you face the world. But you *been* ready, kid. She made sure of it."

He shifts in his chair to dig into his jacket and pulls out a small, square pocket Bible. I recognize the worn, cracked brown leather and the gilded golden edges immediately. It's my mother's. The one she carried with her everywhere.

"Flip to the back." He hands it to me and I take it, pushing my untouched plate of food aside to clear a space on the table. "Probably not something she meant for anyone to see, but . . ." He shrugs. "I love her, and I miss her, and . . ." His eyes fill with tears, and he squeezes them and lets out a breath. "I think she'll forgive us for snoopin'."

I open the Bible with shaking fingers. It feels like I'm touching something intimate and private, and I am. Personal Bibles, even though I've never owned one, always seem mystical. Like the longer someone carries one, the more their spirit lives in the pages. As I flip through the thin, small-print paper, her smell wafts over my nose: verbena and lemon, mixed with a bit of leather. The last section is blank, for notes. On the very last page, in curling script and dated just last year, is a small note.

Lord, she is already stronger than I ever was.

I worry her challenges will be just as powerful.

I worry that I am running out of time.

Please, protect her and give me the strength to let her go.

"Got something else for ya too, kid. It's in the car. Be right back." My dad puts his napkin aside and shoves out of the booth. I nod and stare down at the Bible in my hands, letting the gift of her words wash over me.

My mother had carried so much pain from her own loss. Maybe the exact things Patricia said I had inside me: traumatic grief, PCBD grief. Then, after I was born, it became anxiety. Maybe she'd had the feeling like she could explode. Maybe she'd had my fear and fury. And she hid it from me as best she could.

Just knowing that we have this in common, knowing my feelings are an echo of hers, is a revelation. It makes me sad that she suffered. It makes me wish I could talk to her about it. It makes me want to tell her that I understand. I've been chasing the hidden truth for so long, and now I find out that one of her truths already lives inside me. It makes me feel closer to her somehow, and right now, that feels like enough.

When my dad slides back into the booth, he's laughing under his breath. "I thought about maybe donating her clothes. You know how many clothes she had. And shoes, my God."

I smile. "Tall order. You might have to take a few trips to the donation center."

"Yeah," he says with a sigh. "Bringin' myself to do it's another thing. Rich Glover down at the shop lost his wife last year. He says that once you get rid of their clothes, that's when you know they're really gone." He shakes his head. "Anyway, I was in the closet the other day, and I found this. Thought you might like to have it."

He hands me a square blue velvet box. I recognize it immediately: this is where she stored her golden charm bracelet. She'd only ever had two charms on it—one with my name and one with my father's. It wasn't one of her nicer pieces, but it's the one she seemed to love the most. Even now, the smell of her in the velvet is strong and alive, like she'd never left. It overwhelms me, bypassing any rational parts of my brain and zinging straight to memory. It pulls at a weekend of shopping with her at the mall, unearths the sensation of her hugs, sinks me down into her lap when I was little, rushes me past every single one of her cool hands on my forehead when I was sick. I move to open it, but he stops me. "Open it when you get back to your room."

I eye him. "So I'm going back to my room? You're not gonna tell me not to study too hard?"

"You can study hard, but only if that's how you want to do it." He gives me a wry smile. "No matter what you do, you gotta live *your* life, kiddo. You gotta be in the world. That's what she would want you to do." He reaches across the table to take both of my hands in his. "Don't make your life about the loss. Make it about the love."

42

BY THE TIME I get back to the room after my morning class, the clenched fist of regret in my chest has loosened. I set my book bag down and pull out my mother's velvet box, place it on my bed, think of my father's face and words.

Make it about the love.

Could I do that? Really? As soon as I try, I miss her. I miss her voice and her smile. I miss hugging her and feeling whole.

I look down at the box again and feel ready, pick it up. "Make it about the love," I murmur.

I take a deep breath, flip open the lid—and the room fills with mage flame.

Silver and gold smoke dances up the walls and floods the ceiling with light. Everywhere the flame touches my skin feels like the caress of her hands. My nose fills with the scents of verbena and lemon, bright and sharp and warm. I'm on my knees before I know it, hands shaking.

Inside the box my mother's charm bracelet is pulsing like a heartbeat. When the tips of my fingers touch the gold links, a voice echoes in my mind.

"Bree . . ."

I drop it. I'm gasping, choking, sobbing. "Mommy . . . ?"

As soon as I lift the bracelet and grasp it in my hands, my eyes flutter shut. A memory takes me over.

We are on the lawn outside the fairgrounds. I bounce up and down with unrestrained glee, because today is the first time I've gone to the fair. Ever. Faint screams of joy rise and fall in the background in time to the roller coaster and Tilt-A-Whirl. I can already smell the deep-fried Snickers bars. The sweet, hot scent of funnel cake is so close, I can almost taste the powdered sugar.

I remember this. I was seven. The annual state fair was a monumental experience, one my friends spoke of in excited, envy-inducing whispers. But I don't remember my mother guiding me to a bench outside before we went in. In the memory, she wears a loose white button-up blouse under a lavender cardigan. Her straight hair is pulled back. Our shared strong jawline is lined with tension.

She sits down across from me and rubs her palms down her pants.

"Just for a minute, I promise. Then we'll go inside." My mother's eyes flick over my head, like she's looking at someone behind me. I turn to follow her gaze, but she presses fingers to my chin and turns me back. "Look at me, Bree. Then we can go inside and get fried Twinkies."

"Okay!" I say, and bounce again.

My mother pushes out a short, fast breath, and her gaze sharpens on mine. "Mommy has to say something hard to someone else, like a speech, but I need your help practicing first. Is that okay? Will you help me practice? Mommy's going to say a lot, and I just want you to listen for now, okay? Like the silent game." I nod, and she reaches for my head and pulls it gently down so she can kiss the crown of my hair. "Good girl. Thank you."

In the memory her eyes glisten with emotions I'm too young to parse, but now I can see the determination there, and the fierce pride.

"Okay, here we go." She takes a deep breath. "Bree, if you're seeing this again, it's because I'm not with you."

My younger self opens her mouth to ask what she means, but my mother shakes her head. "Silent game, remember? I'm just practicing. I know it's confusing."

I nod again.

Just practicing.

"I am so, so sorry, because the pain you're in right now is pain I know well, and I

hate that I've caused it. I hope my old charm bracelet gives you some comfort. You can't stop sneaking into my room and playing with it at the moment, so I told your dad that I wanted it to be yours one day. I hope he gave it to you right away, but knowing him . . . it might take a while."

My mother smiles fondly, but I can see the sadness there. An awareness of what my father would go through after her death. She knew she would die.

She sits back and takes another fortifying breath. "I'm going to tell you what my mother told me. Bree, we descend from a line of Rootcrafters. Black folk who can borrow power from our ancestors and use it to heal, or to speak to the dead, or protect others, or divine the future, and more. I use my power to manipulate plant energy for healing and medicine."

I can't help it. I interrupt her. "Magic? Like spells?"

"Not spells." She presses a thumb over her laughing mouth. "Just listen for now, okay? Do that for Mommy? Usually, I would be the one to help you with your Rootcraft, just like your grandmother helped me with mine, and her mother helped her with hers, but things are"—she looks away for a moment, shakes her head—"different for you than they were for me. As far as all practitioners know, if a child has a branch of root, that branch—that gift—manifests early. Five, maybe six, with some small, accidental crafting. That's how it happened to me. It's how it happened to your grandmother. When you turned six, I took you to that nice woman who lived in the country. Do you remember her? Ms. Hazel? She has a special gift too, where she can see light and energy around someone. I asked her if she saw the craft in you, and she didn't."

I make a sad face and cross my arms. This speech sure seems like it's for me.

"Believe it or not, not having root isn't a bad thing for our family," my mother says with a wry smile. I thought maybe our string of bad luck was broken. I'm still holding out hope for that. I want nothing more than for you to have a happy, healthy, normal life.

"But . . ." She sighs, and her eyebrows draw in tight. "I'm telling you all of this now as a fail-safe—a 'fail-safe' is a plan, B, like 'just in case'—because, up until now, the women in our family have never been just regular Rootcrafters. We have something else even more special inside us that we keep secret just in our family. A gift that only we know about, because other Rootcraft users wouldn't like what we have."

Bloodcraft. She means Bloodcraft.

She takes another shaky breath and grabs my hand, leaning down to fix me with a stare. Her dark eyes bore into mine as if I'm an adult, not a child.

"Bree, if you're hearing this a second time, then you already know what I'm talking about. The subtle, persistent abilities, like the one you just used with my bracelet: enhanced sight that lets you see things that other people can't. A heightened sense of smell, touch, hearing, even taste, when it comes to the root in our world. Certain enchantments that work on other people won't work very well on you, if at all. These passive abilities allow us to detect an encounter with root—or magic, or aether, or whatever another practitioner may call it—and avoid it, if you choose to. And there's nothing wrong with that, Bree, nothing at all, because the most important thing you can do in this world, the most neces-sary thing, is to survive it. You can't do anything for anyone else if you don't take care of yourself first. Do you understand me?"

Small me has gone still, but I nod.

"Good. Now, I think of these abilities like fight or flight. This first group allows you to flee if you need to, but if you choose to stand your ground, if you choose to fight . . . well, our gift will help with that, too. But before I talk about that, I want to talk about the cost of these abilities. The reason we don't tell other Rootcrafters what we can do is because this power was done through Bloodcraft—where power was taken forever, not borrowed. Someone, somewhere in our bloodline, bound all this power to our bodies, Bree, and I don't know who or how. Your grandmother didn't know either. As best we can tell, the last of us who knew where these powers came from died in childbirth, so she couldn't pass it on to her daughter, which brings me to my next point. . . .

"The reason they call Bloodcraft a curse is because the universe will come calling for its payment in one way or another. And for our family, that cost is that the power can only live in one daughter at a time. Maybe it's because all that power burns us out, I don't know, but none of us get very long with our mothers. Each mother's final act is to pass these abilities on to her daughter. Which is how I know that if you're hearing this now, it's because you have it. And if you have it, I am gone. I know you're thinking it, but it's not your fault I left you, just like it wasn't my fault that my mother left me. I know you have those feelings now, but don't let them sour inside you. Let the pain be a part of you, but know that it's not all you are. That's what I'm trying to do."

A sob from a small chest. Mine.

My mother pulls me from the bench and holds me in her arms. "Oh, don't cry, baby. This is just me practicing. I'm still here. I know it's confusing."

"I don't want you to go . . ."

"I'm not going anywhere. I'm right here in front of you. I need you to be brave while I tell you the rest of this story. Can you do that for me? Okay? Thank you.

"I said fight or flight, right? The fighting part will only happen when you really need it to, when you're angry or upset enough and you can't escape. It happened to me one time and one time only. I saw something at school that I couldn't ignore: innocent people getting hurt. I made a choice to fight, baby, and it was worth it. I'd do it again if I had to. But a consequence of that choice is that I've had to hide myself since then from people who don't understand who we are or what we can do. And that's why, if there's any chance you don't have these abilities, I'm gonna do all I can to hide this from you. Because if you don't know any of it, then maybe they won't find you. Maybe you won't be drawn to that school the way I was. But that's also why I'm telling you now, in a way that means you'll only hear it if and when you absolutely need to understand who we are.

"I won't say that what I did back then was a mistake. I'd do it again if I had to. I think the mistake was in letting the anger and guilt from my mother's death soak into my bones so deep that I lost a part of myself. I'm working on it. I'm trying.

"I want you to know that you are the greatest thing that has ever happened to me. You're already more of a warrior than I ever was. I believe with all my heart that if you want to, you can change the world."

She takes both of my hands in hers and squeezes our fingers together as if to push her love into me by touch.

"When the time comes, if it comes, don't be scared. Fight. Take risks. Follow your heart. And move forward."

My mother squeezes her eyes shut, and when they open, they're glassy with tears. She looks over my head again and gives a subtle nod. "And she won't remember any of this until . . . after?"

"No." *A woman's voice says from directly behind me. I turn again, but my mother's hand shoots out, gripping my shoulder hard before I can see who's there.*

"Bree, Bree, look at me, baby," *she says quickly.* "Just look at me."

The last thing I see is my mother, holding me still while she whispers, "I love you."

I come back from the memory on my knees. All of it, every word and image and sound, is there now, like a file in a drawer. Like something I've always possessed but didn't have the key to open. The flame on the bracelet in my hands dies down, but her message echoes in the air around me. I let the words flow through me and over me until my eyes close and I'm full of her words.

Move forward.

That's the message my mother planted in my mind for the moment I'd most need to hear it.

When I open my eyes, I know what I need to do.

43

THE AIR IN the cemetery is charged. Unsettled. Even the leaves on the trees stir and shiver, like the whole place knows I'm here for root.

I wait in the unmarked grave section after last class, feeling more bold than frightened.

Two figures in light jackets approach over the gravel path. I recognize Patricia immediately; as she comes closer, I can see that her scarf is a deep copper. Beside her, Mariah is in jeans and fur-topped boots, sleek poof exploding into a puff of curls that add at least eight inches to her petite height. She carries a basket of offerings, just as I'd asked.

"Bree," Patricia murmurs, clutching me in a tight hug that soothes my nerves. "Your call scared me. You said it was an emergency? Are you all right?"

I pull back and swallow hard, take a deep breath. "I will be. Thank you for coming today. Both of you. I know the way we left things was . . . I'm sorry. I'm sorry for my behavior."

Patricia tilts her head, and her eyes roam my features before she nods. "Apology accepted."

"Same here." Mariah shifts the basket to her other arm. "As long as you tell me what we're doing here? Not that I don't mind a graveyard, of course, but I don't come to one lightly." She peers around me. "Restless spirits follow me home if I'm not careful, then I've got to clean house, and it's just a whole process . . . ugh."

"I need your help to speak to someone in my family."

Patricia and Mariah exchange glances. "Bree, what's going on?"

I tell them about my mother's box, and I don't hide any of it, even the Bloodcraft. In the moment of silence after I finish, the wind picks up Patricia's scarf, Mariah's curls and my own.

Patricia has been studying me, and I'm worried she won't help after all. "You deserve to know why this bargain was struck. But even though I want to, I'm afraid I won't be of much help. Bloodcraft among our people is so shunned that those who practice it keep it secret. I don't know how your abilities work or where they came from."

"I know. Which is why I need to speak to an ancestor of mine who can explain. I want to know more about what I am and why." I take a deep breath. "I don't want to get lost in the past. I want to embrace it and understand."

Mariah shrugs. "I'm down to help, but I can't promise you'll hear from any- one," she warns. "And even if you do, there's no promises about who shows up, remember? Could be your mom, could be someone else."

I say hastily, "I actually don't want it to be my mom. I need to go further back."

Patricia considers this and nods slowly. "Okay, Bree."

Five minutes later we've settled into a triangle, hands linked, our knees faintly touching around the offerings in the middle. Since I didn't know what offerings my ancestors would prefer, I'd asked them to bring a small bowl of fruit, some candy, a glass of juice, and nuts. Things my mother liked and I like too.

Patricia repeats her previous instruction in a low voice. "Focus on your love for your mother, to start."

I pull up an image of my mother from memory and there's almost no pain, just a tiny smidge of it around the edges like a bit of burned paper. I see my mother in the kitchen, humming and mixing a bowl of deviled-egg fixin's. She dips a pinkie in to taste and calls me over to test it too. It feels like we're making magic. That's how it always felt when we made food together.

Patricia whispers, "Now imagine the love stretching to your grandmother, and stretching back again."

"Like a strong thread," I murmur.

I hear the smile in her voice when she says, "Yes."

I imagine the thread, thick and wound tight, from my mother to my grandmother—and it stops. I can't go any further. I'm blocked . . .

By a wall.

I've known that this image, this internal construct of my own making, was part of my survival toolbox. I just hadn't found any reason to take it down.

But now I do.

Now I have to.

I imagine my wall crumbling to pieces, one brick at a time. I pull down the chains, the metal, the steel. I peel it all away until I can see beyond it to find that hard, tight knot of pain in my chest, the one wrapped in layers of bright, unending fury—the part of me I call After-Bree.

And then I unwind her.

One strand for my mother.

One for my father.

One for me.

I unravel the rage until it courses through my veins like fuel in an engine. I let it become a part of me, but not all of me. Hot, scorching pain under my skin, under my tongue, under my nails. I let it spread through me—until there is no more "Before" and no more "After."

I am her and she is me.

"I've got the thread," Mariah says excitedly. "I'm following it."

I feel warmth pulling at my fingers, like the tide of the ocean is inside me and it's flowing out to Mariah.

"I hear someone," Mariah whispers. "A woman."

I take a deep breath and focus on the thread. *Please, please. Please help me.*

"She's powerful. She has a lot to say," Mariah says, her voice strained. "No, a lot to *do.* Oh wow, oh wow—" She stops speaking abruptly, and her fingers curl into claws around mine, squeezing the bones of my pinkie and forefinger. I open my eyes to see hers rolled back in her head, her rapid breathing.

"Mariah?" Patricia leans over, but does not break our connection. "Mariah?"

I start to call her name too, when the ocean comes rushing back through my hand so quickly that it sears up my wrist and forearms and swirls in a hot whirlpool in my chest. I cry out, but I can't let go.

A low voice burns into my ears and onto the back of my eyelids. White curls, bronze skin, barely any wrinkles, my mother's eyes and my own. She cracks a wry grin.

'Took you long enough.'

It's a strange sensation, having a whole other person inside your skin. It feels like I'm a human-shaped glass fish tank, and every step makes the water of my grandmother slosh up my sides, almost tipping over the edge.

Patricia holds on to my elbow. "Bree? Talk to us."

"I'm . . ." I blink several times, in what feels like slow motion. "I'm okay. Except I feel drunk."

'And how do you know what being drunk is like?' Grandmother says, jabbing at my ribs somehow.

"Ow," I say, and grab my side. "Is it supposed to feel like this?"

Mariah shrugs. "I wouldn't know. Possession is *really* rare. It's never happened to me, personally, but my uncle Kwame gets possessed *all* the time. Family spirits take his body for a spin, or sometimes they sit inside him and the two of them just talk and fellowship awhile until the ancestor leaves."

"Not every Medium gets possessed?" I cry, panic rising slightly.

"Nope. Mediumcraft is a branch of root with its own sub-branches. All different because ancestors themselves are different." Mariah peers up into my eyes. "Wowwwww. I can *definitely* see your grandmother in there." She stands back and raises her hand for a high five. "Welcome to Club Medium!"

I can feel my grandmother frown at her gesture, so I frown too. It all makes me a little woozy. "Thanks? I don't understand, though. Why didn't I find out I was a Medium when I was a kid?"

"Perhaps it's the Bloodcraft, and the original nature of that spell. You'd have to speak to an ancestor who knows and, as your mother said, you'll need to go back further than your grandmother." Patricia hums speculatively.

"Your mother practiced Wildcraft, which is a different branch. Different power. As a Medium, *your* power is wound tightly with death, and as your family's Bloodcraft is triggered by death, perhaps the two branches intertwined in you until they became tied together in unpredictable ways. I'm afraid I'm not certain."

Mariah cocks her head to the side. "But why didn't both of your branches manifest when your mom died?"

The answer appears in my mind before I even finish the question. "That's my fault." I see the truth of it in my mind's eye. "That night at the hospital was the birth of . . . this version of myself that I named After-Bree. The . . ." I look to Patricia, and she nods for me to continue. "The trauma created her, but I spent all of my energy containing her."

Patricia nods. "Sometimes our brains protect us until we're ready. The most important thing is now you know. And right now, you have help from Mrs. . . . ?"

"Charles," I say instantly. The name sprung into my mouth like it had been launched there.

"Mrs. Charles. So nice to meet you," Patricia says warmly, her accent slipping in slow like molasses. "Will you be stayin' long?"

"No," I reply. "She's just here to act as a lighthouse." I pause and try to turn my vision inward to ask a question. "A lighthouse?" I hear an answer. "Oh, a signpost for an older mother. She'll pass the request on to the ancestor who can show me how to control my power, and where it came from. All she can do is ask. I will have to wait for the answer. It may take a while."

Patricia bows her head. "I understand. Very generous of her. Thank you, Mrs. Charles."

I take another two steps, and the sloshing feeling gets worse. "Jesus, Grandma. Can you get, like, more dense?"

Somehow, she slaps me in the face. I blink, chin twisted over my shoulder. "Ow!"

'That's for taking the Lord's name in vain!'

"Wow." I stare at Mariah. "Did you know your ass can get called out from the grave?"

"Girl, yes." Mariah nods in sympathy. "Happens to me all the time. The worst, right?"

I nod. "I'm just . . ." I stumble slightly, hands out for balance. "I need her to calm down or something. I'll never make it home like this."

"Here." Patricia hurries over from where we'd been sitting. "Eat this." She shoves a pear into my hand and the glass of juice. I eat and drink, and I swear I feel my grandmother's mouth moving long after mine has stopped. After a moment, she seems happier. More settled, like she's found a nice rocking chair in there and has decided to sit awhile.

"Okay." I stand upright, testing my legs. I feel full but not unbalanced. "That's better."

"You need a ride?" Mariah asks.

I nod as emphatically as I dare. "Yes, please."

When Mariah pulls up to the lot by Old East, she stops me before I get out. "Remember, you need to focus. You gotta keep her from spilling out, but keep your guard up so other ancestors from your line don't come knocking," she warns, squeezing my hand. "The hardest part of being a Medium is closing the doors once they're opened. The unsettled spirits, the eager ones, look for ways in and you're much more open to your ancestors now. And listen, this is the South; there are a lot of unsettled Black folk in the ground."

I nod. "Thank you for helping even though you barely know me. It means . . . everything."

"And so it is," Mariah says with a smile.

Before I get out of the car, Patricia's warm fingers rest on my cheek. "Thank you for letting us in. I'm proud of you, Bree. I hope you find your answers."

44

WHEN I WAKE up late the next morning, Alice is already gone, and a text is waiting from her on my phone: At the library!

My grandmother is still there inside me, snoozing.

For the first time all week, I let myself miss Nick. I see the hurt on his face and feel the shame of causing it. What must he think of me now? *That I used him,* I think. *That as soon as I got what I needed, I dropped him and everything we'd found with each other.* In truth, I did. I used him and accepted his kindness along with everyone else's. Leaving was bad, but leaving things like I did was worse.

I can't move forward with this hanging over my head. I tap Alice's text and stamp out a quick response.

Hey, do you have Charlotte's number? I'm gonna need both y'all's help.

While I wait for Alice and Charlotte to come over, I take the rest of the day to wash my hair—and it's the most therapeutic, loving thing I could have done for myself. Condition, detangle, deep condition with a heat wrap, paint my nails and watch a movie while I wait, rinse. I emerge from the shower with my hair wrapped in a microfiber towel and rub the foggy mirror until I can see the genuine, full smile on my face. Tangles gone. Scalp clean. Curls moisturized and bouncy. Head and soul lighter.

More me than I've been in months.

Charlotte ends up bringing over a dozen dresses and a chest full of jewelry—and they aren't just hers. Some are from her friends down the hall and on the floor above us. "Kappas, a few Sigmas," she says. I'm grateful she's such a busybody, because otherwise I wouldn't have any options two hours before the gala.

I expect Charlotte to dig for details about why I need a dress; it's far too early in the semester for most Greek orgs and groups to hold their formals. But Alice already explained that it's for a society gala, and that seemed answer enough for her. When Charlotte doesn't mention Evan getting similarly dressed up, I wonder what lie he told his girlfriend about his plans for the night. Beer and PlayStation? Boys' night? Whatever it was, it's keeping her safe.

I try on ten dresses that are clearly meant for someone with smaller boobs and hips, sending Charlotte running from the room to go on another search, phone in hand.

After I shimmy into the eleventh dress, Alice gasps, clapping a hand over her mouth.

When I turn to the full-length mirror on the back of our door, my witty, self-deprecating retort disappears. A low squawk of disbelief falls from my open mouth instead.

"Oh, Bree. This is the one," Alice breathes. She drops down to where my knees are hidden beneath the long, floor-length layers of tulle and pulls the material out until it fans around my feet. "You look amazing."

When she stands back up, I see in the mirror that her eyes are glistening behind her glasses. "Alice Chen, no crying. It's just a dress," I say, but it's not true.

It's not just a dress. It's a gown, fit for a court.

She wipes at her face and smiles at me in the mirror. "It's just that you look like her."

My chest and throat seize up together, my emotions a swirling cocktail.

There's no way I can respond, so I grab her hand. She drops her head onto my shoulder with a sigh, and we stare at our reflection. We squeeze each other's fingers tight, because there are some moments that are too empty, and too full, for words.

The Carolina Club is a fancy event space used by alumni, faculty, and staff in the center of campus. While its exterior is modern, the interior is antebellum chic. Charlotte insisted on dropping me off at the entrance so I don't walk all the way across campus in my gown, and as I make my way up the stairs in blessedly low borrowed heels from another tall girl on the second floor of Old East, I have to admit, she had a good point. Even with a heel, my dress is long enough that I have to hold the sides up so it won't drag.

A doorman in a black suit and white gloves welcomes me, a smile lighting up the rust-brown planes of his face. As I pass through the door, he murmurs, "All right, sis," and I grin back. It's just the little bit of encouragement I need to cross the elegant foyer with my head held high and walk through the wide double doors leading to the ballroom.

The club ballroom is impressive, with windows along the back wall, a dance floor and stage on one end, and round dinner tables covered in white linens on the other. The jazz band onstage, called "The Old North Greats" according to the logo on their drum, is playing an upbeat swing rendition of a popular song. Overhead, chandeliers hang from exposed mahogany beams that cross the ceiling like great wooden fingers.

There must be at least three hundred people here. News of the demon attacks and murmurs about the imminent gathering of the Table had spread. Nick had said to expect Legendborn and Vassal families from all of the Lines, some even from as far away as Europe, all in attendance to hear an update on the attacks while taking stock of the current class of Scions and Squires. Tables are clustered by color, identifying which Line those Vassals serve.

Older women in long, striking dresses sit together, catching up at their tables while sipping glasses of wine. Several small groups of men in tuxedos gather at the two cash bars in the corner of the room. They look comfortable in their formal wear, smiling and laughing like it's a reunion. I wonder if Sarah's father is here, and if I'll get to meet him. Even with the formal invitation clenched between my fingers, I feel out of place.

"Bree!" Felicity is the first to find me from across the room, waving as she gets up from a half-empty table to walk over with a glass in her hand. When she says my name, Tor's and Sarah's heads pop up, and they shove back from their table to follow her.

As she and the others approach in their Line-colored dresses, I feel the tingling sensation of Sel's gaze, but I can't find him in the crowd. He knows I can feel his attention now. I don't know how I feel about that. Or the fact that, even though he *knows* I can feel him, he's still looking at me.

Felicity makes one long squeal out of a string of words. "OhmyGod, Iloveyourdress!" The tiny bit of slur tells me she must be on her third glass of wine. At least.

"Thanks," I say, passing nervous hands down the front of my gown.

Alice couldn't have known this when she complimented the dress, but the gown is perfect for saying goodbye to the Order and finding my own place in root. While the A-line skirt is simple and elegant, flowing down from my waist in layers of champagne tulle, the halter bodice is an explosion of red and gold. Vines of lace and appliqué flowers climb up from my hips, flow across my chest and ribs, and gather together into a collar at my throat. Charlotte was right about my lacking accessories: I definitely didn't have the strappy gold heels, or the sun-gold earrings, and would have never thought of smoothing my hair away from my face with a wide gold band. Behind the band, my hair stretches in shining black-brown curls that reach upward like the proud crown of a tree.

Felicity's still admiring my dress. "Nick is going to lose his whole entire goddamn mind when he sees you."

In a singsong voice, Sarah says, "Speak of the king . . ."

When I follow her eyes over my shoulder, I see Nick striding toward us, a vision in black and white. He'd opted for a black suit, but Jesus was it tailored for every inch of his wide shoulders and long legs. I freeze, bracing myself for his anger, his rightful disappointment, but I get neither. His expression shifts from shock to something very close to relief, and by the time he reaches my side, it settles into that heart-stoppingly handsome smile that makes my mouth go dry.

"Hey," he says breathlessly.

"Hey."

Nick bites his lower lip, and I want to both run away and fling myself at him. "You look amazing."

"And you," I say, "look like a newly recruited secret agent."

"Oh yeah?" He spreads his arms wide and looks down at his ensemble. "Green and eager, but he's got what it takes?"

"The one that intimidates the aging senior agent at first, but then, begrudgingly, the veteran takes the new kid under his wing."

"And at the end, the new kid's earned the vet's respect. And maybe a new code name."

"Yup."

We hold each other's gaze steadily, the familiar tug thrumming between us, until Sarah clears her throat. It's only then that I realize the others have been watching us intently. Their expressions range from fascination on Felicity's face to annoyance on Tor's.

"Ugh," the blond girl says, walking away. "That was gross."

Nick ducks his head, scratching a thumb across his brow to hide his blush.

"Scion Davis?" An older man appears at his elbow, nodding apologetically for interrupting. I stifle a gasp at the sudden loss of Sel's gaze. I'd gotten used to it and forgotten he'd been watching my entire exchange with Nick. And listening, too, I'd bet. "Your father would like everyone to be seated." The man gestures to a table behind us. "If you would?"

We follow him, sitting at a table with eight place settings. As we walk, Nick leans in close and gives a wry grin. "You don't text, you don't call."

"I know. I'm sorry for shutting you out—"

He wraps his hand around my wrist, his face warm and forgiving. "We can talk later. Right now, I'm just glad you're here."

I nod, because he's right. We can talk later. Our final goodbye, our *real* one, should be in private.

Whitty and Greer are already seated when we arrive, and Evan and Fitz walk up at the same time we do. Tor and Sarah sit across from me and Nick.

Greer tips their head in my direction and waves. "There she is!" They're looking sharp in a navy check three-piece suit and a matching Lamorak red tie and pocket square set. Tonight their long hair is completely up in an elegant crown braid.

The others greet me with smiles and raised glasses. The only sullen expression is on Fitz's face, but even that I ignore. If my friends could accept that I'm here without dragging me over the coals, then I could, maybe, do the same.

Nick catches me looking around the room. "Who are you looking for?"

I smile, feeling rude for not paying attention to my own table. And, for some reason, sheepish about looking for Sel. "Is Vaughn here?" I ask.

Nick's eyes darken. "I asked that he be seated on the opposite side of the room."

Across the table, Fitz rolls his eyes. "He's a good fighter, Nick."

"He fights dirty." Nick pulls his cloth napkin from the table and settles it over his lap.

Fitz snorts. "You think the Shadowborn fight clean?"

"Last I checked, it was my decision who my Squire is, Fitz." Nick's face is the picture of civility, but the steel in his blue eyes says the conversation is over.

"Hey, hey." Evan leans forward, holding out a hand. "Let's not bring drama to the dinner table. Let's talk about how we get the waiters to serve the under twenty-ones instead, hm?" Evan waggles his eyebrows. "Or maybe rank everyone's attire tonight on a one-to-ten scale? Bree, you're a ten, obviously." He makes a chef's kiss motion for effect.

"Agreed," Nick says, raising a glass with a wink in my direction.

A white-gloved hand holding a salad plate crosses my field of vision. When I look up, I see a pair of softly tilted brown eyes in a golden-brown face. The woman smiles and moves on to hand the next plate to Greer. The man to Nick's right pours sweet tea into our waiting glasses, and I see that he's brown too. I feel my brows draw into a line when I see that all of the waitstaff at the other tables in the room—all of them—are Black and brown people. Another reminder that this isn't my world. *I'm just here to say goodbye, the right way.*

The back of Nick's knuckle brushes my hand. "Everything okay?"

I blink. "Yeah," I say, and his smile in response is achingly sweet.

The rest of dinner passes in a flavorful, multicourse blur: seared duck with parsnips, sautéed squash and zucchini with fresh strips of basil and pine nuts, and a vegetable risotto.

It's not until the band starts up again during dessert that I remember that there's a dance floor. We're just finishing our bread pudding when Nick nudges my elbow. "Wanna dance?"

I do a double take, but he seems serious, so I stammer a yes and walk with him to the dance floor to the sound of Evan's not-so-subtle whoops. Luckily, most of it is covered by the movement and noise across the room.

"Does that guy ever let up?" I mutter.

"Not that I've seen."

We stop at an empty corner of the dance floor, but before we can begin, the band transitions to a loud swing beat. Nick wraps a hand around my waist and grins. There's no talking to be done here. All we can do is dance—until a long-fingered hand taps him on the shoulder.

The man standing behind Nick is a silent ghoul in formal wear. Yellow-red eyes the color of dying leaves are set deep in a pale face under hawkish black brows. Underneath his black suit is a dark red shirt and thin black tie. He has a severe and undeniable beauty, but it's been channeled into unsettling qualities; like an ancient Gothic structure, he's all arches and sharp, aggressive features. The acrid, cloying smell of his signature collects in the back of my throat like bile.

A Merlin.

"Isaac." A chill runs up my spine at Nick's stiff greeting.

This terrifying man is Isaac Sorenson.

Lord Davis's Kingsmage.

45

"NICHOLAS."

Isaac inclines his head, but something about the motion feels mocking instead of respectful. His eyes flicker down to Nick's shoulder. Looks like I'm not the only one who noticed that when Nick moved, he'd stepped slightly in front of me.

"What do you want?" Nick says, his voice an octave lower than usual.

"Your father would like you to join him in the antechamber," Isaac says in a deep baritone. When he turns to indicate a side door by the stage, I notice the slight points at the top of his ears.

Nick's jaw is already set in hard lines. They only get harder when Isaac mentions his father. "Right now?"

"I'm afraid so, my liege," Isaac murmurs, holding his hands in front of him like a polite servant, even though the power and fierce intelligence in his eyes suggest he's anything but.

Nick's chest and shoulders rise in a heavy breath meant to calm. He turns back to me, effectively blocking Isaac from view.

"I'm really sorry. I've got to go." His light brows turn down in thoughtful consternation, like he's making a decision that he isn't sure about. "I'll find you after Selection, okay?"

The mixture of worry and hope in his blue eyes sends my heart lurching against my ribs. It finds its footing again when I hear myself say, "Okay."

He lets out another breath, this time with a quiet sort of relief. I think we both expect Isaac to walk away with Nick, but the Merlin simply nods his head toward the door again. Nick's eyes flicker between the two of us for a moment, landing finally on mine with a silent warning that I don't need. I already know Isaac is dangerous.

When Nick disappears in the crowd, I feel the full force of Isaac's gaze on my face. If Sel's attention feels like sparks or embers, Isaac's is a sweltering late July heat. His fathomless eyes bore into mine.

Even still, I don't break our eye contact. I didn't come here to cower.

'Who is this man?'

When I jump at my grandmother's voice, Isaac's thin lips pull back in a horrid smile, revealing the longest canines I've ever seen. No, not canines. Fangs. "You're the Unanedig girl."

Someone bad, Grandma.

"I am."

'I don't like his eyes.'

Neither do I, but I need to concentrate while I'm here with everyone. Can you— She fades, so fast and quiet I worry she may have gone for good. I close the door behind her for now, seal it tight.

Isaac's gaze trails me up and down, and after a moment of inspection, he makes a small, amused sound. "Fascinating." From anyone else, that word might be a compliment; from him, it twists my stomach like spoiled meat.

"Master Isaac."

Sel appears at my elbow, hands in his pockets as if he's just finished a casual stroll. He's in black on black, of course; black suit, black shirt, and black tie. If Nick is a secret agent, Sel is the assassin fighting for the other side.

I'll never be so thankful for an assassin.

Isaac's eyes slide to Sel. "One of my favorite pupils."

A lead weight drops in my stomach; this Merlin taught Sel?

Sel bends his head in a slight bow, but not before I catch the muscles working in his jaw. "I didn't think I'd see you here tonight. I assumed any available

Masters would be at the Northern Chapter. I hear they experienced another attack just last evening."

"I go where the Regents direct me," Isaac responds neutrally. "As you will, when you graduate from this post and continue on in service to the Order."

"If only we could predict the future," Sel says smoothly. "In the meantime"— he turns to me, eyes sparkling with mischief—"I'd like to speak with our Onceborn visitor." He extends his right arm to me just as the band's tempo slows down. It's a clear dismissal of Isaac and one I'm eager to encourage, so I take his elbow.

The fine lines around the older man's eyes go tight even as he smiles. "Enjoy the evening." Isaac inclines his head to us both and turns to walk toward the antechamber door.

I let Sel lead us through the crowd of slow dancers in the opposite direction until we reach the backmost part of the floor. I'd assumed he'd only intervened to help me escape Isaac's attentions, but when I go to pull my hand away, his fingers tighten around mine, sending a sharp zip up my elbow. Before I can protest, he slips his free hand around my waist and tugs me into his arms.

His eyes gleam, like he knows exactly what his skin contact just did to me and thinks it's highly amusing. I roll my eyes and let him lead us into a slow, swaying dance. "A bit of advice. Never look a Master Merlin directly in the eye. At his age, Master Isaac's mesmer is far more powerful than mine, and works much faster."

"I thought you were the most powerful Merlin in a generation?"

"I am the most powerful Merlin of *my* generation." He watches me for a moment, and I try not to squirm under his scrutiny. "After the way you left things, I'm surprised you came tonight." A pause. A frown down at our legs. "Almost as surprised as I am that you're letting me lead right now."

I scowl and fix my gaze on something over his shoulder. "I wasn't going to."

"Come to the gala or let me lead?"

"Both."

He laughs. "What changed your mind about the gala?"

"Disney movies," I mutter.

"Ah yes. The unsubtle propaganda of ball gowns and *charming princes*." The slight scorn in his voice draws my eyes back to his. He swallows it away, a small, resigned smile crossing his face, but he can't hide his feelings about Nick. He never could. "When I saw you enter, I thought you'd come to say goodbye."

"I did."

"If that's your wish."

I tilt my head and examine his face for humor but find none. "You should be happy. You've spent every waking second here trying to get me to leave."

He holds my gaze for a long moment. "Not *every* second."

It's suddenly hard to breathe. I look away. "I have a question."

Sel dips me without warning, sending my stomach into my throat. "I'm listening," he purrs, then pulls me back up with ease. Once I'm upright, I glare at him, but he just smirks.

"Can you use aether to manipulate existing objects?"

His dark eyebrows rise into his hairline. "Have a sudden interest in aether theory, do you?"

"Indulge me."

"Ask nicely."

I roll my eyes. "Please."

He spins me once before he responds, mouth quirked while he makes me wait.

"Theoretically, one could attach an aether construct to an existing material object, or cover the object like a cloak with raw, unformed mage flame, but this would only last temporarily. As with my constructs in the scavenger hunt, the caster would need to maintain the attachment with ongoing attention."

"And how long can a caster keep their attention on an object?"

"Anything more than five, maybe six hours results in a splitting headache, even for a Master. Would not recommend. Why?"

Six hours isn't the answer I was looking for. I didn't have the Sight before my mother died, so for all I know, the aether attached to her bracelet had always been there, hidden from me until her death gave me the ability to See it.

Sel squeezes my fingers to bring my attention back to him. "Why . . . ?"

"What would you say if I told you I have something of my mother's that has aether attached to it, and that that aether had been on that object or in it for . . . several months at least? Maybe longer. Maybe years. And when I touched that object, it unlocked a memory."

Sel blinks. "I would say that's impossible. That any Merlin sustaining a single casting for that long would die from the effort. To 'lock' a memory so that it requires an aether key to open . . . ? That's precision mesmerwork I've never heard of." The warm pinprick of his gaze dances over my cheeks, mouth, throat. "But then . . . I would say that everything about you seems to defy reason as a matter of course."

I nod absentmindedly. The charm bracelet has been in my thoughts since I found it. Manipulating objects with aether feels like the Order's practice, and the vision *had* felt sort of like a mesmered memory surfacing from somewhere deep inside me. But the bracelet had been activated by touch, which feels more like Rootcraft, and the experience of it—being inside the memory as my current self *and* as my past self—felt like a memory walk. Is my mother's bracelet a Rootcraft item or an Order one? And who was the woman with her?

"I know *that* look," Sel says with a sigh. "Tell me, will you *always* be the mystery girl?"

I smile. "Probably."

"May I assist with this quest?" Something harsh and tight in his voice makes me look up. "Or will Nicholas feel left out again?"

"That's not fair."

He shrugs. "It's a limited-time offer." His next words are strained and only whispered. "I may not be here much longer myself."

I stiffen. "Are you really getting replaced? Is that still on the table?"

"It hasn't been taken *off* the table."

"But you're not . . ." I struggle for the right word.

"A raging, feral demon?" His smile doesn't reach his eyes. "After what we learned about my mother, it would be foolish to not keep an eye on myself."

I look away so that he doesn't see how much his last words pain me and because I don't think he'd appreciate pity. I wish he didn't have to carry the knowledge of his mother's actions and worry that he's capable of them too. I wish he didn't have to be scared of himself or live knowing that others were scared of what he'd become. I realize now that his drive to hunt me down must have, on some level, been about a desperate need to prove to the chapter that he was trustworthy. Now that I know his family history and what that could mean about his sanity and when he might lose it . . .

I look back up at him then, and our gazes lock. I put all of my faith into my eyes, so that he can receive it, hold it, remember it when I'm gone. I communicate it with a squeeze of my right hand to his left, and the press of my palm against his shoulder. *I'm not scared of you.* His golden eyes widen, and I think he understands. At least, I hope so.

Sel clears his throat and turns us again. He admires my hair, taking in the size and shape of it; then his eyes follow the line of my temple to my borrowed earrings, down my neck and shoulders. "You look stunning this evening, Briana."

The material of my dress is so thin I can feel the searing heat of his hand against my waist. I imagine his fingertips leaving red imprints on my skin, and the image makes the fine hairs on the nape of my neck stand on end. "Thank you," I say hoarsely.

"It's the truth," he says with a shrug. "You do. Even though you're distraught."

"I'm not distraught."

He leans down so close that his lips brush against my ear when he whispers, "Liar."

When he stands back up with a small smile, I get a whiff of something sharp and pungent, and a bit like sandalwood and vetiver. I wrinkle my nose and say the first thing that comes to mind. "Your magic smells *much* better than your cologne."

His face blanks for a moment. "My . . . magic?"

It hits me a second too late that the conversation has taken a turn toward the intimate and that it's all my fault. I fight the urge to run from his curious gaze by finding a speck of dust on his tie to stare at instead.

"You can *smell* my castings?"

That bit of dust is *captivating.* "Yes . . . ?" He laughs, easy and loud. When I look up, he's shaking his head. "What?"

His grin is completely unguarded, and filled with something like awe. "You are *remarkable*."

"Thank you?"

His eyes dart over my shoulder toward the stage before he spins me in his arms, my back to his front. "And I'm not the only one who thinks so."

At the front, the band is closing out the slow dance, and just off the side of the stage stands a group of Legendborn, with Nick, Pete, and William in a line at the end. Nick's eyes are glued to us, to Sel's body draped around mine—and the anger on his face burns bright as a firework, even halfway across the room.

I pull away, but Sel's fingers hold fast at my hip, keeping me close. He murmurs low, just for my ears, "Oh, the scene he'd make if he could."

I twist to glare up at him. "Are you doing this just to make him jealous?"

His eyes flash. "No. But that doesn't mean I can't enjoy it."

He lets me go, but there's nowhere to move, so the most I can do is avoid eye contact while he chuckles beside me.

Finally the band brings the song to an end and the *ting-ting-ting* of a knife against glass breaks up the murmuring crowd.

Lord Davis steps forward to speak into a microphone on a stand. "If I could have your attention, please." He's in a dark black suit with a deep gold regalia sash that drapes over both shoulders and comes to a point in the center of his chest. A gold star pendant hangs down from the pointed end, and in its center, a white diamond winks in the chandelier light.

The ballroom quiets into a restless silence. On the edges of the room, I notice the waitstaff being ushered out of the side doors by people who look like bouncers. Gillian's there, and Owen too. Lieges, escorting outsiders out of earshot. Once the band members leave too, the doors are locked.

"Thank you, everyone, for coming to the annual Selection Gala of the Southern Chapter!" The crowd applauds until Lord Davis waves them down. "Unfortunately, this year's gala comes at a time of strain for our Order. As you all know, increased crossings have been seen up and down the East Coast at all chapters, including our own here in the South."

Beside me, a woman reaches for her husband's hand. Sel's shoulders stiffen.

"The last uprising of demons was over two hundred years ago." Davis raises his chin. "And while none of us were living in that time, we know from the records that this"—he thrusts his finger down toward the floor, his voice rising as he speaks—"is how Camlann begins. This is how it starts. And we know, as in centuries past, that our ancestors prepared us for such a time and equipped us with the birthright to beat the hordes back!"

Applause from the crowd rises to meet his fervor, and the Tristans pump their fists. Out of the side of my eye, I see Fitz, cracking his knuckles like a prized fighter about to go in the ring.

"And as in centuries past . . ." Davis pauses, tipping his head back to the sky and holding his hand over his chest in reverence. "Let us recommit ourselves to the mission and one another by joining in our sacred pledge."

Around me, the voices speak the pledge in unison.

"When the shadows rise, so will the light, when blood is shed, blood will Call. By the King's Table, for the Order's might, by our eternal Oaths, the Line is Law."

Sel's eyes, swirling with emotion, fall to mine.

Davis fixes the room with a steady stare. "My fellow descendants, let us waste no time in our preparation for what we know comes next." He gestures for Nick and the others to step forward alongside him.

Down on the floor below the stage, the five remaining Pages stand in a line, facing the stage and the three Scions. Sydney, Greer, Blake, Vaughn, and Whitty.

A week ago, I'd have been there too.

"Scion Sitterson, please step forward and announce your choice for Squire."

When William steps to the microphone, I can't help but grin at my friend. His tux is a deep green with near-black aubergine lapels, and tailored to perfection. "I, William Jeffrey Sitterson, Scion of Sir Gawain, twelfth-ranked, select Page Whitlock as my Squire." He raises a long green ribbon with a single silver coin before him, and I know without seeing it that it bears the sigil of Gawain. A token for his Squire to wear. "With his agreement, we will be bonded. For this war and beyond."

A cheer rises up at the Page table before Lord Davis calls the room to order. "Page Whitlock, do you accept?"

Even from behind, I can see Whitty tugging nervously at his tie. It takes him three attempts to get the words out. "I do. I accept Scion Sitterson's offer."

The older crowd—the Vassals and Legendborn parents and Lieges—applauds while wild cheers rise up from the Legendborn table, and from the Pages' tables too. I join their crows and whoops, delighted for my friend, while Whitty walks forward and accepts William's colors and sigil. He gives an awkward wave to the room and sits down as fast as possible.

Lord Davis calls the room to order, then beckons Pete forward. Pete looks scared out of his mind, but duty sends him to the mic. "I, Peter Herbert Hood, Scion of Sir Owain, seventh-ranked, select Page Taylor as my Squire. With their agreement, we will be bonded. For this war and beyond."

A hushed murmur travels through the room. Lord Davis leans down beside Pete. "Page Taylor? Do you accept?"

Behind Greer, the crowd shifts. I track the wary eyes, the hesitation, and the curiosity of some of the parents and Lieges in the room. And some outright sneers. People who don't want to be inconvenienced. Don't want to adapt. People who don't want to get better or learn more, just like Greer said.

I smile for my friend. *Time to break their rhythm.*

Greer's shoulders draw back, and when they speak, their voice is strong and clear. "I do. I accept Scion Hood's offer."

More applause this time, but it's so raucous I'm not sure if it's for Pete and Greer, or for the announcement that's coming next.

"The moment we've been waiting for has arrived." Lord Davis uses both hands to quiet the room. "My son, Nicholas Davis, Scion of Arthur, will announce his Squire."

Nick steps forward beside his father, flinching almost imperceptibly when Davis claps him on the back. I knew this moment was coming, but I wasn't prepared for Nick's face, so solemn and so serious as he surveys the room. When he approaches, the room falls silent, as if the whole of the Order even outside these walls is holding their breath, waiting for their future king to announce his first decision on the path toward the throne.

Beside me, Sel tilts his head in my direction, as if his ears are antennae. His eyes flick down to my chest and back up; the corner of his mouth twitches. *Oh.* My heart is a beating drum in my chest—so loud he can hear it.

Nick takes the mic, and the room takes a breath. He looks down at the three remaining Pages, eyeing them one by one. I wait for him to pick Sydney. Try to be happy for him to pick Sydney. She is a better choice than Vaughn or Blake. She will serve him well.

He holds the gold ribbon of Arthur up and the coin glints in the light.

"I, Nicholas Martin Davis, Scion of King Arthur Pendragon, first-ranked . . ."

Oh God. I turn away. I can't look. I don't want to hear.

". . . select Page Matthews as my Squire. With her agreement, we will be bonded. For this war and beyond."

46

THE ROOM ERUPTS.

Sel hisses, a sharp intake of breath beside me.

I feel hundreds of eyes search the ballroom for the Onceborn girl who would be Squire to the king, but I can't move. Can't think.

Davis tries to calm the crowd. I hear him say something about "respecting the king's decision."

The mic squeals. "Page Matthews?" Nick calls, and everyone in the room turns back to him. "Do you accept?" When Nick's eyes find me again, his new subjects follow his gaze. Everyone turns toward me. "Do you accept my offer?" Nick repeats, and I can hear the uncertainty in his voice mixed with the hope.

Suddenly, all I can think is that tonight was supposed to be an apology and a goodbye, but if I become Nick's Squire and Arthur Calls him, I'll never be able to leave.

Fear wraps its hand around my heart.

I came to the Order to find answers about my mother's death, and I found them. Finding a way to leave the Order afterward was always the next step. That was our deal. But Nick's offer would take me on a new path: accepting the Order's mission as my own. Living with the risk of Abatement.

Sel steps close to my side; I feel the tension in his shoulders. "You *must* respond," he whispers, the harsh sound in my ear jarring me back to life.

"I . . ."

I meet Nick's eyes across the room and across hundreds of people, centuries of history, secrets and truths—and I feel the familiar tug between us. *If you can be brave, I can be brave. If I can, you can.* Call and response. In a way, Nick and I are already bonded. We have been since that very first night. In that second I am in two places at once: here with Nick and back in the hidden memory from my mother. I see the same qualities in his eyes that I saw in hers: faith, hope, pride. Camlann is coming and, like my mother, I have a choice: fight or flight.

Take risks. Follow your heart. And move forward.

I am my mother's daughter.

"Yes," I call, loudly and clearly. "I do. I accept Scion Davis's offer."

As soon as the words leave my mouth, the crowd explodes again.

The ballroom becomes a storm of exclamations, gasps, and outraged shouting. Lord Davis calls for order, even tapping the mic. It's no use. No one is listening. An attendant moves Nick offstage. He's protesting, they're pushing.

"You *stole* this from my son!"

I flinch. The woman next to me sneers, disgust turning her face into a hideous mask. It's Vaughn's mother, Rose member Schaefer, who had been kind to me before. Tonight, the slurs in her eyes rain on me like daggers.

"This is his future, you . . . you nappy-headed little—" Someone pushes her back, but another man with a graying beard takes her place, his teeth bared.

A pair of strong arms—Sel's—wraps around my middle, pulling me backward through hands that grab at me. Hands that try to pull me close so that they can inspect me, judge for themselves. I twist in his arms to find Nick, but he's gone.

Insults fly as I pass.

"Gold digger!"

"Onceborn cheat."

"Charity case!"

"Come on! Her blood is dirty. She'll taint the Line!"

That sets me off. I swing around for the culprit. "Who said tha—"

Sel twists me out of a Vassal's grip. He manages to get me off the dance floor without being harmed, but it takes Whitty, Greer, Sarah, and Evan forming a wall behind us to hold off the grown men and women ready to come after me with pitchforks. Behind the crowd, the stage is empty. Sel hauls me to his side, halfway lifting me off the ground, and bolts to the locked doors on the far side of the room. Two Lieges move out of his way—just in time—before he kicks the doors open and sprints down the long hallway, shifting me onto his back as he runs.

"Fucking assholes!" His curses reach my ears over the rush of air.

"Where are you taking me?"

"Away!" We're heading toward the exit. "From the aforementioned ass-holes!"

"Fuck them!" I bat at his arms. "I need to see Nick!"

Sel growls low in his throat and curses again, but changes course. He runs us down a short, empty hall, and suddenly we're in a dark room that smells like leather and books, striped with amber light streaming in from the balcony windows. He deposits me on the floor, and pain shoots up an ankle when I land awkwardly on one heel, but I barely notice it. Adrenaline roars through my veins along with giddiness, pride.

In the light of the hallway, Sel peers out to see if we've been followed. He shoves a hand through his hair and turns back to me with electricity in his eyes. A surge of fierce triumph, a current of conflict. "Stay here. I'll get him." And then he's gone in a whoosh of black.

I press both palms to my flushed cheeks and whirl around in a circle. Even though I'm still shaken from the mob, endorphin-fueled joy bubbles up in my chest, escaping from my mouth in breathless laughter. I can't find the light switch, but it doesn't matter. I don't need to see. I need to feel. Fresh panic is still bouncing around my chest and against my ribs, but there's anticipation, too.

A click behind me, then Sel and Nick appear together in the doorway, their hair equally tousled from Sel's run.

For a moment, the three of us stare at one another in wordless compre-hension. I look between the two of them—a fallen angel and a king, the dark and the light, and feel a deep, churning thrill at what I've done. What *we've* done. This is how it will be now. Oaths between us. Bound to each other. Forever.

Nick moves first. He reaches me in two steps and lifts me in his arms, laughing into my hair. He spins me until my shoes fall from my feet. On one rotation, I glance over his shoulder to see the door swinging shut, and Sel gone, but when Nick puts me down, all we can do is hold each other's gaze and grin. Then, he covers my mouth with his, and this kiss . . . *this* kiss is nothing like our first one.

I can feel it in the hard heat of his lips and in the tight, firm way he holds my waist like a man drowning. He walks me backward until my spine hits the door, then his hands slide down to my thighs and I'm airborne, held up by the strength of his arms and press of his hips. I dig my fingers into his hair, and he sighs before his kiss presses my lips apart and overtakes all my senses. When he pulls away to drop his forehead to the flowers on my chest, he takes a long, soul-deep breath, inhaling me and us together.

When he looks up, his sapphire-black eyes and kiss-swollen lips pull me in so wholly I feel like I'm falling into all that he is and all we'll become. He sinks his teeth deep into his bottom lip and shakes his head in wonder. "You and me, B," he murmurs. He trails light kisses along my jaw between his words. "We can make things better. Make it good. Together." I tip my head against the door and think of forever.

A sharp rap behind me jars us both. "Scion Davis?"

Nick's head jerks up. "One moment!"

I stifle a giggle, and he pecks me on the mouth before sliding me to the floor.

When he opens the door, it's the attendant who instructed us to take our seats for dinner. The man flushes red. I can only imagine what we look like. Nick's arm is draped low around my waist; my hair must be massive, wild. "Can I help you?" Nick says with a barely suppressed smile. He pinches my hip, and I yelp.

"Your father needs you, sir." The attendant steps back, his eyes everywhere but us. "Immediately."

Nick leans in close. "Five minutes. Then it's you and me. I'll have Sel Oath us as soon as Arthur Calls," he murmurs against my skin. The words set my heart racing all over again. With the Warrior's Oath, I'll be Legendborn. More than that, we'll belong to each other. That feeling between us that has always been there? Now it will be official.

He passes a thumb over my cheek again, and I know he's thinking the same thing. Then, he kisses my mouth and leaves with the attendant.

I've just found the light switch and started looking for my shoes when there's another knock. "Back already?" I rush across the carpet on bare feet and open the door. "That was—"

Isaac pushes into the room, glowing red eyes bearing down on me in a grip that I can't shake. They burn and expand, taking me over until all I see are his black irises, the rings of crimson. I try to scream, but my nose is already filled with the smell of hot bile, my mouth burning. It's too late. Blackness takes me.

WHEN I COME to, the mesmer headache in my skull blooms bright and full. It takes everything I have to simply pull my head upright and open my eyes.

A slow voice finds me in the dim light. "She awakens."

It takes a few blinks for my eyes to focus. I'm in a lamplit office. No, a study—Lord Davis's study, where Sel and I were just last weekend.

Nick's father sits at the desk across from me, his fingertips templed on its inlaid leather writing surface. Lightning flashes outside the window to my right, illuminating the angles of his cheekbones and deep-set eyes. For a moment, he looks like Nick.

"Where is Nick?" I move as if to stand but only get an inch off the chair I'm sitting in. I look down to see rope wrapped around my wrists, tying me to the armrests. Even my ankles are tied to the chair, somewhere underneath the layers of my dress. Dread chills me from the inside out. "Let me go!"

"My apologies about the restraints." His Southern charm and its gentle tones of hospitality and care feel twisted now. Calculated. He inclines his head toward the rope around my arms. "I had a feeling you'd decline my invitation to chat."

"Abduction is not an invitation," I say through gritted teeth. "Where is Nick?"

He ignores me and stands up to circle around the desk, tugging at his tie as he walks. "How much do you know about our heritage, Briana?"

Our heritage. Not mine. The Order's heritage and history. His and Nick's.

"Thirteen knights. Merlin. The Round Table . . ." I turn my gaze inward and search for my Bloodcraft, for the part of me that might be able to burn these ropes, but nothing responds. I've shoved my grandmother away so far I can't reach her. My insides feel like they're full of numbing cotton. Why can't I—

"Don't bother tryin' to get free," Davis says without turning. "Isaac's mesmer is quite draining, even for you."

He looks at me over his shoulder. "Oh yes. We know about your inherent resistance to mesmer. Isaac saw Selwyn's mark inside your skull earlier tonight. Remnants of a memory replacement that, it appears, never took. Further reason to take you in."

I don't bother denying it. If that's all he thinks I can do, the better for me.

He crosses the room to pull down a wall map of Western Europe. "There were one hundred and fifty knights of the Round Table at first. The table bein' metaphorical at this point, of course." He taps the map with his knuckle. "And these knights were known all throughout Europe."

"Wonderful for them," I snap.

Davis hums and turns away from the map. He props himself on the edge of his desk. "Legends of individual knights' feats and chivalry stretch even beyond that, even as far as Africa."

The casual tone in his voice does nothing to hide where he's going. What he might say. Fear grips my body.

His voice is easy, light. A gentleman making an innocent inquiry. "Have you heard of the knight called Moriaen?"

He waits, smile patient and smug, for my response. The moment stretches out between us, endless and strained, until I reply, my voice thin as air. "No."

"Ah," he says, staring down at a silver ring on his left hand that he twists idly back and forth. "That's understandable. Legend tells us that the knight Aglovale, son of King Pellinore and brother to four other knights of the Table including our own Lamorak, once traveled to what were then known as Moorish lands. There he fell in love with a Moorish princess and got her with child. By all accounts, their son, Moriaen, grew up to be a formidable fighter—tall, strong, skilled in battle. Moriaen wore a shield and armor and, as grandson to Pellinore and nephew to so many valorous knights, it must have seemed a sure thing that he, too, would join the Table."

The hot blanket of sudden humiliation suffocates me, makes it impossible to breathe.

Davis looks at me, false concern settling across his brow. "But Moriaen did not join the Table. Do you know why, Briana?"

I swallow around the thick, burning rage in my throat. "No."

"Because he was not worthy." He clasps his hands in his lap, eyes unreadable. "Just as you are not worthy. Not for Camlann, and not for my son."

My voice rings oddly, like someone else is speaking from a room far away. "Nick has already decided that I am."

"Nick doesn't see the grand vision of his ascension. What the return of the king means, and what it can restore. The opportunity of Camlann that I never had."

I glare at him, fresh rage lacing my voice. "You think war is an *opportunity*?"

He looks surprised, as if I've mistaken red for blue. "All wars are opportunities. And I won't let another one pass me by."

"Pass you . . ." I trail off. My heart pounds as details return. "You wanted Camlann when you were a Scion. You wanted Arthur to Call you."

"Of course I did." Lord Davis tilts his head. "You wouldn't understand the frustration of a Scion who has never been Called, but for a Scion of Arthur? To be *that* close to that much power and be forced to wait for it to come to you? The impotence was *intolerable*. But that's not why I am accelerating Camlann. That, I'm doing for my son's future and the future health of the Order." He waves his hand at the paintings on his walls, the old books. "In the old days, Vassals served *us* in exchange for protection. Now, CEOs and politicians expect *Lieges* to follow their whims, give them what they want. Vassal infighting pits Lines against Lines. Once, ladies were respected and honored at court, but then the Order of the Rose fell to the wayside and now women sit at the Table, when Malory tells us that 'the very purpose of a knight is to fight on behalf of a lady'! And now my son's foolishness in choosing *you*, who sits at the crux of two faults. Can you not see the sickness here? How the corruption must be rooted out and corrected?"

Two faults. My race and my gender.

But they are not faults. They are strength.

And I am more than this man can comprehend.

Lord Davis watches me, waiting for an answer with open curiosity on his face. The disconnect in his eyes, the cold way he talks about war and power . . . Suddenly, I remember the records, the affidavit, his signature at the bottom— and sickening horror floods me.

"It was you. You opened the Gates twenty-five years ago. You laid out the welcome mat for the Shadowborn, invited them right into our world."

I expect him to deny it. Call me a liar. But he doesn't. Instead, he wags a finger. "Isaac told me he could smell both you and Selwyn here in my study. I imagine you availed yourself of my archives while he pursued his very inconvenient 'mole' theory?"

"You aren't even denying it," I breathe. "You got people killed! My m—" I start, then stop. He has no idea about who I really am. That my mother suffered because of his greed. I don't want to raise her name here. Don't want to give him any more power over me.

He hums, sliding off the desk. "I admit, it was a failed experiment. I'd hoped to create the threat of Camlann through the sheer numbers of Shadowborn crossin' and the loss of Onceborn life, as you might infer from the tenets of our mission. 'Protect the Onceborns from the scourge.' It took a few more years of research before I realized that the more the Scions *themselves* were threatened, the more the Calling would occur."

"Sel was right. There *was* someone on the inside opening the Gates on campus. You." Memories piece themselves together faster now. "The night of the First Oath, you asked him if his abilities were failing him—that was just to make him question himself. And your threat to remove him as Nick's Kingsmage, that was just to get him out of the way."

"I can't take all of the credit for Selwyn's paranoia, Briana. Gates *are* opening at an increased rate up and down the coast, at every chapter. I simply pushed things along where I could."

"You were going to *torture* him!"

He shrugs. "The Kane boy needs to be leashed."

My teeth grind together at his flippant response to Sel's pain. The disregard for the child he raised.

I cycle through all of the Shadowborn attacks in the past two weeks, starting with the first at the Quarry, the hound on campus, the Oath—"You're the one who brought the hounds and the uchel to the Oath that night, aren't you?"

Lord Davis tips an imaginary hat. "I suppose I have you to thank for that, don't I? Nick's unexpected arrival made things a bit more dramatic than I'd planned, but you helped serve a great purpose. He saw you injured, saw me fall to the uchel." He drops his hands into his pockets, clucking his tongue. "It was a strong start, but I still needed to open the Gates at other chapters so that *all* of the Lines were at risk. And now there are only two Lines left to Awaken."

"You're putting your own *son* at risk," I sputter. "And all the Lines, too. If Nick falls—"

"Nick will not fall. I've trained him far too well for that. He is a natural-born leader and does not tolerate harm to innocents. He's made for this war."

"This manufactured war, you mean," I spit.

"The world is a great chain of being, and everyone has their place. Even you. Even me. The hierarchy that holds the Order together has lost its value because the danger has appeared distant. Once the Vassals are reminded of the destruction we prevent, they will be reminded of their place in things. Their place under the king."

"You mean Nick," I retort. "Your time as the Scion of Arthur has passed."

That makes him angry. "Nicholas is a hero to his core. If it's necessary, I will show him how I have learned to open the Gates, and how I will continue to if he doesn't follow my lead. He will be Called by Arthur and take up Excalibur *tonight* and, as king, he will do as I say. Then the whole of the Order and its Vassals around the globe will bend to our will."

"Well, I won't," I say, clenching my fists against the ropes.

His expression shifts to pleasantly amused just as there's a knock at the door. "Right on time," he says, as if we'd just ordered room service at a fancy hotel.

When the door opens, my whole world cracks into a million excruciating shards.

Alice enters the room in her matching polka dotted pajamas as if sleep-walking, her face slack and eyes half-open—with Isaac holding her tight at his side.

"Alice?" I cry. "Alice!"

She sways, silent, and her forehead glistens like she's sweating out a fever. *"Alice!"*

Davis leans away, wincing with a finger to his ear. "No need to yell. She can't hear you."

Fury races through my body like a forest fire. "What have you done to her?" Isaac bares his teeth in a chilling smile. He holds Alice's hand in both of his, caressing the top of her fingers. "Don't touch her!"

"I'm afraid Isaac has to keep touching Ms. Chen in order for this particular mesmer to continue." Davis walks back to his chair and settles in his desk. "Which it will until we come to an understanding."

"If you don't let her go—" I choke out. "I swear to God, I will tear you apart!"

"Such fire." Davis smirks. "Let's see if we can put it out. Isaac?"

Isaac moves in front of Alice as if wrapping her in a hug and slides his hands up to her cheeks, holding her head still until their eyes meet. A slow, sickly shimmer of silver-gray mage flame circles her from the neck up. A second later, Alice blinks rapidly.

"Bree?" she whispers. Her eyes focus on me. "What happened to your dress? Why are you tied to a chair? What's going on?"

"Alice! Alice, listen to me. I'm going to get you out of here!" Isaac shifts his fingers, and she goes under again, slouching slightly against the Merlin's chest.

"What are you doing to her?" I demand, looking back and forth between Isaac and Davis.

Davis nods to the other man, and he brings Alice up again, like a puppet being tugged awake by its strings.

This time her eyes take a while to find me, and even then, they don't focus. I don't think she can see me at all. I call her name again, but she frowns, disoriented. "Matty? I know you don't have a dress for the gala thing this weekend. We should go shopping after class. . ."

She'd said this exact sentence to me two days ago at breakfast. . . . Cold horror bleeds through me when I realize what Isaac is doing.

He's erasing her memories.

"Stop!" I strain against the ropes, tears burning my eyes. "Stop it, please!"

Isaac grins and clasps his hand tighter against her skull.

"You've been weird all week."

"Stop it!"

"If it feels like it's just the two of you, then it's a date, no matter who else is around."

That was two weeks ago. On the phone the day after Nick kissed me in front of the Lodge.

Isaac had just erased two entire weeks from her mind. Everything she'd learned in her classes, every idea she'd generated, every memory of laughter, of joy. Every conversation with her parents or brother. Everything we'd said to each other. Gone.

And he could do more. I know he could. He could take her from me right before my eyes, just like Nick's mother had been taken from him.

That's what this is. A show of power. A reminder that no matter how much I know, I don't know enough to survive in this world. That I'm not worthy.

"Please," I whimper, the tears running in hot streaks down my face. "Please, stop. Stop it."

Davis signals Isaac to stop, and Alice and I both sag. He taps his fingers on his desk lightly and lets out a tired sigh. "Normally we'd simply mesmer any inconvenient Onceborns, but since you've proven a bit stubborn in that regard, I sent Isaac to collect Ms. Chen for some persuasion. You'll have to forgive the dramatics. Merlins are quite showy beings, aren't they?"

"What do you want?" I whisper, because that's all I need to know.

Davis smiles as if I'd finally asked the right question. "You'll leave Carolina and the program. Tell the dean you were ill-equipped to keep up with the rigor. A poor fit. I'm sure that won't be hard for the administrators to believe, coming from you."

My fingers curl into fists.

"You won't speak to Nicholas or any of the other chapter members ever again. You'll apply to another college when the time comes, out of state preferably, and forget you ever found the Legendborn world."

I glance back up at Alice, who is swaying, eyes fully closed now. Only Isaac's arms on her shoulder seem to keep her upright. Davis follows my gaze toward Alice.

"And if I don't?"

"You're a clever girl, so I'm sure you already know the answer." He sits back in his chair and drums his fingers on the desk. I'm boring him. Even as he tortures my best friend, and through her, me. "But I suppose it's best to make things clear. If you don't comply, Isaac will take you to one of our institutions where his colleagues, the other Masters, will enjoy themselves finding out exactly why your brain won't accept their illusions—whether it's in your skull or out. And while you cannot be mesmered, please understand that we will happily find and manage other loved ones in your life who can. Like Ms. Chen here."

I see my dad sitting in the vinyl chair at the hospital, putting on a brave face while his world crumbled. I hear his voice, warm and laughing in my ear. The texts I've never responded to. How he tried to help me even when I didn't want to hear it.

Lord Davis leans forward and pins me with a pleased smile. "Now tell me, Ms. Matthews. Do you consent to *this* offer?"

All the frustration, all the fight, leaves my body.

"I do."

48

ALICE MOVES AS if sleepwalking, and she falls asleep as soon as I get her upstairs and lay her on her bed. Her thin eyebrows are drawn up tight, and her stringy hair is glued to her neck and forehead. She shivers with nightmares and moans without waking up, not even stirring when I pull her into a sitting position to change the damp, clammy bedsheets. I wipe the sweat from her face and neck and sob, praying for whatever Isaac's done to leave her system.

'This craft is a poison.' My grandmother's voice is loud in my mind. 'I'm sorry, baby.'

"Where *were* you?" I cry. "Where did you go?"

'I am using all of my power to call back to the old mother, like you asked,' she murmurs. 'I couldn't help you back there, and I can't help you here.'

"There must be something I can do!"

She is silent, and I worry she's gone again.

Then my body turns hot, and a new presence stretches beneath my skin. "Who—"

A new voice answers. 'Jessie. A healer. Three generations back.'

"Please—" My voice cuts off in a strangle as Jessie pushes my hands over Alice's forehead.

'My healing and your immunity . . . maybe.' A pause. 'No herbs on this side, so you'll have to do.'

"I'll have to do wh—"

Red mage flame erupts from my palms and flows over Alice's face and hair. Jessie won't let me pull away. All I can do is watch with horror as my root, my aether, cascades down my friend's body and soaks into her skin. Then Jessie releases me, and the flames snuff out.

The threat of fainting shudders through my frame. I'm drained. Weak.

Instead of herbs, Jessie used *me*, my own power and energy.

Alice's eyes flutter open. "Bree . . . ?"

"Alice!" My hands fall to her cheeks and smooth her damp hair away from her eyes.

She pulls at my wrist. "What happened?" she gasps, and her eyes dart back and forth. "There was a man. A man with red eyes . . . and *fangs* . . . and he—he took me somewhere. A house off campus—" She pushes up into a half-sitting position, trembling as the memories return. "You were there. They'd tied you up. Oh God. *Oh God. He took my memories.*"

She starts to hyperventilate. I kneel, nearly falling forward in the process. My blood feels sluggish in my veins, heavy and spent.

"Just breathe," I soothe, for myself and for her. "I'm right here."

"They knew you." Her brow furrows; then her eyes meet mine. "And you knew them."

It's time. I can't avoid this anymore. "I can explain."

When I finish telling Alice everything, she has a dozen questions ready to go. She paces the room, hands moving while she talks, while I kneel on the floor, recovering my reserves by the minute. Then she asks a new batch of questions about the Lines and the Order while changing out of her sweat-soaked pajamas and into jeans and a tee. I answer each inquiry one by one and end with Lord Davis's plan.

Confident that she and I are both well enough, I push to my feet to search for new clothes while considering my options.

No, I consider if I even *have* any options.

I could just leave, like I agreed to do, I tell her. It's my fault Alice is in the

Order's sights, and it will be my fault if they get to my father. I can't risk her or my father falling to Isaac. I care less about my own well-being than theirs.

"But what about Nick?" she asks, standing as I pull on a black tank and leggings.

"I don't know," I say. I draw my hair into a tight, high puff. Battle ready. "No one's texted or called to find out where I am, so whatever Lord Davis and Isaac are doing, they've either convinced everyone I'm gone for good or they're keeping the chapter busy in some other way."

"With demons?"

I bend to pull on my sneakers. "If Davis plans for Nick to take up Excalibur tonight, then he's got to have a plan in motion to expose Nick to more Shadowborn. And putting Nick in danger puts everyone else in danger, including and especially Sel."

My eyes fall to my mother's box.

Our Brave Bree.

"Well," Alice says, pulling her hair up too, "I'm coming with you."

"No, you're not," I say, stunned.

She raises a brow. "You've been doing this by yourself. You need backup."

"No, I need you to be safe. Lord Davis is behind all of this, Alice. He's a monster. He got people killed, he sent my mother into hiding, kept me from my family's truth. And now he wants to start a war, killing more innocents in the crossfire. I'm not letting him anywhere *near* you."

She smirks. "And I could say the exact same about you."

I blink, speechless.

"I won't claim to be some sort of demon hunter, but I am your best friend, Matty. I loved your mother. I love you." She meets me in the middle of the room, close enough that I can see the steel in her eyes. "So if this is your fight, then it's my fight too."

WE WALK WIDE around the perimeter of the Lodge's lawn, taking care not to rustle any gravel. If Isaac's inside, it probably won't matter, but I need to avoid detection for as long as possible. Alice is quick and careful, and follows my hushed orders without question.

By the time we reach the basement-level side door, my grandmother is back, but she's completely asleep. Like, straight-up old person on the couch asleep. Jaw slack, slight snoring echoing in my skull, and releasing a heavy, slow feeling in my chest.

I suppose it's for the best. I check my mental boundaries like Mariah taught me. *Visualize yourself as a house. Shore up each entry point. Close the blinds. Close the chimney flue.*

On the way over, I reasoned that if Isaac and Lord Davis are inside, they'd be upstairs on the main level, but now that I'm here, I'm not sure. What if the reason the upper levels are dark is because everyone's downstairs? What if they're not here at all, and everyone's out fighting the Shadowborn Davis has already released? What if Nick's already been Called and Camlann is here?

All I know for sure is that I'm here now. And if the Legendborn are here too, there's only one person I'd trust right now to be discreet. I dig out my phone and send a quick text.

Two minutes later, the door opens to reveal William, still in his dress shirt and green suit pants, his face a mixture of relief and shock. "They told us you quit. I didn't believe it for a second. I knew the moment you walked in wearing that dress, you were going to steal the show." He pulls me into his arms.

"Then you knew before I did." His bright smell floods my nose. It's fresh. Too fresh. "Who's hurt?"

"You'd better get inside." When he stands back, he notices Alice. "Who's this?"

"Alice Chen. She's with me."

"If she's with you, then I trust her." His eyes slide to mine. "But if you walk in with an outsider, then everyone will know you broke the Oath of Secrecy, and wonder, like I am, how you're still standing."

"Long story."

He nods again, and I notice the sweat on his brow, his rolled-up sleeves. He tugs me into the hallway and then turns an immediate left down the stairs. "Everything's gone to shit in the past two hours. Sel, Tor, and Sar are off hunting some demon, Russ barely made it back in one piece . . ." As soon as we emerge from the stairwell, we hear shouting and set off at a run.

Russ's yelling guides us to a room I've never seen before. "We need to wait!" It sounds like his fist hits a table. That stops me short; I've never seen Russ angry enough to hit something. He and the other Legendborn are standing around a large square table covered with maps.

"No," Fitz says, his voice booming. "Three attacks in less than two hours, and they've all been fully materialized. They're moving closer to campus each time, pushing inward toward the middle. Onceborns will see them, and then what? We need to go out in full force. Now!"

No one notices us walk in. The Scions and Squires are bent over the stack of maps talking across one another, shouting in raised voices. Fitz, Evan, Felicity, and Russ are in aether armor, with weapons across backs or slung around hips, while the others are still in jeans and T-shirts. I spot Greer and Whitty in the middle of it all.

"Felicity, you're fourth-ranked," Russ says. His Scion stands with her arms crossed on the far end of the table, gnawing on a thumbnail. "Tor isn't here. Nick isn't here. You tell us what to do."

I respond before Felicity can answer. "We've got to find Lord Davis. And Nick."

They all turn to me. Russ looks like he's thrilled to see me, and so do a few others, but some, like Fitz and Pete, look unnerved by my presence. Greer walks over to me first and wraps their arm around my neck.

"Bree, what are you doing here?" Felicity says, coming around the table to hug me too. Her armor tingles against my skin.

"Who the hell is this?" Fitz says. Alice is tucked back in the shadows, her eyes wide and bright. She's keeping quiet, just like I told her.

"A Vassal," I say.

William chimes in. "Someone we can trust." That seems to settle the room some.

Fitz's eyes narrow. "Lord Davis said you rejected Nick's offer after the gala."

"I'll tell you everything, but first, catch me up. Where are Nick and his father?" I step closer to the table. In the center of the pallet rests a large piece of paper covered in topographic lines and color-coded circles and squares. A map of campus.

Felicity joins me at the table. "We don't know. They came back after the gala, argued in the foyer. Davis said you were gone, and Nick just—"

"Flew off the handle," Evan says.

Felicity nods. "It was loud enough that we could all hear, even in our rooms. I don't think Lord Davis wanted an audience. He told Nick they should talk privately, and then they left."

"Then shit got real weird," Pete mutters. Several pairs of eyes turn to him. He shrugs. "What? It did!"

William looks nervous. He rubs his thumb over his brow. "Sel sensed a demon a little over an hour ago, just off campus. He, Felicity, and Russ went after it."

Russ takes over. "Full-corp hellhound. Not full-grown, but big enough. We dusted it easily, were on our way back, and *wham*, Sel senses another one on South campus, so we head that way."

"Russ was wounded," Felicity adds. For the first time I notice the smear of dried blood on her glowing chestplate. Russ's blood, by the rattled look on her face. I realize his weight leans more heavily than usual on his left side. "I carried him back. Just as William got started on him, Sel sensed another demon. This time on mid-campus. He went back out right away with Sar and Tor." My stomach sinks at her next words. "We've been calling Nick since the first attack, and he and Lord Davis aren't answering. And now, Sel and Sar and Tor aren't back."

"It's happening," Fitz says harshly. "It's just like Lord Davis said, this is how it starts. We can't wait until we're all in agreement to do something. This is what we're trained to do. The shadows are rising. This is Camlann!"

"No," I say. "It's not."

"Help!" Sarah's frantic scream tears through the hallway. *"Help!"*

William and Whitty are through the door before anyone else has even moved. The rest of us crowd into the hallway to see the two boys take Tor's still form from Sarah and rush her down to the infirmary.

"Move!" William barks as he runs. Tor's head lolls back in his arms, supported by Whitty's steady fingers. Blood, deep crimson in the fluorescent hall lighting, trickles in a line down the side of her mouth and pools in her straw-colored hair. Her chainmail, light and thin for an archer, but strong, has been rent into shreds. Chunks of aether metal links drop from what remains of it, falling to the floor and exploding back into nothing as William passes by.

I tell Alice to hang back and follow William into the infirmary. Felicity and Russ join me, pushing the doors open after I enter. Sarah has already sped past both of us. I didn't even see her move.

Sel must have already bonded the Scion and Squire, because William and Whitty work in unspoken concert over the archer's body on the table, William hovering his hands over Tor's head and Whitty moving his fingers like he's playing a piano inches above her chest and stomach. They speak without looking at each other, without looking at anyone. Their eyes are closed.

"Broken ribs, internal bleeding. Punctured left lung. Spleen and left kidney sliced right down the middle. Damn."

"Explains the blood in her oral cavity. No injuries to her brain or cervical spine."

Whitty hesitates. "I don't know how to—"

"I'll do it." William wordlessly moves into Whitty's space, calling aether into his fingers until it encases Tor's torso like a shining shell. He seems to pull away from us and into another world inside his head. His mouth moves soundlessly, speaking Welsh again, I think, and his eyes move rapidly under his lids like he's in REM sleep.

"What happened?" Felicity asks Sarah, who is hovering over Tor's still form with trembling hands at her mouth.

"I should have been there," Sarah says, her voice quivering. "It should have been me. That's my job. This is my job."

"Sarah, honey." Felicity grasps the smaller girl's shoulder. Sarah flinches, but her lost eyes find Felicity and slowly focus. "Tell us what happened."

Sarah tries several times before words come out. "A . . . a . . . fox, I think? Something that stole Sel's aether and weakened our armor. We—we had it cornered, but then a cougar showed up."

"A hellcougar?" Russ exclaims. "What in the f—"

Felicity silences him with a look. "What happened then?"

Sarah blinks. "Tor heard it before we did. She went to pull an arrow, but it was too fast. Fast as us. It . . . it just jumped, and it—I thought it was going to open her up right in front of me . . ." Sarah sobs. Her face has gone white as fresh snow, and her shoulders start to shake uncontrollably.

"Get her on the table," Whitty orders, already moving to the other table in the room. Russ lifts her like she's made of shredded paper and sets her gently on the table. Whitty grasps her hand, and her body goes limp, but her eyes and face stay alert. A calming injection of aether, right from his hand to her system.

"Where's Sel?" Russ asks carefully, the tension suppressed in his voice.

"He sent me back with Tor. He said he could handle them himself."

Felicity gasps beside me, but I can't breathe at all. Sel is good. He's better than good, but if he's bonded Whitty and William, and maybe even Greer and Pete? He could be too intoxicated to fight.

"Sel said . . ." Sarah moans quietly. She tries to sit up, but Whitty presses gently against her shoulder. Her eyes scan the room wildly until they land on mine. "He said he thinks Lord Davis is trying to force Arthur's hand."

Russ's head jerks up. "What the hell does that mean?"

"Davis wants Arthur to Call Nick," I tell them. "But maybe it isn't working."

I gather everyone who's still standing in the room down the hall, along with Alice, and tell them why I came here and what I know. What Sel and I found, what Lord Davis did to me. And what he said he'd do if his son refused to claim his throne.

I worry that they won't believe the parts of the story that Sel and I uncovered at Davis's home, with Sel's title in the balance as it is, but the Legendborn trust him more than he thinks. It helps that Sarah shared his message and that there were so many witnesses to Nick's argument with his father.

And some of them, I think, have come to trust me, too.

Russ speaks first, the frustration in his voice barely under control. "But how is Lord Davis breaking his Oaths? He's taken the First Oath, the Oath of Service, who knows what else."

William grimaces. "Every Oath comes back to the same common commitment— to be in service to the Order's mission. If Lord Davis's logic is that warped, it could be that, from his perspective, his intentions *are* in service to the mission. Or maybe his Kingsmage has protected him somehow from the Oaths' effects. A Master mage would know more."

"But how would Nick be Called?" Felicity says. "The Scion of Lancelot is at Northern, and he's still dormant."

"As far as we know," Fitz interjects. "Maybe Davis fixed that, too, or he's working with allies. Maybe that Regents' meeting at Northern last week was just a cover."

William runs a hand over his face. "Or the kid at Northern *is* still dormant, and threatening Arthur's Scion will somehow force Lancelot to Call his."

"It doesn't matter!" Russ throws his hands up in the air. "It doesn't *matter* if

Davis is trying to force the Callings if the demons he's letting cross over are *real*. Why is Arthur waiting?"

"Could Nick hold Arthur off?" I ask William, thinking of Nick's confession about trying not to be Called and his desire to prevent Camlann at all costs. "Is that possible?"

William blinks. "No. There have been Scions who wanted to resist the Call before, but they've all failed." He scratches his head. "I mean, I could see it for the other knights, *maybe*, but the strength of will—and life force—it would take to stop the Call of Arthur . . ."

"If it's possible, then Nick will be the one to do it," Evan says from where he's leaning on the back wall. "Especially if he thinks he can talk his father down from starting Camlann. He has faith in us to handle the demons in the meantime. And we can, now that we've got two more bonded pairs. But there's another variable here." He looks over at me. "Nick's in love with Bree."

My cheeks heat. "That's not—"

"Yeah, it is." Evan smiles and pushes off the wall. "The entire gala saw the way he looked at you. Davis made a bad gamble. He thought Nick would believe that you'd accept his Squireship, then quit. Instead, that tightly controlled temper of his finally popped. I bet Nick is *furious*. Angry, heroic, and in love is a formidable combination; he'll hold off Arthur's Call, all right."

Everyone looks at me then, and I feel like I might burst into flames. I'm saved from an internal wildfire when someone knocks, hard, against the back door.

"Sel!" Felicity yells, and runs out the door again. I want to follow, but I can't. My feet are rooted to the floor in terror, my heart suddenly beating so hard that the blood rushing in my ears sounds like an ocean. It doesn't make sense, but my brain tells me that if I don't see Sel injured and broken like Tor, that might mean that he isn't injured at all.

It's not Sel, though. Felicity walks back into the room with Vaughn trailing sullenly behind her.

Greer scoffs. "Didn't you run off with your tail between your legs?"

"My question exactly," Fitz says.

Vaughn watches us warily. "Lord Davis said he had a plan for me. That I should just wait in my room until he called." His eyes slide to mine, but when I look into them, I can see that the arrogance from before has taken a blow. Then it hits me: Davis had reserved Vaughn for Nick.

Russ frowns. "So, what, you got antsy and decided to come here?"

"My dorm's on the sixth floor of Ehringhaus. I looked out the window and I saw some lights over mid-campus. Green mage flame. Blue-white too."

"Sel," I breathe. "When was this?"

"Ten minutes ago," he says, spreading his hands wide. "I ran straight here, but . . . it sounds like you already know?"

Fitz steps forward to fill his Page in. I hope Sel is still alive. The thought that he might not be steals the oxygen from my body.

"Fitz," I say quickly. His head raises. "What did you say earlier about the campus map? About the demons' movement?"

"They're moving toward a central location."

"Why would they do that?" Alice asks, and the room turns toward her. She raises her chin, and soldiers forward with her question. My chest bursts with pride. "What are they drawn to?"

"Onceborns, obviously," he says.

"And aether," Greer says.

My heart races in my chest. "What source of aether is in the middle of campus?"

Felicity's and Fitz's faces blanch. They're the only veteran Scions in the room, and they've come to the same realization at the same time.

"Care to share with the class?" Russ huffs. "Or is this a bloodline secret?"

"Actually . . ." Felicity flushes. "It is."

Somehow, I already know what she's going to say.

"Excalibur," she says, her voice a mixture of fear and awe. "It's the oldest aether weapon in the world. Forged by Merlin himself, it contains so much power that it never dissipates, like ours do. Not even when its bearer releases it. Each king, each Scion of Arthur, adds to its strength every time they wield it. When the last Camlann was over, and we'd won, that Scion returned it to the stone. Shadowborn usually aren't materialized enough to get this far. Or

Sel finds them first, so I didn't think of it, but if a lesser demon doesn't find a specific person to hunt, they'll seek the nearest, biggest source of aether to consume. The more they consume, the longer they can stay. And the biggest source of aether would be the sword."

"Where is it?" Russ demands.

"Ogof y ddraig," I breathe.

She nods. "Yes. Under the Bell Tower. And there are Gates underground too. Tons of them. Merlins sealed them hundreds of years ago, but if Lord Davis wants Nick in position to take up Excalibur . . ."

"Then that's where Nick and his dad are," I say, my chest tightening at the very thought. "We've got to get to them and stop Davis before he opens any more."

Pete throws a hand up in the air. "What about the Gates up *here*? I know they don't spit demons out rapid-fire, but are we going to just let them stay open?"

"I'll go," William says from the doorway. "I can close them."

"How?" Pete asks.

"With this." William produces something small from his pocket and wiggles it back and forth. A vial of blood.

Sel's blood. I'm sure of it.

"You don't need to be a demon to close or open a Gate. You just need demon blood. Or part-demon blood, in this case." He steps forward into the room. "I don't have the same radar that Sel does, but my healing abilities give me a pretty good sense of where aether is. This is sort of like that, except on a bigger scale. And Russ, Felicity, and Sarah can point me in the right direction." He nods to Alice. "I'll take Vassal Chen with me to keep the Onceborns out of the way."

"No," Felicity says firmly. "You're a solid fighter, but it's not even close to midnight, so you don't have Gawain's strength. What if you get hurt? You're our only healer."

William's lip curls. "No, I'm not. Whitty's a fine apprentice already. He's in the infirmary right now finishing up with Tor. What I'll be doing is ten times safer than going into the tunnels to find the ogof. If you're worried about someone still being around to patch y'all up, then you don't want me in there. You want me out here." He smirks. "And if Sel returns, I'll tell him where you've gone and send him in like frikkin' Gandalf the White. It'll be great, promise."

Russ places a hand on his Scion's wrist. Felicity tilts her chin slightly in his direction. A silent conversation passes between them before she sighs and turns back to William. "Okay."

Before she and William leave, I pull Alice aside. "You won't be able to see them coming. If William says run, you run."

She nods, her mouth tight. "You gonna be okay?"

"Yeah."

"You mean it?"

I pull her into a hug. "I mean it."

Before we part, she grasps my arm. "Make him pay, Matty."

It only takes a quick twist of Russ's wrist to break the lock on the door to the hidden weapons room. Well, hidden to me, at least.

"The Lieges don't like us playing with their stuff, aka real weapons that stick around after a fight, but the padlock always makes me laugh." He pulls the door back to let us in. "It's insulting, honestly. Do they forget whose traits we've inherited?"

"Lamorak is known for his temper *and* his wisdom," Felicity says as she steps through the door. "I think they'd hoped the latter would prevail."

"Where's the fun in that?" Russ says, winking as I pass.

The Scions and bonded Squires—Russ and Felicity, Fitz and Evan, Pete and Greer, and even Whitty, with William's help—will all use aether weapons in the tunnels. But since Vaughn and I aren't Squires, we need real weapons in our hands.

I hesitate in front of the rack of shining steel and heavy, polished wood. There are swords, of course, but some are in shapes I've not seen used before. Curved cutlasses, katana, shortswords, and even a thick machete for hacking. There's also a rack of daggers of varying lengths, a double-bladed axe, and what Evan calls a lochaber axe. On the far end are maces, flails, and crossbows.

"Take the sword," a voice says gruffly from my shoulder. To my surprise, it's Vaughn. He selects a blade for himself and hefts it, testing its weight. "You're hopeless with the daggers, and the staff'll be hard in tight quarters. You're passable with the sword and probably won't cut your own arm off," he mutters before ducking his head and walking back out into the training room.

Honestly, it's probably the best compliment I could have asked for.

50

FELICITY TELLS US there's an entrance to the tunnels not far from Davis's home, being the family property of the Line of Arthur. She guesses that's how Nick and Davis will have entered the cave. We don't have time to go that far, and we don't need to.

I should have known the Order founders would want an entrance close by, but even then, I'd have never guessed the door to the tunnels would be the Wall of Ages itself.

"This has been here this whole time?" Russ exclaims, clearly put out that his Scion had kept something from him.

Felicity winces. "I'm sorry, Russy! All of the Scion families are sworn to secrecy. It's a security measure, just in case anyone tries to get in."

He harrumphs, and she goes to squeeze him around the middle, their armor clanking together when she does.

The founders weren't playing around. Not only did they keep the entrance secret and, literally, right under everyone's noses in the basement, but it takes actual Scion blood—at least three Lines in agreement—to open the door.

The group going to the tunnels stands back as Felicity, William, and Fitz step forward to do the honors.

William uses a small needle to prick their thumbs. I reach nervous fingers to the sword strapped to my back. It helps to touch the solid pommel and leather-wrapped grip. I'd selected a blade that was light, sharp, and well-balanced. I'm still scared I'm going to accidentally chop my own arm off. The thought, vivid and violent, seems to be enough to wake my grandmother.

She stirs inside me, in what feels like her chair. *'Oh, finally doing something, are we?'*

"Wow. Just wow," I mutter. Evan looks at me strangely, and I smile back and gesture at the wall in front of us. "It's impressive, right?" He nods in agreement and focuses on the Scions.

You find that old mother yet, Grandmother Charles? I ask inside my head. *I could use some of those red flames right about now.*

'Young folk never listen,' she mutters, scoffing so loud it rattles my ears from the inside out. *'I'm not findin' her. She's comin' to you. And no, she ain't here yet. 'Spect she'll be by shortly.'*

I don't even bother responding, for fear I'll say the wrong thing and she'll find a way to slap me again.

The three Scions bend in unison and smear their thumbs over their names in the carved Lines of the Wall. As they do, the Lines blaze to life, streaking up to the top of the Wall in three distinct colors—red for Lamorak, green for Gawain, and deep orange for Bors. Right as they reach the gemstones at the top, a deep grinding sound shakes the room and the tables and files inside it.

"Oh, shit," Russ says, his irritation now replaced with unsuppressed glee. "Oh, shit!"

We step back as hidden gears, still working even though they must be centuries old, pull the door inward inch by inch. A rush of stale, damp-smelling air blows into the room, and we cover our noses. The passage beyond must be filled with mildew and decay. I can taste it in the back of my throat. It's so strong, even my grandmother pulls back.

Just as the door comes to a squealing, echoing halt, the door behind us opens, and Tor and Sarah walk in. "We're going too," Tor says in a surprisingly strong voice.

"Oh no you're not!" William points a finger at her and Sarah both. "I should have told Whitty to knock you both out."

"Oh, shut it, Will," Tor says, even though her movements are stiff and her breath is already leaving her mouth in rattling pants. "I'll be healed soon enough. And they need more firepower."

"I said no!"

Tor reaches the group and leans against a cabinet to gaze into the gloom beyond the Wall. The tunnel has no lighting installed, so we can only see what the fluorescent lights in the room reveal: a pounded charcoal-black dirt floor, smooth from wind-distributed dust. A pathway about six feet across that disappears ten feet in. No ceiling, as if the Wall marks the boundary between the Lodge's foundation and the passage to another world. An older world. One that is deep, dangerous, and much nearer to the demons' plane. Beyond the Wall, in total darkness, we'd be in their court, not ours.

And what's worse is that just a foot before the light weakens, we can see a rounded antechamber that ends in six openings. The first branch in the network.

William runs his hand down Tor's back, evaluating her condition with a deep scowl on his face. "Impatience is an inherited personality trait in your Line," he mutters. "Fortunately for you, so is rapidity of aether metabolism. You'll be healed in less than an hour, you ungrateful girl."

Tor grins. "Toldja."

"All right, everyone, listen up." Felicity calls us to attention, her back toward the tunnel so she can see our faces.

"Hey!" Tor calls, limping over to her. "I'm here now, and I'm third-ranked. I'll make the pronouncements!"

Felicity fixes her with a truly damning stare. Tor, to her credit, only holds her stance for a moment before she concedes, stepping aside.

"The good news is, according to my dad's stories, there's a tunnel network map that will show us the most direct path to the cave. The bad news is, we don't know where that map is." Our groans echo into the tunnel behind her. "But since all paths eventually lead there, we're splitting the group four ways." She glances at Tor and Sarah. "Five ways." William walks between us, handing out small black flashlights.

There's an odd number of us, so I get put into a group of three with Fitz and

Evan. Vaughn and Whitty agree to join forces, leaving the rest of the bonded pairs to work together.

"There won't be reception down there, so your phones are useless. Remember that the center of the campus is to our left, and hopefully we'll all end up at the cave together. If you get there first, please try talking to Lord Davis." Before using a weapon, she means. "But be on your guard. He might open a Gate to truly force Nick to defend himself."

The pairs file in one at a time. Evan, Fitz, and I will go in last. Just as we take a step forward, William catches my arm.

"You don't have to do this, you know," he says earnestly, his gray eyes searching mine. He glances into the cave and back to me again, and I see the worry there, so genuine it pains me. "It's not your war."

It's not your war. I had a similar thought the last time I was here, when I was leaving the Legendborn world for good.

"I don't want war," I reply. "I want the people I love to be safe."

"I thought you might say something like that."

"You coming, Matthews?" Fitz calls. He and Evan are standing just over the threshold, faces limned in light, bodies already in shadow.

I say, "Right behind you," and step forward into the earth.

51

THE SCENT OF rotting things overwhelms us. It burns the insides of my nostrils so much that I tug my T-shirt up over my nose for relief. The shift of my sleeves up my forearms makes me wish I had a coat; it's freezing down here.

The others have already chosen their tunnel, so once we reach the small antechamber, we take the one farthest to the right.

We walk with our flashlights pointed down mostly, with occasional flicks up ahead, not that it helps very much. The tunnel turns vaguely left, I think. It's hard to focus when the ceiling sometimes drops to just above Fitz's hair and other times rises up into steep, empty columns to nowhere. Often, Fitz's massive shoulders brush the wall, but for most of the way, the tunnel is about four feet wide. Our steps makes a crunching, scratching sound on the gravel under our feet. The sound of dripping water reaches us from somewhere out of sight. Probably where the mildew comes from. Its presence is a constant, deep green and black and slippery. We walk for twenty, maybe thirty minutes mostly in silence and single file. Fitz leads, Evan takes the middle, and I bring up the rear.

I feel a surge of relief that Vaughn warned me away from the staff. It'd never even fit in this part of the tunnel.

"Where are we, do you think?" My voice bounces in loud, jarring echoes in the tight space.

Fitz grunts. "Not sure. Tunnels aren't a straight line. It takes about fifteen minutes to walk to the edge of campus aboveground, then another fifteen or so to the Tower."

I'm not claustrophobic, but the thought of walking in and out of cramped, dark spaces for—at the minimum, if we're on the direct route—another twenty minutes makes my heart pound in my ears. The sound almost blocks out the dripping.

"Do you really think Davis might open the Gates down here?" Evan asks his Scion. "If he does, and Arthur doesn't Call Nick, they'd both be trapped."

Fitz grunts dismissively. "He'd be out of his mind. Fighting in quarters this close would be a nightmare. I'm sure the cave is bigger, but even still. You've got to contain the threat or neutralize it in an enclosed space with limited exits. Tactical nightmare."

Evan hums in agreement.

Fitz leads us into another left turn. I hear his sharp intake of breath about two seconds before I see its cause.

The tunnel opens up completely on one side, turning a narrow passageway into a path with only one wall on our left. On our right, dropping down into terrifying blackness, is a ravine about thirty feet across. Fitz's flashlight shows us the other wall, a series of massive jagged outcrops reaching toward us like giant molars with sharp edges. When he and Evan point their beams down, we see that the ravine narrows as it drops, with stalagmites rising up from an unseen floor filled with shadows that swallow our light.

The path ahead is still four feet across, but everything about it seems more treacherous with certain death on the other side.

Fitz says what we're all thinking: "Better hug that wall, y'all."

We do. I hug it so much that I curl my left fingers into the bumpy, cold, slippery surface, hoping that a small handhold will appear if I need it.

We're three, maybe five minutes into the new terrain when the skittering sound begins.

Fitz's flashlight swings right. "What's that noise?"

"Bats, maybe?" Evan offers.

It seems like he's right; the skittering becomes the flapping of leathery wings. I cringe.

Evan's flashlight pitches up just in time to catch a thick, scaly body and webbed foot before both disappear into the darkness. "That's not a bat, y'all."

"Well, what is i——" Fitz is struck by something solid. He grunts and goes sprawling along the path, dropping his flashlight into the ravine in the process.

I yell *"Fitz!"* and lean around Evan's body, cutting my flashlight long across the wall. Fitz groans, but gets back up on his feet.

"That's *not* a bat!" he roars, holding his hand up to shield his eyes from the light. Heart thudding in my chest, I direct my flashlight down to his feet.

Miraculously, his flashlight must have landed on an outcrop about ten feet below us and at an angle, because a wide beam of light hits the wall and path ahead of us.

"He's right. I didn't see it, but I heard it!" Evan shouts. "Whatever it is, it's strong!"

High-pitched screeching sounds bounce around the cavern, and that's all the warning we get.

A cloud of heavy wings descends on us. I hear Fitz yell again, then, a half heartbeat later, the singing whine of his aether sword when he pulls it from its scabbard. Claws pull at my shoulders. I scream and cover my head, dropping down to the ground. The gravel digs through my pants into my knees as I cower beneath beating wings and what feels like tiny, sharp daggers.

One of them lands on my back. I thrust an elbow back and up. It makes contact with something hot and heavy that howls and dislodges itself from my shirt.

Fitz screams. I drop my flashlight so that it faces his direction and spring up, drawing my sword. The angles of the light hit Fitz just right, and then I see them.

Four flying demons the size of swans swarm Fitz's head and torso. Leathery wings as wide as he is tall carry their bulbous bodies and long, red, scaly limbs. Their hind feet are long and bent back like a wolf, but their hands look human, with long fingers ending in black claws that slash at Fitz's arms and face.

"Imps!" he screams.

Evan is running, and so am I. I swing at the first imp I reach, hacking off its long, pointed tail. Its screech is a railroad spike driving deep into my brain, but it flies back over the ravine, away from us. Fitz manages to drive his blade into the body of another imp. A squelching, wet sound, and the silver tip of it pops out of its back, shining and covered in black blood. When the imp falls, it almost takes Fitz's glowing sword with him.

One of the imps flies over Fitz's head and makes a beeline for me. I swipe high, just slicing into the soft pocket of flesh under its arm. It screeches and wings upward.

Inside my skull, my grandmother screams.

Her wail sends me to my hands and knees—right at the edge of the path. I freeze, my head and shoulders just stopping before tipping me over into the chasm.

I gasp and scramble away until my back hits the wall.

'Protect my grandchild, Lord, oh please . . '

I think *Not right now!* at her as loud as I can, because the imp I injured is still circling the ravine. It loops back around and flies right toward me. It's the first time I've seen one straight on. It has long, curved horns like a mountain goat and green glowing eyes. I drop into a loose stance. Wait for it. Wait for it.

'The Lord is my shepherd . . '

"Not now, Grandma!" I scream out loud, and slash downward with all of my strength, slicing the imp in two from shoulder to hip. Both sides of it fall back into the ravine.

I shove Grandmother Charles into an empty room in my mental house and imagine locking the door tight so I can focus, then turn back to Fitz.

The last imp has sunk its claws deep into Fitz's shoulders and hovers behind him where his sword can't reach. He drops the blade and, face and chest bloody with gouges, reaches back behind his head to try and grab its ankles. It's futile. Before I can take another step to help him, the imp laughs—a sound like nails on a board—and takes off, pulling Fitz up with him.

I watch, horrified, as Fitz's feet leave the ground. The imp leans to the left, dragging Fitz's weight toward the ravine. I run, only to end up standing right where he'd stood. Just in time to see the terror on his face when the imp extracts one foot.

"*Fitz!*" Evan screams, but it's no use.

Fitz shouts. The imp lets go.

He falls.

There's a heartbeat of silence, then a heavy, wet piercing sound—and silence again.

My brain has shut down.

It tries to process what it's seeing in the ravine, but it can't.

Fitz's limbs, loose and limp, hang from his hips and shoulders, but his chest is gone. It's *gone*. In its place is a shining red point of rock protruding up from his body like a spear.

I watch myself raise my sword again as if from a distance. The imp, still hovering, smiles with its double row of dagger teeth and dives again with claws extended.

My feet slide left. It misses me.

I swing the edge of my sword into its back, cutting it into two halves, a top and bottom. It dies against the wall with my blade sunk into the stone behind it.

I hold the hilt, my lungs heaving against my chest and my eyes burning with tears. I want to let go, but I can't. I can't yet. My knees hit the ground.

Evan slowly rises from his knees to his feet, his face stricken. "He's—he's gone." The whites of his eyes shine as he casts a wild gaze at the bloody scene around us.

My brain clicks back into operation. I take a deep breath and unlock my fingers to pull my blade from the wall. The top half of the imp falls with a homey splat that turns my stomach.

We both watch as his Scion's sword shimmers, then fades to dust without its caster. A heartbeat later, and Evan's sword, still on the ground, goes too.

Evan approaches, backlit against my still-fallen flashlight, and offers a hand. I take it automatically, and he pulls me to standing.

"He's gone," he repeats, stunned. His armor disappears before our eyes.

"I know," I whisper, even though I don't know. I don't know what it would feel like to watch your Scion die right in front of you. Would his Oath punish him? Did he feel Fitz's pain as well as his fear?

As I unstrap my scabbard and resheathe my sword, a cold certainty slides into my mind. Davis opened a Gate. He may not have killed my mother, but he did murder Fitz.

No more deaths.

52

EVAN HANDS ME my flashlight with a shaking hand. "We've got to keep moving."

I meet his eyes, unwavering in his familiar face. I take the lead this time, flashlight in hand, although my hand trembles as I hold it.

We walk for another few minutes. It takes that long for my breathing to begin to slow, but nothing about the situation feels calm. My eyes and flashlight fly to every distant drip of water, every shadow of stone.

"Those were imps, right? Isels?" I ask, hoping to fill the quiet. Hoping that talking will keep my heart from racing right out of my chest.

"Yes," Evan replies, his voice cracking.

"Why weren't they invisible?"

"We're underground. Aether is richest close to the earth. Down here every Shadowborn is more powerful than it is on the surface. Harder to kill."

I nod, even though he can't really see me do it. "That makes sense."

"Fifty feet ahead there's another turn left — there's a turn ahead," I call back to Evan. I pitch my flashlight low to keep the path in sight so we don't keep going straight and end up walking right over the edge. That's how I see that the gravel on the path, which had been small and mostly flat, has changed over into heavier, round pieces. "Watch the ground, these rocks are loose." I walk slowly, each step shifting the floor slightly before my foot settles. I pause to catch my breath and turn back to see Evan walking about six feet behind me.

It's only when I turn back to keep going that I realize that while my feet send rocks shifting and crunching . . . Evan's feet make no sound at all.

If the cave hadn't been so silent, I'd never have noticed.

My next step falters, and I have to catch the wall to stay upright.

Goruchel.

Consummate mimics.

"You okay?" Evan asks.

When it facilitates their human ruse.

My heart pounds so hard that I can barely form the words to reply. And I am desperately certain that I have to reply. I push off the wall. "Yep, just slipped." My voice sounds hollow and thin to my ears, but I hope he doesn't detect the lie. I pray he doesn't detect the lie.

I want to run. Run as fast as I can. But instead I walk forward, forcing myself to keep a steady pace and ignore the growing dread in my stomach. I'm so focused on not running, not revealing what I know, that I slip for real and land on one knee.

This time, when Evan reaches a hand toward me, my body flinches without my permission. An instinct. I look up into his dark blue eyes—and see the sliver of something canny move behind them.

"I'm good," I say with a laugh. A laugh that sounds so fake that no one would believe it. I stand up and keep walking, this time a little faster.

He lets me go a few steps.

"Oh, Bree."

"Yes?" I whimper, still moving quickly.

His mouth is suddenly at my ear. "You're a little *too* smart," he whispers in a voice like broken wind chimes falling on rocks.

I run then, feet sliding under each step. I don't know if he chases me. I can't hear him if he is. I only slow when I reach the turn. I make it without getting too close to the edge, but my left ankle twists sharply when I do it. I cry out in pain and drop the flashlight in my left hand, but keep moving.

Without the flashlight, the pitch black of the cave presses from all sides. I'm completely blind in the darkness. Can't see my hand inches from my face.

I'd glimpsed the path ahead before my flashlight went flying. It had been straight, then a dip, then straight. I keep one hand against the wall and move as fast as I dare, straining for any sounds behind me. But I'll never hear him coming.

Drawing my sword would be useless.

He could kill me here, and no one would know it was him.

When he speaks again, his voice is slightly muffled; he's still on the path before the turn.

"Honestly, I have to thank you. If it wasn't for you showing up tonight, I'd never have found the entrance to the ogof y ddraig. Well"—he pauses—"I'd have found it eventually, but my kind aren't the most patient."

Every step sends a lightning strike of pain through my ankle. I don't stop, but eventually my jog becomes a limp. I grit my teeth and push forward. Use the wall to take the pressure off my foot.

"I have to thank Davis, too, you know."

His voice is louder, more direct; he's turned the corner.

"He threw the Kingsmage blood traitor off my scent by opening Gates of his own. I barely had to open any, really. Just one or two, like the night of the second trial. I'd hoped the foxes would take care of Sel, but then there you were. How'd you do that, by the way?"

The pain drives my teeth so deep into my lower lip that I taste blood.

Keep. Moving.

"Did you know the real Evan Cooper played the banjo? Do you have any idea how hard it is to learn to play the banjo? Nightmare." His laughter is a stabbing sound. Devoid of humor.

He's closer now, but I know he's toying with me. He's fast enough to catch me. To kill me, if he wants. The thought is jolting enough to make me trip. I fall forward onto my hands and knees in the darkness. Then I'm crawling. Crawling as fast as I can away from him into black nothing.

A hot hand closes around my bad ankle. I scream, but he drags me back across the rocks on my stomach, my free hand clawing uselessly at the gravel.

With a grunt, I heave up on my left hand. Punch up in an awkward back-swing, knowing full well he'll see it coming; I don't need to wound him, I just need him to let go. And he does.

I scramble to stand, but his hand shoots out and strikes me, palm open, in the middle of the spine. The force knocks the breath from my lungs, and I fall again. I twist around to face him just as the Evan Cooper that I knew goes away forever.

In the light of his flashlight, the goruchel demon grins, his human teeth stretching in his mouth until they look like a boar's canines. His fingers darken and elongate to crimson claws. The skin of his eyes recedes into deep hollows, and his blue eyes bleed to red. The smell that fills my nose is the sour scent of burning flesh.

His new gaze scorches my skin. Like my face could sizzle and peel, melt away until it's only bones and seared muscle.

"It's rude to ignore someone who's talking to you," he hisses. "Evan liked your attitude, Bree. Rhaz does not."

"My bad," I spit. "I don't like listening to murderers!"

The demon—Rhaz—tilts his head to the side. "I didn't kill Fitz. I only called the imps who killed Fitz." When he jerks a thumb behind him, I see the long, fresh cut from the outside of his wrist to his elbow. He'd bled into the ravine somehow as we walked. He'd called those demons in the darkness without us even noticing. He clucks. "Well, no, you're right. I did kill the real Evan Cooper. Took his life. Pretended to be Fitz's new Squire—even copied Evan's humanity enough to take that silly Warrior's Oath right under the traitor's nose. But it was *awful*, Bree. I can't tell you how many times I daydreamed about *ripping the skin* from Fitz's meathead face—"

"Why?" I scream.

A glittering, fanatical glee dark as the cave itself slides into his burning eyes. "To get to Nick, of course. And to wait."

My lungs burn in my chest, but behind them my heart twists and skips.

His scratching voice becomes low and conspiratorial. "Did you know that if a fully Awakened Scion of Arthur dies, the Lines will end forever?" He giggles. "Kill the head, kill the body. It'd be easy if all I needed was for Arthur to Call

Nick like the others do, but that arrogant prick of a king won't fully Awaken his Scion until they take the blade."

I crabwalk away, my sword dragging at an awkward angle, but he follows, one silent step at a time.

"And here I was, planning to go for the father! Then precious Nickie asks for *you* at the gala"—his lips curl in a mocking smile, and he clasps his hands to his chest—"declaring to all that he wants *you* as his Squire. That's when I realized that foolish boy would do *anything* to keep you unharmed. Fight a horde of my demon comrades. Take up Excalibur. Expose Arthur. I had to take you"—he grins—"so Fitz the meathead got kebabed."

My stomach turns. Bile rises in my throat.

"My mistress, Morgaine, will love hearing how I found the Scion of Arthur's weakness." He considers this. "Well, *love* is the wrong word. She'll be quite jealous, actually. She *adores* torture."

I shuffle backward, but he moves faster than my eyes can track, grabbing both of my ankles this time. "Rude!" he hisses.

My fingers dig into the gravel behind me. My only thought is to grab it and throw it into his eyes, but when my fingertips hit the soil and roots below, the doors inside me snap open.

'*The cave is right behind you. Just ten more steps, Bree.*' My grandmother's voice urges me forward. I feel her hands, warm and soft, wrap around my heart and hold it in her palm.

Rhaz registers something in my face. His eyes narrow—and I wrench my legs from his grip with frightening speed. Pull my knees tight to my chest, and kick both feet upward to send him flying into the ravine.

53

MY GRANDMOTHER WAS exactly right about the cave. I reach it in ten limping steps.

I turn a corner onto an overhang—and look down into chaos.

Rhaz meant what he said: he'd called his brethren. And they were doing his bidding, fighting Scions and Squires who'd reached the cave before me.

Tor and Sarah zip around the room like streaks of silver aether, shooting arrows at hellhounds and foxes from every angle.

Felicity and Russ are on the floor, each brawling with enormous green hellbears.

Pete and Greer are back-to-back, facing a pack of hounds closing in all sides. Two glowing lions take on one hound, jaws clamped at its haunches and throat.

Vaughn hacks at a fox of his own and seems to be keeping it at bay.

And in the middle of it all, on a small island surrounded by black water, is Nick. Buckled over on his knees with the effort of resisting Arthur's Call.

My heart leaps into my throat at the sight of him, scratched and bloodied, but alive. Above Nick, his father slashes at circling imps, barely keeping them at bay. There are too many demons here. Whatever Davis had in mind, the goruchel was never part of his plan.

Behind them is a bright sword sticking out of a boulder at an angle. Even at this distance, the clear diamond of Arthur gleams from its pommel.

Excalibur.

I launch myself over the overhang into the curved wall of the cave, sliding down on smooth-hewn rock. I hit the ground floor with a jolt and draw my sword for battle. Test my ankle; sprained maybe. But not broken.

I join Felicity against her bear. She pins it while I stab it through the chest. She takes a flying leap onto the back of Russ's bear. I hack at its arm until it rears back, sending us tumbling. Russ grabs it by the middle and slams it into the rock wall so hard the entire cavern shakes. Rubble tumbles down on us from the ceiling.

"Try not to bring the whole damn thing down!" Whitty yells from where he's fighting his own hellfox in a corner. He dispatches it swiftly, then turns toward us with a grin—

His body seizes into a single, rigid line.

Both daggers fall from his hands.

"Whitty?"

His eyes are wide, blank. His chest angles up. Toes drag on the ground, like he's being lifted—

By the hand buried in his back.

"WHITTY!" I scream, frozen in place. The fighting rages on around us. We're overwhelmed. The demon that was once Evan kicks at Whitty's upper spine to free his hand. My friend falls forward, hitting the cave floor with a heavy thud, head twisted in my direction.

My heart stops, but I search for life.

I don't find it.

Instead I see my friend's unseeing eyes. The wrong angle of his shoulder. Blood on his favorite camo jacket. His jaw open to the dirt.

No one saw Whitty die but me.

I should have guessed that that fall wouldn't have killed a greater demon.

I should have known.

Rhaz points at me with a bloodied claw. "That was very mean of you, Bree! Look at what you did!"

Two black ribs protrude from his chest, oozing green blood down his T-shirt. He doesn't seem bothered at all.

I'm running, screaming, an arrow of hate. I'll kill him. I'll rip him apart—

"I'll order these beasts to kill everyone here," he snarls, stopping me short, "unless you tell Nick to accept Arthur's Call and take up the blade."

A wave of churning anger and fear comes over me, warring in my chest. All around me, there's the clanging of aether weapons on hard isel hides. The roar and cry of battles.

"No."

Rhaz hisses. "Have it your way." He darts forward and strikes the blade from my hand. Twists my arm so tightly I scream and see spots. He yells something harsh and unintelligible—the language of demons. At once, every hellbeast stops. The Legendborn pause too. Stunned. Every time I try to move, the uchel squeezes harder—until I'm gasping for breath.

"Nicholas!" Rhaz yells.

Nick and his father turn stricken faces to the back of the cave. Davis is slack-jawed, but drained and on his knees, Nick takes the scene in all at once: the human mimic goruchel. Whitty's broken body. Me in the demon's arms. *"BREE!"*

"Take up the sword, Nicholas!"

"No!" I manage to scream. "He—will end—the Lines!"

Nick's hands ball to fists. "If you kill her," he grinds out, eyes like fire, "I will *never* touch this blade!"

"You must think I'm bluffing," Rhaz says—and in a blink he is gone.

Not gone. He has Russ by the throat. He lifts him high—and pitches him like a fastball straight into a stone wall.

It happened so fast, Russ didn't even get a chance to scream.

We watch as his body falls twenty feet into a crumpled heap.

Felicity shrieks and launches herself at Rhaz—Tor and Sar reach her first, but it takes both of them, Vaughn, and Greer to keep her down.

Before I can move, Rhaz has me around the middle again.

"Let Arthur Call you, Nick! Or I'll snap her—"

A blue-white dagger hits him in the throat.

His fingers fly to the handle of the blade. He makes a gargling sound and pitches face-forward into the water.

With a piercing screech, a huge eagle owl dives into the cave from a tunnel. Quick and silent, it melts into the shape of a man as it drops to the ground.

A shape I recognize immediately: Selwyn Kane, Merlin and Kingsmage of the Southern Chapter.

A sorcerer—with the ability to *shapeshift*.

Sel stands, eyes blazing, and stalks to the moat. He hauls Rhaz up by the neck; blood drips from the demon, turning the water the color of rot. Sel inspects the unmoving body, a low growl rising out of his clenched teeth, and then drops it.

The hellcreatures yowl and snap, but without Rhaz to command them, they don't make a move.

Felicity breaks free and runs to Russ's body, tears streaming down her face. Her sobs echo throughout the cave, loud and painful and broken.

Which is just the distraction Rhaz was waiting for.

Alive and furious, he launches out of the moat and onto Sel's back. They roll over and over in the water, grunting and striking in a blur of limbs.

Then the demon has both hands around Sel's throat. The Kingsmage claws at the demon's fingers for breath, kicking.

I run, but Tor and Sarah streak past me.

Rhaz is too fast; he sees them approaching.

He wrenches Sel's head *down* just as his knee snaps *up*—a crack, blood— Sel's limp body sinks into the water.

Suddenly, Nick's scream echoes, the sound of agony everywhere. He writhes under the weight of Arthur's Call. He's losing the battle.

Rhaz grins. "That's it, Nickie."

We all watch, frozen, as Nick takes a shuddering breath, then draws up to his knees. His head falls back, and Arthur's deep voice emerges from his throat.

"Though I may fall, I will not die, but call on blood to live."

Nick rises to his feet in one movement, then turns to face the stone that holds Excalibur.

'*She's here*,' my grandmother whispers, her voice so loud in my head that I'm sure everyone can hear it.

The resolve in Nick's shoulders grows with each step he takes to his destiny. *Who?*

Sel heaves up from the moat, gasping for air, searching for Nick. But Nick is already at the stone.

'*The old mother. The oldest. Vera.*'

Nick reaches for the sword's hilt and, with a deep breath, pulls.

My grandmother fades.

The sword does not move.

Tor gasps. Lord Davis makes a choking sound. Even the goruchel's hellish eyes grow wide.

Nick pulls with both hands gripped around the hilt—but the ancient sword does not yield.

He steps away, his face a mask of confusion and shock.

Inside me, a bomb explodes. My house blows part.

Time slows.

Stops.

Freezes.

A single second, suspended.

The old mother of my family fills my every limb. Arrives, just as I'd asked.

Her voice is rich and smooth, liquid steel on its way to a blade. It drapes over me, a warm blanket with sharp edges.

'*What do you want to know, child?*'

"Everything," I whisper.

'*Why?*'

I could say the demons. Davis. Nick. The innocents. The world.

But I don't.

I think of my mother. Her fights. Her triumphs. Her pain. And how they're mine now too. Mine to hold. And mine to wield.

"Because her life counted. And I want to make sure her death counts too."

I feel her appraisal, and pleasure.

'Then I will give you the power to do so, wound tight with truth.'

She pulls me into her memory.

I shatter.

54

A WALK.
Years past.
Years of pain.
The history my mother
and her mother
and her mother never knew.

I see the oldest mother when she is young, standing in a field
behind a great white home.
She wears a plain white dress, or at least it was white, at one time.
Her hair is tied up. Face like glowing mahogany. Eyes like mine.
The sun is low in the sky. She is tired. The day has been long.
The days are always long.
The angry screams of the master's wife
can be heard across the field.
They fight, the master and his wife.
They fight about children, but they do not have any.

Another day done.
She begins the walk to the quarters when

she hears a sound.
A pale man with hair the color of acorns
slips into the yard
through the back gate.
She recognizes him. The man called Reynolds.
A woman with flaxen hair comes out the back door to meet him,
glancing behind her at every step.
The master's wife.
Reynolds pulls the master's wife to him
until they are hidden behind the magnolia,
its branches almost touching the earth.

It's daylight. Another day. Another magnolia.
She has stopped to rest underneath its bows, just for a moment.
Just a moment of rest.
The master appears. She is frightened. Caught.
He holds a hand out. "I'm not here to hurt you," he says.
But he is. He hurts her anyway.
The magnolia tree's fallen seedpods litter the ground.
Their sharp edges dig into her back.

Three months later.
The master and his wife
can be heard fighting from the orchard.
My ancestor wonders
if a child between them would truly make it better.
It wouldn't.
But the next day
she feels one growing inside her anyway.

When she shows,
the master's wife notices
but doesn't seem to care.

When she shows,

the master notices,

and he cares.

He cares very much.

He comes for her. He holds her weathered, soft face

between his hard fingers.

His blue eyes stare down into her brown ones.

The others in the field notice.

He sees them over her head.

"Tonight, Vera," he says roughly, and releases her.

He walks away.

Vera knows this time, he means to hurt her.

She runs.

There are paths to take. Rumors of the way to go.

She leaves as soon as the sun sets

and hopes she remembers the stories.

She tells no one lest he come for them, too.

He may come for them, too.

She takes nothing with her but a bit of fruit and sweet honeysuckle,

nectar still in the stem.

She runs for hours.

Master Davis has the money for pattyrollers, but she didn't expect

to hear them so quick.

The dogs bay in the distance.

She splashes into a creek. Doubles back.

Works upstream with skirts held high.

Climbs a tree whose branches hang low.

Her arms are strong.

She works with the trunk, sends prayers to the roots,

thanks the tree for its help,

drops down fifty yards north of where she started.

She settles into the dark shadow of that helping tree

and spills out the fruit

and the honeysuckle, crushed but still good.

She sits cross-legged on the cool earth and draws a broken blade

down her palm.

The cut is deep, but it hurts less than the blisters on her feet.

She is a memory walker, but tonight she does not want to walk.

She wants to run.

She smears her blood onto the fruit and the flowers, presses the

mixture and her hand as deep into the ground as they'll go, and

calls the ancestors to aid in a rhythmic chant of her own making.

"Protect us, please. All of you. Everyone.

Protect me so I can protect her.

Help me see the danger before it strikes.

Help me resist their entrapments.

Give us the strength to hide and to fight.

Protect us, please. All of you. Everyone.

Protect me, so I can protect her.

Help me see the danger before it strikes.

Help me resist their entrapments.

Give us the strength to hide and to fight.

Give us all we need to hide and to fight . . ."

They hear her. Their voices rise up from the earth.

Up through her wound and into her veins

and directly into her soul.

'Bound to your blood?'

She gasps. The dogs are at the creek. Tears drop into the dirt.

"Yes, please! Bound to my blood!"

'A price.' The voices sigh, sad and heavy.

'One daughter at a time, for all time.'

"Bind us to it!" she cries.

Her body trembles with a wave of desperation,

an ocean of determination.

She and the voices say the words together. *"And so it is."*

A molten core of red and black sparks to life in her chest.

As it spreads through her limbs, burning her up from the inside,

she turns to me, *sees* me.

Her eyes are volcanoes, bloodred fire streaming from the corners.

Power erupting over her skin,

she wraps a hand tight around my wrist.

"This is your beginning."

The old mother's walk, like Patricia's, is only the beginning.

In the grip of her power, I am passed through

eight generations of women.

Her descendants, my foremothers.

A stream of strong brown faces meet me, one life after the next,

one after another into a blur.

Angry faces and sad ones. Scared ones and lonely ones.

Proud ones and ones tired from sacrifice.

Their faces. My faces. Our faces.

They show me each of their deaths,

when the furnace of power in each mother's chest

passes down to her daughter.

Their resilience is bound to my flesh.

I spin, twist, stumble onto grass.

I see my mother when she was young. She walks through campus.

The light inside her shines bright

even through her heavy winter coat.

A girl with smiling yellow eyes walks beside her.
Snow sprinkles the girl's hair;
its black waves hang loose down her back.
They turn together down a brick path, talking and laughing.

I see my mother behind the wheel.
I am sitting in the passenger seat, watching her as she watches me,
our spirits meeting in a blend of Vera's walk and my newfound gift.
The car approaches.
The accident.
Just an accident.
No one's fault.
My mother wraps her hand around mine and squeezes.
"It comes for each of us, honey."
Just before the car strikes, she presses her love against my heart,
and fades.

I am myself, sitting in the hospital. The light in my chest is small,
a flame only just lit.
I revisit my own memory with my ancestor's eyes.
Through her, I see my power, still new, simmering in my chest.
The police officer's body shimmers
like air over hot summer asphalt.
The police officer and nurse brought me and my father into
a tiny, mint-green room.
The mesmered memory returns in full.
I see his badge, him standing while in a door,
the stubble on his chin.
Bushy eyebrows, blue eyes.
I blink, and the shimmer dissipates. The glamour drops.
I see her old sweater, her narrow shoulders,
the tears streaming down her chin.

Black hair like a raven, black brows, face too beautiful to be real.

Features both young and old.

Two golden eyes like Sel's, filled deep with sorrow.

Not like Sel's . . .

They *are* Sel's.

Sel's mother's lower lip trembles. She speaks through the pain.

"You won't remember this,

but I want you to know

that she was my friend."

55

BLACKNESS.

Vera stands before me, bathed in blood and flame,

hair stretching wide and loose like a live oak.

"Answers, but not an ending. Now that you have them,

do you still want to fight?"

I don't hesitate. "Yes."

"Then there is one final truth. A legacy forced, not given.

A burden I did not carry."

A question in her eyes. A choice.

"I'm ready."

She considers this. Nods.

"Then I will release him. And grant him voice."

In the distance, a presence rises.

From the threshold between worlds, he calls my name.

All at once, I become we.

We are in the cave again.

We take one step and we are already at the stone.

We grasp the ancient hilt, warm under our fingers.

We pull Excalibur free.

THE MOMENT I raise Excalibur, the sword sings in my hand, hungry for war.

The blade's aether rockets up my arm and slices through my consciousness, pulling me back to myself.

In the center of the diamond in its pommel, red root rises and bleeds until the stone shines like heartblood.

Engraved letters glint on both sides of the silver: *Take Me Up. Cast Me Away.*

Flames of blue and red ignite and swirl around my body, and Arthur's armor builds in stripes and layers until it gleams like metal on my shoulders. In Excalibur's reflection, my eyes burn crimson.

Vera passes a hand over my brow. Ghostly lips kiss my forehead before she bids me farewell.

"Stop her!" Lord Davis screams. Enraged, he points a trembling finger and calls the Legendborn to action. *"Now!"*

On the far end of the cave, Greer, Vaughn, Felicity, Tor, and Sar startle at Davis's command. But they do not comply. Their eyes follow the sword in my hand.

Sel locks eyes with me from where he stands in the water below, an impossible mixture of emotions on his face.

Inside me, Arthur is the only presence. And his possession is nothing like Vera's or my grandmother's.

He jerks my arm up, leveling Excalibur at Davis. The words burst from my mouth—in both my voice and Arthur's booming baritone. *"Traitor! You levy war against the crown, lure our enemies to innocent blood, and now you dare rally my knights against me!"*

"No, no—" Davis stammers, shaking his head over and over again. Murmuring denials, he stumbles and plummets backward into the water with a splash. He scrambles up like a rat and runs toward one of the tunnels.

Arthur takes me to the edge of the island, full of righteous fury and royal rage as Davis escapes. *"You will not go unpunished!"*

"Bree?"

Nick's voice cuts through us both. Arthur turns my body until I face Nick where he stands with a hand half-raised to shield his eyes from my light. Our eyes meet across flames of red and blue.

I want to cry. I want to scream. But Arthur is in control of my voice and body, and even though he uses my eyes, he doesn't see Nick at all.

"My brother Lancelot. My right hand. Camlann has come."

Nick's eyes go round.

We'd all seen Nick collapse, heard the ancient knight proclaim his presence and Awaken his Scion. Nick *had* been Called. Just not by Arthur.

Because *I* am Arthur's Scion.

A screeching, grating laugh echoes back from the cavern ceiling. All of us turn, reminded of the immediate threat.

Rhaz and his army of demons, prowling on the banks. A hellbear, imps, foxes, and hounds, waiting for his command.

"Abomination!" Rhaz cries, his face split in a wicked grin. "But an Arthur just the same!" The demons yowl and yip, roar and scream—a war cry from the underworld. And now he roars.

The beasts surge forward. Arthur raises Excalibur high. In our dual voice, he shouts, *"To me, my knights!"*

And then I'm sprinting off the island, vaulting in the air over the moat. The Legendborn are running with weapons raised—

I scream mid-leap, my will overpowering Arthur's. "No!" I swing my free hand in a wide arc, fingers splayed. A twenty-foot wall of red flames erupts in front of the Legendborn. A barrier between them and the demons. Arthur's confusion fills me as I land on the bank. "No more deaths!" I say, and switch the sword back to my right hand.

He doesn't argue. Instead, he calls on aether to create a heavy, solid shield strapped to my left forearm, and we go to work.

The beasts converge on us. Arthur thrusts Excalibur down deep into the earth at my feet, sending a hot pulse of swirling aether out wide in a shining circle. The wave hits them all, knocking them back against the cave walls.

The imps recover first and dive at me in one howling flock.

There are three. Too fast and nimble for a single attack. Too far away for a sword.

Root crackles in my ears, alive and ready.

I open the furnace in my chest—and scream. Flame pours out of my mouth in a rolling ball, exploding into the first imp's face. It shrieks, burns, bursts. Smoke everywhere. The second imp pulls up and away. The other is close enough. *Got you.* I use Arthur's strength to jump, spearing it through its scaly belly. It dusts over me in a shower of green aether and smoke that blocks my vision.

A roar in the mist. A paw like concrete strikes me in the face, knocking me back. Crushes my nose and jaw. Pressing me down. Suffocating me. I flail with the sword, reaching for an impossible angle around the bear. I can't *breathe! I can't—*

'Drop the sword.'

I do.

Arthur pushes my left shoulder back, then *heaves* the shield edge first into bone and muscle. The bear rears back with an angry yowl. Arthur sends me surging up with it, following the embedded shield until the bear hits the earth. Now we are on top. Arm out of the shield's straps. Both hands now, digging the metal in farther. The bear roars in pain. The metal hits bone. Arthur's strength, more than I could have imagined. The hellbear swipes, slashing my right shoulder—the skin opens up—and I scream.

The hounds howl at the scent and thunder toward us.

Foxes suck the floating aether away, and the smoke clears with it.

"Sword now?"

Arthur yanks me back off the bear. Flips me stomach-down on the ground to grab Excalibur.

I roll back just in time to whip the flat of the blade up between a hound's jaws. My arm shakes. I can't hold the hound back. Saliva sizzles on the blade, on my cheek—

A crystalline spear shoots straight through its head. I crane my neck back, searching for the source upside down.

Sel stands on the island with the stone, another spear at the ready. He launches it. Impales the second hound. And leaps from the rock to the bank beside my head, eyes on the foxes, a ball of aether already blooming in each palm. "Don't ever do that to me again."

Before I can respond, a high-pitched whizz streaks by my ear. Tor's arrow, striking a fox in the throat. The other Legendborn stream forward, weapons raised against the four foxes. Nick's in the air, bringing an aether sword down across a hound's back as he lands. My root barrier is gone. I don't know how.

I spring to my feet, but my right arm can no longer take the weight of Excalibur. I can't—

'Switch to sinister!' Arthur yells.

"What?"

Sel's head jerks in my direction. "What?"

'LEFT HAND!'

"I'm not left-handed!"

'You are now!'

I toss Excalibur to my left and feel the familiarity there. The surety.

The bear pounds toward me, gone berserk with pain. Sel meets it first, two daggers extended.

Movement to my left. Rhaz springs for me—the bear was a distraction, a setup. The demon's fast—but my Bloodcraft roars to life, and for a second, I'm just as fast.

I spear Rhaz through his broken ribs, and Arthur's strength helps me push the blade forward and in. Rhaz claws at Excalibur, but the blade bites into his hands. I lift the demon up, just like he did to Whitty. I watch him writhe and twist on his own death, and laugh—a joyous sound that crashes around the room. A sound that soars over the cries of his dying brethren and makes Sel and the Legendborn turn to watch us.

"What are you?!" Rhaz croaks.

Three voices answer him in a booming chorus. *"I am a Medium, born from the earth. I am Bloodcrafted, born from resilience. I am Arthur, Awakened!"*

"My death means nothing. Killing me won't stop what's coming. There are others of us in your midst," he rasps, stilling on the sword. "The Line of Morgaine is rising."

"Let her Line rise. We will rise against it."

Rhaz growls deep in his throat, and his eyes roll back. He collapses inward, melting around the sword until all that's left is a slimy stream.

I stand there, sword still raised, chest heaving and blood thundering through my veins. Every eye turns to me. Nick. Sel. Greer. Bloodied and panting, ichor covering their faces and torn clothes. Piles of isel dust around them.

I lower Excalibur, exhaustion overtaking me. All of that power—Vera's, Arthur's, my own. It's too much. My vision blurs, and the cave spins. Nick steps toward me; so does Sel. To catch me, I think, before I fall.

Now that it's over, maybe I'll let them.

But Arthur is not done. To him, it's not over.

Without warning, he seizes me up like a puppet, turning me to the Legendborn in the cave and roars, *"Has it been so long? Do you not kneel for your king?"*

I gasp in the silence after my own words. That's not what this battle was. That's not what this is. That's not who I am.

I had to destroy these monsters, I yell at him. *And we did. But* this *is not about demons. This is about you!*

I fight against Arthur's will, but he will not yield—not on this. He demands obeisance. Homage. And deference. Especially after Davis's public betrayal.

Thankfully, no one moves.

Then, someone does.

"No," I whisper, because I don't want to hear it. But when Sel speaks, his voice is strong and clear.

"Y llinach yw'r ddeddf."

The Line is Law.

He drops to one knee, and bows his head deep.

A second passes. Another voice rises. Sarah's.

"The Line is Law."

One by one, she and the others bend, kneeling to their king. Kneeling to me.

Tor stands still, shock and fury shaking her frame, locking her legs in place. Arthur roars at her insubordination, but I don't care.

I turn to Nick, pleading, but there's nothing he can do. His ocean eyes are kaleidoscopes of emotion, turning so fast I can't read them.

"No . . ."

"Y llinach yw'r ddeddf." On the final word, his voice cracks—and despair slashes across his features like lightning. Then, a smile. Small, worried, sad.

"No."

His weight shifts. "It's okay—"

"Please, don't—"

But Nick falls to one knee anyway and bows until I can no longer see his face.

This isn't what I wanted! I scream at Arthur. *I don't want this!*

"*A fo ben bid bont.*" Arthur speaks through my voice, so that his answer is both for me and every Legendborn present. "*They that would be a leader, let them be a bridge.*"

The king's spirit subsides until I am myself again. Bereft, empty, and buzzing with power. I plunge my attention back into the stone as if to seal Arthur there.

I know it's no use. He's part of me now.

Realization dawns through my dizzy, floating brain: the Legendborn remain bowed, because I am the one who must release them.

"Rise," I whisper, then collapse.

57

I WAKE TO the sun shining through the curtains. Everything, and I mean everything, hurts. I'm so weak that it takes three attempts to turn over on my side in bed. When I do, two sticky notes fall from my forehead.

You collapsed in the ogof, but not
before driving Excalibur back into
the stone. Sel carried you back
through the tunnels.
It was all very dramatic, or so
I've heard. I hooked you up to
an IV for fluids, (cont'd)

but I expect you'll wake up
famished. Alice told me to put
cheesy grits on the stove.
(I like her.) Lots to talk about.
Come down to the great room
when you're ready.
-W

I smile, grateful that Alice knows me so well. Then the memories flow back and take my breath away until my chest feels like it could collapse.

I bury my face in the pillow and cry. For Vera. For my ancestors. For my family. For my mother. For all of my people. For the thread of death and violence forcibly woven into our blood, and the resistance we had to grow to survive it.

I cry for the deaths I witnessed—and couldn't stop—for Fitz and Whitty and Russ.

I cry for me.

I'm not Nick. I'm not some chosen one. I am the product of violence, and I am the Scion of Arthur, and I don't want to be either. I just want to be my mother's daughter. And my father's. I just want to be *me*.

But I know it will never be that simple again. *I* will never be that simple again.

My lineages are bound together in inextricable, horrible truths, and there's no untangling them from my destiny, whether I'm ready to face it or not.

Sel bursts through the doors, and I shoot upright. "Where is he?" His hair is sticking up in every direction, his yellow eyes wild, and his clothes are covered with dirt and leaves.

"Where's who?" I croak. I finally take a hard look at my surroundings and realize I'm in Nick's empty room.

As Sel blurs from one end of the room to the other, opening the bathroom doors and the closet, a heavy, cold feeling settles in my stomach. "Sel?" When he stops in front of me, he roars in frustration. "Sel—"

His eyes find mine, and they are wide, lost. "They took him. They took Nick."

I pace the room calling his phone without success for half an hour before Sarah stops me and pushes me to the couch. She disappears into the kitchen mumbling something about caffeine. Panic and tension have set every Legendborn on edge.

"Has anyone else tried calling him?" Tor asks for the fifth time.

"Kidnappers don't tend to let their hostages call home, Victoria!" Sel bites out. He shifts beside me in the chair, and I feel the heat of aether radiating from his skin.

"How do you know it was Lord Davis and Isaac?" I ask around the catch that has formed in my throat. I'm trying to push fear for Nick out of my immediate consciousness, but the efforts are no good.

"Because," Sel says, shoving himself to his feet, exasperated to be repeating *his* story for a third time, "Isaac mesmered me. I was up late in the kitchen after we returned from the cave because I couldn't sleep. Isaac slipped into the house, I turned around, and he was just there—taking over my vision, eyes locked, full mesmer. Then I woke up thirty minutes ago in the woods two miles from here. He got me out of the picture so he could grab Nick."

"And Nick's not in danger?" Tor demands.

"No. I would feel if his life was being threatened." Sel shakes his head. "Doesn't mean he's safe, though."

"But Nick and Bree were in the same room," Felicity says in a wavering voice. She looks horrible. Her hands won't stop shaking. My heart hurts just looking at her, trying to be strong when Russ is . . . gone. "Why didn't Isaac take her? Control the Scion of Arthur?"

Sel's already considered this. "Because an Awakened Scion of Arthur he can't control with powers he doesn't understand is too risky. Dangerous, even for a Master."

"Speaking of powers he doesn't understand . . ." William enters the room with more records. "A Medium, you said? And . . . ?"

Sel watches me respond as he paces. "I—yes. A Medium and . . . a Bloodcrafter. I can generate my own aether."

William whistles. "Handy. The Medium bit explains why Arthur can possess you the way he did. We sometimes inherit personality traits but . . . what he— and you—did is nothing I've ever heard of—the Pendragon speaking directly *through* his Scion—"

"You've never heard of it before because it's never happened before." Sel drags both hands through his hair. "William, this isn't the time—"

"This *is* the time, Selwyn!" William shouts. "You yourself said you could feel if Nick is in harm's way. He's not. We need to arm ourselves with *information*. About Bree, about Nick, about how this all happened."

Greer shakes their head. "If Nick isn't the Scion of Arthur, then why did they take him?" They've been mostly silent on the couch all morning, eyes red-rimmed with tears for Whitty and Russ. Their grief is the voice-stealing kind. The kind that lives in your throat like slivers of glass.

"Isn't it obvious?" Sel sneers. "To keep the Table from gathering! If they hold him hostage while Camlann has come, the Regents will do everything in their power to get the Awakened Scion of Lancelot back. Give Davis whatever he wants. If they don't, the Table will never be at its full strength and it will fall to the Shadowborn. And to the Line of Morgaine—who are now in league with demons, if what the goruchel said is true."

"That's exactly why we need to understand the Scion we *do* have!" William says, sitting down on the couch. "Bree is something new. Something powerful. We need to understand the situation she's in, and by extension, the situation we're in." He turns to me. "Now, Bree, my theory is that Arthur will inhabit you in ways we've never seen. Not just his abilities, but his spirit, his emotions, memories, possibly."

William's grief has sent him diving into work. He's eager to dig into all that Arthur's possession entails, but I have no desire to revisit it. Not when I can still feel him in the back of mind. I hold William's gaze for a long moment, then look away.

Tor excuses herself just as Sarah walks in with a carafe of coffee and a tray of mugs.

While we've been talking, Greer has been spreading stacks of William's yellowed documents and heavy, leather-bound records across the coffee table. "I still don't get it. How is Nick Lancelot's Scion and Bree Arthur's?"

William rests his hand on my knee. "Bree, this is where we need you to fill in the gaps. Last night when Sel carried you upstairs, you were mumbling about Vera and a baby." He shakes his head. "Who is Vera?"

All eyes turn to me, just as I knew they would.

"My ancestor," I say quietly. "She was enslaved on a Scion of Arthur's plantation."

Greer and Sarah shift uncomfortably on the couch. Sel sucks in a breath between his teeth.

I tell them what I saw, remembering it all myself as the words spill forth. I tell them about everything except the woman at the hospital. When I stop, Sel looks at me closely. He knows I'm holding something back. I shake my head imperceptibly. *Later.* He narrows his eyes, but nods.

"Say the names again," William says, riffling through a large, musty-smelling brown book. "The men's names."

I take a shuddering breath. "Davis. And Reynolds."

William stops on a page, trails his finger down, until, "And there it is."

"There what is?" Sarah says. We all lean in over the table.

William points to a yellow page with columns of names, dates, and locations. "This is Nick's family. The Davis line. In the early 1800s Samuel Davis was the Scion of Arthur. Samuel"—William grimaces—"was a slave owner. He owned a plantation maybe twenty-five miles from town."

The room falls silent around me.

"Davis knew if Vera had his child, that child would be a Scion," Sel says. "If there was even a sliver of a chance she was carrying his child, he'd hunt her down."

"But because she survived, she gave birth to a Scion," William says thoughtfully. He turns to me. "Which means that you and your whole family are a splinter in the Line. The blood of Arthur has been running in your veins for generations."

"And what about Davis's wife?" I ask faintly. "The blond woman in my vision? She was sleeping with Reynolds."

"Her name was Lorraine." William flips to another page in the same book and blows out a breath. He taps a row of notes and names. "Reynolds is the surname of the Line of Lancelot. And Paul Michael Reynolds lived near here around the same time."

"Like Guinevere," Sarah whispers, eyes growing wide. "It's just like the legend. Lancelot is Arthur's most trusted knight, until he sleeps with his king's wife. Lorraine sleeps with Reynolds and passes the baby off as Davis's.

Maybe he was even in on it, since he never found Vera or her child."

William nods, staring down at the book on his table. "Samuel Martin Davis, Jr., born the same year. Their only child on record, and Nick's ancestor eight generations back. Reynolds, on the other hand, isn't recorded as having any children until later. He had three sons and a daughter. The Order has all of their records here."

Sel stands up, pacing the room. "Which means Lord Davis and Nick are not Davises at all, from a bloodline perspective. They're Reynoldses. And the Reynolds at the Northern Chapter right now is from the Line of Lancelot, but he's not the eligible Scion."

"Nick is," I whisper, and all eyes turn to me. "His face last night . . . I've never seen him look so broken."

When I look up, I catch William's worried expression. The glance of concern he shares with Sel.

I'm worried too. I think about my connection to Nick. Our trust and affection. Now I wonder how much of that was me and Nick and how much was Arthur and Lancelot. Call and response. A king to his first knight, tied together by the deep bonds of loyalty and betrayal both.

"What will we tell the Regents?" Sarah asks.

Tor strides back into the room. "Not sure, but I just called their emissary. They're on their way."

"You did what?" Sel roars incredulously.

"I had to!" Tor yells. "I'm in charge now, Merlin, and I say we have two dead Squires, a dead Scion, a goruchel who murdered a Squire and infiltrated us—*for months!* You heard that thing, there are others embedded in the Order. What do you think will happen if we try to hide all of that?"

"That was not your call to make," Sel says between his teeth. "And you are not in charge. Bree is—"

"Bree is what?" Tor demands. "Our king? By accident? This is a mistake!"

"*Accident?*" I growl. "Mistake?!"

Alice is on her feet already, fists clenched. "Is that what you're calling chattel slavery? Three hundred years of *accidents?*"

Tor's face turns red. "You know what I mean."

"I don't think I do!" I spit. A flash behind my eyes of Vera's face as she spilled her own blood into the earth. My fingers curl, nails cutting deep into my palm. William's eyes—and Sel's—stare down to my fist and the strength that lives there now. "What that man did was not an accident. He knew *exactly* what he was doing. He *liked* owning her life. Her body. And he wasn't the only one. *She* wasn't the only one." Suddenly, I want nothing more than to launch myself at Tor. *Would the Legendborn stop me?* I wonder. *Could Sel even stop me?*

Tor catches sight of my growing anger and takes a step back, but she won't shut up. "People gave their lives for the cause last night, and you what? Just showed up at the last minute?"

I take a step forward, and Sel's arm shoots across my chest. "Tor!" he booms. "Bree is your king!"

"Not my king." Tor shakes her head, staring at me accusingly. "Not when she doesn't even want to be."

"I—" The memory of Whitty's and Fitz's and Russ's bodies rises up before me, blood spraying into pools so red it was black. "I . . ."

Alice steps in front of me, arms crossed. "Scion of Tristan, right? Bree doesn't have a choice in any of this, as far as I can tell." She looks Tor up and down. "And neither do you, third-ranked."

Tor lunges so quickly that only Sarah can catch her around the waist. And only Sel is fast enough to move in front of Alice.

Alice doesn't even flinch. She's catching on fast, all right. She'd been up early learning all she could from William.

But William's had enough. "Everyone, calm down!" he yells. "Tor, back off!"

Tor's heaving in her girlfriend's arms. She pulls away, glares at me and Alice both, and speeds out of the room in a gust of wind.

In the ensuing silence, William orders, "Take a breath, all of you! Before I sedate you myself!"

I do, but it doesn't keep the world from tilting. I wonder if I'll ever see it tilt back in the right direction or if I need to learn a new way to move through it. A way without Nick. A way where I'm in charge of all of . . . this.

Does a king imagine strangling her own knight?

The events in the ogof showed me answers, even if those answers are hard and ugly. Those same events only gave Nick questions. And we didn't get a chance to talk about them and what they'd mean for us, for the Table, for everything we both have known.

Soon, Sarah's, William's, and Sel's predictions and plans swirl around me, peppered with occasional references to my new title and rank. Alice holds her own, interjecting with logical questions and demanding answers on my behalf.

Sel is adamant that we stand our ground against the Regents and start the search for Nick ourselves, but even he doesn't sound so sure of our success without outside assistance; the Order's network can cover more ground than we can, and they're better equipped for a manhunt. Sarah wants to wait for the Regents' instructions, but Sel says they'll waste time debriefing all of us about what happened here, me especially. I will have to share Vera's story again. The Mage Seneschals will want to know about my other abilities, maybe even run tests on me. Sel won't allow it. He thinks I need to select a Squire as soon as possible, before I take the throne. William argues I need to recover before taking the Warrior's Oath. In the meantime, the Regents will need to confirm Arthur's presence before they transfer power to me and alert the whole Order that Camlann has come. He says that, as king, the Regents will expect me to promote calm among Order members instead of panic. Then I can gather the Table and designate members of the search committee myself. The discussion goes on and on . . . and right now I don't want any part of it.

"What if the Line of Morgaine and the Shadowborn working with them get to Nick first?" My own voice floats up and around me like mist over a pond. I didn't realize I'd possessed the question until it had made itself known. For a fleeting moment, it makes me a little worried that the question didn't come from me at all. "What will they do to him?"

Silence. Anxious glances.

No one knows what to make of the Morgaine-Shadowborn alliance that we now know exists.

I squeeze Alice's hand and stand. "I need some air."

She lets me go, and no one else stops me, because I am their king.

I know without looking that it's Sel who eases the door to the balcony open and then closes it behind him. Even before I felt the prickle of his gaze on my back, I knew he'd be the one to come to me. Aside from Alice, he's the only one who looks at me like I'm still just Bree.

"I'm sorry." His voice is quiet, cautious.

I nod and grip the wooden railing until it creaks in protest under my fingers. Arthur's strength is *terrifying*.

"Are you going to ask what I'm apologizing for?"

"No."

The evergreens stand like the last hope of life in the crowded wood, pines like needles and blades against the sky. I envy their readiness. Soon, the Regents will arrive with questions that I can't answer and some that I don't want to.

His approach is silent, as always, and then he's beside me, leaning forearms on the railing. "I don't know how much time we have, but the Regents and their Mage Seneschals will be here soon. We need their resources and intel to find Nick."

"I know."

"We will find him, Bree. I swear it." Sel turns toward me, pulling my attention from the trees to his golden eyes. My gaze travels across his dark hawkish brows, the aquiline curve of his nose, and the inky-black hair that curls like feathers over his ears.

I nod. "We will." My chest clenches. "What they did to his mother, his father's abuse . . . all of it was for a lie, Sel."

He regards me with solemn eyes. His sacrifices were based on a lie too.

"Your mother . . ."

He sharpens, tenses. "What about my mother?"

I tell him then—my small lie of omission from inside the Lodge. I tell him that I'd seen his mother in my memory walk, that she and my mother had been friends, and that she'd been there that night at the hospital—in mourning. That she'd posed as the Merlin assigned to my mother's case, if that Merlin had even existed. That his mother watched over my family for who knows how many years to ensure that we were safe from the Order. Our mothers were friends. Allies. Like Nick, our bloodlines are connected in ways we'd never imagined.

When I finish speaking, his mouth has fallen open in silent shock.

"Sel?"

"It's not that I don't believe you. It's just—" He shakes his head, recovers. "Even if she escaped their prison, overpowered and mesmered her Merlin guards as Isaac did to me . . . how could she have survived? At her age and power level? Away from the Order, she'd have succumbed to her blood years ago."

"But at the hospital," I begin carefully, "your mother was lucid, focused. Mourning, but in complete control of her abilities."

His eyelids flutter. "That's . . . impossible."

"It is," I whisper, "if what the Order told you is true."

His dark eyebrows wing upward in shock. "Bree . . ."

"What if Merlins *don't* have to succumb to their blood? Just—just what *if*?"

He blows out a long, slow sigh. "That would change *everything* we're taught about how our powers progress, how our blood works, why we're Oathed in the first place, why they lock us away . . ." His eyes narrow in warning. "If that were true, this would be dangerous knowledge to possess. Or share. Even for you."

"I figured." I nod, picking at the wood beneath my fingers. "It's why I waited until we were alone."

We stand in silence for a long moment, considering how much our worlds have already changed, and how much change is still to come.

I feel Sel's attention on my cheeks—and wonder when the sparks in his eyes had become a comforting heat.

"What?" I murmur, looking up at him.

"You are my king now, cariad." His low voice carries all the intimacy of a caress, and his eyes are a melted gold. I turn away, overwhelmed at the meaning in both.

I don't ask him what "cariad" means, because, in my heart, I'm scared of his answer. Scared to be torn in two once more when my reality has been a slow shatter all morning.

Sel touches my chin, guides my face back to his. "Camlann has come. We are at war. Against the Shadowborn and the Morgaines both. Against enemies that can hide in plain sight." A pause while he searches my features. "You need—"

"You are Oathed to *Nick*," I cut him off, my voice thin.

Sel studies me, sees my twisting heart. Releases me with a quiet sigh. Unspoken words hang heavy between us, but he lets them go until they dissipate in the air to wait for another day.

I know he's right. I need a Kingsmage. I am the most important player on the board now. My life is tied to the Lines, and now that I'm Awakened, the Shadowborn will come for me. But . . .

'We will face the shadows. We always have.' Arthur's baritone is resonant inside my chest. A bell rung too close. Sel lifts an eyebrow but says nothing at the mage flame that leaks from my skin.

Vera hums from within. Even now, I can feel the strength she holds. Enough to hold Arthur, and his Call, back with ease—until I agreed to hear it. *'There is a cost to being a legend, daughter. But fear not, you will not bear it alone.'*

If I concentrate, I can almost feel three heartbeats behind my ribs. Different rhythms. Different origins. All me.

I shudder. "Can we get out of here?"

His mouth quirks into a smile.

58

WE WALK SLOWLY side by side through the open yawn of the field beside the Quarry.

Sel's silence is a balm against the harsh flurry of voices at the Lodge. His hands in his pockets, the clean line of his profile in the sun, the relaxed set of his shoulders as he paces—they ease the harsh edges of my anxiety so I can finally breathe, and finally think.

These are the facts:

Nick helped me find more truths than I'd known to look for, and now he is the one who's lost.

Even though his heritage crumbled beneath the weight of my truths, if it were me in Isaac's clutches and at risk of being hunted by the Morgaines, Nick would fight to bring me home. And so I will fight to rescue him.

I don't know if it's our inheritances or our bloodlines or what we've forged together all on our own, but I can *feel* Nick's absence like an open wound in my chest.

I love him.

Nick is in my heart, and I am in his. This is irrefutable, no matter how it happened or when or why. And I won't lose someone that I love again. Not when I have the power to save them.

Unspeakable evil gave me Arthur, Vera's resistance gave me power, but *I* earned my will.

The Order is my court now, whether I want it to be or not. The Table will look to me to lead.

I'm scared, but like Vera said, I'm not alone.

As I bend to untie my shoelaces, my companion leans against an oak tree, and our eyes meet. A light prickling pressure passes from him to me like a blessing: the exact opposite of what he offered the last time we were here together.

Sel doesn't ask why we're here. He doesn't ask why I discard my sneakers. He doesn't ask why I bundle my socks and stuff them into the mouth of each shoe. His gaze stays warm on my back as he watches me walk barefoot past him and deeper into the woods the way we'd come. Satisfied with the distance, I crouch in the dirt and look to the sky. I dig fingers into cool earth, and it sends whispers up into my arms. I push toes into the buried memories of bodies gone past, bodies running away, and bodies bearing through.

This is why I'm here. I need one wild horizon—one sharp moment that belongs only to me—before I return to battle.

No more Before. No more After. Only Now.

I surge forward, and the strength of armies sings through my muscles. Survive. Resist. Thrive. Each pound of my feet echoes in my joints like a blacksmith's hammer, ringing loud into bones and ligament and sinew until the forest blurs past in a stream of moss greens and umber browns.

I sprint fast and faster.

And then I'm in the air, leaving the earth and trees far behind me.

RANK	BLOODLINE	SIGIL
1	King Arthur Pendragon	Dragon rampant
2	Sir Lancelot	—✦—
3	Sir Tristan	Three arrows sinister
4	Sir Lamorak	Griffon courant
5	Sir Kay	—✦—
6	—✦—	—✦—
7	Sir Owain	Lion couchant
8	—✦—	—✦—
9	—✦—	—✦—
10	—✦—	—✦—
11	Sir Bors	Three-banded circle
12	Sir Gawain	Two-headed Eagle
13	—✦—	—✦—

COLOR	INHERITANCE	WEAPON(S)
Gold	The King's Wisdom and Strength	Longsword
~	~	~
Azure Blue	Marksmanship and speed	Bow and Arrow
Carmine Red	Preternatural strength (enduring)	Axe
~	~	~
~	~	~
Tawny Yellow	Aether lion familiar	Quarterstaff
~	~	~
~	~	~
~	~	~
Burnt Orange	Agility and Dexterity	Longsword
Emerald Green	Enhanced healer abilities; preternatural strength at midday and midnight	Dual Daggers
~	~	~

AUTHOR'S NOTE

In a lot of ways, Bree's story is my story. When my own mother died, I learned that I had just become the third consecutive generation of daughters who lost their mothers at a young age. That we know of. This realization was sharp and quick and impossible—and the exact moment when Bree and *Legendborn* began to take shape.

Death is rife with odd ironies; growing up, I had, on occasion, seen my mother's wound, but not understood its nature. It took losing her to recognize that wound as grief, and, of course, the event that helped me better understand her is the exact event that took her away. I wanted to compare notes, but that's not how my story works. Instead, I wrote my own explanation.

In order to create the magic and legacy that answer Bree's questions, I took hold of the pattern of loss in my matrilineal line, then wove that pattern into the otherworldly qualities of the women in my family. Bree's story is, at its core, a story about someone who wants to understand the role of death in her life. It's about Black motherhood and Black daughterhood. But it's also a story of someone one who wants very much to understand and honor her mother and ancestors.

GRIEF AND TRAUMA

Legendborn addresses several types of trauma. Bree's grief-related trauma is directly drawn from my own experiences. In the book, she suffers from acute traumatic grief, PTSD, and early symptoms of Persistent Complex Bereavement Disorder (PCBD), reflecting my current nonprofessional understanding of those conditions; PCBD is a relatively recent addition to the *DSM-5* amid evolving research. In my case, it took a year after my mother's death to seek the support of a bereavement specialist and ten years before I began focused grief treatment with a trauma professional. In the interim, I'd lost my biological father and the father who raised me. Part of why I wrote *Legendborn* is because I hope to raise awareness of these sometimes comorbid conditions, particularly when they occur due to loss of a parent and/or when they occur in young people. Many people live with these disorders, undiagnosed, and suffer in silence due to how our society treats grief and death. Many people turn away from this type of suffering, even those who are suffering themselves. If that's you, just know you're not alone and that trauma is treatable.

Legendborn also addresses: intergenerational trauma experienced by descendants of enslaved people, the ways in which trauma can manifest between parents and children, and the legacies of racial trauma, oppression, and resilience.

ROOTCRAFT

In addition to drawing on my own life to create the fictional magic system of rootcraft, I took inspiration from African American history and spiritual traditions. In particular, I focused on rootwork, also known as hoodoo or conjure. Rootwork was developed by enslaved Africans and their descendants under American chattel slavery, and it can be traced from its historic origins to varied practices in present-day African American communities. Rootwork is not a centralized tradition, and practitioners from different families, regions, and times have their own gospel on what it looks like. But there are common aspects, many of which can be found in other traditions and religions, including those with roots in West Africa. "Rootcraft" in *Legendborn* borrows four of these common elements: ancestor reverence and communion, the ritual use of organic materials, naturopathic medicine and healing, and themes of protection.

Rootwork is a historic and living folk tradition and spiritual practice, but it is not the practice in my book. While the rootcraft magic Bree explores in the book is fictional, I chose to use the term "root" in *Legendborn* for four reasons:

- To set this type of ancestral, organic magic apart from the magic of the Order.

- Because of the power of this word in my community; imagery using roots exists across Black music, pop culture, and film.

- Because, for me and many other Black people in the South, it feels as if the very soil that helped grow this country is soaked with the acknowledged and unacknowledged blood, sweat, and tears of enslaved Africans and their descendants. And, in truth, it is.

- To hint at the solution to Bree's turmoil in the book, which is to recognize the living nature of love in her life, alongside death, and to literally go underground to find the truth of her origin.

UNC-CHAPEL HILL HISTORY

When I talk about *Legendborn*, I often talk about King Arthur and when I first fell in love with Arthurian legends. (Susan Cooper's The Dark is Rising sequence, in 1995, by the way.) I also say that it's about the ways grief and history walk beside us. UNC-Chapel Hill is many things: my alma mater twice over, a beloved epicenter for some of my favorite memories, the oldest public university in the country to admit and graduate students, a site of local and national history, a school casually abundant with secret societies, and, undeniably, a campus and community still reckoning with its deep connections to slavery.

Legendborn is a contemporary fantasy work of fiction whose setting is a real place with real history. I made up the Order of the Round Table and Early College. The geometry is real, but I added connections, I took some liberties with Battle Park and campus geography. The Unsung Founders Memorial exists, but I moved its location. There is no Carr statue, but the Confederate monument known as Silent Sam stood for over a hundred years on Carolina's campus and was the subject of decades of debate and protest until it was taken down by activists in 2018.

Some of the most painful stories in the book are facts: the unmarked, disrespected, and segregated graves; the open brutality of the real Julian Carr against an unnamed woman; that Black students live and learn on a campus built by enslaved people held in bondage by celebrated men who would have wanted to enslave us, too. These facts and monuments have mirrors in other spaces and at other schools, and I hope light continues to be shined on them.

KING ARTHUR

If one must find Arthur's beginning, I would turn to Wales. Still, I could never list all of my sources for Arthurian lore and legend. Like Nick says, fifteen hundred years is a long time! Arthuriana is absorptive and has always invited invention and reinvention. Arthur exists in a network of narratives; there is no single story, no sacred text, no definitive version, no single voice. Instead there are many versions of many legends, reimaginings, and retellings. Consider *Legendborn* a contribution to the collection.

To me, Arthur represents the seat of the canon of Western legend. Arthuriana is an opportunity for us to reorient ourselves to the stories we preserve . . . and rediscover who gets to be legendary.

ACKNOWLEDGMENTS

This story has lived with me for a long time, and I am grateful for the many people who have supported me in transforming it into a book.

I wouldn't be a writer, much less an author, without the support of my parents: my mother, who introduced me to science fiction and fantasy and made certain that I knew my writing mattered, and my stepfather, the man who became "Dad" and who truly believed I could do anything, and told me so. I miss you both, and I know you're watching and cheering.

Gratitude eternal to the ancestors whose shoulders I stand on. I am because you were.

Huge thanks to Penny Moore, who helped me and *Legendborn* find a fantastic home.

Massive thanks in every direction to my editor, Liesa Abrams. First, for sending that one email to Amy Reed in 2017. Forever, for championing my voice and this project from the very start. I truly believe the universe helped nudge us into each other's paths, and I am so thankful for your hard work, your vision, and advocacy.

Enormous aether-and-eternity thanks to Sarah McCabe, who jumped into the tangled web of demons and Scions with both sleeves rolled up. Thank you for embracing the *Legendborn* world, helping to mold it into its best shape, and helping me become the writer who could put her ambitious vision onto the page.

Enormous thanks to Laura Eckes and Hillary Wilson for a cover that gives me life every time I see it. Enduring thanks to everyone at Simon Pulse and Simon & Schuster for believing in *Legendborn* and working so hard to help it come to life and get into the hands of readers: Mara Anastas, Chriscynethia Floyd, Katherine Devendorf, Rebecca Vitkus, Jen Strada, Kayley Hoffman, Mandy Veloso, Sara Berko, Lauren Hoffman, Caitlin Sweeny, Alissa Negro, Anna Jarzab, Emily Ritter, Savannah Breckenridge, Annika Voss, Christina Pecorale and the Simon & Schuster sales team, Michele Leo and the education and library team, Nicole Russo, Lauren Carr, Jessica Smith, Jenny Lu, Ian Reilly, and Nicole Sam.

To my critique partner, Julia: this book would not be what it is without your careful eye, alpha and beta reader enthusiasm, spot-on feedback, and enduring support for me during the challenging times while writing it. Thank you for everything.

Enormous gratitude to my research consultants, subject matter experts, and authenticity readers: Dr. Hilary N. Green for your work, support, and insight; Dr. Gwilym Morus-Baird for medieval Welsh knowledge and modern Welsh translations and creations (*Diolch yn fawr iawn!*); Sarah Rogers, MA, for playing in the world while dropping medieval wisdom; and Dr. Cord J. Whitaker. To Lillie Lainoff, Brittany N. Williams, and Maya Gittelman. Thanks to UNC-Chapel Hill and Chapel Hill historians, archivists, librarians, memory-holders, and truth-unearthers, for your work and research.

An extra special thank-you to Daniel José Older. You were my first author friend, and I am so grateful for your listening ear and wisdom, humor and support. You're a very good human.

To Amy Reed: thank you for reminding me of who I've always been.

There are so many authors in my life to thank for their support, advice, and love: Kwame Mbalia, Victoria Lee, Elise Bryant, Karen Strong, Justina Ireland, L. L. McKinney, Dhonielle Clayton, Bethany C. Morrow, Eden Royce, Lora Beth Johnson, Susan Dennard, E. K. Johnston, Margaret Owen, Zoraida Córdova, Natalie C. Parker, Tessa Gratton, Graci Kim, Liselle Sambury, Annalee Newitz, Kiersten White, Ashley Poston, Jessica Bibi Cooper, Monica Byrne,

Emily Suvada, Nicki Pau Preto, Akemi Dawn Bowman, Antwan Eady, Claire Legrand, Saraciea Fennell, and Patrice Caldwell.

Special thank-yous to Mark Vrionides, Katy Munger, Jamye Abram, Negar Mottahedeh, Kat Milby, Michael G. Williams, Tina Vasquez, and the ladies of Color of Fandom.

Thank you to St. Anthony Hall and my siblings. I wouldn't be the person, the writer, or the artist I am without the bonds. I very much hope you enjoy this LD.

To Annalise Ophelian and Alyssa Bradley: thank you for the spells and projects, the cauldron, and every other magic we make together.

To Arlette Varela for *always* being ready to brainstorm demon names, magical abilities, and blood curses. Your early feedback gave me the boost I needed.

To Kathy Hampton: thank you for your artistic eye, abundant spirit, and glowing support. You've seen me and Bree from the very beginning, and I so appreciate it.

To Adele Gregory-Yao: I am immeasurably grateful for your unwavering support, brilliant brainstorming, troubleshooting, talent, dark humor, and creative vision during this journey.

To Karin McAdams: you have supported my writing (and my reading) for over twenty-five years. You helped me survive two losses, and then bolstered me in writing about them. You are my sister in arms, and I think she'd be so very proud of the both of us.

Immense gratitude to all of my family members across all of my families, for being enthusiastic about my future and this book without having read a word. Thank you.

To Walter, thank you for keeping me fed and hydrated, for reminding me to rest, and for believing in me every day. You had faith when I didn't. You white-board and sketch and talk through my world until the magic and plot make sense, my partner in storytelling as much as in life. None of this would be possible without you. I love you.

ABOUT THE AUTHOR

Tracy Deonn is a writer and second-generation fangirl. She grew up in central North Carolina, USA, where she devoured fantasy books and Southern food in equal measure. After earning her master's degree in communication and performance studies from UNC-Chapel Hill, Tracy worked in live theater, video game production, and K–12 education. When she's not writing, Tracy speaks on panels at science fiction and fantasy conventions, reads fanfic, arranges puppy playdates, and keeps an eye out for ginger-flavored everything. Tracy can be found on Twitter @tracydeonn and at tracydeonn.com.